THE WEEPING CHAMBER

OTHER BOOKS BY
SIGMUND BROUWER

□ □ □ □ □ □ □ □

Out of the Shadows
Crown of Thorns
The Lies of Saints

THE WEEPING CHAMBER
SIGMUND BROUWER

Tyndale House Publishers, Inc., Wheaton, Illinois

To Kip Jordon
We miss you.

FOREWORD

When I first met Sigmund Brouwer, he was already a very good golfer. Yet he was determined to elevate his game to a higher level. Several years later, I was paired with Sigmund in a golf tournament and discovered firsthand that he had done just that. But this, I've come to learn, is simply characteristic of Sigmund—in all that he undertakes Sigmund ferociously pursues excellence. Nowhere is that more evident than in his writing career, and *The Weeping Chamber* is a classic case in point.

When it was first published in 1998, this powerful novel set new standards for Christian fiction by employing what was then an experimental literary technique of shifting between first- and third-person narratives. In the process, Sigmund successfully transported us into the heart of ancient Jerusalem during the days leading up to Christ's death. Within this milieu, he constructed a gripping and biblically informed story around the intersection of two men: one desperately seeking personal redemption, the other providing redemption for all.

This revision of *The Weeping Chamber* evinces Sigmund's evolution as a writer relentlessly pursuing excellence. He unveils an even more developed and endearing Simeon, who narrates an epic steeped in spellbinding spiritual reflection. *The Weeping Chamber* is a particularly poignant preparation for Passion Week. Readers not only will get to know the villains of the greatest drama in history—Caiaphas, Herod, Pilate, and Judas—but will encounter the all-too-human motivations that we share in common with them. They will also encounter disciples such as Mary and Martha, who did not adequately apprehend God's purpose in redemption until they experienced Christ's resurrection. Readers will come to grips with the fear of the religious establishment at Jesus' monumental claims and miracles, as well as the joy that overwhelmed those who found ultimate healing and forgiveness.

In the end, you will feel that you have been transported back in time as you experience an inexorable march toward crucifixion and internalize the revolutionary impact of resurrection. Prepare for a breathtaking journey that will educate as well as evoke your deepest emotions.

Hank Hanegraaff

PREFACE

I cannot pretend to be a historian. In writing this book, I could only do my best as a novelist to reshape and bring to life what I learned from great writers and historians. I owe them much for enabling me to see these events with new eyes. I especially recommend time with Alfred Edersheim as he shares passionate history and deep faith in *The Life and Times of Jesus the Messiah.*

Because I came to this book as a novelist, I hope readers will indulge my decisions to fix a specific time or place or character to some of the Gospel events. My intent was to remain true to Scripture and to historical facts; I ask forgiveness should my efforts appear to fail in this regard.

I would like to thank Janet Reed, Laura Kendall, and Joey Paul for sharp eyes and excellent editorial intuition. I would also like to thank Reverend John Woods; as tour guide at the Garden Tomb in Jerusalem, his observations gave me the title of this novel and helped me understand what it might have been like to stand in the weeping chamber on that Sunday of hope.

Most of all, I am deeply grateful to my wife, Cindy. During my time with this novel, she was in the process of writing the music and lyrics to *The Loving Kind,* an album that explores these same days of Jesus' journey to the cross and beyond. That she and I were able to share time in Jerusalem as preparation for the novel was a joy; that she encouraged me as she did was a gift; that I was able to listen to her songs was joyous inspiration.

I stand in the weeping chamber of my own tomb. I hear the dry wheezing of my old lungs. As I lean upon a cane for balance, my body shakes and trembles.

Behind me, the mouth of the tomb opens to the sunlight beyond. Despite the day's heat, here in the peculiar silence that fills any resting place for the dead, it is still cool. My cloak does not keep me warm, but I have given up on expecting my frail bones to hold any heat.

I stand in the weeping chamber of my own tomb.

It is not a large tomb. I purchased the rocky hillside decades ago and immediately hired stoneworkers to carve a narrow arched entrance the height of a man. Through this opening, the workers continued to hew into the hill, widening and clearing a space inside. When they finished, the tomb was as high as a man could reach and no more than seven steps in length or width.

They had measured me and chiseled into the rock inside the tomb a basin that would accommodate my body upon my eventual death. Beside it, they chiseled another measured space for Jaala, my wife. As was customary, the workers left the remaining graves rough and unfinished, waiting for our children to grow before determining the size of their resting places alongside ours. We prayed, as all parents do, that our children would outlive us by many years. It was a prayer that would not be answered in the manner we wished.

I stand in the weeping chamber of my own tomb.

After my death, mourners will work in this small area overlooking the graves, washing and anointing my body with oil and perfumes, wrapping me in the graveclothes made of long strips of linen, packing those linens with fragrant spices to take away the smell of death, and binding my head with a linen napkin.

I do not fear the thought of my death. Not after seventy years on this earth.

Nor do I stand in the tomb's weeping chamber to contemplate how eternity will sweep past my still body, leaving me behind to add to the dust of previous generations.

I stand in the weeping chamber because it is my yearly ritual.

While my wife approaches death, her grave remains empty. As, of course, does mine. Our daughter's grave is empty too, and I thank God she is in good health.

It is the fourth grave—far too tiny, the space hewn into the rock—that draws me into the tomb.

The expensive linen there has long since fallen into tattered strips; the body's odor has long since become a dry mustiness; the bones have long since collapsed into a small, sad pile that clearly shows my son died as a young boy.

He was my firstborn son. And the first dead.

I have mourned his horrible death for forty years. . . .

SUNDAY

CHAPTER ONE

My dearest love,
Please do not abandon me. The only solace that I can find is the hope
that you will mourn for the return that I cannot promise.

Thinking of you, I am unable to sleep. The prayer call of the
priests' silver trumpets has yet to mark the dawn, and I write by the
light of an oil lamp, knowing this activity will not disturb my hosts.

First, I wish you to know that I arrived safely for Passover, and
I can report that Pascal and Seraphine are in good health. Now that
my travel has ended, I have the luxury of applying markings to scroll.
Far apart as we are, my intent is to begin each day of this week with
you. I picture you listening to my letter and thus pretend we are in con-
versation. It aids me that I can imagine you reclining on your couch
in our villa far above the harbor. I see your pretty head tilted sideways
as you listen with your half frown of concentration. The sun casts a
shadow across your face, and the ocean breeze plucks at your soft dark
hair much more gently than my rough fingers were ever able. It is how
I like to dream of you.

Does it surprise you that I now take such trouble with words?
Me? Your stony-faced husband who deals so harshly with sailors and
merchants? I have not hired a poet as you might suspect. No, the dis-
tance between us makes my heart ache with sentiment, and it is easier
to be weak for you when you cannot see how I tremble.

Last night, as I fell into troubled sleep, I could not escape thoughts of you: your soft singing as you brush your hair, your flashes of temper and immediate remorse. I remembered, too, our wedding—how you quivered with fear and anticipation and held me so tightly in our first moments alone that I thought my ribs would crack.

All I have are the thousands of memories with you since then. Simple memories. Watching you on the road from our balcony as you returned from the market with your arms laden. The perfume in your hair as we fell asleep together. The sight of you with a suckling child.

All of it. What we have lost in the present, I relive in the past.

Even on the road from Caesarea to Jerusalem, among the pilgrims on foot and riding wagons and mules, I found myself turning to you again and again in the crowd to share comments on the sights and sounds. You were not, of course, beside me, and on each occasion my heart grew heavier.

It is far worse, is it not, when you can only blame yourself for what is lost? when what you have lost becomes far sweeter because you will never have it again? Let us not fool ourselves. You no longer love me. That you are faithful, I have no doubt. But you do not love me.

I warn you now that in these letters I intend to pursue your hand with the same passion I did during our first days together. I want you to love me all over again.

Yet when I find the courage to tell you what I must, I wonder how you could ever offer that gift again. At the least, you will finally understand what has driven us apart. And why we will never be together again.

Until I find the courage, permit me these daily contemplations. Above all, think of my love for you.

Your Simeon

CHAPTER TWO

Incense and silk. Scent and satin. Irresistible, at least to those who could afford it. Absently—a touch once trained is a touch that would not forget—I ran my hand over a roll of dark silk in the front corner of the market shop. My fingers traced a few flaws, but I said nothing.

Three women stood in front of me, their veiled heads bobbing as they simultaneously haggled prices with my cousin Pascal. I watched with as much amusement as I allowed myself in those days. The women had my sympathy. Their nostrils were filled with perfume, their grasping fists filled with draped silk and their husbands' purses of gold coins. Against Pascal's shrewdness, they stood little chance.

I waited patiently, knowing Pascal would allow them the small victory of an extended battle.

Although it was well past dawn, little sunlight reached Pascal's wares. The shading was deliberate. He did not want his colors to fade. As well, dimness added confusion to a shop cluttered with rolls of silk and purple cloth, giving the impression that Pascal's luxuries spilled endlessly and sloppily, waiting for a buyer to take advantage of his carelessness. While the first was true—Pascal did have wealth a king might envy—not a single thread of silk floated out the door without Pascal's knowledge and consent.

When the women happily admitted defeat and walked past me with their armloads of wares, I turned so they could not see the angry burn scar that showed through my beard on the left side of my face. Their veils hid their eyes, but not their sight.

"Simeon," my cousin Pascal said. "Did you sleep well?"

In the middle of his forties, he was fifteen years older than I. The night before, when I had arrived at his mansion in the upper city, I had seen him for the first time with his new wife. They made an interesting contrast. She—young and plump with golden-red hair, a ready smile, and plain clothing. He—old and thin and bald above a scraggly white beard, dressed in layers of luxury and chains of gold. Yet I had no reason to second-guess Pascal's choice of wives; he had already outlived three and could be expected by now to know what he did and did not like in a woman.

"I slept well," I said.

"That is a poor lie." He gave me his toothy lion's grin. "You do not look rested."

I shrugged.

Pascal pointed to where I had been standing. "That roll of silk you examined . . ."

"Adequate quality," I answered, "but merely adequate, despite its rich appearance. I think water has marked it."

"Praise be to God that you do not choose to set up a shop opposite me here in Jerusalem." Another toothy grin. "You are right, of course. Fools and camels and a sudden rainstorm. I paid a fraction of what it is worth. As you might guess, however, I will not take that into consideration when the wives of rich men—"

"Pascal, purchase everything I have," I said bluntly.

My words stopped him flat, probably the first time I had seen him unable to immediately grasp a situation.

"My ships, my warehouses, my shops," I said. "Everything."

He recovered, his grin replaced by serious study. He knew me well enough to understand I did not speak frivolously. He also knew me well enough not to ask for the reason behind my sudden offer.

"For a fair price, of course," he said, not so subtly testing me.

"Perhaps less," I answered. "I am far less concerned about the price than you might imagine."

He studied me, looking past my appearance. "If it is not price, what, then, is your concern?" he finally asked.

"Honor," I said. "That is why I decided to use Passover as an excuse to come to Jerusalem and approach you."

Two women entered the shop. Pascal did not have the opportunity to ask more.

As for me, I was satisfied. I had planted the seed that would rapidly grow. By week's end, I guessed, Pascal and I would come to terms.

I left him with his customers and wandered out to see the city.

***

This was not my first visit to the Holy City. I knew what I would find as the markets came to life over the next few hours.

The streets would be crowded with bazaars peopled with shoemakers, tailors, flax spinners, goldsmiths, wool combers, butchers, food inspectors, and diplomats. The air would be filled with the smell of fish, of incense, of ripe and rotting fruit, of the stench of leather being cured, tanned, and dyed. I would find food- and wineshops, where, if my appetite conquered my dull spirit, I could partake from a selection that varied from fried locusts to fresh fish to fruitcakes. Or I could be tempted by Judean or Galilean wines, or a wide range of foreign beers to break my recent vow to avoid drink.

If I were after excitement, I could have dodged thieves and prostitutes in the lower city, among the dark underground alleys where a man could lose his soul and life to any number of different seductions. Or I could have cheered at the horse races in the Hippodrome, or disappeared into a theater in pursuit of distraction, or lost myself in the hot fog of steam rooms that were as luxurious as any in Rome.

I knew, however, that no amount of activity would console me.

I chose instead to seek the countryside beyond the city, using as my guide the distant smoke of the temple sacrifices, which rippled dark above the altar like a curtain between earth and heaven.

CHAPTER THREE

I spent the remainder of the morning in the dusty groves above the Kidron Valley, on the western slope of the Mount of Olives. From there I could quietly survey all of Jerusalem. A few hours later, I returned to the main road and joined the pilgrims moving into the Holy City. I could not know then, of course, how I was about to become part of an inexorable avalanche of events about to destroy the single innocent man who stood resolutely in its path.

Not until later would I understand more, learning portions of it from those prominent in religious and political circles who welcomed me because of my wealth. Many of the other participants—servants and scribes, women and soldiers—later recounted their witness to His followers. Eventually, when combined with what the followers themselves had seen, this entire story would become clear to me; I lean heavily on their accounts—admitting some speculation at their motives—for what I was unable to see myself.

And what I could not see that morning began on the other side of the hill.

To be more accurate, the events began in Bethphage, which lay on the eastern side of the Mount of Olives. Some considered

9

Bethphage distinct from Jerusalem, for the deep Kidron Valley separated it from the city proper. Others—despite the valley between—considered Bethphage an extension of the city, and during Passover and the days before, the scattered collection of buildings that made up the hamlet were filled with festive pilgrims who could not find room to stay in Jerusalem.

Bethphage is connected to Jerusalem by a caravan road that crosses the bottom of the Kidron Valley and passes by olive groves as it climbs the Mount of Olives. After the road reaches the top, it dips through Bethphage, then continues on a gentle descent into Bethany, a half mile away. From there, the caravan road reaches to Jericho and beyond.

Little traffic, however, followed the road away from Jerusalem at this time of year. Instead, patriarch pilgrims jammed the road destined for the Holy City. The bickering of pilgrims with mothers-in-law, camels, donkeys, chickens, children, and other stubborn beasts irritated by long days of travel provided amusement for the residents of Bethphage who sat beside their homes and watched the parade.

The crowds were at their most entertaining, for so near to Passover, people were impatient to reach the Holy City for purification in the temple. Furthermore, the warming weather had called out the idle travelers fortunate enough to have already secured lodging. The sky was weak blue in the high altitude, painted with wisps of clouds. A slight breeze kept the day from becoming hot, yet the sun had enough strength to banish all thoughts of winter.

Among the traffic, two men approaching Bethphage gave little cause for notice until they began to untie a young donkey haltered to a post near its mother in front of an inn.

Peter—redheaded and red-bearded—wore the rough clothing of a fisherman, with a sword strapped to his side and the perpetual scowl of suspicion common to laborers who understand no way to make money except with their hands. The other, John, taller with thinning brown hair, walked with a staff.

Fumbling with the rope at the donkey's side, Peter and John tried to ignore the hostile stares from a group of men nearby. The older men sat on chairs, surveying the road in dignified disdain; the younger men stood behind them with their arms crossed, trying to appear equally important to passersby.

"You!" the tallest of the younger observers challenged, stepping toward Peter and John. "Red and stubby! Mind giving an explanation?"

Mutters of support came from the others.

Peter said nothing.

"You!" the man repeated. "Are you deaf? Touched in the head?"

Peter straightened, his hands still on the halter rope. "I can hear you with no difficulty. As for my head, there is nothing wrong—"

"Ho-ho," the man laughed. He was bulky with the natural advantages of an athletic body, but his substantial belly showed he took his prowess for granted. "But a few words and I can tell you're from the north. All they grow are simpletons up there."

He paused, looking to his companions for support. Their grins were all the encouragement he needed. "So tell me, country boy," the man continued. "What are you doing?"

The tendons at the side of Peter's neck strained as he tried to control his temper. "This is a rope," Peter said slowly. "The rope is attached to the donkey. My fingers are upon the rope. As my fingers pull apart the knot, the rope becomes untied. Once I untie the rope, the animal will be free. It is a simple concept. Surely even the dimmest of minds can—"

"Peace, Peter," John interrupted him. "Remember our instructions." John turned and spoke directly to the gathered men, recalling how he had been instructed. "Our Lord needs this donkey. He will send it back shortly."

Peter's chest rose and fell visibly as he took in and let out a deep breath.

"Tell me," one of the older men said, speaking to John before a fight could erupt, "this Lord of yours. Would He happen to be the prophet from Nazareth?"

"None other," John replied.

The group's silence became a silence of respect.

"We have heard rumors of His arrival. Will He pass by soon?"

John nodded.

The old man thought for several seconds. "The story about a dead man, Lazarus of Bethany. Were you there?"

John nodded again.

"Was it as described?" the man asked. "A man raised from his tomb?"

"Words do not do it justice," Peter said stoutly. "I smelled the stench of death from the tomb. And from the darkness he came, called out by our Lord."

The observers whispered among themselves.

"Silence," the old man barked. To John and Peter he spoke more quietly. He knew there could be no harm and possibly great gain in extending a favor to a famous worker of miracles. "Take the animal."

Both disciples led the donkey toward Bethany, where the teacher had already begun leading a procession on foot.

As soon as Peter and John turned a corner in the road, the young men at the inn scattered to spread the news in all directions. They took proud ownership in the arrival of the miracle man of Nazareth by being the first to have knowledge of His coming to Bethphage from Bethany on His way to the Holy City.

This news reached me as I walked among the pilgrims on my return to Jerusalem, news that stirred me from thoughts of despair and aroused a little curiosity from my depths of self-pity.

As for the old men, after the departure of the two disciples, they merely waited by the side of the road. They had long since learned that much of life arrived with or without their efforts.

CHAPTER FOUR

W ith pilgrims surrounding the donkey, Yeshua rode in silence, cushioned from the vertebrae of the animal's spine by cloaks provided by His disciples.

Beside the animal, among the twelve of the teacher's closest followers, walked Lazarus, smiling and vigorous, the picture of anything but a man who some claimed had once been dead. Behind them, maintaining a respectful distance, were the women who took comfort from Yeshua's presence and teachings.

The small group of pilgrims traveling from Bethany—close followers and friends of the teacher—was also silent. Politically astute, the followers feared Jerusalem's reaction to their teacher's arrival. For some time, public postings had dictated that any person who saw the man from Galilee must report Him. If He had chosen to arrive in full view and defiance of the temple authorities, however, they were not going to abandon Him. Not yet.

As the procession left Bethany behind and continued toward Bethphage, the caravan road remained a broad, easily traveled mountain trail. The footing was rock, loose stones, and sand, paler brown than the reddish soil of the arid lower hills of Jericho. The Mount of Olives sloped upward on one side of the road and dropped steeply on the other.

Unexpectedly, as the travelers neared Bethphage, they saw a

stream of pilgrims heading toward them, away from Jerusalem. These pilgrims were loud, almost boisterous in their enthusiasm.

Peter, walking a few paces behind the donkey, squinted as he tried to make sense of it. But too many hours of fishing with sunlight bouncing off the lake had made his sight notoriously untrustworthy among his friends.

"What's that?" he whispered to Judas. "A mob? Why?"

Judas Iscariot, a thin, handsome man with a well-trimmed beard, grinned. "Ask the teacher. He knows everything."

"He doesn't appear to be in the mood for jokes," Peter said.

Judas had a knack for ill-timed humor.

Peter squinted again. "All those people, what are they carrying?"

The redheaded fisherman's hand had unconsciously fallen to the hilt of his sword.

"Relax, hothead," Judas said. "Those are branches."

The large crowd swept toward them.

□□□□□□□□□

I was among that crowd. After hearing the babble and rumors and excitement and stories regarding this man, my curiosity had grown.

And so, I was about to see Him. I had no idea how the intersection of our lives would change who I was.

"Is this the prophet from Nazareth in Galilee?" a man near me shouted.

"It is," one of the followers called back.

Shouts and cries carried back to reach those behind me. The crowd swelled forward. A few in the front removed their cloaks and placed them on the road.

Others began waving their branches. And yet others shouted for Lazarus to step forward, to prove he was alive.

Somewhere from the middle of the throng came the first

cries of praise. "Hosanna! Blessed is he who comes in the name of the Lord! Hosanna!"

As I well knew from my previous Passovers in Jerusalem, people were shouting the welcoming chant extended to pilgrims from one of our ancient psalms. According to tradition, the pilgrims would respond with the second clause of each verse, with both parties singing the last verse together.

This occasion proved to be different from tradition, however. Much different.

Before us walked Lazarus, whose miraculous rising from the dead provided heated debate, speculation, and awe among the pilgrims to the Holy City. Lazarus was the proof, they cried, proof that all the other stories about Yeshua could be believed! Proof that a new Messiah had arrived to fulfill the ancient prophecies—a new Messiah with powers to break Roman oppression!

As a man of wealth and education, I did not need such stories to entertain me. Still, I understood how the stories could affect common people who had little variation or hope in their daily lives.

The crowd's fever grew, and the hosannas became hoarse, broken utterances. From voice to voice, from soul to soul, the fire of unencumbered joy spread.

"Hosanna! Blessed is the King of Israel! Blessed is the coming kingdom of our father David! Hosanna!"

Yeshua did not alter the pace of the donkey. People had plenty of time to rip down more branches to throw onto the road before the animal.

As the long procession spilled over the highest ridge to begin descending the Mount of Olives, the twelve followers finally saw the true extent of the crowd behind me and understood how the joyful noise could have reached such deafening levels.

The followers were dazed by the wonder of it all. This was no death march, they told themselves! This was a celebration of thousands streaming out through the gates of Jerusalem to join a spontaneous parade up the Mount of Olives. The majority were visitors to Jerusalem, most of them hardly aware of why they were dancing and singing with strangers.

This was no death march! Surely now the teacher did not have an execution to fear in Jerusalem. Not with the support of so many people.

"Hosanna! Hosanna! Blessed is the King of Israel! Blessed is the coming kingdom of our father David! Hosanna! Hosanna!"

The singing was so joyous, it almost lifted me from my despair. The singing remained joyous for some time—until a group of Pharisees pushed through the crowd.

These men were set apart by their religious caps and the tassels on their cloaks. Disgust showed obviously on their faces. Disgust at the possibility of contaminating themselves. Disgust at the spectacle of the public worship of a man they hated.

As the religious authorities began to shout and strike those around them, the hosannas quieted. Silence fell, all the more eerie in contrast to the almost frenzied shouting that had preceded it.

"Teacher, rebuke Your followers for saying things like that!" the lead Pharisee commanded with the full power of a man accustomed to making people shrink back simply by lifting an eyebrow.

Another spoke. "You are not worth this adulation. Call out now and send them away!"

The teacher slowly pulled His gaze from the view of Jerusalem. From where He sat, He could not see the temple or the northern portions of the Holy City. But to the south and east of Mount Zion, He could see rising terraces and the large homes of the wealthy Jews of the upper city. Yet the magnificent homes seemed dwarfed by Herod's palace with its great towers and lush gardens. The white walls of the buildings glowed in direct sunlight, looking like the entrance to heaven.

Yeshua stared at the Pharisees. He pointed at the rocks visible on the road, those not covered by the branches and cloaks spread before His donkey. Then He spoke slowly and clearly, so the crowd could hear His restrained anger. "If they kept quiet, the stones along the road would burst into cheers!"

The Messiah had spoken! New shouts of acclamation drowned out anything the Pharisees might have said in reply.

Unbidden, the donkey moved forward. The teacher swayed gently with its movement and ignored the Pharisees as He passed them.

The procession surged toward the final descent into Jerusalem.

And because I remained on the outskirts of the crowd, drawn to the prophet yet not committed, I heard one Pharisee say to the other, "We've lost. Look, the whole world has gone after Him."

I did not hear the reply.

Yet I would remember that prediction when they chose their course of action to defeat Him.

CHAPTER FIVE

A girl and a boy—scruffy, dirty children whose parents obviously had little concern for their whereabouts—dodged and twisted among us as we moved closer to Jerusalem.

The girl chased the boy past me, under the waving branches and palm leaves, both children unaware of the reason for celebration but giddy with laughter and the joyous mood of the adults around them.

They shrieked with play until the boy shot into a gap in the crowd. Although space opened for him, he stopped so quickly that the girl tumbled into him. She lifted her hand to slap the boy in mock vexation, but the sight that had mesmerized him stayed her hand, and she, too, froze to stare upward in awe.

A man on a donkey rode beneath the branches held aloft like a royal arch.

They saw what I had first seen.

The man's features were neither ugly enough nor handsome enough to set Him apart from other men. His hair was neither shaggy nor cut in a fashionable style. His physique was compact from carpenter's work, but not overwhelming. This was a man easy to overlook on a crowded street. Except for His eyes.

Men and women looked into His eyes and felt eternity tug at

their souls; a music of peace seemed to still time until finally, reluctantly, they were able to pull their eyes from His. These were eyes with the authority to cast aside demons of torment, eyes that with a single look could make a person whole. Eyes that made His smile unlike any other man's.

It had been this smile that had first riveted the boy. When the girl joined him, the man cast it upon her too. He focused His gentle attention on them with a gaze of such presence that a silence of instinctive, untroubled yearning covered them like the cloaks upon His donkey, a silence so powerful that years later, in occasional quiet moments, this memory could soothe their souls as a caress.

I understood why the children stared. His eyes kept me there in the crowd, unable to leave with a cynical snort of derision at the madness of the crowd's behavior; His eyes cast the first doubts on my disbelief of the Lazarus miracle.

Then the moment ended for the boy and the girl.

The throng surged forward, moving the animal down the road. Pilgrims swept in front of the children, blocking their view of the man riding it.

In unison, without exchanging words or glances, the two turned, squeezing and bumping around the legs of the changing adults in their need to follow. They stayed with us as the road dipped into a shallow depression. When the road rose again, it suddenly brought the Holy City into full view for the first time.

The temple tower dominated the line of the sky as easily as it lorded over the vast courts spread beneath it. And the monstrous temple walls were cliffs—unassailable and as fixed as eternity. The white lime paint of the buildings, the burnish of hammered gold on the temple, and the softness of the green of the gardens gave an impact of unearthly splendor, an ache of beauty that could never be captured by words.

What the children could not see, the man they followed did.

I can only imagine what brought forth Yeshua's next words, as if time's curtain had rippled, shifting until it parted to give Him a ghastly vision of the same city with earthen ramps heaped to the top of the walls, of legions of soldiers swarming triumphantly, of the sky marred by the smoke of destruction, of temple walls shattered to rubble, of hills stark with hundreds of rebels groaning and impaled on crosses so numerous it was like a charred forest, of wailing mothers searching the ruins for their children's torn bodies. And then, with another ripple of the curtain of time, a new vision: of dust swirling in an eerie dance to a haunting dirge sung by the wind as it blew across a plateau lifeless and desolate for centuries, the rejection by God as a horrible, cold punishment for a city that had butchered His Son.

This is what the children could not see and what I would not understand until decades had passed: the beauty of the city and the inexorable tragedy ahead.

Yet at that moment, Yeshua knew.

The force of the contrast tore from Him a wrenching sob so loud it startled those beside Him. His sorrow deepened into heaving lamentation that cast the circled followers into an uneasy, puzzled silence.

It was as if He spoke to the women of the city when the agonized words left His mouth. "I wish that even today you would find the way of peace. But now it is too late, and peace is hidden from you. Before long your enemies will build ramparts against your walls and encircle you and close in on you."

Yeshua closed His eyes but was unable to shut out the vision. "They will crush you to the ground, and your children with you. Your enemies will not leave a single stone in place, because you have rejected the opportunity God offered you."

His weeping did not stop.

The boy and the girl crept forward. Unlike the adults, they were not frightened by the terrible sorrow of the man on the donkey, but they were filled with a longing to comfort, as if He were a smaller child in need, and His sorrow drew them slowly to the donkey, where each shyly rested a hand on its flank.

For as long as He wept, they wordlessly shared His grief.

CHAPTER SIX

As the procession continued on toward Jerusalem, a conversation took place, one that I would learn of later from well-placed friends who enjoyed telling me of their successes. Friends, I am ashamed to say, accustomed to political intrigue.

If that says something about my character—to have these friends—I accept the judgment. It is part of the danger that comes with accumulating wealth, and there was a time in my life when I found it exciting to associate with such people—before I realized the price I was paying for my gold by giving it more devotion than I did my wife and children.

These friends I mention had sent spies to fish among the twelve followers of the man of Galilee. Later, they conveyed the conversation to me.

"Hello, my friend."

Walking behind the others, Judas glanced at the man who joined him. Older and of medium height, the most striking portion of the man's face was a bulbous nose, skin thick and pitted. The man's smile was ingratiating, dulled by several missing teeth.

"Who calls me friend?" Judas asked. He carried the money-bag for all the disciples. His natural shrewdness with money also made him naturally suspicious.

"Does it matter in this great crowd? We are all for the Messiah, are we not?"

Despite the ringing of song and cheers that had resumed around them, Judas caught the duplicity in the man's voice. "We are," Judas said evenly.

"And you are one of His closest followers. Judas Iscariot. A Judean when all the others are Galilean."

That the man knew Judas's name was one thing. That he was prepared to show this knowledge was another. It was the essence of Judas to understand cunning subtlety. He knew the man was playing a game and was unafraid to show it. What game, however, roused Judas to curiosity.

"It is a great thing to be close to someone with such power, is it not?" the man continued.

Judas lifted an eyebrow, not agreeing, not disagreeing. At this point, it was in his interest to listen without committing any kind of answer.

"After all," the man said, "if He ever led crowds like this to a successful revolt, He would need capable administrators. Which, of course, is another sort of power."

The man alluded to the position Judas held among the disciples, showing he had even more knowledge about their workings. Outwardly, Judas hid his enjoyment of the intrigue.

They walked without speaking for a few steps. Halfway down the Mount of Olives now, they passed through the mottled shadows of olive trees.

"After all," the man said, content that he had Judas's interest, "if half of the stories of His miracles are true, with a single word He could fell Roman armies."

"They are true," Judas said. "My own eyes claim witness."

"Yes, yes," the man answered, still smiling his ingratiating, toothless smile, "but in the region of Dalmanutha, a group of Pharisees challenged Him to show a sign from heaven, and He was unable to produce a miracle. Had He but taken that opportunity . . ."

"My own eyes claim witness to His miracles," Judas repeated.

"Then why has He not taken the cloak of Messiah? I have spoken to other followers who left Him. Followers who tell me that in Capernaum, He commanded them not to rise up against the Romans. Surely you saw how many fell away from Him?"

Judas did not rise to his teacher's defense. For somehow, this grubby man had squeezed juice from the very same doubts Judas held.

"Yes," the man mused, "there is such a thing as a sinking ship. I, for one, would never hesitate to swim to safety. There is nothing noble about drowning unnecessarily, particularly if power is to be found elsewhere."

He winked at Judas. "You asked me my name, friend? Should you ever want to know, you may find me among the Sanhedrists. Those who hold true power."

He gave Judas a final oily smile before blending back into the flow of pilgrims.

CHAPTER SEVEN

S imeon, you are quiet this evening."

I brought my attention back from the flame of the oil lamp. Dusk had yet to arrive, and although the room received ample sunlight through the slatted window overlooking the central courtyard, Seraphine had insisted on the flame and incense to accompany the meal.

I found both Seraphine and Pascal staring at me. Pascal, I guessed, was curious because of our earlier conversation in his shop, a curiosity I did not wish to attend to immediately. Seraphine, perhaps, was still accustoming herself to the sight of a scarred cousin from a distant land, trying to match my appearance to all the wild stories Pascal had undoubtedly told about me before my arrival.

I attempted a wan smile at their concern. "Travel has left me weary."

"That was your excuse yesterday," Pascal said. He paused to swirl his wine, sniff it, and leave some on his tongue several seconds before swallowing. "You are beginning to sound like an old woman."

"Pascal . . . ," Seraphine began in admonishing tones.

"Don't start on me, wife," Pascal told Seraphine. "He and I are cousins and business partners, and I also lay claim to the privilege of old friendship." Pascal took another swallow, grimaced, and handed her his wine cup. "We have better. Find it."

"Only if the steward delivered more today," she said tartly. "And don't show off by attempting to treat me as chattel."

Pascal lifted his bearded face to stare at her directly. For a moment, I saw the iron that made Pascal the king of Jerusalem silk merchants. So, obviously, did Seraphine.

"My darling," he said, meaning it, "would you please bring us some better wine?"

She hesitated only briefly, hid a smile, took the wine cup, and left with a defiant swish of her dress.

"I'll pay for that later," Pascal said a few seconds later. His grin was crooked, showing large yellowed teeth. "A man's a fool if he thinks he rules his own home."

I thought of my home overlooking the sea and of my wife on the balcony as the wind blew her dark hair when she loosened it to dance freely. Regret must have crossed my face. When Pascal spoke again, his tone was much gentler.

"What is it, my friend?" he asked. He gestured at the table loaded with salted fish, sweetmeats, fried locusts, grapes, figs, honey, and breads. Jugs of beer, wine, and water sat among the plates. It was a feast for many although there were only three of us. "You have eaten little and refused all my wine. And this morning, the unexpected offer to sell everything you own . . ."

"One matter is not related to the other," I said. "We shall find time this week to discuss business. As for my appetite, again blame travel. I am older now. I do not recover as quickly."

"A few weeks at sea exhausted you?" If our business matter was foremost in his mind, Pascal did a masterful job of pretending otherwise. "With a stopover in Alexandria? And a few days of rest in Caesarea? Don't lie to me, Simeon. I sent Seraphine away to give us time alone here, as you seem to disappear during the day and retire early upon your return."

"It is nothing." If he was trying to give me the opportunity to talk about the fire that had left me scarred, I had no desire to oblige him.

"A dozen times over the last twenty years, you have joined me here for Passover. Each of those dozen Passovers, I was hard-pressed at any meal to keep your wine cup full. And now? All you take is water and bread. Is that why you have become so gaunt?"

"In the last months I have fasted," I acknowledged.

"You? A religious man?" Pascal laughed. "I thought you were far too practical for that. And your love of wine and beer was—"

"It no longer suits me!" I said, surprised at the vehemence of my voice.

Pascal closed his eyes in instant remorse. "Forgive me for prying."

"There is nothing to pry," I said, trying to keep the edge out of my tone.

A moment later, I sighed. "And there is nothing to forgive. As you said, it is a privilege of old friendship to speak openly."

Pascal nodded as if he understood. But he didn't know my secret.

The day before, I had overheard him speaking to Seraphine: "Simeon has always been robust," he'd told her; "he always had an air of dangerous wildness that attracted the wrong kind of women. Now, he is a different person. Where he once kept his thick dark hair long, it is nearly shorn and dull. And if that doesn't show something seriously wrong," he'd added, "all you have to do is look at his skin, loose and parchment gray. Yes," Pascal had concluded, "today's Simeon is not the Simeon of old."

Seraphine's only response had been a cluck of sympathy. They both knew of the tragedy that had befallen my family. A son lost. A daughter crippled. And, of course, even if they had not received a letter from my wife, Jaala, there was the damaged flesh of my face, mute testimony to the accident eighteen months earlier.

□|□|□|□|□|□|□|□|□

"Since we speak of religion," I said, looking to stop Pascal's speculations regarding my troubles, "tell me about this prophet from Nazareth. I was near the temple today, and He caused a tremendous stir."

Pascal poured himself some beer. He did not remark on the unusual aspect of my spending more than the required Passover time at the temple. *If he has gone as far as to fast*, he was undoubtedly thinking, *how far will Simeon go with his new religious efforts?*

"As you know," Pascal said, "a good many of my friends belong to the Sanhedrin. Caiaphas, the high priest, in fact, is one of my best customers. Of course, with the proceeds from temple sales, he can afford to be. Do you know what kind of profit there is in simply changing coins to the half shekels demanded for the yearly tribute? Let the peasants grumble if they will, but you have to admire the strong business sense of Annas and his family. They——"

"The prophet." I brought him back to the subject that was on my mind. "The one they call the Messiah."

"We have had dozens of messiahs," Pascal snorted, unfazed by the directness of my question. "The countryside is rife with them."

"Dozens who raise men from the dead? Dozens who refuse to call for action against the Romans and instead preach love and compassion? Dozens who are followed by crowds of thousands?"

"You've heard the stories then."

I nodded.

"Understand that it is unsettling for those of us in Jerusalem."

"A dead person brought to life?" I snorted. "'Unsettling' is an understatement. If it is true, then—"

"Truth has nothing to do with the situation," Pascal said. "This Yeshua could be a magician. Or He could be working with the devil, as some of the Pharisees say. Besides, what does truth matter against hard practicalities? This country is dry tinder, ready to be set ablaze by the tiniest spark. A so-called messiah with a following is more than a spark; it is an open flame. Surely you, as a merchant, understand the implications."

"A revolt is bad for business," I said dryly.

"When business is good, life is good. Would you rather watch soldiers go through the city, killing men, women, and children? I've heard Caiaphas say it myself. Better that one should die than we all perish."

"So the prophet is marked for execution?" I asked.

"I'm surprised He marched publicly into Jerusalem. If you want to hear His teachings, you had better do it as soon as possible. If they can ever get Him away from His adoring public . . ."

"Perhaps He is unafraid. If He can raise a man from the dead . . ."

Pascal dismissed me with a gulp of beer and a wave of his hand. "Don't give that rumor a second thought, my friend. Only God Himself could do such a thing. And I doubt He would come from the backwaters of Galilee."

MONDAY

CHAPTER EIGHT

My dearest love,

Another day begins. It is so early that I again write by oil lamp, but soon, although the passage of time seems endless, the sun will rise.

I am tired. The night does not treat me well whether I sleep or not.

When I lie awake in my bed, I am at least able to distract my mind. I run through calculations on anticipated prices for this year's silk. I judge the chances of losing ships in storms. I plan mild revenges on the harbormaster for his annual tax increases. And when I feel I can bear the sadness, I open the gates to my memories of moments with you.

Remember the evening we evaded the guests at our own party and sneaked through the silent city to be alone on a hillside? Beneath the moonlight, we giggled not like a long-married couple but like teenagers. Remember how, at a passionate moment, the appearance of a herd of wild swine wandering the hillside sent us running?

I also remember a time when you fell asleep curled against me, with your hand on my chest and your face resting on your hand. When you woke—for I had been watching the rise and fall of your breathing—you blinked and lifted your head, and I saw the line of your rings in the skin of your lovely cheek. My heart burst to think that someone as beautiful as you would have accepted those rings as gifts from me.

Do you know what I worship most about your beauty? Your nose. The small freckles of perfection. The delicate curves. A profile of grace. How your nostrils flare during your quick surges of anger. It is a nose I can gaze upon for hours. Think me silly if you will, but I love your nose.

Now, this far from you, I am grateful for all the times early in our marriage when I woke in our chamber and silently watched you in the silvery moonlight, my near reverence as much for the beauty of your face surrounded by the hair draped on your pillow as for the love inside me that would thicken my throat with sadness and joy and longing and gratitude.

Even now as I write, I smile, because for all your perfection in flesh and soul, it is not difficult to recall how thoroughly you have caused me vexation. I will remind you, as I have on many occasions, that a bath is not meant to take more time than the rebuilding of the temple. Nor was it intended by marriage vows that a husband be forced to pace for hours while his wife leisurely applies perfumes and chooses attire for a public occasion, all the while hearing assurances that the final result is but moments away.

But as I remember now, my smile fades, for I know I threw it all away. Even before the horror of the fire and your unspoken blame, I had lost much of the love you once gave me. Now, looking back, I see it happened in the way that dust settles. Slowly. Layer by layer.

How could I have been such a fool to let my ceaseless work become more important than my time for you and with you? Yet slowly, layer by layer, day by day as I pursued the wealth that would give us comfort in our old age, I was losing you. Worse, you even warned me many times, begging me to spend more time with you. All those days I threw away, days I could have idled hours with you and listened to you sing lullabies to our children.

Yet I spent my days at the harbor and at the warehouses. How could you not finally believe that gold was more important to me than your love?

Thinking of it, I sigh here in my lonely chamber. I long for you, more so for the final reason for our separation. I believe that I truly could win back the love we once had if not for that final, irrevocable event that put the chasm between us.

Yes, all of this remorse I carry and ponder during my wakeful state here.

Yet no sooner do I find the blessed relief of sleep than the demons begin to hiss and coil around my unconscious soul. I do not dream, but instead see the startled wideness of our daughter's eyes, the fear on her face. I hear the screams of panic. I feel the panic and strength in her arms, as if once again she is clutching me in the throes of her agony. And then—as if once was not enough pain, I am cursed with it again and again. I see the flames. These details are inflicted on me so clearly that, as she screams in my nightmare, I see flames licking at her oil-drenched skin. And I smell the scorch of tortured flesh. The smell brings me back to wakefulness, trembling and sweating and determined never to sleep again.

Pray for me, I beg. You embrace our Yahweh with far more devotion than I have ever shown Him. I have distanced myself from any hope of mercy from Him . . . pray for me.

Your Simeon

T he blind beggar cocked his head. In the early quiet of the city, even before the priests blew the trumpet calls to prayer, did he hear footsteps crossing the plaza?

Yes, his ears told him. Coming from the west.

The footsteps were soft. Slow. A man not in a hurry.

The footsteps belonged to me. Pascal's guest chamber had become too much of a prison. I had dressed quietly, trying to run from my memories by walking the city streets in the pale gray of the new light.

Later, I would come to know this man better. Well enough to guess that as I began to cross his path for the first time, he concentrated beyond the cramp of his hunger pains to visualize what his milky cataract-covered eyes could no longer tell him. He knew from memory the imposing sight presented by the temple behind him. Indeed, in his youth, he had been one of thousands of laborers who had worked on the massive reconstruction under Herod the Great. Each block of stone of the temple wall was almost the height of a man and easily several paces long. Hundreds of these blocks, piled hundreds of feet high, formed the massive walls. Here at the south entrance, two sets of wide steps led to the gates of the temple compound. In a few hours, it would be crowded with Passover pilgrims coming to make offerings, awed to stand in the temple's shadows.

Now, however, only he and I shared the vast plaza. The markets had yet to open, the wailing of public prayers had yet to begin, the wind had yet to rise.

The air was so quiet and still that the crowing of a rooster easily crossed the valley from the top of the Mount of Olives.

As the first rays of the sun warmed the beggar's shoulders and ribs, he might have found it pleasant to sit and think of earlier days when a hard day's work was enough for bread and wine. Pleasant, except for the hunger that tortured him constantly. Pleasant, except for his nervous tension. At this hour, he did not have the teeming public around him as protection. There was a strange intimacy in sharing this open empty place; how could he know what I might do to him, a helpless, blind old man?

My footsteps approached. Closer . . . closer. I could see on his face that the sound made my approaching presence the total concern of his world.

My footsteps faded as I passed him by, telling him that his hopes and fears and past were worthless and insignificant to me. In anger, even more than from the need for money, the beggar rattled the two coins in his bowl.

I stopped and looked at him more closely. His beard was streaked with gray and grease. He stank. Flies crawled across his rags.

I walked back toward him.

He knew I was there.

The beggar stared straight ahead. Who was I? Soldier? Priest? Cruel? Kind? With just the two of us there in the plaza, I held power over him because of his handicap.

"I once was strong," the beggar said, speaking to me, the stranger he could not see. "Now I can no longer work. My wife died before I lost my sight, and we had no children to support us." He spoke simply, maintaining his dignity.

"You have not eaten in some days," I said. Did the beggar

hear the accent in my voice? "There is a smell to a starving man. His body begins to burn impurities."

I knew this because I had recently fasted, almost to the point of death. What I had found interesting was that after the first week, my body lost its hunger. What I had found discouraging was that my self-imposed fast had not relieved the burden of my soul. And that I hadn't found the courage to take my fasting to its final stage.

"I have not eaten in some days," the beggar acknowledged.

Undoubtedly, the beggar heard rustling as I opened my money purse. I poured coins into the bowl between his legs. After all, what did money matter to me?

"May God's peace rest upon you," the beggar said. From the shakiness in his voice, it seemed he might weep in gratitude.

"And upon you." But my mind was already elsewhere as I turned away.

I took a few steps. Then I realized he did not know me; I could speak to him without worrying about his opinion of me.

I returned and crouched beside the beggar. "Tell me," I said. "If you were to die, what method would you choose?"

I saw him recoil in fear. There were men, of course, who killed simply for the pleasure of inflicting pain on another. For all the beggar knew, I was holding a knife. A sword. A length of rope. I could kill him swiftly, with no witnesses.

"P-please," the beggar stuttered. "Keep your coins. I mean no offense by stopping you."

I laughed softly. "I should ask your apology," I said. "I have startled you when I simply meant the question in a philosophical way. After all, if one attempts to discuss such things with friends, they become nervous. But you and I are here alone. You do not know me. I do not know you. Strange, how that makes it possible to share thoughts that would not be possible with someone you knew."

I paused. "So tell me, what do you think is the least painful way to die? My own opinion is that the Romans do it best. They sit in a steam bath and open a vein. Death approaches as a faintness that comes with the loss of blood. Of course, the mess is very inconsiderate to those left behind."

The beggar relaxed somewhat. This was an eerie topic to discuss.

"There is, however, the matter of the obvious sin of taking one's own life," I continued. "Especially with the iron rod of Moses and his commandments hanging over one. So instead, should a man attempt to deceive those close to him? Perhaps a fight might work best. One could throw himself into battle against Roman soldiers. This would give the appearance of a heroic death. God Himself might be fooled into believing it was not suicide. And a wife . . ."

I sighed. "A wife, too, might find it at least forgivable."

"If it's only a woman's opinion that concerns you," the beggar said, "I would give it no more thought. If she loves you, no method of death would be forgiven. If she doesn't love you, any death will suffice, as long as you leave behind enough to attract the next suitor."

I thought about his words. From the lower part of Jerusalem, we heard the first arguments of vendors at the market as they set up their wares.

"Well spoken," I finally said. "You have responded well to a question designed to amuse me."

Before the beggar could reply, I straightened and walked away. What troubled me most was that I had meant my question for more than amusement.

I t would be a wishful twist of memory to say with certainty that I noticed Yeshua and His disciples as they journeyed to Jerusalem early in the day.

Yet, for all I know, I could well have seen them. Again, a need for solitude had drawn me from the city. In the countryside, the sunshine and solitude gave my soul the illusion of freedom.

But it was only an illusion.

Resting on a large boulder on the side of the hill, I gazed at the faraway road that led down the Mount of Olives. The burden that had weighed heavily upon me for the previous eighteen months stayed squarely with me.

To Pascal—when we sat down to complete our transaction—I would give truth. A fire had destroyed one of my warehouses. I was tired of business.

Yet I would not tell him the entire truth: that my wife had only coldness in her heart, that my daughter recoiled from my touch, that I had discovered far too late what was truly valuable.

As for my intentions once Pascal and I came to terms and I had ensured the well-being of my family, I was still unsure. I wondered whether I could find comfort in a quiet life in some far corner of the empire. I also realized there was another possibility, the one that was frightening me less each day and tempting me more.

Deep in such thoughts, I would barely have paid attention to the pilgrims as they descended the Mount of Olives. Of course, at that time I did not know that Yeshua stayed in Bethany each night, nor did I care that He was determined to return to Jerusalem each new day.

Still, had I actually been looking, I might have seen Yeshua and His followers among the stream of pilgrims. Had I noticed, however, I still would not have understood why they stopped near a fig tree. Or what that stop could mean to the one named Judas Iscariot.

Halfway down the Mount of Olives, the unseasonably early leaves of a solitary fig tree were obvious from a considerable distance. While shrubs and wildflowers had begun to emerge, dotting the hillsides with color, the season had yet to woo anything but the fig tree into such a luxurious cloak of green. It stood in welcome contrast to the rocky soil around it.

Judas, however, had no eye for the beauty of the wild hills or the oasis of shade the fig tree promised. Of all the disciples, he walked farthest behind the teacher. Inside his purse, the fingers of his right hand played with layers of shekels as he sought relief for his uneasiness, which felt like black blood coursing through his veins.

He'd brought up the rear of the small procession since they'd left Bethphage, shuffling his sandals at an unenthusiastic pace with little energy. The crisp air of the morning had not roused his spirits; rather it seemed the cheerfulness of the pale blue sky and a sun not yet hot, along with the promise of a new season in the beginning bloom of wildflowers, all served to taunt him for the darkness his soul could not shake.

He'd slept poorly, waking again and again to remember pieces of his short conversation with the stranger in the crowd:

"Why has He not taken the cloak of Messiah?"

"In Capernaum, He commanded them not to rise up against the Romans."

"Nothing noble about drowning unnecessarily, particularly if power is to be found elsewhere."

"Should you ever want to know, you may find me among the Sanhedrists. Those who hold true power."

These statements surely worked like a slow poison, and when Judas felt guilt at his traitorous thoughts, it would be all too human to wash the guilt away with anger. After all, Yeshua had the entire world at His command. If He did not act upon it, should Judas be blamed for the natural result of resentment?

Judas was so deep into his bitter contemplation that when the procession stopped, he stumbled into Peter, striking him squarely between the shoulder blades.

Judas blinked. The small group had bunched at the side of the road. He saw no reason for the sudden halt.

"What's this?" Peter joked, spinning to see Judas. "A blind sparrow flutters against my neck?"

Some of the others laughed at Peter's affectionate remark.

Judas raised his lips in a smile to hide his thoughts. Earlier, Judas had always fooled himself into believing such jokes were meant to include him. Now he knew differently. Had not the teacher deliberately excluded him earlier—taking only Peter, James, and John up to a mountain one night for meditation? Inside, Judas flamed with anger at where his thoughts began to take him. After all the work he had done, after all he had given of his life over the past three years . . .

Again, Peter interrupted Judas's thoughts, grabbing him by the elbow, fully expecting this unspoken, imperious Galilean command to focus Judas's attention. Judas frowned in irritation.

More and more the arrogant fisherman was taking a position as second-in-command. Had they forgotten Judas was the one trusted with the band's funds?

Nonetheless, Judas turned his attention to where Peter pointed. Yeshua was walking a delicate path through low thorny bushes.

"It's a fig He wants," Peter said.

So now, Judas thought with scorn, *the fisherman knows the teacher's thoughts?*

Yeshua stopped at the base of the tree and looked up into its wide branches.

"As we left Bethany this morning, some of us warned Him to break His fast," Peter said softly. "It was plain that a night of prayer had worn Him into a faint of hunger. But He insisted on leaving for Jerusalem."

"It is not the season for figs," Judas said. Yeshua was still searching the tree for fruit. "Surely He knows that."

"You have a head good with figures," Peter said with a smile. "But it is easy to guess that you are not from the country. See the tree's greenness? It is well known in Galilee that the fruit on a fig tree always appears before the leaves. Failing that, there should be old fruit from last season, just as edible as new fruit. Don't be surprised when our master finds a fig."

"Thank you for increasing my limited education," Judas replied. "How I ever lived without such knowledge is beyond me."

Peter did not hear the sarcasm and patted Judas on the shoulder. Before, Judas would have accepted such an action with a glow of fellowship. Now it seemed condescending.

Beneath the tree, Yeshua gave up His search and picked His way back through the brush.

"Barren," Peter said quietly. "In any man's garden, it would only be good for kindling."

"Again," Judas said, taking satisfaction in his ambiguous tone, "I thank you for your valuable teaching. It will undoubtedly serve me well in my own orchards."

Judas enjoyed Peter's response, a quick strange look as if the big man had finally suspected something amiss but did not have the intelligence to understand.

Peter's jaw began to move—Judas nearly laughed at the thought that the fisherman was so slow he needed to have his mouth in motion to think—but the teacher interrupted whatever reply Peter might have given. He surprised them all by speaking His first words of the day's journey not to them but to the tree.

"May no one ever eat your fruit again!" Yeshua said; then He turned toward Jerusalem.

His followers also turned and exchanged puzzled looks. Not even Judas—ever alert for hidden meaning in any man's words— could make sense of the teacher's utterance, for His tone had been completely flat.

Judas had, of course, noticed one thing. In the intimacy of sharing shrugs, none of the other eleven—all Galileans, when he was Judean—had bothered to glance at him.

Judas decided he would remember that. Just as he remembered all the injustices in his life.

To my surprise, on my return to the city, I saw the blind beggar again. He was not begging but awkwardly shuffling through the temple.

To enter the city, I had done what most who arrive from the direction of Jericho did. Instead of taking the longer route past the Pool of Bethesda and around the north side of the temple, I came through the East Gate, which allowed me to cut directly through the temple to the lower quarters of Jerusalem on the other side. The bedlam of the money changers and livestock in the temple had hardly distracted me.

But when I caught a glimpse of the man shuffling uncertainly as people moved quickly around him, I stopped. Twice, as I watched, uncaring pedestrians knocked him to his knees.

I'm not sure what moved me to help him. Perhaps it was the pitiful sight of someone struggling to reach a destination he could not see. Perhaps I felt the role of his guardian; I had already assisted him with a gift of gold. Or perhaps seeing his misery was a balm to my own. Regardless, I reached him quickly and took him by the elbow.

"Don't be alarmed," I told him at his startled flinch. "We spoke this morning."

He recognized my voice and smiled toothlessly as he turned

his face to me. Then he frowned. "I cannot return your money," he said quickly with a shiver of apprehension. "It is already—"

"I am not here for your coins," I said. Passersby jostled us. The din was so loud I was forced to lean toward his ear. The smell of his unwashed body and sweat-soured clothing caused me to regret our proximity. "Rather, I offer assistance. Where do you wish to go? And what madness has you venturing into the temple crowd?"

He answered. At first I did not believe I had heard correctly. Not with the shouting of money changers, the noise of livestock, and the ceaseless noise of bartering. I asked him to repeat his words.

"I want to see!" he shouted. "I have heard that the prophet has arrived again. If I find Him, He can heal me!"

Did I want to be party to this beggar's disappointment? After all, even if we actually found the prophet among the thousands in the temple, the only certainty awaiting this old blind man was tomorrow's blindness. Not healing.

However, as we stood, the prophet and His followers approached us. Although I witnessed what happened next, I later heard it retold in complaint—as I hid my smile and pretended ignorance—from a friend of Pascal, a friend who had a far greater stake in the event than I had.

O ren, son of Judd, stood hardly taller than the heads of the goats in the enclosure behind him. His robes were of fine woven cloth, and his fingers heavy with thick rings of gold. What did it matter that the stench of manure clung to his shoes, or that he was often covered with the dirt of livestock? He was a man of power.

Oren had earned his wealth over the years in the same way he was earning it at the moment—examining sacrificial animals, priding himself on his ability to concentrate on his task even when the pace of commerce was at its most hectic and demanding during the madness of Passover.

Around him, filling the Court of the Gentiles, thousands of pilgrims streamed past the animal enclosures and money tables, creating a babble of noise punctuated by merchants' shouts and children's cries. Cramped against each other in their respective pens, lambs and goats and oxen and cattle milled in nervous circles; the smell of fresh dung scattered by their hooves was ample proof of their instinctive fear of the unaccustomed din.

Dozens of pilgrims waited sullenly for Oren to inspect their offerings—small lambs tucked under arms, goats led by ropes, doves in reed cages. An old woman with a lamb stood directly before Oren.

He turned the lamb upside down and frowned at a spot on its belly. "Impure," he announced to the elderly woman. "Not fit for the sacrifice."

"What's that?" She cupped her ears with her hands, trying to hear above the din.

"I cannot give my approval to an animal with blemishes," he said, guessing she was too dim sighted to realize the spot was merely dirt. He could clean the lamb later and sell it for great profit. "Without my approval, the priests will not accept it at the altar."

"I brought my best lamb," she protested. "It cannot be blemished."

"Ignorance like yours is why the priests engage a *mumcheh* like me."

"I am offering God the best I have!" She was close to weeping.

Oren shrugged. "Have you spent a year and a half with a farmer learning what faults are temporary and what faults are permanent?"

"No, but—"

"I have. The priest will take my word over yours." He held out his hand. "I have been authorized to charge six *isar* for my judgment." Oren clucked self-righteously. "You could have avoided this trouble and bought your animal at the market here."

"From thieves who ask for a pigeon the price of a month's food?"

Again, he shrugged. "Do you wish the inconvenience of carrying this impure lamb, or do you wish to leave it with me to dispose of for you?"

At this final outrage, the elderly woman lost her patience. "I traveled three weeks to get here. I paid two *denarii* to change my coins to shekels for the temple tribute. And you propose to steal the very lamb you have rejected?"

Oren's thick ruddy lips formed a waxen smile. "You are welcome to have another mumcheh examine your lamb. For another six isar, of course."

The elderly woman screeched with anger. "You are all thieves! Working together to squeeze blood from our bones! If I were a man I would—"

Voices behind her rose in agreement. Until louder shouts distracted them.

"The prophet! He arrives! It is Yeshua, from Nazareth!"

Oren hoped they were wrong.

Then he heard a roar of approval. Although suspicion told him what to expect, he needed to see for himself. Oren remembered very clearly a time when Yeshua had visited before. Oren had been one of the prophet's first victims. He had no intention of seeing his money scattered again.

Oren groaned with effort and somehow squirmed his fat body onto his table. The table sagged. He tottered as he stretched to look over the crowd. What he saw confirmed his dread. The lunatic from Nazareth had begun another rampage.

CHAPTER THIRTEEN

From my vantage point, one hand still firmly clasping the blind beggar's elbow, I saw everything clearly. And with some degree of fascination.

The prophet Yeshua was less than a dozen steps away.

He showed no anger. Instead, great resolve was etched into His face. Already, He had turned over two money tables. Shekels and pagan coins had scattered like grain; the money changers were on their hands and knees, trying to scoop the coins together.

The next table held cages of doves. Had He wrenched the table on its side, the doves would have been crushed. Instead Yeshua leaned on the table and stared at the much taller, angry merchant behind it.

But the stare was enough. Instead of shouting, the merchant snapped his jaw shut and stepped away. With quick flicks of His fingers, the prophet opened the cage doors. Blossoms of white freedom, the doves whirred into the air above the crowd.

Yeshua upended two more money tables in silence. Several money changers down the line had lifted their tunics by the hems with one hand, uncaring of the indignity of exposing their skinny white legs as they scrambled to throw coins into the makeshift pouches. Despite their frantic efforts, they were not fast enough and fell backward as Yeshua flipped their tables.

He stopped abruptly and spun toward the gates of the animal enclosures. Pulling open the gates of the goat pen first, He waded in, waving His arms to drive the goats into the crowd. Then the cattle, the sheep and lambs, and finally the oxen.

The animals did much of the remaining work, knocking over tables and benches, bumping into merchants so greedy to guard their money that they refused to move away from the stampede of frightened beasts.

Around me, the confusion multiplied as people panicked. Twice I had to pull the blind beggar from the path of oxen. People flowed around us, at first trying to stem the escape of livestock, then fleeing it. Sheep, goats, and oxen barged in all directions.

The blind beggar kept crying for an explanation of the noise and confusion around him. I shouted to him to stay with me and wait. I did not know it at the time, of course, but the chaos had extended far beyond this portion of the temple.

Above all of it, I could hear pilgrims cheer. They thrilled to watch Yeshua's righteous anger. This man dared to stand alone against corruption. While the pilgrims needed animals for sacrifice at the altar, a proper market had been established on the lower portion of the Mount of Olives. The family of Annas had no scriptural authority for its stranglehold on these tainted profits.

Yeshua's moral certainty, like a physical force, at first made the merchants fall away. Then, as His methodical action gained momentum, the crowd's approval of His stance against the thievery was too much for any one merchant to overcome.

Still, as Yeshua continued, I could not help but wonder when the temple police would arrive.

I can thank Pascal and his love for passing on gossip from his well-to-do customers for the answer I eventually discovered.

When the first priests reached Caiaphas, the high priest, they were out of breath. It had been a long run from the Court of the Gentiles.

Caiaphas turned from conversation with a chief priest and raised his eyebrows in question at the noisy approach of the two men.

"He is at the money tables," one gasped. He waved his arms in a rapid gesture of confusion. "The animals! Coins! Benches everywhere! Send the temple police!"

Caiaphas froze him by raising a single bony finger.

"Do not ever tell me what to do." Tall and angular, with a reach as wide as a vulture's wingspan, Caiaphas's looks caused some to say his face mirrored the wrathful countenance of God. Caiaphas prided himself on the image and was as miserly with his smiles as with his shekels.

Confronted by his full anger, the second Pharisee actually twitched in fear and tried to suck back his own sobs for air, hoping not to be noticed.

Caiaphas looked back and forth between them until he was satisfied at their level of terror. "Tell me," he said. "Is the crowd in favor of His actions?"

Both nodded.

"Then we do nothing," Caiaphas announced. He glanced over their shoulders at the tower of Fort Antonia, where six hundred Roman soldiers were garrisoned and ready to quell any public riots.

Caiaphas closed his eyes. He spoke softly, more to himself than to the others. "This is not our time. When our time arrives, it will be formed at our choosing, without the people around to protect Him."

CHAPTER FOURTEEN

The animals left behind fallen tables, the litter of empty money bowls, merchants searching for coins on the ground, empty stock pens, and near silence. In that silence the crowd watched a man lift high one final dove cage.

Somehow, although the gesture was plainly symbolic, Yeshua did not appear theatrical as He released the latch on the cage.

The dove burst skyward, its wings audible in the vast open area.

Yeshua looked at the crowd and called out a text I recognized from Isaiah. "The Scriptures declare, 'My temple will be called a place of prayer.'" He paused and surveyed the remaining merchants. "But you," He called out again, "have turned it into a den of thieves!"

Behind me, in the quiet that followed the man's echoing words, I heard the *tap-tap* of a stick on stone. I turned my head to see the uncertain progress of a stooped and twisted cripple, his head covered with rags.

"Heal me," the man begged, weeping. "Oh, Lord, let me walk again."

"Where," my blind beggar groaned as he heard the other man, "where is the prophet now? Point me to where He is and let me go."

All focus centered on the cripple, who was undaunted by the

crowd with all its stares. I told myself my own rapt attention was intellectual curiosity. The rumors of miracles—could they be true?

The blind beggar tried to pull himself from my grasp. I held tight. Somehow, this moment had dignity. Even at my most cynical and weary, I would find no humor in watching a blind beggar race against a cripple.

With gentle grace, Yeshua moved to meet the crippled man. He took him by the hand and led him toward the inner courts of the temple.

"Let me take you to Him," I said to the blind beggar.

I followed the crowd, guiding the beggar, who clutched my arm with hands that quivered in hope and excitement.

CHAPTER FIFTEEN

A t the evening meal, Pascal was still dressed in the fine clothing he had worn during the day. Seraphine had tied her hair back, and it added a beauty to her face that surprised me and brought me some sadness, for it reminded me of the beauty of my own wife's face.

The wide assortment of food arrayed on the table before us looked no different from the table of the previous evening. Pascal's hospitality was generous—partly because tradition demanded it of a host, partly because of his affection for me, and partly, I suspect with no cruelty, because he always wanted me to be keenly aware of his status and wealth.

As with the night before, I remained quiet. Less from weariness than from shock. I had left the temple in a daze so profound that I did not remember the steep climb along the streets to Pascal's mansion nor the details of giving my cloak to the servant who greeted me at the door.

To this point in the meal, Pascal had made no mention of my earlier offer to sell my entire estate, nor had he questioned why I had not visited him during the day to discuss it further. While the matter was probably uppermost in his mind, Seraphine's presence again kept us from talking business.

"You drive Seraphine to tears," Pascal said to break the long silence that had fallen around the table. I had yet to say a single word; their forced conversation had brought the meal this far. "Please, eat, drink. Seraphine's beginning to think you have no respect for her efforts."

"Cripples walked," I said, hardly a response that either might have expected. "Blind men saw."

There. I had said it aloud. I still could barely believe what my eyes had forced upon my mind. By speaking it, fully expecting wild crazed laughter as response, I had taken the first step toward accepting it.

"What?" Pascal's beard was soaked with grease, his mouth half full of bread. He gestured with the chicken leg in his hand, waving it to get Seraphine's attention. "My cousin's first words of the meal, and he sounds drunk. Yet I have not seen him taste any wine."

"Cripples walked," I said. "Blind men saw. I was there."

□‖□□‖□□‖□□‖□□‖□

They had approached Him in the afternoon sunlight in the courtyard of the temple. He had spoken to them softly, one at a time. Then He had bent His face toward them, listening intently to their replies. Never before had I seen such compassion on a man's face, such naked love for the weak, the ugly, the infirm.

Then—and my body still trembled to think of it—He had laid His hands upon their afflicted limbs. And somehow, the stooped straightened, the crippled dropped their canes. At His command, the blind turned their faces to the sun and blinked at the light, tears streaming down their cheeks. Children had danced, singing hosannas that not even the temple authorities could silence, reaching for heaven with their souls, their sweet voices ringing off the high temple walls like the distant melody of angels.

He had healed them.

Nothing in my entire life had prepared me for this. It was as if I had seen objects fall up, not down.

He had healed them.

□│□│□│□│□│□│□

"Come, come," Pascal said. "Explain this nonsense."

"The prophet from Galilee. The one they say raised a man from the dead. At the temple today, He overturned the money tables, ran the thieving traders out of the market. He—"

"Yes, yes," Pascal said, grinning. He paused to drink deeply from his wine cup. His eyes shone in the flickering oil light. "I heard of that business. I wish I could have seen it! They tell me it was chaos. Men and beasts everywhere. I wonder if tomorrow the market will be shut down or if—"

I slammed an open palm down on the table in sudden rage. "Listen to me!" I roared. "He . . . healed . . . them!"

I found myself half standing, looking down the table at Pascal and Seraphine. They stared back at me with their mouths open wide. Pascal had wanted to treat the entire matter as a trivial joke, yet he had no understanding that merely thinking of what I had seen was enough to make me feel as if I were swaying on the edge of the world. How could it be that a man healed cripples and blind men by touching them? It defied my common sense of how the world worked, the one strength I had learned to use as my foundation for life.

He had healed them.

I wanted to weep in my confusion. Slowly, the emotion that had driven me to my feet drained away.

I sat.

"Forgive me," I said. "This day has been a strain."

Like the well-mannered hosts they were, my cousin and his wife continued the conversation politely, as if my outburst had not occurred.

"So, you were in the temple today," Pascal said after some small talk, nodding with a smile of cultivated interest.

"Pascal," I said, hardly trusting my voice, "I saw the prophet touch them. He healed them. Had you been there, you would be just as afraid as I am."

"Afraid?" It was probably the first time he had heard me admit fear.

"It is not rational," I said. "That He could touch a cripple and cause him to walk is not rational. If I had not been there, I wouldn't believe it. And, frankly, I don't expect you to believe it from me. But I saw it. He healed them."

I could not get my mind away from that one thought. *He had healed them.*

"Well," Pascal said, "in philosophical terms, I agree with you. Men are notoriously fickle and will only believe what they want to believe. Were I an ignorant peasant with little hope beyond far-fetched stories, I would desperately want to believe you. And so my belief would be certain. But I am not a peasant. I have carved my own comfortable place in the world. My range of experiences and education does not put me in a position where I need to clutch at desperate hope. So, no—and do not take this as an insult—I don't believe you."

"I don't want to believe it myself," I said. "Because then I would have to accept that there are things beyond my understanding."

"Exactly." Pascal took a fried locust, regarded it briefly with satisfaction, and popped it into his mouth. "Dear cousin, let me comfort you."

I waited for him to finish chewing. He washed his mouthful down with more wine.

"You see," he said. "Rumors of this man and His so-called wonders have come to us for nearly three years. We are not provincials, willing to accept any type of hearsay. Everything He has done can be explained easily if you realize He is just another messianic fraud. It is simple to 'heal' a cripple who was never crippled in the first place. Bring in strangers on canes, wave your hand, and send them on their way—healed. And well paid, of course."

"Why?" I asked. "Why go to all that trouble?"

"Influence. Once you have a great enough following, you have power. Whatever He did in the temple today was showmanship timed to impress the pilgrims at Passover. Most of them come from small towns far away and are ready to believe anything as a miracle."

Pascal shook his head. "This Lazarus. All he had to do was sneak into a tomb and wait there until called forth a few days later. Those who believe a dead man walked again are fools who deserve to lose whatever money they spend on His cause."

"I haven't heard the prophet ask for money," I said.

"Once He has power, the money will follow. Any man shrewd enough to be as patient as He appears to be knows that." Pascal smiled. "You see, this Nazarene might have following outside of Jerusalem, but here in the city, among those who count, He is nothing."

Pascal set down his well-gnawed chicken bone and stared at me. "Consider this a mild warning," he said. "Any man who wishes to do business in Jerusalem must consider his own reputation. One who is linked to the rebel will find few to support him. Even those who might wish to do business with him would face pressure from others to shun the follower."

I understood. It was far from a mild warning. Pascal was telling me that he would not be able to involve himself with me or my business if I did something as foolhardy as publicly joining the throng at Yeshua's feet.

Pascal dropped his voice to a conspiratorial whisper. "As I told you yesterday, that man is in danger. Trust me; I know this from those who count. The matter will be taken care of shortly."

So it was that Pascal told me about Caiaphas.

Later, alone with my thoughts in the guest chamber, I desperately wanted to believe Pascal—that Yeshua was a magician, a fraud, a messianic imposter like dozens who had tried the same before Him. It was easier to not believe than to believe.

Yet . . .

There was the blind old beggar whom I had guided to the prophet. Because I had seen the same blind beggar before in the temple plaza, I doubted he was an actor hired by Yeshua. And when I left the old man this afternoon, his eyes were no longer milky with cataracts but shiny with tears of joy.

I lay down on the bed but did not expect to sleep. For the eighteen months since the fire in my warehouse, that luxury had been denied me—except in short stretches when my body's needs overcame my sorrow and horror. The most impoverished peasants slept deeply while I, with all my gold, could not buy a single night's sleep.

It was an irony that had long since failed to amuse me.

As the lonely wakeful hours passed, my mind kept returning to the prophet and the people I had seen Him heal.

What if Pascal was wrong? What if—against everything rational—this man truly could heal the afflicted? It would skew my entire view of the world.

It took a long while for another thought to push its way to

the surface, probably because for too many months I had believed there could be no solution for my problems.

If this man truly had the power to heal—in some way I could not fathom—He could heal my daughter's legs.

And if there was hope for her, was there then hope for me?

Hope was something that had become so foreign that I barely recognized it. When it arrived at that moment, shining a light where darkness had reigned so long, I began to weep.

At that moment, I realized what I had kept hidden from myself the entire journey here—I desperately wanted not to die alone, far away from my family.

TUESDAY

CHAPTER SIXTEEN

My dearest love,
I promised I would write to you as if I were courting you again.
I have been speaking to you from my heart. I cannot continue honestly
without admitting to the mistresses who drove us apart over the years.

My first mistress, of course, was ambition. Now, as I contemplate
what a man's life is worth, I see the futility of pursuing power and wealth.
When I am gone, those accomplishments will be divided and fought over
by other men who also vainly pursue the emptiness. They will also some-
day feel the disappointment of discovering that all they have managed to
grasp is a meaningless bubble on the waves of an eternal tide.

What is worth more than gold?

Your love, freely given. The love of our sweet daughter instead of
the legacy of horror that is her inheritance. And, more than anything,
the life of our son.

I have failed you all. Now I understand too clearly how my actions
have hurt you, how the pain continues to mold you. Truly, the stones a
man casts send ripples through time; the spirit of a man and the love
that he gave, or did not give, continue in his children and their children
long after his wealth and power have disappeared.

Perhaps this is something I have known all along but could not
admit to myself. For as I look back, I see how the empty promise of
that first mistress led me to seek solace in the arms of a second.

Let us not pretend she did not exist. Let us not pretend I did not serve her willingly. Let us not pretend she was not my escape.

It is not possible that this second mistress was a woman, for no other could have competed with your beauty and charm. If you still had some affection for me, you could easily have banished such a temptation from my life.

But the solace of wine is like none other. A mistress who calls like a Siren and punishes like a banshee. But in the arms of this mistress, cares disappear, and in the glow of well-being the spirit seems to become full where it was empty.

That you kept our household in some semblance of order during my months of constant drink is a testimony to your strength. I would ask your forgiveness if I thought I deserved it. I would pursue redemption if I thought it possible.

What stands between us is the fire.

You have never blamed me aloud, but I always know it is there. The night of the fire, you think I could have done more. You are right in blaming me, yet also wrong. The truth of that evening is why I am now in Jerusalem, fleeing you.

Yet today, my love, I go forth with small hope when yesterday I saw nothing but good-bye.

I make this promise.

If, somehow, through this ridiculous hope that I clutch as fiercely as breath itself, I find a way to give our daughter back her legs, I will return to you. I will read these letters aloud to you myself. You will hear the truth about the fire from me, not a servant who delivers these letters with word that I am out of your life, never to return.

Then, and only then, will I get on my knees and beg you to allow us to begin anew.

Your Simeon

CHAPTER SEVENTEEN

I did not go early into the countryside as I had on previous days. I intended to seek solace in another way and had even begun to hope that I might not sell my estate to Pascal.

So it was that I found myself walking directly to the temple, hoping the prophet might return.

Broken clouds sent shadows drifting across the great plaza at the south end of the temple. A quickening breeze promised rain later. I felt the chill and pulled my cloak tighter around my body.

Although it was early and the monstrous temple gates were still closed, as many as two hundred people had already gathered in the plaza, standing in clusters as they gossiped or alone as they set up assorted wares on blankets to sell to pilgrims later in the day. Still, because of the vastness of the plaza, it seemed empty.

At a distance, I had no difficulty picking out the one person I could recognize. The blind beggar I had met the day before. Except he was no longer blind.

I knew he would not recognize me; I had led him close to Yeshua and, before his vision returned, had retreated to lose myself in the temple crowd.

I watched him for several minutes without approaching.

Other ragged beggars—crippled, blind, old—had begun to take their regular positions near the temple gates, armed with canes and bowls. Soon, when the thousands upon thousands of pilgrims streamed into the plaza, the beggars' clamor and wailing would add to the general din of temple activities.

My beggar—I smiled faintly when I realized I thought of him in this manner—walked from one to another, stooping as he talked to each. His back was to me, and I was too far away to clearly see his actions, but I could guess them by the excitement he left behind each time he moved to another beggar.

I walked closer and confirmed my guess. The man I had given gold to the day before was now handing it to the other beggars.

I stood in front of him.

He flicked his eyes up and down my body. Briefly, I wondered if he recognized me. Perhaps he had not been blind and was indeed a part of a trick by Yeshua.

Then I decided his interest might be from the joy of registering as many tiny details as he could. He took in my luxurious clothing and my expensive cloak. His eyes stopped briefly on the scar of my face. Other men might have grown their beards longer to cover such a reminder. I would not.

"Shalom," I said.

He recognized—or pretended to recognize—my voice. "It is you! Yesterday's rescuer!"

I nodded.

He reached out and clasped my right hand, shaking it vigorously. In those close quarters, I did not smell the unwashed odor that had clung to him the day before. His clothes were not expensive but new. And he had trimmed his beard.

"I cannot thank you enough," he said. "You led me to the Messiah."

Uncomfortable, I pried my hand loose. "I see you are dispensing money as if you are Solomon himself."

"Yes, yes," he said. His voice was as animated as his movements. This man could not contain himself. "I feel as if I am Solomon."

"Where will you find shekels tomorrow?" I asked. "And the day after?"

"With the gifts I have received, how can I think merely of myself? Others here have greater need. Of all people, I should know how keen that need is."

His answer shamed me. Would a paid actor have done this?

"What is your name?" he asked. "I am Nahshon. My family has been in Jerusalem since before the Romans."

It occurred to me that I had been content to think of him as "my beggar." With a name and this meager information, I was now forced to acknowledge him as more than an object of pity. This was the danger of helping people directly instead of helping charity.

"I am Simeon," I said. "My family has roots in Alexandria."

I saw little need to tell him how I had struck out on my own after my youth in the harbor area, and where my endeavors had taken me since then.

"You are a young man," he said. His eyes flicked briefly back to my scar. "Wife? Children?"

My natural inclination is silence; I'm often too busy to worry about the niceties of everyday conversation. But because this man was a stranger with whom I'd already been candid, and because of my emotional rawness, I did not retreat into privacy as I would have normally.

"I have a wife," I said. "And a daughter—Vashti."

Jaala and I had called our daughter Vashti because the name meant "fairest, loveliest woman"; now her name served as cruel mockery of what she would never be.

"I will pray that God will bless you with a son," Nahshon said, on the assumption that any man would proudly mention a son before a daughter.

I kept my face a blank. We had called our son Ithnan—"the strong sailor." One who was to inherit my ships, my warehouses, my shops. One who had laughed as he ran, taking pleasure in the motion of his sturdy little legs.

"My young son died recently in a fire," I said.

I touched the scar on my face. "It was the same fire that gave me this." I was acutely aware of how the scar pulled at certain expressions—a constant reminder of that horrid day.

Nahshon's eyes widened. But not for the reasons I expected.

"Yesterday, you took me to the Messiah when you could have stood in my place to beg for mercy. You are a kind and self-less man! I will pray for you in your grief."

I could not tell this joy-filled man that it had not been self-lessness that had kept me from the Messiah, but lack of faith.

"How long had you been blind?" I asked, weary of talking about myself.

He was more than eager to answer. I learned about his time as a temple worker. And his now-dead wife. And the years between.

I cut his enthusiasm short a few minutes later.

"What did you feel?" I asked, aching to understand. If Nahshon was a hired actor, pretending blindness in the morning and a new vision in the afternoon, he was well worth any money a false messiah had paid him. "What was it like?"

"I felt a silvery light," he said without any hesitation. As if all that had occupied his mind was that moment of healing. "I did not see it, but I felt it. Like a bright star alone in a dark sky, grow-ing brighter and warmer until it filled the heavens. When He took His hand from my eyes, the star's warm light became the sun; I could see it shining down on the temple. . . . And peace. I felt peace. No words can explain the strength of that peace."

I closed my eyes briefly, wishing against all knowledge that I could believe this man before me.

"He may return today," Nahshon said. "Go to Him. He can heal you!"

We both knew the unspoken. Yeshua could not give me back my son.

I shook my head.

"My daughter was burned in the fire that took my son. It is she who needs healing," I answered. "I do not."

CHAPTER EIGHTEEN

Nahshon, old as he was, sparkled with the exuberance of a boy. I easily saw that in his renewed joy he wanted to be moving, exploring. It soon became apparent that only a sense of obligation kept him in further conversation with me. So I offered him an excuse, pleading business of my own, and set him free.

By then, the temple doors had opened. I joined the crowd moving inside, hoping to see the man of miracles.

My hope was not in vain. As I learned later, He was delayed only briefly on His journey from Bethany to Jerusalem.

On their descent of the Mount of Olives, Peter, of all the disciples, saw it first. Where once green had softened the outline of the fig tree, a framework of drooping branches now showed through leaves turned brown, curled, and dry, rustling in the breeze.

"Yeshua, look!" Peter cried. "The fig tree You cursed has withered!"

Peter's large hands flailed as the words tumbled from his mouth, his excitement so great that he shared his news with the other disciples as if they could not see for themselves.

"Yesterday. Remember? The teacher spoke to the tree. Did you not hear? He said that no one would ever eat fruit from it again. And look! It's withered."

With the scorn that the cynical use as a defense against enthusiasm, Judas rolled his eyes as Peter continued to point.

"To its roots," Peter said. "Look. Withered to its roots. Just as the teacher commanded and more!"

"Tell me, Peter," Judas said, sounding like an adult patronizing a child. "Has something happened to the tree?"

"Yes, yes," Peter said. He was too caught up in the marvel to hear Judas's tone. "Overnight! The tree has died. See for yourself."

Judas looked around to see if the others enjoyed the humor of his sarcasm. He felt doubly pleased by Peter's oblivion to it. But none of the other disciples paid Judas any attention. Of late, they'd grown accustomed to his sourness. Besides, Judas's attempt at attention paled beside what their eyes beheld. The tree had actually died overnight at the mere words of their teacher.

"Master," Peter said, slowing down, "the tree . . ."

Yeshua continued to walk. Often He would not answer until a time of silence and contemplation had passed. They had almost come abreast of the tree when Yeshua spoke.

"Have faith in God," Yeshua answered, pausing deliberately. Would they understand? Without faith, Israel in its appearance of glory was as barren of God as the tree had been of figs. And whatever resisted God would most surely be swept away.

Yeshua waited for a glimmering of comprehension, but the faces around him remained rapt with awe. The miracle itself had impressed them. A storm calmed, the lame healed, a man raised from the dead. In all of it, as with the withered fig tree, they had failed to look beyond.

The common rabbinical expression for doing the impossible was "rooting up mountains," and as a Jewish teacher, Yeshua gave His followers the comfort of the familiar in His attempt to lead them further.

"I assure you," Yeshua continued, "that you can say to this mountain, 'May God lift you up and throw you into the sea,' and your command will be obeyed. All that's required is that you really believe and do not doubt in your heart."

Still He faced the blank, rapt awe of children. Should it not be obvious? Faith not only gives power to prayer but is also its foundation. He had, on another occasion, told them the two great laws of faith: love God; love man. True prayer demands by extension a spirit untainted by selfish ambition or unforgiveness. Could they not see? In true prayer, a man bound to earth can reach up to heaven. Such is faith.

Yet Yeshua did not show any frustration. He smiled at His listeners. These men had traveled with Him for three years and shared His pains, joys, hopes, sorrows, and disappointments. They were young, unlearned. Any teaching He shared could only be an outpouring of love and compassion.

"Listen to me!" He said. "You can pray for anything, and if you believe, you will have it. But when you are praying, first forgive anyone you are holding a grudge against, so that your Father in heaven will forgive your sins, too."

Would they understand? With faith, they could have everything. Without faith, whatever resisted God would most surely be swept away.

Yeshua, still smiling, looked from one face to another.

When His eyes met those of Judas, the slender disciple flinched and looked away. One of the twelve, it seemed, understood too well the judgment against the fig tree that had denied Yeshua.

Although I had been waiting in a corner of the courtyard, when Yeshua arrived I did not approach Him or His disciples. Not many pilgrims had arrived yet, but there were enough that I could remain among them and watch without being noticed.

The clouds had begun to thicken. With the breeze came an occasional waft of incense, reaching my nostrils like an unseen butterfly moving randomly through the air.

I had not minded the wait. Hope was so precious, I was reluctant to test it. And, with the habits of business I could not escape, I preferred to size up my prospective client.

As I watched the group, their conversation continued, and Yeshua laughed with His followers and the few pilgrims who sat on the outer edges of the gathering.

I found myself liking this man. He had entered this lions' den of His own free will, knowing His very presence would be a challenge to the religious authorities. Yet He did not tread lightly as if fearing to wake the lions, nor did He posture with bluff braveness as a man with a sword, daring the lions to attack.

He was relaxed, handsome when He smiled. Yet, unlike some attractive men, He did not have the oiliness that repels other men. I could imagine Him as comfortable helping fishermen as He would be accepting a gift from a patroness.

Those gathered around Him shared His degree of comfort. It struck me that if this temple truly were a house of God instead of a monument to religious rule, this is how God might want His creatures to enjoy time in His presence.

This sanctuary of carefree enjoyment, however, ended as dozens of men entered the courtyard. The delegation marched with the size, unison, and determination of a small army. Of the thousands of priests who served at the temple, nearly fifty had been released from duty, and they formed the largest part of the wedge of men that now approached Yeshua and His followers.

The priests wore white hats and long white gowns tied with girdles. Each had risen before dawn to take a ritual bath as part of his daily duties. The clash of a gong thrown onto the pavement in front of the temple had called the thousands to hours of ceremonial music and singing. Other priests had been scattered earlier to perform the usual duties—offering sacrifices for pilgrims at the altar in front of the temple, lighting lamps, cleaning the altar of blood. These priests had been ordered to march here.

A much smaller group of elders and scribes—gathered from those who held places of honor among the highest tribunal of the Sanhedrin—led the priests. These men wore ordinary clothes that reflected their occupations, but the stiff dignity in their shoulders and faces clearly set them apart as men of power.

Leading the delegation, Caiaphas set the pace. He alone, in the entire land, had the authority to wear the vestments of the high priest. On this occasion he had dressed to show his supreme position. A blue robe hung to his feet, covering his traditional white priestly garments except for the sleeves. From the bottom of the robe tassels with golden bells and pomegranates hung in alternation. Over the blue robe, he wore the ephod, a cape embroidered in bands of gold, purple, scarlet, and blue. A gold purse inset with twelve precious stones was attached to each shoulder of the ephod by gold broaches inset with sardonyxes. Caiaphas, a tall man already, had added to his height with a blue headdress banded with gold.

The delegates had chosen the early hour with purpose; few pilgrims had gathered around the prophet yet to hear His teachings. The market in the Court of the Gentiles was nearly deserted by the merchants, for not many were brave enough to change money or sell livestock after the previous day's rebellion. In the relatively quiet temple, the audible padding of the priests' bare feet against the pavement made an ominous sound on their approach.

Caiaphas with his dozens of men against Yeshua with a handful.

As the delegation neared, Peter was the only one to rise from the steps where Yeshua sat among the disciples. He stepped forward and waited, arms crossed, the hilt of his sword obvious from his girdle. However, at a few whispered words from Yeshua, Peter sat again.

When Caiaphas stopped, the men halted with him. He stared across a distance of twenty paces at the prophet from Nazareth. To any other Jew in the land, such a hostile glare from the highest religious authority would have been like a roar from God Himself.

"Shalom," Yeshua said. "May God's peace rest upon you."

Caiaphas refused to answer. He had chosen to intimidate, to stand silent as the supreme judge. He nodded for one of the elders to move up beside him. They both stared at Yeshua.

"Shalom to you too," Yeshua said to the elder. "God has granted us a wonderful day in His presence."

"You have been teaching in the temple," the elder said. He was the same age as Caiaphas, almost as tall, but much heavier.

He was completely bald, but his beard, streaked with gray and braided, touched his chest. "Do you deny this?"

Yeshua shook his head no.

"Let me be clear in front of all these witnesses," the elder said. "I am not suggesting You are a mere Haggadist, a teller of legends and stories. I am declaring that You actually teach. Do You deny this?"

Yeshua let a half smile touch His face. He understood. To the assembled priests and elders and scribes, this was a question of great importance.

To teach meant to follow a tradition, handed down from teacher to disciple, who, once granted the teacher's authority by the teacher, passed on the same information, unchanged. The most respected scholars were those who recited teachings word for word, nothing lost, nothing added. In any discussion, the ultimate appeal was always to an authority, whether a famous teacher or the Great Sanhedrin. Anyone who disagreed with the set authorities was seen as an ignorant scholar or a rebel to be banned. And anyone who did not teach from an authority could not truly be teaching.

"Do You deny that You teach?" the elder demanded again, his anger rising at the lack of fear on Yeshua's face.

Again, Yeshua shook His head no, acknowledging that yes, teaching had taken place.

Caiaphas, the imperious observer, smirked. The previous night's meeting in council had planned this perfectly, right down to the time the delegation would approach this peasant. Now, as calculated, the trap had been set. There was no way for the Nazarene to retreat.

"By whose authority did You drive out the merchants from the temple?" the elder asked. "Who gave You such authority?"

During last night's meeting, there had been a long, heated debate as the exact wording of the questions had been decided upon. It had to publicly appear that they were not merely challenging this man because of His teachings; instead, they would be seen as following the duty that forced them to verify His background. After all, if Yeshua had done everything attributed to Him, the elders had to protect the people by confirming that these acts were not from Beelzebub, the devil who opposed God, did they not?

"By whose authority did You drive out the merchants from the temple? Who Gave you such authority?"

Caiaphas licked his lower lip, anticipating one of three answers. Unlikely as it was, the fool might actually answer Beelzebub, the devil, and the priests would have every right to take Him to the temple wall and hurl Him into the valley.

If He quoted a great Jewish teacher as His authority—the revered Hillel, for example—then the people would lose faith in Him, for no Messiah would be lesser than another man.

The anticipation of a possible third answer, claiming authority from God, made Caiaphas's muscles twitch and tremble. Would this man actually blaspheme and claim it came from God? Caiaphas had more than once engineered the immediate stoning of a rebel for heresy. And it would give him great pleasure to watch stones bite into the Nazarene peasant's flesh.

"By whose authority did You drive out the merchants from the temple? Who gave You such authority?"

Yeshua had not yet replied. He turned His gaze from the elder to Caiaphas, as if He were reading the high priest's thoughts. For a missed heartbeat, Caiaphas felt the juice of fear wash against his stomach walls. Then he remembered the dozens of priests behind him and put the curl of scorn back onto his lips. In that moment, the hatred he held for the prophet's teaching became a personal hatred for the prophet.

"Will You not answer?" the elder demanded. "By whose authority did You drive out the merchants from the temple? Who gave You such authority?"

Yeshua leaned forward. Still sitting on the marble steps, He transferred His weight and leaned His elbows on the tops of His thighs. "I'll tell you who gave Me authority to do these things if you answer one question," Yeshua replied. He began so casually, listeners not paying attention might have guessed this was simply another matter of teaching under discussion. "Did John's baptism come from heaven or was it merely human?"

Abruptly, Yeshua pushed Himself up and stood. "Tell me!" He commanded. His face, previously gentle and amused, had stiffened to match the sudden anger in His voice, as if an invisible mantle of power had been placed upon Him, as if Yeshua were now judge and the delegation on trial.

Caiaphas actually took a half step back. He hated the peasant with a cold personal rage that he wanted to satisfy by plunging the sacrificial dagger into the man's liver.

The nearest elder whispered to Caiaphas in panic. "If we say it was from heaven, He will ask why we didn't believe Him."

Caiaphas did not answer. John the Baptist was believed by all to be a prophet sent directly from God. His stature was so great among the people that Caiaphas thought of John with envy and idly wondered at times if it might be worth it to be martyred.

"But if we say it was merely human, we'll be mobbed because the people think he was a prophet," the elder continued, his high whisper such a ridiculous squeak that the Galilean peasant and His disciples could most surely overhear it.

Caiaphas, forearm muscles roped with the stress of his

clinched hands, wanted to slap the elder for his indiscretion. He closed his eyes. With incredible willpower, he held himself in a pose of indifference.

"I have duties at the altar," he finally said in a low voice to the elder. "You will remain and debate this among yourselves to keep Him waiting. Then finally tell Him that we don't know the answer to His question."

Caiaphas did not wait for the elder to affirm his order. The high priest turned with great dignity and walked back through the delegation. As he walked, he made his face a mask of peaceful contemplation. But thoughts of murder—savage murder with his own hands—heated his mind.

For Caiaphas could not fool himself.

They—the rulers and great legal scholars of the temple—had challenged a solitary uneducated peasant-carpenter. And lost.

Walking away was retreat.

As he left the courtyard, Caiaphas silently vowed to use all of his wealth, power, and cunning to end this peasant's life.

CHAPTER TWENTY

I spent another two hours watching. Waiting. The crowds around the prophet grew larger. My view of Him was reduced to glimpses as He moved and spoke.

I watched His unfailing patience and cheerfulness. Laughter. Compassion.

From those gathered around, I saw adoration. Awe. Skepticism. Occasional ridicule.

As entertainment, I could not think of a better way to spend my time.

All the while, I let the seed of hope inside me take root and spread its branches. The reluctance I felt had gone. I no longer wondered whether I should approach Him but how.

Still, I was in no hurry.

But others were.

Oren, son of Judd, nursed anger and a sore leg suffered in the chaos of the market the day before. He limped toward the residence of Caiaphas the high priest, protected from the direct heat of the sun by the walls lining the street. The noise and bustle of the lower city were long behind him. Here, in the enclave of the wealthy in upper Jerusalem, overlooking the hectic confusion of the near slums below, little activity took place on the streets.

The palace of the high priest stood directly before him. Just inside the western wall that enclosed the city, it overlooked King David's tomb. It boasted an outer courtyard, an inner courtyard, a terraced garden, and dozens of luxurious rooms, including halls big enough to hold informal assemblies of the Sanhedrin.

Servants guarded the gates. With faintly hidden distaste, they surveyed Oren's flushed, sweaty face as they listened to him wheeze his visit's purpose. At each successive gate, each servant hesitated unnecessarily before letting him through. As was the master, so were the servants—haughty and highly conscious of their status.

Caiaphas met Oren in the garden. It was a clear indication of Oren's standing that he had not been invited into the palace.

"I know who you are," Caiaphas said, imperiously waving away Oren's introduction. "Let us not waste time."

The tall high priest stood in the shade of a fig tree.

"It is the market," Oren said. With the back of a fat, oily hand, he wiped sweat from his forehead. He had become acutely aware of his thirst, made deeper by the fact that Caiaphas had not sent a servant for refreshments. "The Nazarene has disrupted it completely."

Oren's anger at the situation flared. He pulled up his tunic and twisted to point at the fat hairy calf of his right leg. The pasty flesh showed a deep purple bruise.

"Yesterday," Oren continued, "I was standing on my table to better see the confusion when an ox knocked it over and stepped on me. The commissions I send to you should be ample payment for protection."

"The peasant will be stopped," Caiaphas said. "Even now as we speak, He is being challenged."

"Like this morning?" Oren asked, happy for the chance to poke at the high priest's arrogance. "Word has spread wide that the entire ruling authority failed to move Him from the temple courts. It has only increased His popularity among the people. If this continues . . ."

Oren was rewarded with a clenched smile from Caiaphas.

"It will not continue," the high priest hissed. "Even as you and I speak, a new trap is about to be sprung."

CHAPTER TWENTY-ONE

I continued to stand patiently among the crowd, leaning against a pillar at the side of the court, content to listen to the ongoing arguments and discussions. I had no need to strain to look over the crowd at the man named Yeshua.

The voices carried to me clearly; like me, none of the spectators engaged in idle conversation, and any noise from the crowd came in whispered reactions to points of debate, then stopped as all waited to hear the counterpoint. We were like an audience at an athletic event, except much less boisterous.

Occasionally, however, I did stand on the tips of my toes to see if any of the scene had changed. At first glance, the contest seemed overwhelmingly unfair.

On one side, lawyers and scribes—white-bearded, white-clothed Pharisees armed with scrolls; Sadducees dressed in the wealth that comes with success in politics; fresh-faced students in black robes, eager for the chance to show their verbal skills. Jerusalem's intellectual elite had gathered in full force.

Facing them—alone—was the carpenter from Nazareth. As if His unassuming clothing did not give enough indication of His lack of status, every word He spoke in His rough Galilean accent reminded the audience of His lack of formal education.

"Didn't you ever read this in the Scriptures?" Yeshua continued. " 'The stone rejected by the builders has now become the cornerstone.' "

"Yes, yes," one of the students called, "from the book of Psalms. By excellent use of a pun, the author implies that the cornerstone is also a leader. As part of a victory celebration, the author undoubtedly meant to exhort the people to song." The student smiled at the crowd, proud of his feat of immediate recall.

Another spoke to Yeshua in the thrusting manner of debate the pack of intellectuals had been using. "It is only a fragment of Scripture. What does this have to do with a tale about the tenants of a vineyard who kill the landowner's son when he arrives to collect the grapes?"

"What I mean is that the kingdom of God will be taken away from you," Yeshua replied, "and given to a nation that will produce the proper fruit. Anyone who stumbles over that stone will be broken to pieces, and it will crush anyone on whom it falls."

"No!" one of the white-bearded men shouted, his voice surprisingly powerful. "No! You cannot speak to us like that!"

Yeshua raised His eyebrows as reply. His quiet defiance brought murmurs of shock and worry and even some muted laughter from the crowd, for few of the poorer pilgrims missed the implications. These Pharisees and the rest of the elite felt Yeshua was speaking directly to them as the tenants who rejected the son; their guilty consciences had been pricked to immediate anger.

Some of the older Pharisees turned away, seething with frustrated rage, grumbling for the man's arrest.

Everyone else in the crowd stayed, however. Never before had one of them—one of the lowly—tweaked the ears of the high and mighty.

Yeshua turned to answer some questions quietly, and the rest of the crowd began to talk in low tones, marveling at Yeshua's poise.

It was during this pause in public debate that I stepped forward.

Earlier, I had made my decision to speak with the red-bearded man named Peter.

His wide, young face made him appear approachable despite his scowl. From his simple clothing, I assumed he would be easily impressed. And the fact that he kept his hand on the hilt of a half-hidden sword showed me he was the one who watched guard. He, then, was the one who could get me into the inner circle.

Peter was at the edge of the crowd surrounding Yeshua. I moved closer to him, greeting him with "Shalom."

His eyes narrowed as he appraised my expensive clothing and neatly trimmed beard and hair. I hoped he would see what all others did in dealing with me: a man of even features despite my scar, tall enough to be imposing, with a smile to offset any intimidation rendered by my size.

"Are you another of the Pharisee spies?" Peter asked. "Testing to see if I tire of following the teacher? Looking for someone to betray Him?"

"No," I said.

"You dress like one of them."

I removed my cloak and set it on the shoulders of a beggar near me. He turned to me in surprise, and I waved him on, indicating that he could keep the cloak.

"No longer," I said.

"What do you want?" Whatever sympathy I might have gained was offset by Peter's suspicion of my generous gesture. The cloak was worth a month's wages for a laborer.

"An audience with your master," I said.

"He makes time for everybody."

Why was this man impatient with me? Usually the lesser privileged treated me with deferential respect.

"I wish to see Him privately," I said.

Peter pulled his own cloak back to further expose the hilt of his sword. "How do I know this is not a trap?" he demanded. "Men like you want Yeshua captured. It is a simple matter to pretend you need healing."

"No," I said quickly. This was not going as I intended. "I mean Him no harm. I merely wish to speak with Him . . . to ask Him something."

Peter stared at me, yielding no ground.

I felt the stirring of desperation. Without servants around me to establish my importance, I was failing quickly in my efforts to impress this man.

"It's my daughter," I said. "She . . . she . . ." I drew a breath. "She needs help. I have nowhere else to turn."

The sun-beaten wrinkles around Peter's eyes softened. His hand fell away from the hilt of his sword.

His obvious sympathy came as such a relief that I pressed on. Stupidly. "I have gold," I said. "Tell Him I will give generously to His cause. Whatever price He names."

Had I slapped the man, the change in Peter could not have happened faster.

"The teacher cannot be bought." Peter's shoulders tightened. His face became a mask again. "Take your gold elsewhere."

"But my daughter . . ."

"Go," Peter said. "If you offer payment, it is obvious you do not understand."

"But—"

Peter put his hand on my shoulder, ready to push me away. Before we could argue further, something compelled me to turn toward the prophet. The crowd had parted slightly, and I saw that He was looking directly at us.

Peter had also turned to look. He caught his master's gaze and dropped his hand.

Again, I was held by those eyes. Compassionate. Gentle. Eyes that drew me forward. I even took a step toward Him but was stopped by sudden muttering from within the crowd.

Important-looking men had begun to push their way through the crowd.

"Herodians," someone near me whispered. "I have seen them arguing politics in the plaza."

"Herodians with Pharisees?" another asked. "What has brought them together?"

CHAPTER TWENTY-TWO

erodians. A political party determined to see Herod rather than a Roman governor rule. They were hated by the religious authorities, who knew that Herod would strip them of their power at his first chance.

Their politics were in direct conflict with the Sanhedrin, who, as much as they despised Roman rule, despised Herod even more. After all, his tyrannical father, Herod the Great, had not only replaced the high priests at whim but had also murdered many of the great sages who dared protest his acts.

Herodians joined with Pharisees. The cause that had brought them together, I knew, would prove interesting.

I stepped back again, not wishing the attention that would fall on me if I persisted in trying to reach Yeshua at this moment.

Once again at the back of the crowd, leaning against my comforting pillar, I noticed something that did not bode well for Yeshua.

Temple police—discreetly waiting among the columns at the rear of the courtyard.

The Pharisees Elidad and Gaal—both handsome elderly men with the dignity of fully white beards—expected this to be their finest public moment. Even so, Elidad's legs trembled, and he hoped his tunic hid the movement. Gaal stood with his chest puffed, secure in the knowledge that they had been sent by Caiaphas, who had assured them that the peasant would recognize neither of them. So certain were they of success that they had brought along temple guards.

Each man made a great show of bowing in respect to Yeshua. When He acknowledged them, Elidad began, speaking with the greatest sincerity he could muster. "Teacher, we know how honest You are. You are impartial and You don't play favorites."

Yeshua had a habit of cocking one eyebrow in an expression of gentle inquisitiveness. His face was set thus as He waited for the men to continue.

"Yes," Gaal said, with his hands stretched and open in welcoming friendliness as he had practiced, "You sincerely teach the ways of God."

At that precise moment, a flock of pigeons passed overhead, their shadows rushing away like disappearing fish. One, however, left more behind than the quick dappled movement of shade across pavement; it had deposited a large sticky pellet of white directly into the center of Gaal's open right hand. He closed his fingers over his palm quickly, hoping no one in the crowd had noticed, for if anyone drew a symbolic conclusion about the pigeon's judgment of their speech, the laughter would never cease.

"Now tell us . . ." Elidad said to Yeshua, unaware of what had happened to his partner. As planned, he let a dramatic pause hang as a prelude to his question, one that would end the peasant's teachings.

As Gaal felt the discomfort of the messy liquid seeping between his fingers, it crossed his mind that if Yeshua was the Messiah and capable of raising the dead, perhaps the pigeon's gift had not been coincidence. Worse, it seemed Yeshua was enjoying a secret smile as he surveyed them both during Elidad's dramatic pause.

". . . is it right," Elidad resumed, "to pay taxes to the Roman government or not? Should we pay them, or should we not?"

Silence. To Gaal, it was a wonderful silence, one that more than made up for the indignity of the pigeon's droppings. Silence. The crowd was not whispering or laughing or cheering the prophet. Everyone understood the importance of His answer. No true messiah would acknowledge an earthly power. Answering yes, then, would destroy Yeshua's power among the people.

Yet if He answered no to keep His popularity with the masses, He would immediately be taken away and charged with sedition, for the Roman authorities only tolerated local religions to a certain extent. Nor could He decline to answer, not if He wanted to keep His reputation.

The silence lengthened. The question, in its cunning, was masterful.

Yeshua stood and moved toward the two Pharisees. When He finally spoke, He began so softly that all had to strain to hear Him. "Whom are you trying to fool with your trick questions?" He said, all humor gone from His face.

Facing the full power of the man's character, neither Elidad nor Gaal could stammer a reply.

"Show Me a Roman coin, and I'll tell you," Yeshua ordered.

Elidad patted his pockets. Gaal remained frozen with fear and the discomfort of his soiled right hand.

Elidad finally found a denarius. He reached across the short distance and handed it to Yeshua.

"Whose picture and title are stamped on it?" Yeshua asked them both, loudly enough for the crowd and all the intellectual elite to hear.

"Caesar's," they both said quickly, feeling like delinquent children under full inspection.

Yeshua turned. He gathered the hem of His robe, walked back to the steps, and with great dignity, seated Himself again. His deliberate, slow movements further chastised Elidad and Gaal, as it left them alone before the crowd, the center of attention.

When ready, Yeshua flipped the small coin back toward Gaal, who tried to grab it with his left hand and feebly missed. The light clink of the coin on pavement was obvious testimony to the incompetence he felt in front of the teacher.

"Well, then," Yeshua said, "give to Caesar what belongs to him. But everything that belongs to God must be given to God."

The Pharisees' stunned silence settled like a cloak of total defeat.

And the crowd burst into delighted applause.

CHAPTER TWENTY-THREE

I n the tumult of amazement and laughter that followed Yeshua's deft answer to a seemingly impossible question, He took opportunity to refresh Himself with food and drink, served by women from the crowd.

I did not blame Him. As it was, His stamina impressed me greatly. He had spoken publicly for several hours. From the few political dealings I had had, I understood fully the strain and exhaustion of concentrating intensely under such pressure.

Later, when Yeshua began to speak again, it was in parables—short, interesting stories that held simple yet powerful messages. The bulk of His audience were uneducated peasants. It was easy to see why they preferred His teachings to the dry, scholarly, legalistic lectures of the Pharisees.

I, too, enjoyed listening but not without a degree of restlessness. I greatly wished to speak to the man alone but saw no good opportunity.

Worse, when He had finished teaching, He retreated with His followers to another courtyard, requesting some time of privacy after promising to speak again in a few hours.

I stayed back, like the entire crowd, out of respect. But I did not fall too far back. During our short few seconds of contact earlier, His eyes had spoken to me. I was determined to get my audience. So I trailed Yeshua and His followers from an appropriate distance.

As they rested on the steps in the Court of Women, I saw as He pointed over the hundreds of people milling about.

I was too far away to hear His words, of course. Much later, after all the bad and good that happened, I learned what had caused Him to stop and draw attention to an elderly woman who walked slowly, apart from the crowds.

Not one, not even His followers, ever spoke to her then or later, so I admit to speculation in trying to describe the courtyard through her eyes.

□ □ □ □ □ □ □ □ □

The old woman had inexplicably become uncertain of her name. At times, she wept with frustration, trying to recall it. Other times, especially at night with the chill of the street pressing into her cold bones, she listened for the sound of it, certain that somewhere in her life others had spoken it to her.

As she strained to hear it, fragmented memories of people once important to her flickered through her awareness like ghosts in a dark chamber. When she clutched at their hems to beg for conversation, the ghosts became smoke in her fingers, leaving behind a sadness and sense of loss all the more overwhelming because she had no memories to structure her grief.

To the people in the temple court who moved around her slow, unsteady progress like water streaming past a worn boulder, her stricken efforts to find her identity were mumbled incantations from a living skull pasted with thin white hair. To them, she was insignificant—bowed, shrunken, trembling flesh wrapped in filthy rags.

It was Passover. Despite the disease that had eroded her

mind, the old woman understood that. The instinct drew her to the Court of Women and the thirteen trumpet-shaped boxes beneath the roofed pillars. Perhaps deep in the mysteries of her mind, a framework set by her years of dwelling with her husband and children and her faithful devotion to Yahweh still served her. Or perhaps, shorn of every worldly distraction, her spirit had emerged in a triumph of sorts, freely seeking its Creator before her life force left her old body, and in doing so providing the woman the only glow of joy she could carry until her last breath left her chest.

She did not remember her name.

But she knew the shards of round metal biting into the flesh of her palm had value. Had any of the passersby forced open her hand, they would have torn from her two *perutahs,* which added together were only a ninety-sixth of a denarius, all that she could expect to earn in a day of labor, and by law, the least any person could contribute to the temple coffers as sacrifice.

With her head down, she shuffled, confused, toward the treasury boxes, a solitary figure in the vastness of the temple courts.

The self-righteous, armed with gold and silver, ready to demand God's presence, passed by her without a glance. The cheerful, thinking not of the tithes they were about to drop but of families and meals waiting as soon as they finished their temple duty, also passed by her. Children passed by. Women lost in thoughts of love passed by. Priests, afraid to defile themselves with any contact with a female, passed her.

And slowly, unaware of Yeshua's presence, she passed Him where He rested against a pillar.

She remained unaware of Him as she dropped the coins into the treasury, unaware as she prayed before the rising incense of her sacrifice, and unaware as she turned to retrace the long painful journey to the streets where she would sleep the night. She was unaware that He turned to His disciples and told them that her gift, which had reached His Father, was far beyond any wealth on earth.

As she neared the peasant man again, however, something beckoned her spirit. The woman rarely lifted her head—it was a habit she had developed in the days when she'd had enough comprehension to feel her humiliation, when she'd realized it was easier not to see pity or scorn in the eyes of those who noticed her.

She heard the call to her soul, however, as strong as the light from the sun. His call overcame her years of habit, and she stopped, balancing on her cane as she peered through her milky white eyes almost completely filmed with cataracts.

She met the man's gaze.

Sunshine flooded the dark sad chambers of her memory.

With her head lifted, she saw not the man named Yeshua. Rather she saw flashes of images—the tall dark handsomeness of the man she'd married, and their girl-child at her breast, and a reflection of herself in a mirror when her flesh was smooth and her smile not vacant.

Yeshua did not speak to her. She did not speak to Him. She did not know He was a prophet. Or that many followed Him. Or that, as young and strong as He was, He would find death before she did.

People stepped between them, and she moved on.

Only now, joy gave her new strength.

The light that had returned her memories had given her one more thing.

She remembered her name.

CHAPTER TWENTY-FOUR

I did not have another chance to approach the prophet until early evening. He had spent the afternoon teaching, again in parables, denouncing the religious orders, and making prophecies.

Everything about Him fascinated me. I allowed my hope to grow stronger. I stayed on the fringes of those around Him. Invisible. Quiet. Watching. Waiting.

And, as many of the pilgrims departed from the temple, I saw my opportunity. Some Greeks had asked Yeshua to explain His teachings, and when He finished, I was able to move close.

He greeted me with a smile. The evening shadows had begun to fall, and the light was soft on His face.

Because so many people had been pulling at Him all day, I felt I needed to keep my time with Him short. "I am not here for Passover," I said quickly. "I have left behind my wife and daughter."

His beautiful smile did not waver.

"My daughter suffers," I continued. "Everything that I have, I would willingly trade for her to be healed."

"Understand who I am," Yeshua replied. He spoke so softly that no one overheard us. "Then return to Me."

"Please," I said. "She is horribly scarred. There was . . ." I debated with myself, then decided my burden did not matter. Only hers.

"There was a fire," I said. "Started by a lamp. The oil spilled on her legs, and she was trapped in the flames. She lies in bed, unable to move. She cries constantly from the pain. Please, let me pay for Your journey. Come to my town. Or wait until I bring her to You. Heal her. Every possession I have earned I will give to You and Your cause."

If only He could see what I had seen every day. When the sound of laughter of children playing in the street reached her, she bowed her head in defeat. The slowly healing skin—mottled and rough like a toad's back—had tightened, bending her legs like bows, forming a web behind her knees. Some days, even the light pressure of a blanket on her legs raised shrieks of agony. I doubted my once beautiful daughter would ever draw another breath without pain, and there were days when I wondered if she might be better off in the release of death.

Surely, if Yeshua saw her, He would have compassion on her. Others turned away from my once beautiful daughter in horror at her agony, but this man, I knew, would reach out to her.

"You would give all your possessions?" He asked. Again, softly.

"Yes," I said without hesitation. I could always earn them back again. What did a few years of poverty matter against the possibility of redemption? Hers. Mine.

"Thus it would be your doing that heals her?"

The disciples had begun to move close to us. I could see they were ready to send me away from Him.

"My doing?" I answered in confusion. "I don't understand. You have the healing touch. I've seen it. Other cripples have walked at Your command. Surely You can restore my daughter's legs. You can take away the pain that prevents her from sleeping. You can—"

"Understand who I am before you ask. Understand how you have chosen to ask—and why it is wrong. Then return to Me."

He rejoined His disciples. In the growing darkness, I could not read the expression on His face. Was it disappointment? sorrow?

I recognized that I had been dismissed. Many times I, too, had dismissed others. I knew it would be futile to chase after Him.

I watched the prophet from Galilee walk away.

As my hope disappeared, anger began to fill the hole it left behind.

I am told you spent much of the day following the rebel prophet," Pascal said without any preliminary small talk.

We sat together in a small private courtyard within his mansion. The day's heat had passed, and evening shadows darkened the flowers on the shrubs that surrounded us. Except for the matters to be discussed, it would have been a pleasant place to idle the time before our meal with Seraphine.

"You have spies who watch my every movement?" I said it mildly, but we both knew I was angry.

"No," he answered. "But you must admit that your scar makes you an easy figure to notice. I am not unknown among the Sadducees at the temple, and many people know you are my guest. In this city, most gossip of any importance reaches me."

"I will not deny my presence in the temple," I said. "I would not, however, call myself a follower."

"What you are is much different—and from my viewpoint, less important—than what people perceive you to be." Pascal also spoke mildly, but I felt his anger. "I warned you last evening of this danger."

I shrugged. My pretended indifference was a mistake.

He leaned forward, no longer concealing his anger. "You and I have arranged to sit here to discuss the purchase of your holdings. But first you must understand that already some of my customers, the wealthy and elite of Jerusalem, have threatened to cancel orders because of my association with you."

"What is more important?" I asked, feeling my blood heat too. "Family and friendship? Or customers?"

"I could ask you the same thing. We carry the same blood, and we have been friends for years. But when I asked you to stay away from a foolish rebel, you chose Him over me."

"I have not chosen Him!"

"That is irrelevant. To all of Jerusalem it appears that—"

"Hardly all of Jerusalem. You speak of a handful of stiff-necked, arrogant men who think the world should bow to them."

Pascal's voice tightened. "The world does bow to them. At least the world in which we live. If they think you are a follower, then to them you are a follower. And that hurts me. So my point carries: You have chosen Him over me."

He glared at me. "In practical terms, it is also an unintelligent decision. This lone peasant of yours has angered the entire spectrum of established religious and political parties."

Pascal gestured wide with both hands. "It's remarkable, actually. He has done the impossible and managed to unite them. Usually when one group wants something, the other will block it, just for spite. This prophet's success, however, means it serves everyone's best interests to see Him dead."

"Dead?"

"All you have to do is listen to how you and I have just argued. He provokes severe reactions."

"But dead?" If the miracles were truly miracles, if He was truly the Messiah, surely He had the power to save His own life.

"Simeon, you have lost your hard edge, your ability to assess any new situation. How can you expect to thrive among the other keen businessmen when you fail to read the political winds?"

Pascal's chastisement was accurate and deserved, although I wasn't going to tell him that I no longer cared to thrive in business. I didn't defend myself but listened as he continued.

"It's simple," Pascal said. "The Herodians see that as Yeshua assumes more earthly authority, Herod has less chance of gaining control of Judea. As for the Pharisees, He not only insults them publicly, but He also outright contradicts them and has gained such a following that people may actually leave the synagogues. Furthermore, with all this talk about losing the lucrative income from the temple markets, it is clear that He is a threat to more than their religious beliefs."

"But killing Him," I protested. "That's murder."

"All they need to do is get Him before the Sanhedrin. The trial won't be fair, but that doesn't matter. The powerful elite want Him dead. And so He will die. You of all people should know that is the way of the world."

Pascal softened, opening his arms to welcome me as he had upon my arrival. "Simeon, let us not argue over this man."

I let him believe my silence was agreement.

"I think I understand why you want me to purchase your ships and warehouses and shops," he said quietly. "And I will if you insist because in the long run, it will make me a considerably richer man. But I am begging you to reconsider and go home. If in six months you still feel the same, return to Jerusalem and we will discuss it seriously."

"You mean in six months your friends will have forgotten that I listened to a rebel's words and your reputation will be intact." I was bitter.

"You are unkind. I am concerned about you." He hesitated, searched his mind for a way to continue, drew a deep breath, pushed on. "If you can forgive me for saying this, as one friend who cares for another, I am afraid grief is pushing you to a rash decision."

"Yes," I said, careful not to reject his sympathy despite my irritation with him. "I do grieve."

Again it flashed through my mind. The screams, the flames, the blackened walls falling in, the confusion of the smoke, the searing heat, the agony of my face, my daughter's burned flesh. Pascal could never understand.

"Listen to me, cousin," I said. "Nothing will change my mind. I intend to give you a list of what I believe my estate is worth. I request you pay me only half the value. Once you agree, I will leave you instructions on how to make payment."

"Leave me instructions? Are you going somewhere?"

"I am sorry," I said. "What I meant to say was that I will give you instructions."

He stared at me. I returned his stare.

I needed to become a better liar.

<hr>

The evening meal I shared with Pascal and Seraphine was muted by my low mood. All I had ahead of me was a long, sleepless night, an ordeal whose difficulty would in no way be diminished because of my familiarity with the dark hours of remorse and sorrow.

In another part of the city, a small drama was about to begin. I later learned of it from the servant girl who stood outside the door and listened to every word.

CHAPTER TWENTY-SIX

Oil lamps set every few paces gave uneven light to the long corridor in the palace of the high priest. An elderly man robed in purple walked vigorously behind a maidservant, highly aware and desirous of her youth and freshness. When she reached a door at the end of the corridor, she stopped and bowed.

The elderly man smiled a snake's smile above his neatly trimmed beard. He smoothed back thick gray hair, showing off the wide gold bands on his fingers.

"He awaits you here," the maid said, hiding her instinctive revulsion behind cold politeness.

"Go then," he said, not the least disappointed. For every maid put off by his advanced years, there were two others who saw past his wrinkled skin and understood the warmth and vigor of gold and jewels.

She stepped away, and he pushed the door open.

Inside, more oil lamps flickered, illuminating the tile floor covered with luxurious carpet, the furniture made of oiled cedar, and bronze statues brought from Greece. A man stood at the far end of the room looking through a window that offered a magnificent view of the darkened buildings of the lower city.

The old man shut the door. "Yes, my son, you sent for me?" he asked.

Caiaphas turned from his thoughts at the window. He frowned at the amused solicitous tone of the elder man's voice.

"Don't posture with me," Caiaphas said sourly. "This is far from a public gathering where the great and hallowed Annas must preserve the pious sanctimony of a former high priest."

"A son-in-law must show more respect," Annas said. His laughter sounded like wind shaking dry husks. "Regardless of the irritations of office."

"That is easy for you to say. With respect and wealth and connections, you have all the advantages of holding office and none of the grief."

Annas reached for a jug of wine and poured some. He took a long drink before answering. "Why do you think I appointed one son after the other and finally turned to you? It is far better to have been a high priest than to be one. Especially with the current situation at the temple."

He took more wine, then smiled his snake smile at Caiaphas. "Which, I presume, is why I am here."

Caiaphas began to pace. "Without the temple market, have you any idea how much revenue we have lost in the last two days?"

"Of course," Annas said, still amused. He set the wine goblet down. "Years ago I supervised the delicate negotiations for the 'commissions' to our family coffers."

"If the prophet is not dealt with soon," Caiaphas hissed, "your delicate structure will never rise again. If the people see that the temple can exist without the market, they'll never let us begin again."

"Well, well. The prophet has destroyed your profit." Annas chuckled at his play on words. "And you led us to believe that it was for the safety of our country He must die, not because of money." Annas tapped his chin theatrically as he mused.

"Ah yes," he said moments later, "wasn't it in front of the entire Sanhedrin that you declared it better for one man to die than for a whole nation to perish?"

"Politics and convenience do not lessen a truth," Caiaphas answered. "Even Joseph of Arimathea and Nicodemus remain silent, understanding that the peasant must not be allowed to bring this country to rebellion."

"More wine? From the heat in your voice it sounds like you have already indulged—despite the ritual purification necessary for an acting high priest."

"You are attempting to provoke me further. I know your nature. You stir with a stick and see what rises. Some day you will uncover a nest of bees, and then I shall laugh at you the way you laugh at me."

Annas walked to the window and faced away from Caiaphas as he spoke. "I am amused because I believe this is the first time I have seen emotion from you. Not even when you married my daughter did I detect any flow of blood."

"The man must die."

"Even in the face of the miracles He has wrought within the temple these last few days?"

Caiaphas snorted. "He is nothing more than a magician, hiring people to walk in lame and run out leaping."

Annas turned back from the window. For the first time since entering the room, his voice lost its banter. "I have made queries about some of those people. Neighbors swear they have been lame or blind from birth. I am not so certain it is fraud. This man intrigues me. Someday, I would like time alone with Him."

Caiaphas stopped pacing. "If He is not a magician, then He is from the devil."

"Oh my. You do want Him dead."

"You weren't there when He publicly denounced us." Caiaphas had to lean against a nearby table to keep his hands from shaking with rage. " 'Whitewashed tombs,' He called us. Beautiful on the outside yet full of dead men's bones."

Annas shrugged. "The poor always vilify the rich. I learned long ago that wealth is a wonderful balm against insults."

"Insults? He called into question our integrity, our teachings, our authority. You were not there to see the people cheer His words. This man must die!"

Caiaphas swept his arm across the table, sending the wine jug and goblets smashing against the wall.

"You have gone far past amusement," Annas said in the resulting silence. "There is great danger in passionate action not grounded in cold thought. If your foolish rage threatens everything I have built . . ."

Had Caiaphas not been so flushed with the joy of hatred, he would have quailed; only rarely did Annas show the steel of his absolute rule.

"I shall have both His death and my satisfaction!" Caiaphas continued, riding the wave of his emotion. "Here, in this very room, will I send Him to His knees!"

Annas stepped toward Caiaphas. He reached up and grabbed the younger man's angular chin and squeezed until Caiaphas was ready to listen.

"Do not act in haste," Annas said in a soft voice. "If you take Him publicly, there will be a riot. That could very well spark the people to the rebellion you fear if you let Him live." Annas continued to squeeze until all resistance had left his son-in-law. "Do you understand?"

"We will take Him in private," Caiaphas said, almost dizzy with his hatred. First the humiliation in the temple court. Now this humiliation with Annas.

Annas dropped his hand. "How? Have you thought this through? It is difficult to track His whereabouts. He comes and goes at will."

"One of His followers could solve that difficulty," Caiaphas answered. "Over the past days, I have sent spies out to test His disciples one by one. Not in such a way as to raise their suspicions but simply to discover any disloyalty."

"And?" Annas asked.

"Eleven of the twelve are as resolute as stone—so totally worshipful that they either did not comprehend the subtlety of my spies or turned their backs and walked away."

"I take it you are suggesting that one might be persuaded to betray Him."

"Yes, there is a possibility," Caiaphas said. "He is a poor man; his father was sent to debtors' prison. A resentful loner and obviously lustful for power. We can appeal to that and make him feel important."

Caiaphas pressed his fingers together and smiled. "His name is Judas."

WEDNESDAY

CHAPTER TWENTY-SEVEN

My dearest love,

Remember our days of innocence? The first few years after our wedding? If only I could find a way back to those easy hours of reclining with my head in your lap as you stroked my hair. We happily traded stories of our childhoods, laughed, joked, and hummed silly melodies. Oh, the wonders of love with you, the joyful mystery of abandon in each other's arms, the drowsy smiles as we woke together, the way the bumps rose on your skin when I lightly ran my fingernails across your arms, your shoulders, your back.

If, somehow, I could find my way back to you, I would pledge myself again. This time, knowing the dangers that destroy love, I would guard against the gradual selfishness that eroded what we had. I would be a man you could trust and love. Never again would I neglect the small touches and smiles that I now know matter more than the wealth that supplies the clatter of servants in a large, empty house.

Oh, that I could be with you again.

Yesterday I woke with the hope that I would be able to return to you, to start over.

Today I wake with disappointment. The man I approached to heal Vashti sent me away and did so in a manner that neither confirmed nor denied that He could help her.

My disappointment is all the more bitter against the hope I had allowed myself. I was a fool for entertaining the ridiculous idea that anyone could take away our daughter's pain and make her whole again. As this day begins, after hours of reflection through the night, I see I was a fool, too, for approaching a crazed man with that hope.

"When a man believes in Me," I heard this man say yesterday in the temple, "he does not believe in Me only, but also in the One who sent Me. When a man looks at Me," I heard Him say, "he sees the One who sent Me.

"I have come into the world as a light," I heard Him say, "so that no one who believes in Me should stay in darkness."

My love, can you see me waving my arms in exasperation as I tell you this? (Remember the days when I was eager to share with you all the happenings in my daily life, and you laughed at me for how my arms moved as I spoke?)

My love, what kind of man tells others to believe in Him? As if He is a god. Or the God.

Only an insane man would declare this. Not a great teacher as some call Him, but an insane man.

Yet . . .

I did see Him perform miracles.

It seems to me that everything rests on that. If the miracles are real, my rational mind can accept the premise that He is more than man. And at the same time, my rational mind cannot accept the premise of God among us as a lowly peasant.

My mind circles and circles.

(Here I am, thinking aloud in your presence, as I did in the days before silence settled on us like a frost, unaware it was there until far too much of the cold had arrived.)

The evidence of my eyes and ears tells me it is preposterous to believe that the world is moved by an invisible hand; preposterous to believe that if such a Spirit does exist, it has chosen to reside in the body of a man; preposterous to think that this man Yeshua could turn water into wine, stop a storm with His voice, or raise a man from the dead.

Yet . . .

During the long sleepless hours last night, I realized it is equally preposterous to contemplate a world that is not moved by an invisible hand. My flesh and blood and bones come from the very soil of this earth, nourished by bread made of wheat that draws from moisture and sunlight and soil, strengthened by the meat of animals that feed upon those plants, sustained by the water that falls from the skies and collects in rivers and lakes.

My body gurgles and groans, and somehow, despite the vulgarity of decay that comes with this flesh, there is something unseen in me that fills with love or hate or greed or compassion—and remorse and regret, which weigh so heavily that I tire of life.

That the world exists, and that I exist in the world are great mysteries themselves, dulled only because I see and live it every day without giving it thought.

Thus, I am forced to admit it is a preposterous notion to believe our world exists without the unseen hand of a Creator. If then there is a Creator who breathes spirit into me, could He not have the power to choose to become flesh Himself?

So my mind circles.

One is as preposterous as the other. God cannot be. Or we cannot be without God.

How am I to know? And why, after all these years of comfortable life, am I suddenly tormented with these questions?

It is this man Yeshua. His message and His deeds confront me.

I tell myself He is a lunatic.

Yet . . .

As He spoke yesterday in the temple, indeed in the moment He finished declaring glory to God, a loud noise split the skies. Some said it was thunder, but the sky was cloudless. Others fell to their knees, believing they heard angels. Still others in the temple declared it was the voice of God.

Miracles, the voice of God . . . Yeshua is a man impossible to ignore.

God or man?

I cannot rest until I know. Against all rational thought, in the depths of my disappointment, there remains in my heart a small ember of hope. I am in desperate need, stuck in the darkness of this deep hole I have fallen into. If He is light . . .

God or man?

Today I will seek Him.

God or man?

That is what I must decide before I write any final farewell to you.

Your Simeon

CHAPTER TWENTY-EIGHT

I waited but did not find Him. I spent hours at the temple, sitting on the steps among the columns of the Outer Court, made more miserable by a gloomy cloud that passed over and dropped a light rain. Neither the gloom nor drizzle slowed the hectic activities of pilgrims and priests around me; men and women bustled in all directions, with obvious purpose.

As for me, I did nothing. I was waiting for redemption.

As the long minutes passed, my heart became heavier. Why, I wondered, did nothing in this temple promise me relief from the one single action that had cost me so much?

I knew I owed the truth to my wife before I died, and I hoped there would be a small measure of relief in lancing that heavy boil of conscience. But as I watched the activities of the temple, I could not imagine finding consolation in approaching a somber priest garbed in white robes to confess what I had done. I had already judged myself; I did not need another's stares of superiority to confirm the vileness that shrouded me.

Nor, despite my proximity to the temple altar, did I believe I could find forgiveness by brutally taking the life of a creature as much unaware of my sins as of its impending death; no amount of innocent blood could wash me clean.

I knew this because I had tried with repeated sacrifices.

A Gentile might recoil from this brutality, not understanding the significance of the sacrifice.

Our Hebrew word for sacrifice—*korban*—comes from the same root that means "to approach." Those who believe in God see man as living between the spiritual and natural worlds. Caught in a battle between the darker desires of fallen flesh and the soul's desire to reach God, man constantly struggles to overcome this contradiction. In bringing korban, the death offering serves not only as the demonstration of what man would deserve were God to judge him but as appeasement of God's holy wrath.

He is a God of love who offered Jews this sacrificial system as a way of restoring spiritual life because we all fall short of His righteousness and truly deserve His eternal wrath. The sacrifice, if offered with true repentance, represents the death of man's fallen nature, freeing him to bring his true self into connection with God, elevating him by temporarily giving his spiritual nature victory over his physical.

But months of weekly sacrifices had not redeemed me.

Yes, I was filled with repentance, with remorse beyond self-hatred. And yes, a lamb's blood allowed me *korban*, to approach. But God, I had decided, would not listen to me, no matter how closely I approached.

I was miserably conscious that, for what I had done, any creature's death was too little a price to pay. I did not believe any atonement was possible for me and my sins.

I could buy hundreds more sheep and spill enough blood to overflow the cracks of the stone floor. Yet that river of life would merely cost me more of my surplus of gold. Where was my punishment in that?

Sitting, waiting, dwelling on all of this, it simply became clearer that only one death would suffice.

Mine. Unless I found a miracle.

And the rain fell harder.

CHAPTER TWENTY-NINE

I was destined not to find the prophet, for as I would learn before the day ended, this, the day before Passover, was a day on which He rested in seclusion near Bethany.

Where Yeshua had peace, another, like me, had a horribly restless soul, though for different reasons from mine.

The other was named Judas.

He probably passed almost within my reach among the crowd as he hurried to find the high priests. There is only a field of blood to speak for him now, and I cannot pretend to know his heart and what sent him into Jerusalem.

Still, for me, speculation is inevitable, as it probably is for any who later heard of his secret visit to the temple.

In the gloominess on the Mount of Olives, donkeys brayed at the city gates across the valley. Singing and chanting came from behind the temple walls. But none of these sounds broke into Judas's mind.

He'd been sent to purchase a lamb for Passover. It gave him the perfect excuse to be alone in the city, away from the eyes of the other disciples.

During a poor night's sleep, he had spent his wakeful times alternating between vindictive satisfaction as he thought of his revenge against the slights he had endured and renewed lapses of guilt as he realized the path his vengeful thoughts were taking him.

Now they took him on a literal path, down the Mount of Olives. Jerusalem drew him like a Siren of the Greek myths, beckoning him not with promises of the flesh but with the much sweeter prospect of power among the city's elite—power that Yeshua had chosen to discard, and in so doing, had wasted three years of Judas's life.

Not just three years, Judas thought, but everything he had held dear before meeting Yeshua.

Outside his Judean hometown, his brother now tended the small herd of goats Judas had built from a sickly pregnant nanny over the course of ten seasons. Why was Judas no longer there? Because in a moment marked as clearly as a watershed on the nearby ravines, Judas remembered the messianic impulse that had swept him to run home and sell those goats for a mere note of promise; as part of a crowd, he'd watched the teacher send a lame man dancing away in joy.

All his life, Judas had used aggressive hard work to bury the shame of watching his father go to a debtors' prison for gambling. All his life, Judas had lusted for the security and respectability of wealth, seething at the injustice of belonging to the poor while men of lesser intelligence and character strutted in mastery. Yet on that incredible afternoon, when the teacher's glance had fallen upon him, the gaze had felt like hot water scathing dirt off crusted old leather. The teacher, Judas had known without doubt in that moment, understood the filth of the meanness of spirit that had been forced upon him and, in that depth of complete understanding, had also accepted Judas without reservation.

From that one watershed moment, Judas had worked hard—

with the same flailing, scrabbling ambition he had applied to growing his goat herd—to gain his position among the followers the teacher most trusted. The teacher had even appointed him among only twelve to preach and drive out demons and take the teachings to the people.

More and more, however, Judas had begun to feel like the shamed outsider he had been as a teenager jeered by the village boys. A Judean among close-knit Galileans. A slender man among broad-shouldered fishermen with tough hands scarred by years of handling heavy wet netting.

Judas could mark that first moment of isolation, too—the moment when the teacher had first thrown a shadow over Judas's hopes. Word had come that John the Baptist had been beheaded. This John had proclaimed Yeshua as Messiah, no less! This John, a man with a great following, had once insisted he was not even fit to untie the thongs of the teacher's sandals.

And what had the teacher done for a prophet who had been beheaded at the request of a teenage harlot? Nothing. The teacher, whom Judas had seen command storms into silence, had not sent fire or earthquake or plague to destroy a man as evil as Herod, but instead had shared in grief with the others through prayer. Worse, later the teacher had fled Galilee in fear of Herod. Where was power in that?

Judas had brooded on this many nights near the flickering campfires in the countryside—until the miraculous feeding of the thousands on the far shore of the Sea of Galilee. In the joyous thunder of fervent hosannas that called the teacher to be king, Judas had found hope again, had swelled with pride to be one of the twelve closest to Him.

To what end? Judas now asked himself, his heart dominated by angry memories of the synagogue in Capernaum the day after the miracle of the feeding.

Yeshua that day was easily at the height of His popular support. He had not taken the mantle but had spurned the vast crowds, weaving no stories with His usual charismatic speech, but wearily telling them to drink His blood and eat His flesh.

Yes, the spy sent from the Pharisees had known well to touch upon this incident with Judas. In Capernaum back then, legions of followers had turned away, their disenchantment verging on disgust, for who could make sense of someone who claimed to be "bread sent down from heaven"?

Worse, in private conversation with the twelve shortly after, Yeshua had not only repeated the teaching but had also turned to the group and accused one of them of being from the devil.

It was as if Yeshua had spoken to the bitterness within Judas.

Could a man be blamed for turning love and hope into hatred at such a betrayal? Could a man be blamed for seeking a way to force Yeshua to take a stand and prove His power?

Anger drove Judas to walk faster and faster.

The chief priests awaited him.

CHAPTER THIRTY

While Judas's dark spirit drove him to the city and into the temple, mine eventually drove me out. I could contain my restlessness no longer.

I went to the theater, the horse races, the gymnasium, but all the entertainment failed to distract me.

Eventually my wanderings led me beneath the city.

Jerusalem's subterranean alleys are a world set apart from sunlight, laughter, and hope. They were built almost by accident as the city grew; it became easier to build on top of some of the ancient structures than to tear them down and haul the rubble away.

It is also a world of danger. Whispers bounce from unseen sources through the dim corridors. Movements are furtive. Shadows dance and are lost in deeper shadows. Thieves and assassins hunt each other and prey on the weak.

Here, too, status means little. It is the refuge of the desperate, the unloved, and the poor who take comfort in shared misery and in escaping the shame that awaits them in sunlight.

Perhaps I wandered below the city following an unconscious wish to have the decision regarding my death taken from me. If so, I failed that unacknowledged desire.

Before I had ventured a hundred steps into the darkness, two men stepped out from behind a pillar, daggers extended.

"Strip yourself," one snarled.

The other laughed. "You'll save us the work of pulling the clothes from your dead body."

So they wanted not only my possessions, but also my fear.

I measured them.

They were pitiful. Small to begin with, hunger and alcohol had reduced them to grimy husks. They could not even hold their daggers steady. Had I turned and run, they would have collapsed within their first dozen steps of pursuit.

As they blustered more threats, I discovered that I was still capable of an emotion beyond the deadening sensation of guilt—anger.

Here was a place I could focus my frustration and hatred.

I roared and threw my right fist at the first man's head. Savage joy filled me at the pain of a popped knuckle in my hand, while my victim fell immediately, sobbing.

The other had more spirit. He slashed at my right side, bouncing the edge of his dagger off my ribs, giving me more pain that burned a swath across my side and into the front of my consciousness.

Without thinking, I spun and lifted a knee, catching him in the midsection with such force that his feet left the ground. As he crashed onto his back, his head made a resounding *thunk* against the stone of the alley.

I stood poised to flail again, but neither moved. I heaved for breath as I waited over them. The fight had been brief, but exertion in battle comes as much from the mind's fear as the body's actions.

I touched my ribs. The dagger, rusted and dull, had not even cut through the cloth of my robe.

Between the sobs of the first man, I heard bubbling as he breathed through the blood that streamed from his nose. The other, I only half feared, was so inert as to be dead. Had I killed him, it would have mattered little to me. I would not have to face a court, and if I did, I would be applauded as a hero.

Yes. Wonderful me. Tall and well nourished, I had defeated two broken men.

To further demonstrate the emptiness of my victory, a little girl pushed past my legs and fell upon the motionless man, crying and pleading for him to wake.

She was as grimy and pitiful as they. I became aware of their stench, a collective soured warmth on the damp coolness of the alley.

The man—I guessed her father—groaned. He was not dead, then.

Where my next impulse came from I do not know. My reputation is one of stern severity. While I do not pinch every shekel before I spend it, I do not spend foolishly, and every bargain I drive is one that could not be driven harder or further. I was not known for charity. Yet here I was, moved to it for the third time since entering Jerusalem. First the blind beggar, then the cloak to a stranger, now this.

These two men were so utterly crushed and the little girl's tears so wrenching that I took my purse from beneath my robe.

I pulled the child up by an arm. In the dim light, I saw only the shiny tracks of her tears etched through the dirt of her face.

She tried to pummel me with her fragile fists.

I caught both her wrists and squatted to look her as clearly in the eyes as the bad light permitted. "This is for you," I said. I gave her the purse. Her feral eyes widened at the clink of shekels.

I did not wait for gratitude. I doubted it would come.

I also expected that the men would take the money from her as soon as I departed. I only hoped the father, when he woke, would have the same fierce love for her that she had shown for him, and that he would spend some of the money on her.

I turned away, leaving the popping sound of bubbling blood.

As I reached the light, I discovered my guilt had eased. I felt an unfamiliar joy, and I began to wonder if I could shed my remorse like a snake's skin simply by unexpectedly granting gifts to those who had less than I.

But my joy did not last long.

Before I had stepped into the city proper, I remembered the blind beggar. I had given him more money than he expected in a month of tending his bowl, yet that largess had left me empty.

Why had I not felt this same joy with him? It came to me. He was not a miserable young girl like the beggar at her father's side. Miserable and young, like my daughter.

My heart had been lifted because of the beggar girl I'd been able to help. As I realized this, I also knew my daughter I could not help.

At that realization, my joy became ashes.

CHAPTER THIRTY-ONE

Too much of the afternoon remained. I went back to the temple without sighting Yeshua and so decided to seek Him among His friends. Against the flow of pilgrims making their way to Jerusalem, I walked up the Mount of Olives and down the ridge on the other side, past Bethphage, to Bethany, searching for Yeshua among them. I did not see Him or His followers.

From what I had heard, it seemed the best place to make inquiries would be at His friend's abode.

"Where is the house of Lazarus?" I asked a boy sitting on a pile of rocks at the side of the road.

The boy raised his smudged face to me, gave me a sly glance, then looked back down at his hand. He opened his fingers and a small lizard scooted to freedom.

"My hand is now empty," he said. "The lizard made room for a shekel."

"One shekel to give directions?"

The boy shrugged. "Many others have paid me to take them there."

So I was to be just one of the many curiosity seekers. I should have expected it. Not many men are raised from the dead.

"Half a shekel," I told the boy.

He grinned. "Half a shekel. I'll take you there myself." He'd spoken so quickly that I knew I'd paid too much, but other things occupied my mind.

He led me on a narrow path between the houses. Bethany was a small village. I could imagine it in the middle of the summer, the white walls of the single-level dwellings shimmering in the heat, weeds struggling for a foothold in the cracks between the rocks.

We rounded a corner, and the boy pointed out a house with two goats tethered in front. "Half a shekel," he said.

"First," I answered, "tell me if any share this house with Lazarus."

Another shrug. "Two old women. Mary and Martha."

I gave him his money, and he dashed away as if expecting me to call for it back.

<hr />

I smiled when a woman with high cheekbones and a suspicious glance answered my call. The boy and I had differing opinions on what defined old. My guess was that she had not even reached her thirtieth year.

"What is it?" she asked without stepping out from the doorway. I smelled fresh bread baking inside.

"This is the house of Lazarus?"

"Yes," she answered. "And yes, he was dead. Yes, he is now alive. No, it wasn't the work of the devil that brought him forth. And finally, even if he were here, he would be too busy to be poked and prodded."

A second woman appeared in the doorway. She was taller, slimmer, and younger. The same high cheekbones showed they were sisters, but this one did not have a face creased with suspicion.

"Martha," she told her old sister, "this poor man asked a simple question."

"Just as all the others have bothered us with simple questions to take us away from our work."

Before they could argue further, I slipped in another question. "I am actually looking for Yeshua. Do you know where He is?"

"No," Martha said firmly. "You have wasted your time."

Her sister placed a hand lightly on her forearm.

Martha shook it off. "See how he is dressed?" Martha said to her. "He's probably been sent by the Sadducees."

"No," I said.

The younger sister kept her eyes on my face as she spoke to Martha. "He has need of the teacher. Grant him some peace."

"The bread will burn. I have no time," Martha said as she stepped into the shadows of the house. She was out of my sight when she called her parting words from inside. "And, Mary, you have your cleaning!"

"Forgive her," the woman in the doorway said. "She is worried these days for our teacher. It makes her short-tempered."

"Worried for the teacher?"

"You have probably heard," Mary said. "After He healed our brother, the religious authorities called for His death. Yet He persists in going to the temple."

"Not today," I said. "I waited for Him there."

"He has gone into the hills," she said. "He has taken a day of contemplation and quiet."

I was conscious of standing awkwardly in front of this woman. I was a man and a stranger; it would be improper to ask her to leave the house and join me in a walk. As she did not invite me in, I received a clear unspoken message: I was imposing upon her graciousness.

"My daughter is crippled," I blurted. It was a naked bid for her sympathy—appealing to her heart with news of a hurt child—but I was desperate. "He is my only hope."

"I tell you the truth," she replied. "I do not know where He is or when He will return."

Her eyes lingered on the mutilated left side of my face. I resisted the impulse to rub my scar.

"But He will return?" I persisted.

"He makes His plans known to no one. Spies are everywhere, and the religious authorities lie in wait to capture Him away from the crowds."

I slumped. "How can He be the Messiah, then? How can He lead the nation if He lives in such fear?"

Mary understood that my questions were not meant as criticism. She answered softly. "It is not fear. This leadership is what others want for Him. He Himself walks a different path."

I stared at her. "Who is He then?"

"We all ask that question," she said. "Even those closer to Him."

"And you? What do you think?"

Mary smiled. "He is a man of love. One who not only heals people, but also forgives them of their sins and sets them free."

"No man has the power to forgive sins," I said.

"No man has the power to raise someone from the dead. Yet my brother walks and talks, even after four days in the tomb."

Four days' time was significant. Many of us Jews believed the soul stayed near the body for three days, waiting in hope that it might reenter the body. Not until the fourth day, we believed, did true death arrive with a drop of gall from the sword of the angel of death. This gall changed the body's face, forcing the soul to leave its resting place.

"If He can raise your brother," I said, "He can heal my daughter. I must see Him."

"He does no one's bidding," Mary said. "Were I you, I would try to understand His teachings first."

In so many words, He had told me the same.

Martha called from inside the house. "Mary! Time grows short. We must prepare for the Passover."

Mary apologized for her sister with a quick grimace. "I wish I could help you more. . . ."

"Please," I said, hiding my disappointment, "return to your sister. I will look for Yeshua in the temple later."

I turned back toward Jerusalem. For all the time and effort I had spent to visit Bethany, I had learned little. I should have expected Mary and Martha to confirm the raising of Lazarus; if it had been a carefully worked fraud, they would not reveal it to a passing stranger.

Even if I chose to believe in that unlikely miracle, it has still brought me no closer to what I needed. "Understand His teachings"—there was nothing practical about that. This man seemed to be a whimsical, unpredictable mystic.

It was a shame, I thought, that neither money nor power seemed to tempt Him. What could I do to bend His will to mine?

CHAPTER THIRTY-TWO

I fear for you," Pascal said. Seraphine had left us alone, disappearing after the meal to supervise servants. Candle flames wavered and made it difficult to read Pascal's face.

"Fear?" I smiled, as if his statement had not risen a snake's head of worry in my belly. *Has he or one of his servants found my letters to Jaala?*

He sighed. "Surely by now you understand that a fly does not land in this city without my knowledge. Take your hand, for example. The knuckles, bruised and scraped. The way you wince with every movement. Even had I not heard about your encounter with the thieves, I would have noticed something during our meal tonight."

"Pascal, I will find it unforgivable if you had me followed during the day." I had told no one of the happenings in the alley beneath the city. If he knew, it was because he had made efforts to track my movements.

Pascal sighed again. "Must I remind you of your appearance? How long do you think it took for word to spread through the underbelly of this city that an expensively dressed, unarmed man with a distinctive scar attacked two with knives and defeated them?"

My smile was grim, unamused. "You have friends among thieves."

"Don't be a fool. Of course I do." He grinned, trying to relieve the tension between us. "Most of them live here in the upper city."

I was not in the mood.

Neither was he; his grin faded. "Admit it," Pascal said. "During any of your other visits, your mind found nothing of interest but the price of glass, silk, and other luxuries. You worked ceaselessly, securing shipments at prices far below market rates. Yet this past week, the only mention you've made of business is a cryptic offer to sell me what you own, and even then, you've ignored any opportunity to discuss that offer with me further."

"Other matters seemed more important. I will make a list of the assets tomorrow and present it to you before the Passover begins."

"I'm not sure that will be necessary—which is why I fear for you."

"I don't understand," I said.

He rubbed his face pensively before looking at me again. "You went to Bethany today. You made inquiries at the house of Lazarus. Do you deny this?"

I half stood, immediately angry.

He put up a tired hand. "Simeon, I did not have you followed. The Sanhedrin have spies everywhere around this man. As always, their reports reached me through friends of mine."

I remained half standing.

"Sit. Please," Pascal urged. "Understand that I am willing to see things from your point of view. I have never had the joy of a child, let alone a son to carry my name. I can only imagine how deeply it would hurt to lose him had God given me such a gift. . . ."

For all my anger and all my faults, even I could recognize that Pascal had acknowledged his one deepest pain, sorrow, and shame—the lack of an heir. Seraphine was his fourth wife; he was long past being able to blame a barren womb instead of his own infertile seed.

I sat, as weary as he was.

"A good charlatan can deceive the best, and I pray that in your grief you have not fallen into this Yeshua's power," Pascal said. I had never seen his face so softened with the gentleness I saw in the candlelight. The quietness of his voice matched the compassion of his gaze. "I think of you as a brother, and it would break my heart to see that the rumors of a man raised from the dead have led you to false hope."

"You need not worry about me."

Pascal shook his head and tightened his lips in sadness. "Simeon, listen to me. He cannot bring your son back. Nor can He heal your daughter."

"I'm not sure I wish to continue this discussion."

"We must," he said. His face had lost none of its concern for me. "The Sanhedrin believe you want to join Yeshua's movement, and that leaves me no choice. I cannot consider any dealings with you, at least not now. In a year perhaps, when this false messiah has been forgotten. But not now. I hope you understand."

Before I could reply, Pascal continued. "What makes this conversation so difficult is that your interest in the false messiah has been in vain."

I waited.

"One of His followers visited the temple today," Pascal said. He carefully watched my face. "Obviously a shrewd man, he sees the end. Undoubtedly, he has decided that if he helps the religious authorities now, they can't prosecute him later with the other disciples when Yeshua is gone."

Pascal's narration was not one of triumph but resignation. "Think of it. The chief priests are deep in discussions that must not be recorded by any scribes. Their priority issue, of course, is this prophet from Galilee, who threatens each of their areas of temple jurisdiction. He must be stopped. But He is too popular. If He is taken publicly, the people will riot. Pilate will send in his troops. But how can He be taken in secret when He comes and goes so unpredictably? Then this man Judas approaches and offers them the prophet."

Pascal shook his head in mild disgust. "Our holy representatives did not merely accept the gift but still fought for a bargain. To get this Yeshua would be worth half the temple treasury. Yet they bartered until Judas agreed to betray his master for the legal price of a slave."

I felt the muscles in my chest squeeze. "Betray?" I echoed.

"The prophet will die. And the price of His life was only thirty pieces of silver."

CHAPTER THIRTY-THREE

As I stared sightlessly into the darkness, lost in my miserable world, much higher-stakes politics were occurring not far from my guest chamber.

After all, no place was far from another here in the wealthy upper quarters of Jerusalem. Pascal's mansion lay roughly halfway between the palace of Caiaphas the high priest and Herod's palace, where the Roman governor of Judea sequestered himself when he stayed in the city.

And, as best as I can guess from what I later learned from a bowlegged Greek servant, at some time during my thoughts, Caiaphas himself must have passed nearby on the street—in secrecy, in darkness, without guards—on his way to see a man named Pontius Pilate.

Caiaphas waited with concealed impatience in the warm room of the bathhouse in Herod's palace. He knew exactly why Pontius Pilate had chosen the location for this meeting—the heated, moist air made waiting uncomfortable for anyone dressed in full clothing. Furthermore, Pilate constantly wanted it clear that Rome ruled; his possession of the palace built by Herod the

Great said it much more eloquently and pervasively than words. Finally, Pontius Pilate enjoyed lording his physical prowess over others.

The floor and walls of the warm room were tiled with exquisite mosaics, and an elegant low table stood against the far wall. Other than that, the room was empty. Heavy grunts and groans from the hot room and the roar of the furnace below that heated water to steam was all that distracted Caiaphas from his thoughts.

Caiaphas knew why the location was chosen but not why the meeting had been called, nor the hour for it. His spies, who informed him of every public move made by Pilate as well as most of his private ones, had told Caiaphas nothing unusual. What could be so important that Pilate did not wait until morning?

Fifteen minutes passed. His clothing grew heavy from moisture. To torment him more, his palate began to click with dryness, and the insides of his thighs began to itch with the beginning of a rash.

Still, he had enough discipline to hold himself tall and rigid as the grunts and groans continued just out of sight. The barbarians spent too much time in the hedonistic pleasure of muscle massage and skin scraping.

The first indication that Pilate was ready came when his servant, a large bowlegged Greek, stepped out of the hot room and moved past Caiaphas. Pontius Pilate arrived moments later with a towel wrapped loosely around his lower belly and legs. He held the towel with his left hand, making no effort to hide the stubs of his first two fingers, each long ago sheared at the first knuckle and healed like blunt sausages.

"So," Pilate said. He looked Caiaphas up and down, making it obvious that his soldier's judgment found Caiaphas utterly weak.

Pontius Pilate was wide and thick, almost totally dark with chest and stomach hair beaded with water droplets. Long, narrow scars—sword and spear—covered his upper arms and shoulders. His gleaming red face held full lips beneath a nose crooked from a poorly healed break. The hair that crowned his head formed a bowl in classical Roman cut.

Caiaphas hated Pilate for his smug reliance on the bearlike power of a middle-aged body not yet soft from age. Caiaphas hated as well the intimacy of standing in the presence of a nearly naked man. Most of all, Caiaphas hated the feeling of physical inferiority and weakness that Pilate inspired in him.

"So, High Priest," Pilate said, "Passover is upon us. Once again, the Jews celebrate a miracle that let them cast off the shackles of subjection to a world power."

Caiaphas felt the first wave of dizziness overcome him. Standing in the heat had taken its toll.

"Yet here you are," Pontius continued, "in shackles again. Roman shackles."

The servant returned carrying a heated pot of oil in a thick towel.

Pontius Pilate dropped his own towel and smirked at Caiaphas's stony, straight-ahead look. He walked to the table, settled on his belly, and allowed the servant to begin oiling the skin of his back.

"Isn't it wonderful to be enemies?" Pilate said. "We can trust that we distrust. We can love our hatreds. Each side knows where the other stands because each side watches the other as surely as if they were lovers."

In the dizzying heat, Caiaphas had to widen his stance to keep his balance.

"And this is what I know," Pilate said. "A few years ago, when a delegation of Jews came to Caesarea to protest the military insignias above the temple in Antonia, you were not among them. They were prepared to die before leaving, yet you, their religious leader, conveniently remained in Jerusalem."

Pilate hummed with pleasure for a few moments as the servant continued to knead oil onto his broad muscles.

"I know, too, that you and I agreed to have the Romans build an aqueduct into Jerusalem with temple funds," Pilate said, "and that once it was built, you then made it appear to the populace that we had robbed the temple."

Pilate closed his eyes. "And since then, I know that you sent word to Tiberius, going over my head, to protest the gold shields that honored him, even though they were here in the hall of this palace, not within the temple where I could understand any claims of sacrilege."

Pilate opened his eyes again. "As I see it, you do not fight openly as an honorable soldier, but hidden, as a snake in the reeds."

"I doubt you requested my presence at this hour to go over old history that reflects more your poor judgment than any failings of my own actions." Caiaphas allowed a smirk to rest on his own face. There had been rumors of a letter from Tiberius, the unpredictable dictator from Rome. "I suspect, if anything, you are an honorable soldier about to lose your position as governor if news of any more Judean disturbances reaches your beloved Tiberius. And because of that, you need help to keep the peace."

By Pilate's sudden, rigid silence Caiaphas realized his jibe had hit the mark.

Pilate recovered, but too late. "Isn't hatred refreshing? Who would have thought a dried-up old Jew could harbor the passion that you do. Let us keep this hatred out in the open, where it fools no one."

"Why did you call me here?" Caiaphas asked. "Surely not to establish that I need you. Or you me. We have known that for years. It seems to work rather well, as long as we each stay out of the other's way."

"Then we shall speak plainly," Pilate said. "I have brought in extra garrisons of soldiers for the Passover. See that I need not bring them into use."

"What could you possibly imagine as trouble?"

"Anything that involves Jews," Pilate snapped. "Let me repeat myself. I want no trouble. Do you understand?"

Caiaphas understood. The letter from Tiberius was more than rumor. Pilate could afford no more trouble, or he would be recalled in shame to Rome. And as more than a rumor, it gave Caiaphas the leverage he needed in future dealings with Pilate.

The smile that played at the corners of Caiaphas's mouth was not directed at Pilate but against another. Yeshua.

Caiaphas had his betrayer. Now he had the power to direct Pilate's judgment.

Thus armed, a man of hate could dream of triumph against the man of love.

THURSDAY

CHAPTER THIRTY-FOUR

My dearest love,
The stylus is now in my hand. However, just moments ago I was not thinking of words to send you but of holding yesterday's letter near a candle flame. By burning it, I would have kept you from hearing how far I have fallen in the seemingly hopeless pursuit of reclaiming our lives.

But I promised you my honesty. That commitment kept me from thrusting the scroll into the flame. So, by the time a servant reads you this letter, you will know that in the dark of the previous night, I had actually wondered if the Messiah was among us. I had actually hoped He might heal Vashti.

Now I have lost that hope. He is only an ordinary man, betrayed in squalid circumstance, about to die an insignificant death.

It probably matters little to our circumstances. If I am promising honesty, I must admit to you—and to myself—that I am not sure that I could have found my way back to you, even had He restored Vashti's legs.

I could probably rightly say that your unspoken blame has been a wall between us since the fire. It is a wall, I believe now, I could have climbed if not for the burden I dared not share.

I have never been unfaithful to you. But I imagine it is no different for a husband who has strayed. His wife may never know of the infidelity, but for the man it is a secret of shame that festers and drives him away in hundreds of small ways.

As too is my burden. How could I allow you to love me when I hated myself? So I allowed the little love that remained between us to be slowly destroyed.

I know I cannot find your love.

I know I cannot hope in the Messiah.

Finally, because I foolishly pursued that hope, I cannot expect to sell my estates to Pascal as I had planned.

What do I have left?

Nothing.

The daughter who once sang loving lullabies to me, the daughter who once whispered silly things in my ear—she now screams with agony and will not even meet my eyes when I attempt to comfort her.

The son who once climbed my back and shouted with glee, the son who once followed me into the shops, imitating my every move—he is now cold and still and alone in a tomb.

And you? All I have are my memories. Once sweet, and now more bitter because of the sweetness I shall never taste again.

I have no peace.

Today I begin the final steps to reclaim peace. Not in pursuit of a charlatan messiah. But through my own efforts.

You are my love. I have asked before and I ask again: Pray for me. Against the chance that there is no God, I must hold the chance that there is. It cannot hurt for you to place your heart before Him on my behalf. If there is no one to listen, neither of us has lost anything. Because we cannot lose any more than what we already have lost.

And for what we have lost, I will pay the price to set us both free.

Your Simeon

CHAPTER THIRTY-FIVE

S hortly after the dawn's trumpets called the city to prayer, I began to walk the streets, paying little attention to where my feet took me. Because I had long since chosen to deny myself wine as escape, and because I could not sleep and thus find refuge from myself, it seemed my only relief came in movement.

It was poor relief.

I took no pleasure in the beauty of the soft blue sky above, scrubbed clear by the rain that had passed through the mountains. Lungfuls of the morning's cool air did not invigorate my blood.

As for my other senses, food was tasteless paste. The thought of fleshly pleasures left me cold; no woman's embrace but my wife's mattered, and even if I returned to her, she would never offer me open arms.

Despair congealed around my heart.

So I walked.

I descended from my cousin's mansion in the upper quarters. I crossed over the aqueduct that marked the lower boundary of the wealthy and restlessly wandered into the crowded filth of the lower city, barely aware of the pain of those hunched in doorways or limping through tiny alleys with staggering loads on their backs.

My feet kept me in motion. I reached the main street of the lower quarter. Had I turned left, I would have passed the temple, then the Roman fortress on its northwest corner. Farther on stood the blacksmith shops, the wool shops, the clothes market near the underground quarries at the north end of the city.

I did not make a conscious decision to turn right, but I moved slowly in the direction of the Siloam Pool. Fifteen or twenty minutes later, I reached the end of a street where the outer city wall abruptly blocked my progress. Built for defense, it was easily higher than the flat-roofed houses it contained in this corner of Jerusalem, wide enough that a horse could pull a cart along its top edge.

I stared at the heavy stones for several minutes.

With a grim smile, I realized I had indeed found my destination. A set of narrow, rough steps jutted out from the wall, leading to the top. I climbed, and since the outer edge had no support rails, I leaned for balance against the wall to guard against a painful fall. That, considering my intentions, struck me as ironic.

From the top of the wall I surveyed the breathtaking drop down the sheer cliff of the Kidron Valley. A half mile to my left was the temple, towering over the poverty within its shadows. Ahead and across the valley stood the Mount of Olives, dark against the rising sun behind it.

But it was the drop that held my attention.

Idly, I kicked a small rock into the vast emptiness. It fell with the swiftness I expected, but as it gained distance, it seemed to float until finally, a dozen heartbeats later, it clattered off the boulders below.

That could be me, I thought. In that short a time, I could have total escape from my miserable life. With a slight flex of my legs and the small price of the brief flash of a smashed skull, I could leave behind all that weighed my soul.

How badly did I want to live? Less than a day before, my fury against the thieves had shown me the spark was bright.

Yet . . .

I saw again the oil spilled across my daughter's legs and the snakelike flame licking the path of the oil. I saw again my son's body, the fragment of cloth clutched in his small hand.

I swayed on the edge of the wall with my arms lifted against the breeze.

Yes, I thought. I could do it. I could step out into the emptiness and welcome my death as the air tore at my robe and the boulders rushed toward me.

I might find peace.

Soon.

First, I needed to ensure that Jaala and Vashti would not become paupers in the wake of my departure. If Pascal would not purchase my estates while I was alive, he would find it easily possible after my death. Before taking my life, I needed to make arrangements to protect my wife and daughter.

I moved away from the wall, having found a peace of sorts.

My figure had been outlined against the sky, but it is fanciful to think that it would have drawn the attention of thirteen men in their place of refuge across the valley.

Up there, I was as unaware of them as they were of me. Events would follow later that compelled me to learn what I could about Yeshua and His movements that day.

They rested in a garden at the base of the Mount of Olives.

The walls of the garden contained a hundred gnarled, ancient olive trees—ten rows of ten in a rough square spaced several paces apart, each with a gray, weathered trunk double the thickness of a man's body and hardly taller than double a man's reach. From the massive trunks, webs of low, wide-spreading branches reached out, shading the garden with the delicate patterns of their tendrils of new shoots and curls of new green leaves.

Gethsemane. Nearby residents called it the "garden of the oil press." It was a garden in the traditional sense as well, for while its owner made profit from the olive oil he sold for cooking and lamp fuel, he saw no reason to leave the open ground surrounding the trees barren and had planted small fruit trees and flowering shrubs. Later in the heat of the year, with everything in bloom, it would be a medicine of peace to sit there in the honeysuckled sweetness of an early morning.

As it was still early, however, the peace of the garden came not from blossoms but from the timeless dignity of the scarred solidness of the olive trees, the new grass, the still air, and the distant burbling of the Kidron.

Here, Yeshua rested with His disciples. Nearby, tied by a halter to a low-hanging branch of an olive tree, the white lamb that Judas had purchased the day before tugged at the grass, unmindful of the men nearby.

All reclined against the tree trunks—but one.

Judas. He had been walking the garden ever since the disciples had arrived following their early meal of leavened bread.

He was thirty pieces of silver richer, but there remained the problem of earning that silver. He had to arrange a time and location where the authorities could arrest Yeshua.

This was no easy matter. Worried about riots, the chief priests had instructed Judas that it must be a private place.

This garden and this morning, of course, would have been perfect. But if Judas left now, there was no certainty that Yeshua and the others would still be in the garden when the religious authorities arrived.

No, Judas needed to know a time and place in advance. Especially since that would allow Judas to be among the disciples when the authorities appeared, leaving him unsuspected as the betrayer.

But, Judas asked himself again and again, *how can I know where Yeshua will be?*

When the solution struck Judas, it was so obvious that he smiled. He hid his urgency as he walked toward Yeshua, who leaned comfortably against a tree, smiling, eyes closed, face tilted to the sun.

As Judas's shadow fell upon Yeshua, the teacher opened His eyes.

"We must begin to prepare for the Passover supper," Judas said. "As You know, room is scarce in the city. Let me tend to our arrangements."

This was the solution. If Judas knew where they were going to share the Passover meal, he could tell the priests when and where to expect to find Yeshua.

At the question, nothing about Yeshua's expression changed, but slowly, tears filled His eyes as He looked wordlessly at Judas.

Judas felt an unspoken reproach. Had the impossible happened? Had someone seen him enter the palace of the high priest? Had someone drawn the easy conclusion and informed Yeshua? Or was his own conscience so plain upon his face?

A black shivering void swept through Judas. A void brought on by his urgency to betray and by the fear of the magnitude of that betrayal. A void brought on by his possible failure. And by his possible success. Judas tried to cover his cold dizziness by pushing the conversation.

"I am the keeper of the common purse," Judas said. He had planned his arguments. He hoped his voice didn't tremble. "And I know how important this Passover supper is to—"

"No." Yeshua shook His head at Judas. His voice was quiet. The other disciples would not overhear. "Yesterday, you went into the city and purchased the lamb. You have already done enough."

"You have already done enough." Should he look for a double meaning in the teacher's words?

Yeshua closed His eyes again and tilted His head back to the tree.

Later Judas would convince himself that if only Yeshua had not dismissed him, he would have returned the silver to Caiaphas that morning. Instead Judas stepped away, his face burning with shame and anger, his alienation heightening his sense of determination.

If the other disciples noticed the quiet conversation, none showed interest. Judas wandered deep into the garden, thinking only thoughts of self-pity.

The others continued to rest.

And the lamb, unaware of the few hours left to its short, innocent life, remained content in the new grass.

□|□|□|□|□|□|□|□|□

The echo of silver trumpets rang through Jerusalem, signaling to the pilgrims that the eating of leavened bread must cease. This early division of the festive day, however, was strictly a rabbinical hedge of safety. Not for another two hours would the official abstention begin.

The same echo of trumpets reached Gethsemane. Yeshua rose from His comfortable meditative position. He called for Peter and John.

His voice, after the long silence, naturally drew the attention of the rest of the disciples. Judas moved closer, too, but still found himself on the outside fringe.

"Teacher?" Peter asked.

"Go and make preparations for us to eat the Passover," Yeshua said. His voice held not command but near resignation.

"Where do You want us to prepare for it?" John asked.

Judas leaned forward, straining to hear the answer. His heart thumped and he swallowed hard, as if this were the actual moment of betrayal. Now he would get the answer he needed. And later he would find an excuse to slip away and deliver the information to the authorities.

Yeshua will be defeated.

"As you go into the city, a man carrying a pitcher of water will meet you," Yeshua said. He looked past Peter and John briefly, catching Judas's intense interest. "Follow him. At the house he enters, say to the owner, 'The teacher asks, Where is the guest room where I can eat the Passover meal with My disciples?' He will take you upstairs to a large room that is already set up. That is the place; go ahead and prepare our supper there."

Judas saw plainly that Peter and John exchanged quick frowns of mutual puzzlement. Anger stabbed Judas with a dagger of savage heat. They were so close—these two Galileans—and shared an intimacy they never would with him, the outsider Judean.

The real heat of Judas's bitterness, however, came from something far more significant.

Neither Peter nor John—nor the other disciples—understood why Yeshua's instructions were so vague.

Judas, however, knew.

Carrying water was woman's work, out of the ordinary for a man. This was an extraordinarily simple method to make a man recognizable.

Yeshua must have already made arrangements for a room for the Passover supper; Yeshua must have already planned this simple method of connecting as a way to keep the location unnamed ahead of time. For it was equally simple to choose the trumpet call as the time for the man with the water to go forth and be found.

Judas knew. Yeshua had not only foreseen Judas's intentions but had also taken steps to thwart him.

And Judas knew even more.

Yeshua remained in control.

CHAPTER THIRTY-SIX

I climbed off the wall, knowing I still had business to attend to. The rest of the morning held less pain; I had, for the moment, a purpose. I searched out a lawyer and dictated to him the contents of an agreement I intended to deliver to Pascal.

The lawyer's fees were double what I would have paid had my thoughts not been lured by the prospect of death from the temple wall. The lawyer had protested it was too close to Passover to finish the document before sunset that dictated all work must cease—I was so distracted I did not bother to fight such an obvious ploy for extra fees.

I left the lawyer with a scroll in the sleeve of my robe and returned to the mansion of my cousin, where I hid the scroll with the letters for my wife. Thus suspended from the sharper edges of torment, I managed to wait on a couch in a cool inner chamber until Pascal called for me. Together we made our way to the temple for the sacrifice of our Passover lamb.

There was no enmity between us. I understood the practical reasons why he could not purchase my holdings, and indeed found it a comfort that he insisted we remain together in the temple despite the raised eyebrows my presence drew when his Sadducean friends greeted us. He could not purchase my business, but he refused to publicly abandon me.

Among the crowd in the temple, I would have recognized the disciple named Peter had I seen him; his rigid rejection of my offer for money had left a vivid memory. The crowd around us was too thick, so I did not see him or the other disciple named John.

They were close by, however. Waiting, as we were, for the gates to the altar to open.

▫ ▫ ▫ ▫ ▫ ▫ ▫

In front of the massive Nicanor Gate inside the temple courts, Peter held the lamb that Judas had purchased. He and John were hemmed in by a packed crowd of noisy pilgrims, each representing groups waiting to celebrate the Passover feast that evening.

On the other side of the tall, heavy doors, the Priests' Court was filling with hundreds of white-robed priests and Levites as they prepared for the afternoon ceremonies; this was the one day each year that every temple priest was called to duty at the sacrificial altars.

While the trussed lamb in Peter's arms remained silent, the bleating of other lambs rose above the babble of the crowd. The musky smell of the lambs mixed with the pungent aroma of fresh dung and the general odor of hundreds of people sweating in the afternoon heat. Of this dense crowd, it seemed to Peter that only he and John were silent. Peter could only guess that John felt the same terrible loneliness, for neither had the heart to discuss with the other his sense of foreboding.

Without realizing it, Peter soothed the animal in his arms with slow strokes along its neck and back, as if trying to allay his own fears.

As Yeshua had predicted, there had been a manservant carrying a water jar. And as Yeshua had predicted, the servant's

170

master—the father of young Mark, a follower of Yeshua—had shown them an upper chamber ready for the Passover.

Earlier in the week, Yeshua had correctly foretold where they would find a young donkey. And that they would be able to take it simply by asking. These were just two more uncannily accurate predictions among many.

Including a very grim prediction—the grimmest of all.

More than once on their journey to Jerusalem, Yeshua had foretold His own crucifixion. The day before, again Yeshua had predicted it.

Crucifixion. The end of their teacher. The end of their dreams.

If all the other predictions had come true, then this one . . .

Peter tried to shake away the image.

Peter even held a sense of danger for himself and John. After all, once the gates opened and they lined up before the priests on the other side, it seemed easily possible that either or both might be recognized as followers of Yeshua. These were the religious authorities that had posted notice that Yeshua must be reported if seen in public. For that reason, Peter and John, in the manner of their Galilean countrymen, had each hidden short swords beneath their upper garments. As followers of Yeshua, they were in as much danger as He was.

As he waited, Peter finally became conscious that, in his nervousness, he had been stroking the lamb. For the first time in his adult life, he became aware of an animal as a fellow creature; the rough fisherman's life in Galilee did not allow for the luxury of considering animals as more than beasts of burden, sacrifices, or food. Peter ran his thick fingers through the lamb's delicate wool, watching how its thickness parted and fell back, marveling at its softness. He felt the animal's warmth against his arms and stomach, felt the quick thudding of the lamb's heart against his ribs, noticed the liquid depths of its wide eyes. The lamb was tiny, helpless. To Peter's surprise, a tenderness surged within him. The big, strong, stubborn fisherman swelled with sympathy for the lamb and its fate.

And ahead, priests finally began to open the gates.

□|□|□|□|□|□|□|□|□

The crowd's anticipation was twofold. Passover was different from the regular sacrifices because ordinary people participated in the ritual killing; it was also one of the few yearly occasions when Israelite worshipers were allowed to enter the priests' inner-temple domain.

The size of the altar was enough to silence any pilgrim entering for the first time. The altar had been built on the same site on Mount Moriah, where centuries earlier Abraham had bound his son Isaac for slaughter. The altar was a perfect square of stones and earth, twice the height of a house, with an ascent ramp leading to the top, where three fires burned. The largest—for burning sacrifices—was a pile of glowing, crackling wood taller than the priests tending it with long metal tongs.

Pascal and I shuffled with the crowd through the gates into the inner temple. As did, somewhere behind us among the massed crowd, Peter and John.

The court filled and priests closed the gates again. Later, a second wave of pilgrims would enter. Then a third. Peter and John had hurried to be in the first group as they were anxious to leave quickly to meet Yeshua and the others in the upper room promised them.

Inside, priests lined the steps of the altar, from top to bottom in a long double row that spilled beyond the steps to the center of the court. Each priest had gone through a lengthy purification process of cleansing and ritual. Each was ready for his sacred duty. The spilling of blood.

Nearby, but unaware until much later that Peter and John were there too, Pascal and I waited in the crowd.

A threefold blast from the silver trumpets of the priests echoed against the hewn marble and stones. There was a pause, like a heartbeat stopped. And then, like a heartbeat pulsing back to life, hundreds of Levites began the ancient chant of the Hallel.

"Praise the Lord!" the Levites called. The deep symphony of male voices rolled across the inner court.

"Praise the Lord!" the pilgrims chanted in return.

The Levites continued the verses of the psalms. The pilgrims only repeated the first line of each psalm. Every other line they responded to by singing, "Hallelujah."

The repetitive hallelujahs and the mesmerizing chant of the hundreds of Levites raised us to an emotional level of yearning joy, an awesome inner movement of souls stirred to reach for God.

As the chant rose and fell, the first pilgrims at the base of the altar began to sacrifice the animals they had brought with them. The priest at the front of each line caught the blood of the dying animal in a golden bowl and passed the bowl to the priest behind him, getting in return an empty bowl. The priest behind passed the blood-filled bowl back. Each new bowl went up the long line of priests until the final priest threw the blood in a spray at the base of the great fire of the altar and passed that bowl back down again.

No Gentile would ever witness this; the penalty was death for a non-Jew who dared defile the inner temple with his presence. Only Jews could see the slaughter of thousands of lambs and the river of their innocent blood.

I could not fool myself, of course, into placing any hope in this ritual. I was only here because I had to maintain an untroubled pose until I had departed from Pascal's household.

For the fierce disciple with red hair, this too became an unexpectedly different Passover ceremony, but not for the same reason as me.

The chanting flowed over Peter and moved him in a way he'd never been moved. Because of his unexpected tenderness toward the lamb in his arms, this was the first Passover in which he truly began to understand in his heart what he had been taught in the synagogues since childhood. With his unexpected sorrow for the lamb's destiny and the reason for its death, an awareness of God's love began to fill the crevices of Peter's soul.

It was a mystical moment. Peter looked up to the cloudless sky, half expecting to see in the sun the blinding brightness of God's face.

In his arms, the lamb began to twist and struggle in panic as it smelled the fear and blood of the dying animals ahead. With his new understanding of the significance of sacrifice, it pained Peter to hold the lamb prisoner as he and John moved up in the line of pilgrims.

"This is the day the Lord has made," the Levites chanted in the strange thunderous roar of men caught up in the vicarious taste of death. "We will rejoice and be glad in it."

And the people around Peter and John shouted in return, "Hallelujah!"

At the priest's feet, Peter knelt with John. Peter pressed the struggling lamb's fragile body against the floor of the court. The priest's flowing white robe was soaked with blood.

"O Lord, save us. O Lord, grant us success."

And the people shouted in return, "Hallelujah!"

With one hand against the lamb's head and with a knife in

his other hand, John slashed through the quivering tendons of the lamb's neck to slit its throat. As the lamb thrashed, blood jetted in spurts against John's and Peter's sleeves.

"Blessed is the one who comes in the name of the Lord."

And the people shouted in return, "Hallelujah!"

The awareness of the warmth of the blood against Peter's arm mingled with the wonderful awareness of his soul, which now seemed to flutter—like the torn muscles of the lamb's neck—between incredible joy and incredible sadness. As the lamb's blood flowed into the golden bowl, and as the lamb's life drained away, Peter's voice rose in hallelujahs with the tumult around him.

Peter wept in the beauty of the moment.

"Hosanna in the highest. Hosanna in the highest."

And the people shouted in return, "Hallelujah!"

Peter averted his face from John as they stood. The tears ran into his beard, and with his hands still occupied by the burden of the dead lamb, he could not wipe them away.

John wisely made no comment.

All that remained was to lay the sacrificed lamb on staves, where other priests would expertly skin it, removing the innards for burning at the altar, taking care that the bones of the lamb not be broken.

Later, as Peter and John walked through the city with the lamb's carcass on a wood frame between them, the sight of hundreds of special ovens set in public places for the pilgrims' use brought back the memory of the sacrifice. And something else surged in Peter's memory.

"Blessed is the one who comes in the name of the Lord."

"Hallelujah."

"Hosanna in the highest. Hosanna in the highest."

"Hallelujah."

Those same triumphant cries—the cries heard over the dying lamb—had also rung through the valley on Sunday past as thousands had cheered Yeshua's approach to Jerusalem.

THURSDAY EVENING

CHAPTER THIRTY-SEVEN

I would argue that where faith or meaning diminishes, ritual fills the void. The Passover supper commemorated my people's last meal in Egypt before the Exodus led by Moses.

I imagine to the generation that first celebrated it, gratitude mattered far more than layers of ceremony. To them, a roasted lamb and unleavened bread were sufficient reminders of their newfound freedom and the angel of death that had passed over their firstborn because of the lamb's blood smeared on their doorframes.

I, on the other hand, found myself prisoner to centuries of adornment as I reclined at the Passover supper with Pascal and Seraphine. I squirmed with boredom as prescribed prayer and hymns followed the order that had been regulated by dusty old men with dusty old scrolls. Where among these rites was the Spirit of a mighty God who had inflicted plagues, parted the sea, and rained desert manna upon a people unworthy of His considerations?

I did not mention these thoughts to Pascal as he raised the first cup of wine for a traditional prayer. It was easier to suffer in silence than deal with the questions my thoughts would have provoked. After all, from his point of view, it would have been too surprising to discover that after an adult lifetime as a ruthless merchant of glass and silk, I was suddenly wasting time in philosophical discourse.

And, because I did not want to draw the least amount of attention to myself, I drank from my goblet. It was the first wine I had tasted in months. When I wiped a few drops from the corner of my mouth with the back of my wrist, it looked like blood gleaming in the candlelight.

I would think of that sight later when I heard the account of another Passover supper that began in a hidden room in Jerusalem as our own Passover meal drew to an end.

▫ ▫ ▫ ▫ ▫ ▫ ▫ ▫ ▫

As the disciples followed Yeshua into the upper chamber, they saw the table set according to Passover custom.

Jewish law specifically dictated that pilgrims not sit at the meal but recline on their left elbow and side, leaving the right hand free to eat. Such positioning of the guests made it impossible for a servant to reach over them to serve. Because of this, the upper two-thirds of the elongated oval table was surrounded by a horseshoe of cushions, and the extended lower third held the Passover dishes—unleavened bread, bitter herbs, radish, and vinegar in a bowl—within reach.

Yeshua, lost in thought, moved to the cushion customarily held for the head of the table. On the left side, it was the second cushion from the end, deemed the middle. John took the end cushion, immediately to the right of Yeshua, below the master's feet.

The others moved to various other cushions as Peter, who had supervised the roasting of the lamb, set the meat beside the other dishes. This gave Judas a chance to squeeze past Peter and unhurriedly take the cushion above Yeshua, to the master's left. The place of honor.

Peter waited for Yeshua to command Judas to move. Instead, Yeshua took the first of the four cups of wine that were to fulfill the Passover and began the formal ceremonial benedictions.

Peter had no choice but to finally recline on the empty cushion directly across from John. The place of least honor.

Divine serenity filled Yeshua. All things were under His power as given by the Father; He had come from God and would return to God. With majestic dignity, He continued the prayer.

"Take this and share it among yourselves," He said, passing the cup. "For I will not drink wine again until the kingdom of God has come."

The disciples exchanged puzzled glances, but Yeshua passed the first cup, and the disciples dipped herbs in the vinegar.

Yeshua took one of the three flat cakes of unleavened bread and broke it, putting some aside, as custom dictated, for after supper. It was also custom at this moment for the youngest to ask the reason for Passover. Yeshua answered, telling the story of Moses and the first Passover. When He finished, the men joined their voices to sing Hallels from the ancient psalms.

Yeshua reached for the second ceremonial cup of wine and began the traditional prayers. The meal resumed after the second cup of wine had been passed.

Yeshua looked around the table as the others ate. "The truth is," He said, "one of you will betray Me."

Some of the disciples froze, hands halfway to their mouths. Others set the unleavened bread down and stared at Yeshua. It took a half minute before anyone recovered enough to break the silence.

"I'm not the one, am I, Lord?" two asked, their words overlapping.

"One of you who is eating with Me now will betray Me." Trouble filled the master's face. He was unable to speak with much strength as emotion choked Him. "For I, the Son of Man, must die, as the Scriptures declared long ago. But how terrible it will be for My betrayer. Far better for him if he had never been born!"

The table filled with the babble of each disciple twisting and turning and speaking at once.

In this noise, Judas leaned over and spoke softly to Yeshua across the short space that separated them. "Teacher, I'm not the one, am I?" he said, deliberately echoing the words of the others to avoid their attention. How could Yeshua have known?

The light in Yeshua's eyes fragmented to shards of pain. Although He stared at Judas, it was as if He saw beyond to a night of utmost loneliness, a night with the monstrous depths of hell at His feet, with the fires of torment licking at the edges of the soul.

Yeshua did not answer Judas immediately. His silence, perhaps, was a final appeal to Judas to turn back from the fires of a soul damned to eternal separation from God.

Judas waited, barely breathing, not using the long silence to ponder Yeshua's warning of woe to the betrayer but selfishly hoping for confirmation that Yeshua did not suspect him.

"You have said it yourself," Yeshua said.

CHAPTER THIRTY-EIGHT

At the meal's end, the oily smell of roasted lamb clung to our clothing; custom demanded that we burn all parts left over, and with only three of us, much of the lamb had gone uneaten, to sizzle and spit smoky grease as the fire devoured it.

"I have made arrangements with my friend Caiaphas," Pascal said abruptly. "Shortly, one of his servants will arrive to escort you back to his palace."

Seraphine's puzzled look reflected my own response.

"For what purpose?" I asked.

"Have you forgotten our conversation yesterday evening? The prophet has been betrayed. His arrest will happen tonight. I want you among the priests and soldiers."

"I am tired," I said. "It is not something I wish to do."

"It is a chance to redeem yourself," he persisted.

I laughed. Neither understood.

"You must be seen with the priests," Pascal continued. "My Sadducean friends must know you are for them, not Him. Once they are satisfied of your allegiance, you and I can begin discussing the matter you brought before me at the beginning of the week."

I shook my head no. I'd already made my decision on how to dispose of my estate. "I am tired."

"Tired? Or afraid to discover that your man of miracles is not a man of miracles? Tonight you will know one way or another. Your own eyes will give witness."

There was a reason Pascal was among the wealthiest in Jerusalem. He knew exactly how to manipulate a man's weakness.

And he had found mine.

When the servant arrived within the hour, I made the short journey to the palace of the high priest.

We waited for the arrival of the one named Judas. He was about to be sent by Yeshua.

When the noise of conversation died, Yeshua referred again to a betrayer.

"I am not saying these things to all of you," He said, trouble and pain thickening His words. "I know so well each one of you I chose."

Yeshua stared at the bloodred wine of the third cup. He absently lifted a piece of bread, then dropped it, the actions of a man so deep in thought he had little conscious realization of what his hands did.

"The Scriptures declare, 'The one who shares My food has turned against Me,'" Yeshua said, lifting His eyes to those around the table again. "And this will soon come true."

Peter lost himself to his impulsiveness and strong nature. The very thought that a man might share a meal with a host then behave in any traitorous manner was so vile to the honor code of society that Peter opened his mouth to protest. And to think Yeshua believed this so strongly He referred to it a second time.

Yeshua cut Peter's protest short with a quick shake of the

head. "I tell you this now, so that when it happens you will believe I am the Messiah."

He paused. Although Yeshua's next statement made little sense to Peter when he first heard it, he later understood it was meant to contrast with the actions of the betrayer. "Truly, anyone who welcomes My messenger is welcoming Me, and anyone who welcomes Me is welcoming the Father who sent Me."

Yeshua's shoulders slumped. His face softened in sad defeat. He knew the future. He already felt the pain of betrayal. "The truth is, one of you will betray Me!"

The repeated emphasis of this predicted betrayal threw the table conversation into excited disarray.

Peter, directly across from John, motioned for his friend to lean forward. "Ask Him which one He means," Peter said.

John nodded and leaned back against Yeshua.

"Lord, who is it?" John asked in a low voice.

Yeshua had begun to assemble a sop of unleavened bread wrapped around bitter herbs and meat from the Passover lamb. "It is the one to whom I give the bread dipped in the sauce." Yeshua dipped the sop into a sauce of stewed fruit and handed it to Judas.

Obvious as the message was, John did not understand it. Judas was in the place of honor, and so would be expected to receive the first sop.

Before John could ask Yeshua to clarify His answer, Yeshua dipped another piece of bread into the dish of sauce and handed it to the disciple beside Judas.

John gave Peter a silent shrug to indicate that the master had not really answered.

Yeshua began to dip more bread, and, although He did not speak loudly, John overheard Him.

"Hurry," Yeshua said to Judas, "do it now."

John misunderstood for the second time, so inconceivable was it that Judas—the one who worked hardest, the one trusted with the money—might be the betrayer. Yeshua, it seemed, was now sending Judas on an errand to buy something for the Passover feast or to give something to the poor.

Judas Iscariot, bread from his master still in hand, rose and departed into the night.

CHAPTER THIRTY-NINE

I spent most of my wait at the palace in a shadowed corner of an opulent hall. Other men arrived. As they talked among themselves, I had the opportunity to find solitude with short strolls into the courtyard beyond.

Naturally, my thoughts turned to the man of miracles. I wondered whether a meeting with Him would have changed the course of my plans. What if I had found Him the day before? What if He had promised to heal my daughter? Would I now be frantically running through the city, trying to find and warn Him? Would I have used my wealth to offer Him safe escape? And would I now feel this utterly lonely, counting down the dark hours to my final day?

But I had not found Him. He had not promised to heal my daughter. And somewhere in the city, a man was slipping through the dark streets to arrive at the palace and earn thirty pieces of silver.

When Judas left the upper chamber, the slight wrinkles of worry around Yeshua's eyes disappeared. Surfacing to replace that tension was His love for the men who had stayed with Him through all the troubles of the previous months.

The disciples slowly ate the sop Yeshua had given them. In the lamplight, the juice of the roasted lamb shone off their lips and the edges of their beards.

"The time has come for Me, the Son of Man, to enter into My glory, and God will receive glory because of all that happens to Me," Yeshua told them. He alone was not eating. His arms rested lightly on the table. His hands were relaxed and open. "And God will bring Me into My glory very soon."

Every man around the table had been raised in the Jewish tradition, taught in Jewish synagogues. Every fiber of their conscious beings, all their collective understanding of religion, should have recoiled at the blasphemy coming from Yeshua. Yet a great power was descending upon them, opening their hearts to understand the mystery in Yeshua's words.

They heard, too, the affection as He continued to speak. "Dear children, how brief are these moments before I must go away and leave you! Then, though you search for Me, you cannot come to Me—just as I told the Jewish leaders."

Peter set down his food, ready to disagree with Yeshua.

Yeshua smiled, reading his mind. "So now I am giving you a new commandment," He said, slipping into the role of teacher. "Love each other. Just as I have loved you, you should love each other."

He paused to give emphasis. "Your love for one another will prove to the world that you are My disciples."

Peter broke into Yeshua's discourse. "Lord, where are You going?"

Yeshua smiled again. Indeed, He had known where Peter's impetuousness would lead. "You can't go with Me now."

Peter brought his arms up, his usual preliminary to the hand waving that accompanied his passionate speeches.

Yeshua forestalled Peter's obvious reply by adding, "But you will follow Me later."

"But why can't I come now, Lord?" Peter asked. "I am ready to die for You."

Yeshua lost His gentle smile as His lips tightened in a grimace of pain. He shook His head. "Die for Me?" Yeshua said, "No, before the rooster crows tomorrow morning, you will deny three times that you even know Me."

The silence hung.

Yeshua took the remaining unleavened cakes of bread. He began to break them as part of the ritual to end the Passover meal. He gave a prayer of thanks and raised the bread to all the disciples. "Take it and eat it, for this is My body."

This unexpected break from the usual words of the Passover ceremony and the strangeness of the command deflected all attention from Yeshua's somber prediction for Peter.

Yeshua continued, filling the fourth cup of wine, the traditional close to the Passover supper. He spoke as if confident that now or later these followers would understand the symbolism; the outward elements of bread and wine were to a man's body what the act of accepting each in Yeshua's memory was to his soul. Physical nourishment. Spiritual nourishment.

"Each of you drink from it, for this is My blood, which seals the covenant between God and His people. It is poured out to forgive the sins of many," He said to them. "Mark My words—I will not drink wine again until the day I drink it new with you in My Father's kingdom."

Because the disciples were quiet in their efforts to grasp His words as they passed and shared the wine, Yeshua tried to reach out to them. "Don't be troubled," He said, first looking at John. "You trust in God, now trust in Me."

Yeshua waited until John gave Him a tentative smile. Then He turned to another disciple. "There are many rooms in My Father's home, and I am going to prepare a place for you." Again Yeshua looked into the eyes of His disciple. He waited until the man's heart heard the call of God before moving on to search the eyes of the next. "If this were not so, I would tell you plainly," He said.

One by one, Yeshua soothed them, comforting them with new promises. With each new declaration, He turned to another disciple, so that those promises were not simply a long discourse. "When everything is ready, I will come and get you, so that you will always be with Me where I am."

To Thomas, He said. "And you know where I am going and how to get there."

Thomas, conscious of Peter's earlier unanswered question, refused to accept the comfort of Yeshua's gaze. "No, we don't know, Lord. We haven't any idea where You are going, so how can we know the way?"

By then, the cup had been passed all around the table. Yeshua took it from John, set it down, and turned back to Thomas to answer him directly. "I am the way, the truth, and the life. No one can come to the Father except through Me."

Yeshua spoke to the others, almost as an appeal. "If you had known who I am, then you would have known who My Father is."

The knowledge of the night's future clouded Yeshua's face, and He spoke more softly. "From now on you know Him and have seen Him."

Philip broke the mood. "Lord, show us the Father and we will be satisfied."

What could have gone through Yeshua's mind? So close to the end of His earthly time with them, and at this moment so close to heaven that surely the awareness of God was reaching their souls, illuminating the prisons of their frail mortal bodies. Yet Philip still insisted on clinging only to the pitiful limitations of his external senses, as if Yeshua were offering them the actual sight of God to quell their doubts and fears, when faith came from—and gave—spiritual vision. Yet had not the miracles of Yeshua—and indeed the miracle of creation itself of the world around them—given enough of a foundation for any faith?

"Philip, don't you even yet know who I am, even after all the time I have been with you?" Yeshua asked.

Then He addressed all the others. "Anyone who has seen Me has seen the Father! So why are you asking to see Him? Don't you believe that I am in the Father and the Father is in Me?"

They appeared frightened. At His exasperation? At the force of His words? At the almost inconceivable notion of the God of the universe sitting among them? At the overwhelming shift of perception a man must make if he acknowledges with heart and soul and mind that God had become man?

Yeshua softened, unable to avoid His compassion for them. "The words I say are not My own, but My Father who lives in Me does His work through Me. Just believe that I am in the Father and the Father is in Me."

He paused to think, as if searching for a way to set these fledglings free from the pull of gravity and linear time—a way to help them understand there was One who superseded nature in the very act of creating it, One intent on opening their wings for flight through the eternity they could not see beyond their short lives.

When Yeshua was ready, He spoke so softly they had to lean forward to hear. "Or at least believe," He finally said, "because of what you have seen Me do."

There it was.

As plainly said as possible. If they were only able to view the world from the bodies of men—not with the eyes of their eternal souls someday destined to be free—then it should be enough that they had seen Yeshua shape events in the natural world with a power from beyond it. As it should be enough for anyone who later heard witness of His miracles.

There it was.

He was a lunatic. Or He was God.

And too soon, they—like every generation to follow—would have to make that choice based only on the memory of His short time on earth.

CHAPTER FORTY

Hindsight can provide piercing, and sometimes regretful, clarity.

But regarding Judas, a backward look offers only his actions; his mind is curtained by his silent grave. My own guess—and it is merely a guess, no better or worse than any other I have heard since that night—was that Judas fell prey to the talent given him at birth.

Our greatest temptations generally arise from the areas closest to our hearts. A man with no weakness for food cannot become a glutton; neither can a lazy, unambitious man be tempted by power. As Judas was the keeper of the purse, we can guess at his administrative skills and a sharpness with money, two ingredients for ambition. That he was trusted during Yeshua's entire ministry shows that the others thought highly of him; engaged in what suited him, he was likely content for most of his time with the prophet.

Yet behind this aptitude he probably had—as we all do—a darker side. Once his ambition was thwarted, honesty too easily soured to dishonesty; ideals decayed to disillusionment; service became frustration, resentment, and thoughts of betrayal.

Until finally, these thoughts became action.

When Judas arrived at the temple, I happened to be near a

decorative, imitation-marble panel at the rear of the hall. It was the fashion these days, and I had made considerable profit shipping and selling the deep, rich pigments to mix into plaster.

My pretended intense admiration of the workmanship allowed me to avoid conversation with those around me, and only their sudden collective silence alerted me to Judas's presence. I simply turned and saw him, a slim man with an even-featured, handsome face bearing a well-trimmed beard, eyes distorted with the shine of desperation.

His voice broke as he promised to lead us to the chamber where the prophet celebrated Passover with the remaining disciples.

My first impression of him—and the others' reaction to him—brought to my mind a picture of a dog slinking sideways as it approached its master, uncertain of reward or punishment.

Judas received only grunts of acknowledgment for his information along with disdain, obvious in the curl of lips and the shaded looks down noses.

I think I understood why everyone disliked him. The obvious reason was that his presence served as a reminder of the shamefulness of hating a man who rightfully reminded them all of their failings.

I believe, however, there was more.

In the heated passion of ideological disagreement, men can accept, even admire, another who is compelled to such a defined act as betrayal for a greater cause. But all found it repugnant that Judas had requested money for his betrayal, and more repugnant that Judas had agreed to the legal price of a slave for his deed.

(I've often wondered if this price was offered so the Jewish leaders could later balm their consciences by telling themselves they had purchased Yeshua like any other slave, giving some sort of mock ownership that would allow them to legally hand him over to the Roman authorities.)

Thirty pieces of silver.

At this price, Judas had not joined in their cause, nor had he become an associate of the powerful and elite as perhaps he had hoped.

Instead, Judas was seen as a contemptible slave trader, a hireling.

The men in the hall treated him accordingly. He was ordered to follow, then ignored as their assembly moved through the night to gather armed reinforcements.

Cold high moon, pale, almost blue. Stars shivered in a blanket of black. Dim square outlines, houses crammed together in poverty. Temple gates shut.

A small group of men—once thirteen, now twelve—crossed the south plaza, the shuffling of their footsteps a broken cadence of retreat. Ahead of them stood the city gates leading into the Kidron Valley—behind them, a city stilled in solemn observance of religious ritual.

The remaining eleven disciples had no sense of the events ahead, no sense that their beloved teacher would truly die before the next sunset. Later they would look back and understand that Yeshua knew His future as He led them from the upper city through the narrow dark streets of Jerusalem. He had abandoned the teaching style of parables and spoken quietly to them in plain words of the world beyond the body, promising a Spirit to comfort them in His absence.

Yet as He spoke, Thomas and Philip clearly struggled to understand. Midway across the plaza and near the back of the group, Philip, afraid of being chastised again, leaned over to Thomas and whispered his question. "What does He mean when He says, 'You won't see Me and then you will see Me'?"

Thomas shook his head.

Philip whispered again. "And what does He mean when He says, 'I am going to the Father'? And what does He mean by 'a little while'? We don't understand."

Yeshua could not have overheard. Philip and Thomas knew that without doubt. Yet Yeshua broke off teaching to answer Philip. "Are you asking yourselves what I meant? I said in just a little while I will be gone, and you won't see Me anymore. Then, just a little while after that, you will see Me again. Truly, you will weep and mourn over what is going to happen to Me, but the world will rejoice. You will grieve, but your grief will suddenly turn to wonderful joy when you see Me again. It will be like a woman experiencing the pains of labor. When her child is born, her anguish gives place to joy because she has brought a new person into the world. You have sorrow now, but I will see you again; then you will rejoice, and no one can rob you of that joy."

None understood, and a gloom seemed to fall on them.

Yeshua turned away from them and continued His slow, steady walk toward the darkness beyond the city.

The others followed.

CHAPTER FORTY-ONE

I stamped my feet and shivered, as did many of the men milling around me. I regretted that I'd listened to Pascal at all. We stood at the gate at Antonia, the square stone fortress that butted against the northwest corner of the temple walls. Its ramparts overlooked the courts. Intimidating in height and bulk, it was still a poor second to the temple itself. The temple, however, did not have a moat. Nor did the temple hold six hundred Roman soldiers.

Antonia, of course, had both. The reason for the moat was self-evident, and the soldiers were assembled to keep the peace during Passover.

Armed only with torches, we had been a quiet procession crossing the bridge over the moat. The light of our flames bounced off the placid water beneath us. A sentry had seen us, and when we arrived at the gate, it was a simple task to send a message to the captain, who hurried out for a quick consultation with Caiaphas.

I overheard only snatches of their conversation, enough to understand that the captain was unsure of procedure, which was what had forced our wait in the cool night air.

When the captain finally returned, he announced that we should follow him and the soldiers to Herod's palace, so named because it once belonged to Herod the Great. Roman governors, as Pontius Pilate, used it as residence when in Jerusalem. Herod, tetrarch of Galilee and beheader of John the Baptist, made his Jerusalem quarters the Maccabean Palace, near the chief priest's palace. We would not proceed this night without permission from Pilate.

About sixty soldiers escorted us back through the city, armed with swords and shields. Volunteers and onlookers joined us as we walked. By the time this group reached Herod's palace, there might have been as many as a hundred and fifty people.

Later, when I had a chance to make more sense of this hurried night, I would realize the herald who disturbed Pilate's sleep also woke his wife, Procula. For her, the sight of so many men gathered on the street beneath the palace balcony must have been disturbing; over the previous few years, Pilate's previous miscalculations had resulted in other night mobs howling loud protest, and our torches flickering up at her would only remind her of those earlier times. Thus, it came as no surprise when I later heard that bad dreams that night inspired her to write a note of warning to Pilate as he tried Yeshua.

Having obtained Pilate's approval, the mob followed Judas as he led the soldiers to the upper room, where he had left Yeshua celebrating Passover. As we walked, we could not know that Yeshua had His own agenda and, like a canny fox, had long since bolted during our delay.

⬚|⬚|⬚|⬚|⬚|⬚|⬚|⬚|⬚

At the entrance to the garden of Gethsemane, Yeshua paused. The twisted deep shadows of shrubs and olive trees, innocent in daylight, looked sinister in the countryside darkness. Yet often He and the disciples had used this garden as evening fell into night, staying for hours, sometimes until dawn. This was a sanctuary, a place of peace and beauty, where the breeze caused the leaves to flutter pale gray in the moonlight, where the tall grass in the open places among the trees caressed sandaled feet that moved through it.

It wasn't fear of the garden that halted Yeshua's approach. He paused among His disciples because He faltered. He had begun to walk slowly, almost stooped with the weight of sorrow and desolation.

His voice was almost a croak. "Sit here while I go and pray."

Without question, all the disciples obeyed. It was usual for Yeshua to take time alone.

"Pray that you will not be overcome by temptation," He said. Was this a warning for their trials ahead? Was He hoping that they, too, would take advantage of this time of contemplation to ask God for strength?

Yeshua began to walk away, then turned back.

Had He been flooded with the cold of utter loneliness? If so, His anguish caused Him to seek out the three closest to Him, the men who had witnessed His transfiguration, the men who had been with Him when He raised the daughter of Jairus from the dead.

Yeshua placed one hand on Peter's shoulder. With His other hand, He lightly touched James and John, the two sons of Zebedee, so that all three understood to follow. Yeshua took them on a diagonal path through Gethsemane. Well before reaching the oil press, He stopped them.

"My soul . . ." A shudder choked His words.

Arms rigid at His side, He clenched His fists and looked to heaven. The moonlight draped His shoulders and head with soft light and made visible the glistening trail of tears on His face. He drew a deep breath to find the strength to begin again.

"My soul is crushed with grief to the point of death." He turned to them. "Stay here and watch with Me."

He had not begged, but the need was in His voice. The obvious agony in His soul terrified each of them. This was the man who they had dimly begun to believe might be God incarnate. What did He see that they could not? And what thing of horror could this vision be to bend Him to this point of defeat?

Terror muted them.

Yeshua walked away, but not so far that they were unable to see Him collapse face forward as He knelt to pray.

CHAPTER FORTY-TWO

The house where Yeshua had shared His last supper with the disciples belonged to a widower who lived there with a son, John Mark, who was nearly grown. The widower was called out by the captain at our arrival. The man, who had dressed in haste, stood helplessly on the street before the crowd as soldiers marched inside to the upper chamber.

I noticed Judas did not accompany them. He passed back and forth nervously on the fringes of the crowd, head down, trying to ignore the stares sent his direction. Every person who had joined to swell this procession had heard, in immediate whispers, of Judas's role in this drama. By morning, it would spread rapidly among the general populace how he had betrayed the Messiah of their hopes.

I, too, watched Judas closely, idly curious at how he would react when Yeshua appeared as the soldiers' captive.

But the soldiers returned to Caiaphas's house almost immediately—without Yeshua.

Caiaphas screamed at them to search the widower's house. They ignored him, waiting for an order from the captain, who sighed and told them to go through all the rooms.

Again they returned without Yeshua.

Caiaphas stepped close to Judas. "You make us look like fools," he snarled. "Where is He?"

The torchlight threw dancing shadows across Judas as he screwed his eyes shut to think. "There is only one place He would be at this hour," Judas said. "In a garden. It is called Gethsemane."

□ □ □ □ □ □ □ □

As Yeshua prayed a stone's throw away, there was no one to explain to the three who sat against the trunk of an olive tree.

A man is born with the seal of death's claim already stamped on his soul. Body and soul are fused from the beginning to be torn apart at the end, this dissolution a mystery so unknowable that every instinct and every breath fights against the moment of death and the soul's rebirth beyond.

To One born into the world without the taint of death upon His soul, without the lifelong struggle of flesh dimming the spirit's awareness of God, the approaching dissolution of body and soul would hold not fear but the sensation of an ultimate loneliness of being caught between God and man, unable to take comfort from either side.

Yeshua, in the conflict the men could not share, prayed aloud, and His voice carried to the three. "Father, everything is possible for You. Please take this cup of suffering away from Me. Yet I want Your will, not Mine."

Born only of flesh, Peter and the two sons of Zebedee could only hear, not understand, the prayer uttered by Yeshua.

Through Yeshua's prayer, His body and soul cried out to God. Both agonized in the contradiction of a perfect duality submitting to the humiliation of death. It was the spiritual anguish of a single star shrinking to oblivion in an eternal midnight of infinite black. And a physiological anguish so great that the body responded by squeezing the vessels near the skin into a bloody sweat.

Drops of blood fell from Yeshua's brow, marking the grass with the scent that drew the stalking presence of the hunter Satan.

We marched through the city and into the countryside. Some of the soldiers carried torches set on high poles, casting light far and wide to aid their search.

I wondered if I should try to slip away and circle ahead, out of range of the torchlight. If Yeshua was ahead, I could warn Him. Even now in my disbelief, I still held that remnant of hope—and perhaps in His gratitude He would help my daughter.

Or perhaps once we arrived, I could help Him escape among the confusion of so many men.

It was a thought. I held on to it as we proceeded deeper into the countryside.

Where His soul's agony led Yeshua to deep and passionate prayer, inexplicable dread settled on Peter and the two sons of Zebedee like a heavy blanket, and their stress-fatigued bodies escaped into sleep.

Utterly alone in the garden, Yeshua returned for comfort to the three men who knew Him best and found them oblivious to His suffering.

"Are you asleep?" He asked Peter. "Couldn't you stay awake and watch with Me even one hour? Keep alert and pray. Otherwise temptation will overpower you."

He admonished them gently, for to Him they were children in need of compassion. "For though the spirit is willing enough, the body is weak."

Yeshua again left them.

The hunter waited in the shadows beyond to wrestle with His soul.

□|□|□|□|□|□|□|□|□

I was near Caiaphas when the Roman captain stopped him.

"This man you seek," the captain said. "How will we know Him?"

Perhaps Judas was anxious to redeem himself. More than a hundred men were walking along a country road at night because of him. And what if he was wrong about the whereabouts of Yeshua? *Fool* would be added to the name *betrayer.*

Thus, Judas anxiously answered before Caiaphas spoke. "There will be no mistake," Judas said. "I will greet Him with a kiss."

□|□|□|□|□|□|□|□|□

At Yeshua's second departure, Peter and the sons of Zebedee had tried to straighten to alertness. The hard coldness of the ground and the nip of the night air should have been ample discomfort to keep them awake.

But a palpable presence of evil in the garden pushed them down, so that in utter weariness they were already sinking as Yeshua's renewed prayer reached through the fog of heaviness on their eyes.

"My Father!" He cried, "If this cup cannot be taken away until I drink it, Your will be done."

None knew how much time had passed before Yeshua's second return for comfort and companionship. He found them in slumber, and stood over them, smiling sadly at the peace of their sleep.

Peter stirred, dimly aware of Yeshua's presence. But Peter's sleep was so deep he could not rouse himself. He dropped into unconsciousness again as Yeshua stepped back into the darkness for a final savage, silent battle with the hunter.

We were almost at the garden. I told myself I did not care about the prophet's fate.

I was lying to myself, of course. Otherwise I wouldn't have been among the mob arriving to take Him captive.

Part of me perversely hoped He was not the Messiah but a fraud.

I could not deny, however, that a greater portion of me hoped for another miracle.

Dozens of torches lit the approach to Gethsemane's low garden walls, throwing warning flares of brightness that reached like fingers through the trees where Yeshua finished His prayer.

Without hurry, He moved to Peter and John and James. He crouched beside them and gently shook each one to wakefulness. Peter's hair had fallen over his eyes, and Yeshua softly pushed it away for him.

"Still sleeping? Still resting?" Not questions with the base of anger, but more like a father upon finding his children asleep in the corner of a host's house, waking them to carry them home.

As the men blinked and yawned, Yeshua pointed at the bobbing light of the torches, now almost at Gethsemane's entrance, where the other eight disciples waited.

Yeshua said, "Look, the time has come. I, the Son of Man, am betrayed into the hands of sinners."

Groggy, they didn't quite understand.

"Up," He commanded. "Let's be going!"

They stood and lurched on uncertain legs as they followed Him through the trees, not fleeing but instead going forth to meet the mob.

In the darkness, even with the torchlight, it was hard to distinguish how many men approached. It was clear, however, by glimpses of swords and clubs and armor that among them were Roman soldiers.

The other eight disciples were huddled in a nervous group, waiting for Yeshua. He stepped through them, calming them with low words.

While they peered through the confusion of the darkness, Yeshua spoke, for His vision was different from theirs. "See, My betrayer is here!"

And Judas and the soldiers stepped through the garden entrance.

CHAPTER FORTY-THREE

Judas broke away from the crowd and quickly crossed the short gap to reach Yeshua and the disciples behind Him. Illuminated from behind by the torches, to the other eleven Judas was just a dark figure detaching itself from other shadows.

He, however, had no difficulty discerning the features of the men who awaited him. With unerring line, he reached Yeshua. Raising both hands in enthusiasm, Judas called loudly. "Greetings, Teacher!" He brought a hand down on each of Yeshua's shoulders and hugged Him closely, kissing first one side of Yeshua's face, then the other.

"Judas, how can you betray Me, the Son of Man, with a kiss?"

It was a sad question that needed no answer. Judas had expected Yeshua to react with anger or shock. Either would have given him great satisfaction. Either would have allowed Judas to spill his bitterness and tell Yeshua He had been a fool to forsake the chance of becoming the Messiah and conquering the Romans, and an equal fool to slight Judas in as many ways as He had. It would have allowed Judas to remind Yeshua of all that he had sacrificed and how he had worked hardest of the followers to please Yeshua. And for what? he had been prepared to ask with proper indignity. All this would have given Judas justification for the kiss of betrayal.

Instead, Yeshua's resignation became a heart blow to Judas. In one horrifying moment, he realized the full magnitude of what he had done—feeling the desperate shame of a straying husband who, before the sin, had enjoyed the intoxicating temptation and the shivers of false expectations, only to see clearly after the sin and pain he had caused his wife.

"Judas, how can you betray Me, the Son of Man, with a kiss?"

Would that he could have turned and sent the soldiers and the chief priests away. Would that he could have fallen at Yeshua's feet and begged for forgiveness. Would that it could have been any other moment along any of the dusty Galilean roads when the sun shone brightly and the future was filled with the hope that Judas had first carried in the presence of Yeshua.

But behind milled the mob that Judas had led to his master's garden. As much as black remorse overwhelmed him, Judas could not turn back.

"My friend," Yeshua said, "go ahead and do what you have come for."

Judas was too stricken to reply.

▫▫▫▫▫▫▫

I had been considering without much seriousness whether to try to help the prophet.

It wasn't Pascal's insistence that I be seen as Yeshua's foe that stopped me from action. I did not care how my reputation might suffer among these Pharisees and Sadducees and curiosity seekers. As with possessions, a reputation is only worth something to a man when he is alive.

Instead, I held myself back because of logic. Pascal had persuaded me to accompany Caiaphas by telling me it was a way to prove—or disprove—the messiahship of the man of miracles.

I still wanted proof.

So I would watch.

If He failed to rescue Himself, I would know He was a fraud.

Yet if the miracle occurred and He proved that He was the Messiah come to deliver the Jews and He saved Himself from these soldiers, I wanted to stay within following distance. When the first opportunity presented itself, I would approach Him.

Yes, it was cowardly of me. But I was far beyond worrying about my own opinion of myself.

The Roman soldiers neared Judas and his teacher. Yeshua stepped around the betrayer to challenge the crowd.

As the soldiers arrived, Yeshua asked, "Whom are you looking for?"

"Yeshua from Nazareth." The reply came from one with the bravado and contempt of a bully soldier facing an unarmed civilian.

"I am He," Yeshua said.

His calm, regal assurance seemed uncanny to the soldiers. This was not a man frightened by the full authority of the Roman Empire but one who acted as if He, not they, controlled the situation. A man, then, who might have actually performed the rumored miracles that had reached their ears in the fortress above the temple. Their instinctive reaction might have been from a superstitious fear of some magical retribution, and the soldiers closest to Yeshua stepped back and stumbled on the feet of the soldiers directly behind.

Yet it was more than something human within them. I can explain it no other way than this: Filling the dark grove around us—in that moment that seemed to stretch and stretch—was an uncanny supernatural presence that brought chills to my skin.

I shared the fear that the soldiers showed as they lurched away from Yeshua. More than a few tripped and fell to the ground.

The moment passed. Like a wave of powerful sound, gone so completely it could have been imagined, leaving behind only its resonance in my soul.

Swords and shields clanked as soldiers scrambled to their feet. The rest of the mob had begun to press in, and there was no place for the soldiers to flee.

"Whom are you searching for?" Yeshua asked again.

"Yeshua of Nazareth." This time, the answer was respectful.

"I told you that I am He," Yeshua said. He swung His right arm to point at the disciples behind Him. "And since I am the one you want, let these others go."

Lightning had not struck. No ghosts or demons had appeared. The soldiers' fear passed, and Yeshua's reminder of the other eleven men snapped the centurion from his brief paralyzation. His military mind assessed the immediate danger; if the eleven men rushed them, fighting would be difficult in the crowd. A Roman sword could easily strike one of the chief priests. Such a political disaster would end his career.

"Now!" the centurion barked. Once they held Yeshua, the others would not dare attack. "Seize Him!"

In the milling confusion of figures and shadows in flickering torchlights, Peter moved to the edge of the mob, surreptitiously withdrawing his short sword from his clothing. It would have been suicide to attack one of the armed soldiers and equally suicidal to injure anyone with the political standing of chief priest, so he moved toward one of the servants.

No doubt Peter did not want his defense to go unnoticed by Yeshua. Judas, who had taken the place of honor, had betrayed Yeshua. Peter, forced into the seat of least honor, would do the opposite.

"Lord!" Peter shouted as he swung. "Should we fight? We brought the swords!"

Peter's target jumped sideways at his warning cry, and the sword sliced along the servant's skull, shearing off part of his ear.

"Don't resist anymore!" Yeshua commanded. Although a soldier was about to grab Yeshua, He stepped away unhindered. None made a move to stop Him as He reached the whimpering servant.

Yeshua put His left arm around the servant's slight shoulders to comfort him. With His right hand, He touched the man's ear. When Yeshua pulled His hand away to examine it in the torchlight, He saw blood.

"Put away your sword," He said to Peter. "Those who use the sword will be killed by the sword."

Yeshua's irritation was obvious. That Peter had swung at a defenseless man instead of a soldier spoke plainly of the act's true meaning. Did Peter not yet understand that Yeshua was not here to establish a kingdom on earth?

"Don't you realize that I could ask My Father for thousands of angels to protect us," He snapped at Peter, "and He would send them instantly?"

Quick as the irritation had struck, it left. Yeshua allowed that Peter still needed instruction, as did all children. "But if I did, how would the Scriptures be fulfilled that describe what must happen now?"

As calmly as He had stepped away from the arresting soldiers, Yeshua returned to them. Because all attention was on Him, none immediately noticed the servant He had left behind, who was touching his ear in great wonder, amazed that the bleeding and pain had ended.

The appearance of resistance had been enough for the centurion. He commanded the soldiers nearest him to immediately bind Yeshua.

Other soldiers moved to capture the disciples, but they fled into the shadows of the trees. One, John Mark, the son of the man who had given the use of his house for Yeshua's Passover, twisted in the hands of a soldier and spun away only by slipping through his outer garment, expensive fine linen instead of the usual wool. That he had dressed in haste was obvious by the flashes of pale flesh that showed his nakedness as he ran.

A soldier began chase.

"We have who we need!" barked the centurion. "Return and regroup!"

The last thing he wanted was to have his soldiers running around in the confusion of the dark grove beyond the torchlights. He'd seen night battles where Romans actually attacked Romans, such was the adrenaline and panic of men fighting for their lives.

The soldiers returned as the ropes were tightened around Yeshua's wrists.

"Am I some dangerous criminal, that you have come armed with swords and clubs to arrest Me?" As He spoke, Yeshua looked over the soldiers at the chief priests and their servants. "Why didn't you arrest Me in the temple? I was there every day."

He let the rhetorical questions hang briefly, then continued. "But this is your moment." Another pause. "The time when the power of darkness reigns."

THURSDAY
NIGHT

I remained with the soldiers and the priests and the captive. I knew I would not sleep anyway in the solitude of my cousin's guest chamber. And because I had watched the captive heal the lame—unless it had been fraud—I still believed there was the smallest chance that the man of miracles was biding His time, waiting for the moment when messianic drama would be its most impressive to the largest number of spectators.

The walk back from Gethsemane was hardly more than a mile. But uphill, at night, and with Yeshua stumbling at the prodding spears of the soldiers, it took close to an hour to reach the gates that led to the courtyards of the high priest's palace.

Well behind us, John and Peter watched. They had not run far from the garden, and while their devotion did not extend to sharing captivity with their master, neither could they completely abandon Him.

"They know me there," John said, pointing at the crowd as it disappeared through the gates. "My father does business with that family. I'll go in and find out what I can."

Peter nodded, dumb with fright and cold. He wanted to flee

yet was drawn to stay with Yeshua. His helplessness and uncertainty made him miserable. He hung back while John walked ahead.

A cassocked priest passed by Peter, accompanied by a servant to guard him in the late night.

At the gate, John spoke briefly with a woman servant, and she opened it for him.

Peter stamped his feet, crossed his arms, and jammed his hands in his armpits for warmth. As the wait lengthened, more and more men began to pass him on the street, heading to the palace gate like dark, silent bats converging on a cave's entrance.

The call had gone out. Yeshua was captured. Those of the leading priests, elders, Sanhedrists, and Pharisees who had not been part of the arrest were assembling to cast judgment on the carpenter from Galilee.

<hr />

I had lost sight of Yeshua among the servants and soldiers and men of religion. More and more men arrived, so I assumed Yeshua was still somewhere within the palace. I had no worry that I was missing anything of significance; as all of these arriving men remained in the courtyard where I waited, it was doubtful that He was being tried.

At least not by the Jewish Sanhedrin. Not yet.

<hr />

Annas, the former high priest, sat on an ornate chair in an inner chamber of his son-in-law's palace. Beside him stood a personal attendant with the build and face of a gladiator. He had been a wonderful find; in the course of business, Annas often rankled others and found it convenient to have the protective cloak of this man's intimidating presence.

Annas had been expecting the soldiers to arrive first. When they brought Yeshua to the inner chamber, he instructed them to wait outside the door. Because of the influence Annas had with Pilate, the soldiers obeyed without question. It was also a sign of the power of Annas that Caiaphas was not in attendance but was pacing a corridor of the palace.

When the door closed behind them, Annas examined Yeshua with the cynical eye of an experienced slave trader.

"Somehow, I expected more," Annas said. "At Your touch, the lame walk and the blind see. Or so I have heard."

Yeshua, hands still bound, gazed back at Annas without shame.

Annas lifted his tunic to expose his gnarled legs. He pointed at his knee. "I have an ache when I walk. Will You heal it for me?"

No nod. No shake of the head from Yeshua. Just calm dignity.

"Truthfully," Annas said, "I admit to some curiosity. Show me a miracle, and I will do my best to save You from my son-in-law's hatred. Indeed, perhaps we can join forces. With the reach of my influence, we could both profit magnificently."

Yeshua closed His eyes briefly. Then opened them. Still silent.

"You cannot speak?" Annas asked. He dropped his tunic, suddenly embarrassed at his exposure. "Is it from shock that we have finally acted?"

Silence.

Annas curled his lips in a smile of derision. "I think of a monkey throwing sticks at an elephant, running up and down its back, shouting high-pitched taunts. It grows bolder and bolder because the elephant does not respond. And then suddenly the great beast swings around and grabs the monkey with its trunk."

Annas laughed at Yeshua's continued silence. "And as the elephant shakes the monkey in the air," he went on, "the monkey discovers how insignificant it is and how powerful the beast it thought it could tame."

Yeshua merely kept His eyes intently on Annas's face.

The strength in His silence unnerved Annas. "Jibber, jibber, jibber," Annas continued, unaware of the irony of his own taunting against Yeshua's stoicism. "The monkey goes jibber, jibber, jibber until the elephant snatches it and squeezes it. And the monkey dies."

Still no response.

Annas would never have admitted it to himself, but Yeshua's dignified silence had become a power of its own. So, trying to establish his superiority, Annas leaned forward and pressed his interrogation. "Tell me, are there other little monkeys to throw themselves at the elephant?

"Let me translate for Your provincial mind," Annas said, making his scorn obvious. "How many followers do You have? Do they contribute money to support Your cause? Are they armed?"

Annas had hoped he could anger Yeshua and, in so doing, trick Him into incriminating His disciples.

Yeshua smiled peacefully. He could have answered that a judge attempting to extort confessions to which he had no right was not a fair inquiry.

"And Your teachings," Annas demanded, moving on so that the continued silence was not a victory for Yeshua. "What of them?"

"What I teach is widely known, because I have preached regularly in the synagogues and the temple." Yeshua said slowly and clearly. "I have been heard by people everywhere, and I teach nothing in private that I have not said in public. Why are you asking Me this question?"

Yeshua's simple logic caught Annas off guard. The old man could think of no sarcastic or cutting reply.

"Ask those who heard Me," Yeshua continued, implying

that if the inquiry had been fair, the judge would have sought witnesses. "They know what I said."

It was not the craven servility that any other man would have offered the most powerful religious authority in the Jewish world. Annas's attendant bore it no longer.

Stepping forward and lashing out at the same time, he swept the back of his massive hand in a crashing blow against Yeshua's face. "Is this the way You answer a former high priest?" he snarled.

Yeshua's top lip cracked, and blood began to film His teeth. When He spoke, however, His calm patience concealed any pain. "If I said anything wrong, you must give evidence for it." Again, the challenge to produce witnesses in a fair trial, something both knew Annas could not do.

Yeshua spoke to the attendant. "Should you hit a man for telling the truth?"

It was enough for Annas. The superiority he had first felt in front of Yeshua had disappeared. He did not see any way to regain the upper ground against this man, and that realization, too, was further defeat. He was beginning to understand why Caiaphas had such a hatred for this carpenter from Galilee.

"If this man will not answer questions," Annas said, "this hearing is finished." He did his best to affect an air of boredom as the soldiers reentered the chamber to take Yeshua away.

□□□□□□□□□

Dozens of men had passed Peter, and seeking the safety of numbers, he had drifted closer to the iron bars of the gate. He was debating whether to bluff his way past the woman at the gate when John rejoined him.

"Enough of the Sanhedrin has gathered," John said. "They are about to begin."

"Begin what?" Peter said. "I know little about the law but enough to know any trial must take place during the day."

"Better yet," John grinned. "Much as they would like it, they can't pass a death sentence on Yeshua. It's a Roman prerogative." He clutched Peter's arm. "Even if somehow they convinced Pilate to crucify Him as our teacher predicted, there is not enough time before the Sabbath."

He began to pull Peter toward the gate. "Think of it, my friend," John said. "Whatever happens in there, we will have until the new week to raise the support we need to free Him. You just watch; everything will turn out right."

Peter stopped. "What if they decide to kill Him themselves?"

"Sanhedrists?" John said. "Men who bind themselves with regulations? Much as they would like Him dead, they won't taint themselves with something they cannot legally justify. We will have time to rally support."

Much encouraged, Peter finally returned John's grin. It did not dampen Peter's spirits at all when the girl at the gate gave him a hard, questioning look before she let him in with John.

CHAPTER FORTY-FIVE

A charcoal fire in the center of the inner courtyard threw a small glow on the bearded men as they talked in excited tones about the capture of a rebel messiah.

Peter sat among the servants at the fire and warmed his hands with them. Minutes later, he stood and began to pace. Despite the reassuring words of John, he could not calm himself.

His agitation drew the attention of the maid who had first admitted him to the courtyard. The fire's light was uncertain, so she said to him, "You were one of those with Yeshua the Galilean."

Peter thought of the servants behind him. One, a cousin to the man whose ear Peter had sliced, had spoken loud and long about what he would do to the Galilean coward who had attacked an unarmed man. What might happen if these Judeans realized Peter had wielded the sword?

Peter told himself, too, that it would hurt Yeshua's case if he were brought forth as a witness to testify against Him, especially in light of John's predication that they could rally support for Yeshua over the next few days. Not only that, he convinced himself, true denial would have been leaving the city instead of staying as near to Yeshua as possible.

Quick anger surged through Peter at the defensiveness he felt at her question. This was only a woman, and a servant at that.

Who was she to expect Peter's answer, needless and potentially harmful as it might be?

He drew himself tall with cold indignation.

"I don't know what you are talking about," he said, loudly enough for all those around to hear.

While Peter protected himself with his first denial, I remained in the great hall in the palace of Caiaphas with a couple dozen spectators. Naturally, I cannot say for certain what went through Caiaphas's mind, but I saw and heard enough to feel confident my witness to the record is as close to truth as anyone might offer.

The great hall was not much more than an open court with an arched ceiling. Smoky torches along the walls blackened the limestone with oily resin. The light, although dim, was strong enough to give shadow outlines to the cracks of the flat, interlocked brick that formed the floor. Rows of mats had been thrown down in three semicircles to provide seats for the council members.

Caiaphas, in his official high priest's robe, stood at the side of the great hall. He watched with satisfaction as Pharisees and elders and teachers took their seats. At least twenty-three were needed for a quorum of the Great Sanhedrin; it appeared that all seventy had arrived.

Israel had three tribunals. The lowest—consisting of three judges—held limited jurisdiction in towns with a population of fewer than one hundred and twenty men. The next highest—for larger centers—consisted of twenty-three judges, whose authority, while still somewhat limited, gave them jurisdiction over some capital causes. Finally the seventy men of the highest tribunal, Jerusalem's Great Sanhedrin, presided over all matters and met in the temple's Chamber of Hewn Stones under the direction of the seventy-first man, the high priest, called Nasi, "prince." There were no greater powers of authority in Israel.

As the men took their places, there was little noise beyond the rustling of clothing. Part of the silence stemmed from the lateness of the hour. As well, each man had been warned to expect the meeting and thus knew the seriousness of the matter.

When they had seated themselves, Caiaphas strode to the front to face them. Two court scribes, also facing the tribunal, prepared to note the speeches.

"As you have heard," Caiaphas said without preamble, "the rebel has been placed under arrest. He will be brought before us shortly."

Immediately an ancient Pharisee named Jochanan, whose long bone-thin neck was wattled with loose skin, stood. "There are legal difficulties with this," Jochanan said. His fanatic adherence to rabbinical teachings was notable, even among Pharisees. "I would like it recorded that I have made formal protest to this."

Caiaphas smiled to hide his irritation. Jochanan, in his fanaticism, hated Yeshua deeply. Which meant Jochanan was playing politics. It was his not-so-secret intent to one day act as high priest; he probably hoped this evening would also end Caiaphas's career.

"What is your protest?" Caiaphas asked.

"This trial grossly violates every tenet of Jewish law and order."

"How so, venerable judge?" Caiaphas had not risen to his position by letting challenges appear to intimidate him.

"Rabbinical law dictates that such a case as this be tried only in the regular meeting place in the temple. Furthermore, capital punishment may only be pronounced in the same place."

"Capital punishment?" Caiaphas responded. "Surely you are not suggesting—" Caiaphas bared his teeth—"that you have determined the outcome before listening to the testimony of witnesses. Such prejudicial leanings are not fitting for a Sanhedrin judge."

Jochanan gave himself time to think by losing himself in a coughing fit. When he recovered, he said, "If the Nasi had let me finish my sentence before reaching such a quick conclusion, the tribunal would have heard me add a simple phrase—capital punishment—if necessary."

"Thank you for that clarification." Caiaphas bowed, reveling in Jochanan's brief humiliation. "Please continue."

"According to rabbinical law, no process of trial shall begin at night. Or even in the afternoon. Nor may trials proceed on Sabbaths or feast days. As the court scribe will note, it is well past midnight on the Passover, a highly unusual and unprecedented occasion for a tribunal gathering."

Caiaphas watched Jochanan's large bald head totter on his impossibly skinny neck and enjoyed the thought of hearing those bones snap. He observed the shifting and muttering of the rest of the tribunal and realized the impact of the man's words.

"Last," Jochanan said, "in all capital causes, the judges must obey an elaborate system to warn and caution any witnesses. I do not see any outside witnesses, and I wish to ask for the record whether normal trial procedures will be used to safeguard the accused."

Jochanan sat, smugly happy that he had trapped Caiaphas, who would lose face if he sent the tribunal home after his urgent messages to set up this night gathering. Yet if Caiaphas continued, Jochanan could sanctimoniously protest Yeshua's inevitable death sentence, keeping the moral high ground while seeing both Yeshua and Caiaphas suffer.

Caiaphas pounced immediately. He wanted the entire tribunal to realize how easily Jochanan could be outmaneuvered.

"In answer to the noted protests," Caiaphas said, smiling condescendingly at Jochanan, "this is not a trial, and I extend my pity to Jochanan for his inability to understand this. It is also unfortunate that he chose to waste the tribunal's time by bringing up something already known to all."

Caiaphas directed his next words to the entire tribunal. "Obviously this is a matter of supreme importance. I cannot recall any other occasion that has merited the gathering of Jerusalem's religious leaders on the holy Passover night. Your united attendance shows, however, the great danger facing us. If Yeshua is not silenced and stirs the land to rebellion, the Romans will have every excuse to slaughter thousands of innocents and remove all authority from this tribunal. Or perhaps Jochanan has also lost the ability to understand this?"

Jochanan stared ahead stonily, knowing any answer would only add to Caiaphas's victory.

Caiaphas enjoyed letting the silence of triumph linger. "Let me repeat," Caiaphas finally said. "This is not a trial. As learned men, we are simply gathered to determine whether Yeshua from Nazareth should be sent to Pontius Pilate for judgment." Caiaphas gazed over the Great Sanhedrin. "Are there further comments?"

None came.

"Then we shall proceed," he said. He motioned to attendants at the back of the hall.

They brought Yeshua forward.

CHAPTER FORTY-SIX

Near the fire at the gate, another one of the servants overheard Peter talking to John. She cocked her ear at Peter's strong accent.

She listened a little longer, then remarked loudly. Her observation became an accusation that those around him could hear. "This man," the maidservant said, "was with Yeshua of Nazareth."

During his small talk with John, Peter's mind had been on the first girl and his reply to her. He'd convinced himself he had done the right thing by maintaining anonymity. Peter was trapped firmly in one of the peculiarities of human nature; sometimes the more wrong a man is in his stance, the more strenuously he argues it, for a justification needs continued and further justification for the self-deception to survive.

"I don't even know the man," Peter said now. He pushed up from where he was squatting and walked away from the fire.

An hour later, it was obvious to everyone that for Caiaphas, the sweetness of victory over Jochanan had faded. His frustration stemmed from two sources. The first was rabbinical law, which dictated that two witnesses must agree to support a given charge. Caiaphas had called witness after witness to bring evidence against Yeshua. No two, however, had been able to agree on the same charge.

Some had tried exaggerating or distorting different portions of Yeshua's teaching. Others had pointed to His acts of healing on the Sabbath—it was unlawful, but the politically shrewd Caiaphas had realized condemning Yeshua on that charge would also legitimize His miracles. It had reached the point where even the most ridiculous accusations were put forth, but with no results. The only thing proved by all of this was that Caiaphas had too hastily assembled the Great Sanhedrin and in his excitement had done little planning as prosecutor.

The second source of Caiaphas's frustration merely stood silently before the assembly, showing His canny understanding that He needed no defense; it was far better to let the false and contradictory statements fall by themselves.

Caiaphas beckoned for one of the young teachers from the rear semicircle to come forward. Caiaphas had no great hopes of him, which is why it had taken him so long to turn to the least experienced of the Sanhedrin.

The young teacher said, "This man said, 'I am able to destroy the temple of God and rebuild it in three days.' "

Hope flared in Caiaphas, and he marked the young teacher in his mind for reward later. Any threat against the temple was blasphemy that demanded the death sentence. Properly manipulated, this testimony could prove that Yeshua was a seducer of the people, calling them to tear down the temple while promising them magical power to rebuild it. It would not necessarily hold as a capital charge in Jewish law, but Caiaphas had no intention of making this an official trial. He simply wanted something he could take to Pontius Pilate so the Roman procurator could pronounce a death sentence. And most surely, if the Sanhedrin could show Pilate that Yeshua was calling for rebellion . . .

Caiaphas called out, "Is there another witness who will testify for or against this?"

"Yes," another elder replied. "I heard Him say the same."

Muted conversation rolled through the gathering. They all understood the significance of this.

The Pharisee named Nicodemus stood. "It should be brought to the attention of the tribunal that those words could be interpreted as 'the temple of the body.'"

Caiaphas glared at Nicodemus. Spies had brought word months earlier that Nicodemus had sought nighttime audiences with Yeshua. Nicodemus was not raising his point as a matter of law to protect the Sanhedrin from a sentence that would not hold up under examination. Nicodemus was actually trying to protect Yeshua.

The muttering grew louder.

Caiaphas raised his voice to silence everyone. He turned to Yeshua. "Well, aren't You going to answer these charges? What do You have to say for Yourself?"

But Yeshua remained silent.

Caiaphas felt his own heart pound against his ribs as his rage and hatred rose.

Yeshua, showing the wisdom of an experienced scholar, was taking advantage of the very laws they were using against Him. No proven evidence had been laid forth in these hearings; legally, Yeshua did not have to reply.

"Will you not answer?" Caiaphas demanded.

All muttering stopped. The other seventy men waited. Even the scribes, who normally showed no interest in testimony, leaned forward.

Yeshua said nothing. His head was bowed so the swollen upper lip that distorted His face was not visible.

Attention shifted to Caiaphas as the elders and teachers of the Sanhedrin sensed a crucial point in the hearing. Unless a proven charge was introduced for their vote, the prosecution would have no case. They would have no choice but to set Yeshua free, making Him even more popular with the people and setting up extreme humiliation for the religious establishment in Jerusalem.

Caiaphas felt his composure washing away to waves of hatred and rage. It had taken him months to get this detestable peasant in his grasp.

He commanded himself to think. Did he want to ground an accusation on Yeshua's claim to messiahship?

No! Israel's holiest and highest hope should not be exposed to mockery before the Romans.

Yet . . .

Yeshua lifted His head and smiled peacefully, as if at that moment He knew exactly what choice remained to Caiaphas.

Caiaphas wanted to destroy Yeshua because the peasant was a false prophet preaching false doctrines, because He publicly abused and ridiculed Jewish religious authority, because of the great likelihood that Yeshua would lead a popular rebellion against the Romans, and finally, because He did not deny messianic claims.

Over the last hour Caiaphas had not been able to build a case on the first three charges. Yet the fourth charge . . .

Yes! Caiaphas told himself. There was a way to make Yeshua incriminate Himself. Caiaphas would not need to find witnesses to prove and bring to Pilate Yeshua's claim to messiahship, not if Yeshua claimed it Himself.

Caiaphas could find seventy witnesses! Right here!

As his eyes met Yeshua's through the uneven yellow light of the great hall, Caiaphas raised his right arm and pointed a long, craggy finger at Yeshua. "Are You the Messiah," Caiaphas asked, "the Son of the blessed God?"

Somehow, the previous silence grew even heavier. The question was genius in its formulation. Once Yeshua denied it, His popular movement would cease. The Sanhedrin could set Him free to do no more damage among the people. If He didn't deny it . . .

"Are You the Son of God?" Caiaphas demanded.

"I am," Yeshua said, speaking His first words of the hearing.

A near roar went through the hall as the members of the San-hedrin absorbed Yeshua's reply.

"I am."

The hallowed unspeakable phrase that only God could speak in reference to Himself.

"I am."

Blasphemy!

Yeshua turned to face the assembly. "And you will see Me," Yeshua began, cutting short the babble, "the Son of Man, sitting at God's right hand in the place of power and coming back on the clouds of heaven."

Son of Man.

Sitting at God's right hand.

Coming back on the clouds of heaven.

Claiming to be Messiah in itself was not blasphemous. Dozens had done so across the land over the previous decades. Significant as it was to speak against the temple, this too, was not blasphemy. But here, as Yeshua cited and applied and linked messianic texts in Daniel and Psalms, He essentially claimed authority over the temple, claimed He would share the very throne and glory of God, and that—by using a scriptural phrase for God's judgment, "coming back on the clouds of heaven"— claimed Yeshua Himself would ensure God's righteous vindication as these men were punished for their unbelief.

This, unless it was true, was blasphemy of the worst kind!
And Caiaphas would never accept it as true.

Rabbinical law dictated that when blasphemy was spoken, the high priest rip both his outer and inner garments, tearing them so completely that neither could ever be repaired.

There was nothing judicial, however, about the manner in which Caiaphas tore his clothing. Fury animated him with such passion that no elder in the assembly had ever seen him show, and Caiaphas shredded his upper garments so completely that wisps of gray hair were visible on his bony, narrow chest.

"Why do we need other witnesses?" Caiaphas shouted, releasing his months of brooding hatred. "You have all heard His blasphemy. What is your verdict?"

Starting from youngest to oldest, so that the opinions of the elders would not unfairly sway the first votes, Caiaphas asked for each man's decision.

"Guilty," the first man said. As did the second. And third.
So it continued.

When the first thirty-seven members had all agreed that Yeshua was guilty of blasphemy, Caiaphas permitted himself a small smile of victory. Only a majority of two was required; with only thirty-four votes left, Yeshua's sentence had been pronounced. As Caiaphas continued polling the final votes, the only exceptions were the man named Nicodemus and another, Joseph of Arimathea, who each abstained, drawing glares from Caiaphas and whispers from the Sanhedrin.

The final count showed sixty-nine votes of guilt and two abstentions.

Technically, it had not been a trial, so Caiaphas did not pronounce a formal sentence. He would reassemble the Sanhedrin at first light at the temple for a second vote, which would legally seal the fate of the rebel.

Which, for the grave offense of blasphemy, would be death.

Still at the back of the hall, I waited for Yeshua to show everyone He was the Messiah.

He did not.

CHAPTER FORTY-SEVEN

They began to beat Yeshua after the mock trial; I was sickened at the joy lesser men took in trampling one they had feared.

This final injustice after the mockery of a trial I had witnessed pushed me to unreasoning anger. Perhaps I was looking for a way to vent my frustration, much as I had taken savage satisfaction in fighting the two men beneath the city earlier in the week.

Ten men had gathered around Yeshua, vying with each other to swing at Him with fists or kick Him.

I rushed in and tried to throw them away from Him. My efforts were useless. They briefly turned their fury on me. Three men tossed me to the ground. Others kicked at me until I managed to roll away.

Two of the men made moves to pursue me, but Caiaphas stopped them. He looked down at me in scorn. "Leave this fool," he told them. "He is the cousin of Pascal. We will hurt him as we hurt any wealthy man—by restricting his business."

I pushed to my knees and dusted myself, feeling powerless.

I knew there was now no way for Pascal to associate himself with me by purchasing my estate while I lived. And, oddly, I began to feel relief at the only alternative left to me.

When they tired of beating Yeshua, they placed Him in a

small room above the courtyard to pass the final hours until dawn and His sentence of death.

From there, Yeshua perhaps witnessed something that must have hurt Him far more than the blows, insults, and spittle of His enemies.

□|□□|□□|□□|□

Peter was well to the side of the fire, conspicuous by his solitary outline. Intent on trying to overhear the results of the trial, he did not notice until too late that one of the servants had moved beside him.

The man tapped his shoulder. Although it was dark, Peter saw enough to recognize the man. It was the servant who had complained loudly about the coward with a sword.

"You must be one of them; we can tell by your Galilean accent," he said.

Before, anger had surged through Peter. Now it was fear. By the aggressive tone of the remark, Peter knew he could be mobbed and beaten badly if found out.

Peter called a curse on himself to swear the truth of his words. "I swear by God, I don't know the man!"

As the words left his mouth, a distant rooster crowed.

Yeshua's words flashed through Peter's mind: *"Before the rooster crows, you will deny Me three times."*

The horror of the accuracy of the prediction lifted Peter's head. He saw the One who had predicted it. In the torchlight that had illuminated the trial proceedings, it appeared to Peter that Yeshua was staring directly back at him.

Peter shoved away from the servant and stumbled in a half run, looking for any place that offered him privacy. Deep wrenching sobs overcame him.

Yeshua, too, wept.

FRIDAY

CHAPTER FORTY-EIGHT

My dearest love,
If our servant has read you these letters in order, you will remember
easily that I would not write my final letter until I had decided the truth
about this man of miracles.

Last night I saw Him captured and tried by ordinary men.
Greedy men. Vain men. Self-righteous men. Men who wanted Him
dead because His teachings were a threat to them. Men who had the
power to murder Him publicly and make it appear lawful.

For the events that transpired against Him, He has my sympathy.
He was innocent and, by trying to help others, condemned Himself.

Yet if He were who He claimed to be, He would not have let this
injustice occur. Nor would He have taken the beatings and insults
rained upon Him. If He were the Messiah, He would have had the
God-given power to prevent all that happened.

Thus I am satisfied that He cannot help me.

I am also satisfied that I have tried everything possible to redeem
my wrongdoings. Altar sacrifices failed. As did fasting. Self-denial.
And the pursuit of a miracle man.

Nothing in my power will set our daughter right, or our love
right, or myself right again. Knowing I have done everything possi-
ble within my considerable means and talent allows me to seek my
solution in peace.

Please be assured that my beloved cousin Pascal will take care of my estate and ensure that you will never want for money.

In farewell, let me tell you again that you are blameless for the death of our love. I am the one who failed. Grieve the man you remember me to be in the beginning—I beg this as my final wish. Then find a man who will cherish you until your last breath.

As I do not want my confession to reach the ears of the servant who reads this, I will write it on a separate scroll, sealed, to be included with these letters.

Have Vashti read my final confession to you from that scroll. I know she has been seeking education; books are now her only freedom. As she reads my confession aloud in your presence, it will grant her another freedom of sorts, for she will be telling you the truth she has kept hidden from you on my behalf. Tell her my death is payment for the burden I gave her.

Once you hear my confession, I ask you to forgive me if you can.

I beg of you to ask Vashti to forgive me.

I want you both to know I would have given everything I owned to undo what I did; instead, I am giving my life, and not even that is enough.

Lastly, at the first star on the evening you receive these letters and the news of my death, sing a song for me from our balcony.

I will cling to that image. The thought of your sweet voice will bring some happiness to me over the next few hours.

Good-bye.

Your Simeon

I n the prison of my cousin's guest chamber, I set aside my final letter and wrote the promised confession to Jaala, half expecting that act to somehow set me free.

It did not. In my mind, I saw my wife's face as she heard the truth as Vashti read the confession to her. In my mind, I watched my wife sit back slowly, absorbing what it meant. This vision of the woman I love increased my pain.

I rolled the parchment of my confession carefully and set it with the other letters that would be delivered to her with the possessions I had brought to Jerusalem.

I let out a deep breath of resolution. With the arrival of the dawn, my self-imposed trial had finally ended.

For another, too much trial remained.

Pilate sat in his magistrate's chair, his shoulders covered with a cloak. The sun had yet to warm the courtyard of Herod's palace, and he knew it would be another hour before he could set the cloak aside. This early hour and the judicial task that went with it were two of the reasons he disliked coming to Jerusalem.

As Roman governor, Pontius Pilate's duties included moderating all local disputes between Jews and Gentiles. Because of Jerusalem's large Gentile population, a huge backlog of cases always awaited him during his infrequent visits from Caesarea. Pilate was also responsible for overseeing appeals, capital cases, and any political offense that threatened Roman administration. Other duties had delayed his first hearings until Wednesday. Since then, he had held two sessions a day—dawn until noon, and midday to early evening—and still expected to be stuck in Jerusalem until the middle of the following week.

His role as provincial judge demanded full concentration. Roman courts usually had large juries, but in the provinces, because of the scarcity of Roman citizens, the governor was both jury and judge. Pilate had no room for legal sloppiness; the transcripts of all his trials were subject to review in Rome. His advancement in part depended on his reputation as a magistrate.

Pilate considered it a small mercy that the current case had required little time and even less legal skill. He looked down on the two bearded men shivering, as much from fear as from cold, before him. Both were stripped to the waist, both mongrel thin with dozens of bruises and abrasions across their ribs; the soldiers who had captured them had not been gentle.

During a court session, there is always one totally quiet moment, the pregnant pause before the verdict is delivered. This was that moment.

As Pilate drew a breath to pronounce his deliberations, sandals scuffling over bricks broke the moment. The spectators turned to watch a slave rush into the courtyard.

The slave stopped short, seeing by the scowl on Pilate's face that it had not been a good moment to interrupt, no matter how urgent the message.

Pilate turned his attention back to the two prisoners. "The court shall note that no less than five witnesses have described without variation your attempt at highway robbery," Pilate said. "Accordingly, I judge you both guilty."

The larger of the two men, whose nose had been broken by the butt end of a soldier's spear, emptied his bladder in a spasm of fear. He had expected the verdict, but to be in the moment when it was delivered was too much. For he also knew the penalty.

"Take them away," Pilate said. "As they are not Roman citizens, flog them first; then crucify them."

The second man bore his sentence stoically, but his wife rushed forward and tried to pull him away from the Roman soldiers. A fist knocked her to the ground, and she lay moaning in pain and misery as soldiers led the men away.

Pilate waved for more soldiers to remove her as well and sighed at the wearisome drama of human nature. He beckoned the slave forward.

"Excellency, a delegation waits for you outside the palace. Sanhedrin. With the rebel," the slave said.

"I have been expecting them." Why else had they requested a cohort of soldiers in the middle of the night? "Send them in."

"They request you meet them outside, Excellency. They wish to avoid religious defilement. If they enter now, they will be unable to participate in the remaining Passover celebrations."

"They expect me to go out to them?"

The slave hesitated.

"What is it?" Pilate said.

"Caiaphas instructed me to let you understand that he foresees dangerous rioting if this matter is not handled soon. Already, hundreds are gathering in the square outside the palace."

More hesitation.

"Out with it," Pilate snapped. When would these servants realize he was first and foremost a soldier, not a capricious emperor who vented cowardly anger on the helpless?

"I have also been instructed to let you know that their own criminal investigation has found the man guilty. Caiaphas promises this will not delay your schedule."

Pilate slammed an open palm against his chair's armrest.

"Excellency?"

Pilate was a soldier, but no soldier reached a governorship without political acumen. Much as Caiaphas wanted this Yeshua dead, he was trying to force Pilate to bear the blame for any rioting that might result from the prophet's death. Furthermore, Caiaphas expected Pilate to accept the judgment of the Sanhedrin when the very essence of Roman law was a public hearing. Any disturbances over Yeshua's death would hurt Pilate twofold in Rome: for the disturbance itself and for the legal improprieties. For Caiaphas, it was a shrewd attempt to hurt both of his enemies at the same time.

"Excellency?" the slave asked again.

Pilate realized his attention had been on his disdain for Caiaphas and his anger at the leverage of the high priest's office.

Pilate uncurled his grip on the armrest. "Tell Caiaphas I will thoroughly judge this case."

Before the slave could move ten paces away, Pilate stood. "Wait," Pilate commanded. He threw his cloak aside. "I have changed my mind. I will tell him myself."

CHAPTER FIFTY

J ust before leaving the guest chamber, I took the opportunity to review, for the final time, the legal documents I had had prepared shortly before the Passover. Listed in full detail—if nothing else, I had a good head for numbers—were the total values of all my holdings.

Pascal would see this and trust me for accuracy.

Following this list was the price I had requested for the full estate, not including the villa where my wife and daughter could comfortably spend the rest of their lives if they chose. This price was only half of a conservative estimate of the estate's value, yet more than enough to allow my wife and daughter to live extravagantly each year of their lives.

Pascal would gladly pay this amount to add to his holdings.

The bargain included the provision that Pascal oversee the transfer of wealth and administer this money in such a way as to protect my wife and daughter.

My death would force Pascal to honor this deal despite my foolish actions against the Sanhedrin. And because I would be dead, none would speak against him for associating with me.

I had decided upon this as the simplest and least wearisome way to handle my holdings. I was tired of life and wanted no more burdens. If I actually entered into a discussion with

Pascal, negotiations could take days to resolve. Days I did not care to see.

I had one last note to write.

I began without hurry. In the same manner, the Roman governor began to deal with his problem in the public square not far from where I sat at my window.

◫◫◫◫◫◫◫◫◫

Pilate sent guards ahead with his magistrate's chair and orders to set it on the top of the steps, then to clear a large space in front of it.

He also sent word to Fort Antonia that reinforcements should move to the Herodian palace but position themselves out of sight of the Jews in the square.

Finally, Pilate waited fifteen minutes before marching majestically into the public square, accompanied by guards and personal slaves. After he settled himself into the chair, he placed his forearms on its armrests.

And waited.

The crowd already filled most of the square. White robes marked dozens of priests. Long gray beards indicated the Sanhedrists. Poorly dressed peasants from lower Jerusalem, some of them obviously drunk, filled out the crowd.

Pilate waited longer. Despite the impatient mutters and grumblings around him, each passing minute gave him more satisfaction. The space cleared before his chair ensured that every person would see when Caiaphas moved forward in supplication to Pilate.

The tension increased.

Caiaphas remained as stubborn as Pilate. He stood at the front of the crowd, expecting Pilate to summon him.

Pilate contented himself by examining the prisoner. There

was but one man with His hands bound, so he knew it must be Yeshua. Unlike the hundreds of prisoners Pilate had seen in his career, this man's eyes held no fear, no shame, no defiance, no plea for lenience. Still—after hearing rumors of miracles for months, after seeing the efforts Caiaphas had expended to capture this prophet from Galilee, after the threats of rioting and public disorder—Pilate had expected more. A bigger man, perhaps. Or striking features. But, aside from His dignity, this man appeared as ordinary as the carpenter He'd once been.

After several more minutes, Pilate let a smile curve his lips. Enough time had passed. Caiaphas could no longer claim that Rome had not been prepared to dispense judgment. Pilate stood, smiled once more, and began to walk back toward the palace.

His bluff worked.

Excited rumblings in the crowd told Pilate that something was happening behind him. He continued to walk.

"Your Excellency!"

It was Caiaphas.

Pilate pretended to hear nothing but didn't keep the gleam out of his eyes. Let Caiaphas grovel.

"Your Excellency!"

Pilate sobered his features and turned back to the crowd. Caiaphas, two chief priests, and the prisoner were now at the foot of the steps, below the magistrate's chair. Pilate returned, happy that he'd forced Caiaphas to supplicate, and resumed his position in the chair.

"What is your charge against this man?" Pilate asked.

The question seemed to stun Caiaphas. Pilate's question had been the opening statement of an official Roman trial. A nearby scribe, in fact, was copying the words for the transcript.

Pilate hid his satisfaction and amusement. Let the Jews condemn Yeshua. Let them bear the brunt of public opinion.

Caiaphas recovered badly. "We wouldn't have handed Him over to you if He weren't a criminal!"

Pilate shrugged, but it was pretended indifference. This exchange was going exactly as he had planned. "Then take Him away and judge Him by your own laws."

The scribe continued marking Pilate's words. None of the previous night's discussion, nor Caiaphas's expectations because of that discussion, would be on the record. To any legal authority reviewing the case later in Rome, then, Pilate would be without blame.

"Only the Romans are permitted to execute someone," Caiaphas said.

Pilate nodded wisely, as if agreeing with Caiaphas. "I am to understand then, since you seek His death, that you have found this man guilty, although you have not laid charges. I am also to understand that somehow, during the night, you were able to give Him a fair trial. Again, without laying charges."

A blow to the kidneys would not have had more impact. Pilate was beginning to think he had actually cornered the old gray snake before him.

Caiaphas began a heated whispered conversation with his chief priests.

Pilate kept careful watch on Yeshua, expecting some of the conversation to visibly affect Him. After all, it was His life at balance. Yet the prophet remained in a near meditative calm.

"This man," Caiaphas announced, "has been leading our people to ruin by telling them not to pay their taxes to the Roman government and by claiming He is the Messiah, a king."

Inwardly, Pilate winced at the slightly scratching sound as the scribe continued to transcribe the accusation. He could not walk away from the trial now.

Pilate waited for Yeshua to defend Himself against the

charges. The man said nothing. While it intrigued Pilate—defendants often shouted counteraccusations, pleaded for mercy, made excuses, but never just stood silently—it all placed him in a difficult situation.

One that Caiaphas saw. For if Yeshua said nothing, Pilate would have to address the charges.

Caiaphas took his own opportunity to smile in triumph. The three charges would alarm any Roman governor. Sedition? Opposition of tribute? The high treason of a claim to kingship?

Caiaphas knew that Pilate knew. Emperor Tiberius, in Rome, would be far less likely to understand the local situation than Pilate. Tiberius would think Pilate stupid or insane if he didn't simply and cheaply execute a non-Roman citizen to eliminate the slightest risk to Roman rule.

Pilate beckoned Caiaphas forward. He kept his voice low so the scribe could record none of their conversation.

"I tell you this for my own satisfaction," Pilate said. "We both know this Yeshua has avoided all political causes. As for your second accusation, the nonpayment of tribute, I have had a good laugh at His now-famous response to give to Caesar what is his. You are only fortunate that what He said could be distorted in Rome."

Pilate leaned forward so he was almost nose to nose with Caiaphas. "Do you see the hypocrisy of publicly defending tribute to us when you and your Pharisees spend your days protesting Roman rule?"

Pilate's spittle flecked the high priest's beard. "And finally, it is totally contemptible that you and your Sanhedrin claim religious defilement prevents you from entering my court when what you are attempting is judicial murder. Why should any man with intelligence believe you serve God?"

The only thing that held Pilate from physically pushing

Caiaphas away was the certainty of the riot that would result. So Pilate leaned back and made his pronouncement. "Send the prisoner to my chamber," he said. "I will interview Him there on these charges."

CHAPTER FIFTY-ONE

My final words, the note to Pascal, were simple. I explained that I was going to take my own life. I thanked him for his hospitality and assured him that as a younger cousin, I would have approached him for help with my problem if I had at all thought there was a solution.

I told Pascal the general area where my body might be found and asked him to keep the note to him secret and to arrange it so that it appeared I had been a victim of crime, as it would allow my wife the comfort of a synagogue funeral if the world believed I had died at the hands of highway robbers.

I asked him to honor the document of sale he would find with the note, explaining that I doubted any harm would come to his reputation if he did so after my death; assets are never held accountable for the character of the man who owned them. I requested that he send along the nearby letters to my wife without reading them.

Then I wrote my good-bye to Seraphine and wished her and Pascal my love and shalom for the rest of their lives together.

When I discovered I had nothing else of importance to add to the note, I stood, wrapped myself in my cloak, and set the note on my bed where Pascal would find it.

I was ready to die. And I was delighted to feel a sense of calm.

As I departed the mansion of my cousin unnoticed, I pondered this calm. I decided it came to a man once he truly accepted the finality and consequences of a decision.

So, too, it must have been for the man of miracles.

□│□│□│□│□│□│□│□│□

"Are You the king of the Jews?" Pilate asked Yeshua.

The scratching of stylus on parchment reminded them both this was a private interview only in the sense that it was done out of the hearing of Caiaphas.

"Is this your own question," Yeshua asked, "or did others tell you about Me?"

The man's utter calmness fascinated Pilate. This peasant should be quaking in the presence of the single man in Judea with the power to order soldiers into instant war against the Jewish nation.

And the man's eyes—Pilate had to harden his own soldier's heart against the gentle appeal of the prophet's compassionate gaze. As if Pilate were the one who needed pity.

Pilate shook off this unexpected softness by replying brusquely to Yeshua's question. "Am I a Jew?"

When Yeshua did not reply to Pilate's implication that he could not understand Jews, the governor continued. "Your own people and their leading priests brought You here." He pointed at Yeshua's bound wrists. "Why? What have You done?"

"I am not an earthly king," Yeshua said. "If I were, My followers would have fought when I was arrested by the Jewish leaders. But My Kingdom is not of this world."

Pilate found himself in a quicksand he had never experienced. His world was the harsh competition of soldiers and politics. As a man excelled, so his rewards increased. It was a simple world.

But there was a subtext to this conversation, a tugging at Pilate's view of the world, that made him uneasy yet vaguely hopeful of some peace he could not define.

"You are a king then?" Pilate said, glad that the words recorded by the scribe would not contain the texture of his near helplessness.

"You say that I am a king, and you are right," Yeshua said. "I was born for that purpose. And I came to bring truth to the world. All who love the truth recognize that what I say is true."

Pilate felt himself sinking deeper into the quicksand. He was not a man of philosophy. Yet as he grew older, he was becoming more conscious of his mortality. There, too, was his wife, Procula, who insisted on speaking of spiritual matters, as if a man actually had a soul.

The soldier's world was simple. These other matters were not. Perhaps the world was not as simple as Pilate wished.

Here he was, the governor of Judea, a direct representative of Rome, engaged in conversation with a man persecuted by His own people for no crime that Pilate could see.

Nonsense. Any soldier would call it that. Nonsense.

Pilate also had the honesty of a soldier. The honesty to allow himself other questions. This near the pinnacle of his political career, what did he really have? Why did nothing really satisfy him? What was the hollowness that filled him when everything he possessed should have fulfilled him and brought him peace?

Beyond this brief conversation and the thoughts whirling through his mind, Pilate sensed something out of his vision and touch and hearing. As if instinct were searching for a home he did not know. An instinct heightened by the man in front of him. What was it about this man? Who was this man?

A man who claimed that everyone who belonged to the truth listened to Him.

Pilate set aside his confusion and went for the safety of responding cynically. He reached for the only philosophical statement he knew. Yet as the words came out of his mouth, he heard more than the cynicism he was trying to posture. Pilate heard his own half plea of hollow despair. "You tell me," Pilate said to the man before him. "What is truth?"

CHAPTER FIFTY-TWO

I did not want to be overwhelmed by indecision as I walked through the city for the final time of my life, so I defeated it before it could strike.

My face was resolutely set toward the countryside, and with the will that had vaulted me from poverty to wealth, I did not allow the sights and sounds and smells of the city to distract me from my purpose.

Perhaps I was afraid that if I looked for beauty or nostalgia, I would change my mind. After all, I was my own executioner. If I wanted to turn back, I could.

Across the city, however, another condemned man did not have that luxury. Nor did His executioner.

Back outside Herod's palace, Yeshua stood beside the magistrate's chair as Pilate made his announcement to the Sanhedrists. "I find nothing wrong with this man!"

Pilate crossed his arms, defiant against the immediate uproar. He was aware of Yeshua's continued calm dignity, as if He had no fear of death.

This man was no rebel. Pilate knew it with certainty. And reflecting on their time alone in the chamber, Pilate realized how much he had revealed to the prophet, even implying a sort of homage by appealing to Him with the philosophical question of truth. Was it an accident that they were standing side by side as they faced the crowd?

Caiaphas marched directly to Pilate. "Tiberius will hear of this," he hissed above the crowd's shouting. "The letter will present a case to show the man's teachings have inflamed people from His beginnings in Galilee. Even to the point that tax collectors have followed Him. And you know Tiberius and his expensive habits well enough to know how he will react to that."

"What was that?" Pilate asked.

Caiaphas repeated himself, this time so that others could hear. "But He is causing riots everywhere He goes, all over Judea, from Galilee to Jerusalem!"

Pilate only heard one word. *Galilee.*

Much as Pilate's conscience had been stirred by the presence of Yeshua, he could not escape his political nature.

Galilee.

Herod, the tetrarch of Galilee, was in Jerusalem. With diplomatic genius, Pilate could place the troublesome issue in Herod's hands and at the same time appear to be respectful of Herod's territorial claims. Perhaps Herod would see this as a conciliatory gesture in light of their current strained relations.

"Oh," Pilate said mildly, setting the trap, "is he a Galilean?"

"It will give me satisfaction to see you recalled to Rome," Caiaphas was saying as he nodded affirmation to Pilate's question. "Most surely—"

"Take this man to Herod," Pilate said.

"Herod?" Caiaphas went from artificial outrage to calculation.

"Herod. It is a case within his jurisdiction." Thinking it through, Pilate was satisfied. Both for how it saved him from trouble and because it would probably save the innocent man beside him. Herod would be extremely reluctant to judge Yeshua guilty. Not after the trouble he'd faced for beheading the other popular prophet, John the Baptist.

"There is ample legal right for you to preside over it yourself," Caiaphas said.

"Herod," Pilate repeated. "Your charges have religious overtones within Jewish law. He is far better qualified to judge than I am."

Pilate stood and motioned for his attendants to return the magistrate's chair to the inner courtyard of the palace. He ignored Caiaphas and gave a slight nod of acknowledgment to Yeshua as he retreated from the crowd.

As far as Pilate was concerned, there was nothing left in this affair to trouble him.

CHAPTER FIFTY-THREE

I did not carry a purse or valuables as I headed to the countryside. I had stripped myself of jewelry before departing.

I did not fear the possibility of bandits here on the lonely highway; rather that possibility was part of the reason I had chosen the countryside, for it would have been much simpler to return to the city wall above the Kidron.

I did not know how long it would be before my body was found. But I wanted to be shorn of valuables, leaving the easy conclusion that I had been robbed and killed, discarded over a cliff.

My death must not appear self-inflicted. My beloved wife, Jaala, had already faced so much grief that my suicide would have little extra significance for her. But I didn't want her or my daughter to have to face questions. If others accepted my death as one at the hands of bandits, they would have no occasion to wonder or gossip about why I had killed myself. After all, to the world, I had everything.

But, as I had discovered, everything tangible can be nothing. I am certain I am not the first, nor will I be the last, to learn this.

Knocking at the door roused Herod from a restless sleep. He couldn't even remember getting beneath the blankets.

"Go away," he groaned.

"Worthy Tetrarch," a voice from the other side said, "a delegation from the Sanhedrin has arrived to see you."

"Castrate each of those pompous fools and send them back to their mothers." Herod ran his tongue over his teeth and grimaced. The taste and texture were as if a small animal had crawled into his mouth and died. When, Herod asked himself, would he learn not to mix wine and beer in such great amounts?

"They insist on seeing you. It is a delegation sent from Pilate."

"Unless you leave me in peace," Herod shouted, "you will be castrated with them!" Herod immediately regretted his foolhardy exertion. His head throbbed at the slightest movement.

"Worthy Tetrarch . . ."

Herod vowed to whip the servant himself, even if the man had served the royal family for three decades.

"Go away!" Herod tried to spit on the floor but could not work any moisture into his mouth. "No! Bring water!" He owned an entire kingdom yet suffered hangovers like any mortal man. What justice was there in that?

"They have with them the prophet from Galilee."

Herod pushed himself upright. Blankets fell from his massive belly. "Yeshua?" Herod asked, wobbling for balance on the side of his bed. *That* prophet?"

"Indeed, worthy Tetrarch."

"Tell them I will see them as soon as I am ready," Herod said. "Then hurry back and help me dress."

Facing the delegation of elderly Jews from his throne, Herod wondered if their faces would crack and bleed the next time they smiled.

So arrogant, so self-righteous. Herod had half an urge to order them to stay and watch his dancers. Then he'd see just how much their rules and regulations meant to them. All except the most withered, Caiaphas, who would probably collapse with shock at the flash of the first wiggling navel.

It was Caiaphas who started to rattle off a long string of accusations against Yeshua, and his passion surprised Herod. Maybe the old man did have some life in him.

Herod listened as long as he could bear it, then waved Caiaphas to be quiet. "Bring in your prisoner," Herod said. "I'm quite familiar with your complaints."

Too familiar. It was all these rabbis did, moan and complain. They weren't happy unless everyone around them shared their misery. Parasitic fools.

As Herod waited, he eased his throat by drinking from a goblet. *Let the fools think it's water,* he thought. But it was a hearty red wine—much needed to get his blood coursing at this early hour.

Herod's guards escorted Yeshua to the throne.

"Finally," Herod said to Yeshua. "I've been wanting to see You for some time."

The wine had heated Herod's veins, and he found the energy to lean forward with interest. "I have heard of Your exploits for years. The great healer, You have been called. Then those stories about fish and loaves and feeding the thousands. Truly amazing. Perhaps You heard I actually sent soldiers out looking for You. But never to harm You, despite what You might have heard about John the Baptist. After all, he never performed a single miracle. . . ."

All this talk scratched Herod's throat. He drank deeply and sighed. "Would You grace us with a miracle right now? Nothing spectacular. It is early, and I wouldn't want You to tax Yourself too much on my behalf."

Aside from Yeshua, twenty men crowded the throne hall. Five were the limited delegation allowed. Fourteen were Herod's soldiers. And, of course, Herod.

Forty eyes stared at Yeshua. Caiaphas and the other Jews with some dread, for they feared a miracle. Herod and his soldiers with curiosity and expectation, for they hoped for the miracle.

Yeshua merely closed His eyes as if lost in deep thought.

"Come on," Herod said. "You are here because these great religious leaders want You dead. All I need is one miracle, and You can go free."

Yeshua opened His eyes.

What Herod saw in his gaze was pity. "Listen," Herod snapped. "I'm offering You Your life. Show me a sign from God, and I'll bow down before You and Him. One miracle is all I need."

Yeshua only smiled sadly.

Angry, Herod gulped another mouthful of wine. "Make the rope drop from Your wrists. That's all. I'll know You are a true prophet, and we'll send these Pharisees on their way."

Silence.

Caiaphas cleared his throat. "Noble Tetrarch, there is a good reason He will not perform any miracles. He cannot. He is a false prophet. You are well within your rights to have Him stoned."

Herod's headache returned with his loss of interest in Yeshua. "Don't tell me what my rights are." He focused his irritation on the high priest. "Word of this failure will become public, and the people will stop following Him. He doesn't need to die to lose His power among them."

Unspoken—and both of them knew it—was Herod's fear of stirring up more trouble by killing another popular prophet.

"But He calls Himself the Son of God," Caiaphas tried. "He is a heretic."

"Only an insane man would call himself such. You are to be pitied as much as He for giving His foolish claims attention."

"The Sanhedrin has found Him guilty," Caiaphas said.

"Take Him back to Pilate. You can continue the trial with Him where you left off."

"Pilate?"

"You will notice I have not set this prophet free. Push me further and I will acquit Him immediately."

Caiaphas gaped briefly, almost protested, and thought better of it.

Seeing the high priest at a loss was the first moment Herod had enjoyed since hearing the knock on his door.

Herod carefully set his goblet on the armrest of his throne. He stepped down. With two painful, gout-slowed steps, he reached Yeshua. "If You can't perform a miracle, at least talk. Let me hear You tell me You are the Son of God."

The satisfaction Herod had felt in humiliating Caiaphas dissipated when he saw the strength in Yeshua's eyes. The knowledge and power there brought Herod's insecurities into focus through his wine-deadened senses.

"You have my apologies," Herod said sarcastically. He removed his elegant robe and draped it over Yeshua's shoulders. "Guards," Herod called, "here is your king. Bow down. Worship Him. Then take Him to Pilate."

Herod's guards pounced on the opportunity for fun. They blew trumpets in Yeshua's ears. They dropped to their knees in front of Him. They taunted Him with vulgar comments about His ancestry.

Not once did Yeshua show any sign of discomfort. The laughter began to die.

"Enough," Herod said. "On your way."

The guards began to push Yeshua forward.

"Wait!" Herod called. As ordered, the procession stopped.

"Galilee man," Herod said, holding his goblet aloft. "Turn this water to wine!" Herod shook the goblet as if a great force were taking hold of it.

Seconds later, with the goblet a few inches above his mouth, Herod poured the remainder of the red liquid into his mouth. "Look, look," Herod laughed. "It has become wine! A miracle!"

Fat and wheezing, incapable of enjoying his wife's favors, wearying of exploring luxury and sin more with each passing year, he did not feel like a king.

Moments later, when all had left, Herod leaned against the throne in defeat.

CHAPTER FIFTY-FOUR

I walked through the northern part of the city, through the Tower Gate, unaware of how soon Yeshua would follow the same route. I barely noticed the houses built beyond the second wall of Jerusalem.

Bezetha, the new city, was growing rapidly past the underground quarries and the timber market, where wood was stored away from the dense inner city as a safety precaution against fire.

North, there were plateaus and small cliffs, which I had observed from the highway on my travels into or away from Jerusalem. These would suit my purpose. While I did not have a specific site in mind, I anticipated that I would know it when I saw it.

The highway was quiet. It was early on the morning after Passover. I had my solitude and my resolution to find final peace.

It wasn't until I passed the public execution site at the Hill of the Skull that I thought, for the first time that morning, of the man of miracles and the fate that awaited Him.

Herod had sent Yeshua back to Pilate.

Because of it, the governor faced the Sanhedrists and the

crowd again. Some of those gathered near the back were drunk and amusing themselves with fistfights. In the middle, hundreds of ordinary Jewish citizens—residents of Jerusalem, not pilgrims—massed together to show their support at the request that had been put forth by their religious leaders. At the front of the crowd, Caiaphas stood proudly and visibly among the priests and elders.

As for those who might have supported Yeshua, it was so early and this trial had convened so quickly that none of the many who followed Him even knew of the trial.

Pilate assessed the people. Yeshua's words echoed through his mind: *"But My kingdom is not of this world."*

Pilate had smelled this tension before among the frantic Jews. It was a supercharged sweat of heated emotions, of people unified in the unreasoning passion of a mob. As Caiaphas had reminded him earlier, three other times the Jews had pushed Pilate almost to the point of bloodshed: the riot in Caesarea, the aqueduct riot, and the removal of the golden shields. This gathering, too, had reached that boiling point, and Pilate wondered if he would have to call for soldiers.

"But My kingdom is not of this world."

Pilate had first sent Yeshua away to simply thwart Caiaphas. Now, however, his determination to resist the crowd's call for the man's death came from the brief time he had spent with the prophet. Yeshua's peace spoke loudly, and His single statement of defense echoed through Pilate's mind.

"But My kingdom is not of this world."

Nothing in Roman law could convict Yeshua. If Pilate took pride in any institution, it was Roman law and tradition. Aside from his unexpected admiration for the prophet, Pilate had no intention of betraying his personal convictions as a soldier and citizen of the republic.

Pilate began loudly, intending to forestall a formal trial. "You brought this man to me, accusing Him of leading a revolt. I have examined Him thoroughly on this point in your presence and find Him innocent. Herod came to the same conclusion and sent Him back to us. Nothing this man has done calls for the death penalty. So I will have Him flogged, but then I will release Him."

Some of Caiaphas's men had been circulating near the back. They shouted as previously instructed, "Take this man away! Crucify Him!"

In the shocked silence that followed Pilate's quick verdict, those shouts rang as clearly as trumpet blasts.

Within seconds, a few of the drunks took up the cry, looking to generate excitement. Their hoarse voices prompted the conservative Jews in the middle of the crowd to join in. "Crucify Him! Crucify Him!"

The shouts soon became a unified chant. Others, at Caiaphas's orders, had spread dissension by telling people this had become an issue of autonomy; Rome was refusing to do the bidding of Jerusalem. Still others went through the crowd, spreading the story of how Yeshua had failed to perform a miracle in front of Herod. Rage at Rome and disappointment in a failed messiah were fueling the discontent.

Caiaphas, near the front, sat serenely, delighted that his masterful plan was working so well.

Pilate beckoned Caiaphas forward. "If a riot occurs," Pilate said in a near yell, "I hold you responsible. To keep peace, I suggest you withdraw the charges. That way I don't have to declare Him innocent. As for my part, I am willing to have the man flogged to save face for you. Later, if you build a case against Him that will stand up in court, bring Him back to me."

Caiaphas merely backed away, smiling his contempt for Pilate.

Caiaphas lifted his hands, as if accepting the orchestrated shouting of the crowd in triumphant tribute.

"Crucify Him! Crucify Him!"

Pilate saw a solution.

CHAPTER FIFTY-FIVE

I left the highway and pushed my way through low brush, sweating despite the coolness of the early morning. My progress was impeded by loose sand and rocks and by the steepness of the climb.

I would not be stopped, however.

By following the empty wash of a ravine as it narrowed upward, I could reach the highest point of these hills. Then, at the top, walking along the edge of the cliff, I would see the bottom of the ravine at its widest and deepest. I would find a place where the drop was far enough and steep enough to be certain of quick death.

But certainty in this world is deceptively slippery.

Pilate knew his solution would not fail.

He had remembered a recently captured notorious insurrectionist named Barabbas. A member of the Sicarri, infamous for the short curved swords they used to assassinate Jews they marked as traitors, Barabbas had proudly confessed to killing more than twenty Jews, usually by sneaking up behind them in a crowd and stabbing them in the liver. The Romans had arrested him as he led an attempt to steal a supply train of mules.

It was the custom to release one prisoner to the Jews at Passover. Few were those who might want this killer loose among the general population.

Barabbas, of course, was the solution.

Pilate stood. Silence rippled back through the crowd, so that when he spoke, all heard him clearly.

"Which one do you want me to release to you—Barabbas, or Jesus who is called the Messiah?"

Pilate sat again, expecting the obvious answer to the artful dilemma he had placed upon the Jews.

He might have received it, had he not attributed kingship to Yeshua. But his reminder of Yeshua's messianic claim played directly into the anger of a crowd fanatically determined to preserve its religion by ridding themselves of a heretic.

"Not this man!" It was a roar that surged forward. "But Barabbas!"

Among the crowd there were a few weak shouts for the prophet, but in the confusion of the swaying mob, these people were beaten and dragged away by Caiaphas's men. No others dared to resist the outcry for Yeshua's blood.

"Barabbas! Barabbas!"

Pilate was astounded. Before he could react, however, a slave brought him a wax tablet with a message from his wife: "Have nothing to do with that innocent man, for I have suffered a great deal in a dream because of Him."

It was an ominous inscription arriving at an ominous moment. The night before Caesar's assassination, Calpurnia, Caesar's third wife, had dreamed of Caesar's torn and bloody toga and had unsuccessfully tried to prevent his departure in the morning. All Romans knew of the dream, and all Romans treated dreams with respect.

For Pilate, however, it was far too late to take his wife's advice.

Pilate stood. It took five minutes for the crowd to settle. Five minutes with sweat growing heavy on Pilate's face. Sweat he dared not wipe for fear of showing weakness.

When finally he could speak without yelling, Pilate asked, "So what should I do with Yeshua, the one called the Christ?" He not only unwittingly repeated his mistake, but he had also thrown it at them with the imperial arrogance of Rome.

"Crucify Him!" The roar from the crowd was like an army charging forward. "Crucify Him!"

Pilate looked sideways at Yeshua. The prophet was cloaked with resigned sadness but had not lost His air of deep, intense peace.

"But My kingdom is not of this world."

A soldier who reaches governorship is not bullied easily.

Pilate raised his arms and held them high until he had the crowd's silence. "Why? What crime has He committed? I have found no reason to sentence Him to death. I will therefore flog Him and let him go."

"Crucify Him! Crucify Him!" The shouts became more frenzied.

Pilate wondered for a moment if the mob would attack. He didn't wait to give it the opportunity. Above the deafening noise, he motioned to his soldiers to take Yeshua back inside the palace.

CHAPTER FIFTY-SIX

I stood at the edge of the cliff. Wind pushed against my face, its freedom mocking me.

The sky. The corner of the distant city. The red stone of the hills. All of it filled my eyes. As a last sight of the world, it was better than a sword slashing downward, or disbelief at blood pouring from a speared belly, or fevered thrashings against dirty sheets, or dark cold water closing in, or any of a number of possible final images.

I was hopeful, too, that my death would be quick.

Eyes closed, all that remained was to dive forward into emptiness. The blue sky and red stone hills in my mind would be a balm in those final seconds. Time would have no meaning once my skull exploded against rock.

There would be only nothingness.

At the whipping pillar, as the soldiers gathered around Yeshua and began to strip Him, Pilate knew what to expect. During his long career, he had often been among the enlisted soldiers who engaged in the ancient custom—the games of mockery that followed after a criminal had been whipped bloody.

One soldier already held a purple robe. Another soldier had gathered thorn branches and woven them into a crown to force upon Yeshua's head. From the vulgar banter Pilate overheard, these soldiers found it humorous that this lone, naked figure had claimed to be king. They would savage Him for it and, in so doing, vent their hatred for Jews, a conquered people who refused to play the role of the conquered.

Several soldiers forced Yeshua to bend over the waist-high pillar. Runnels had been gouged into the ground below to drain blood, and flies collected on the small pools of red that lay stagnant from the earlier whippings of two convicted robbers.

A burly man stood ready on each side of the pillar, each holding a whip of leather strands woven around dozens of small shards of pottery. They waited for a signal from the governor.

Pilate told himself he was letting an innocent man be whipped for a good reason. He hoped the intense pain of the scourging would force Yeshua to defend Himself against the accusations. Pilate hoped, too, that once he showed a bloody, beaten man to the crowd—especially a beaten Jew to a crowd of other Jews—a collective pity would satiate the lust for His death.

Pilate nodded.

Soldiers kicked Yeshua's legs apart to expose all parts of His body equally.

With a grunt of effort, one of the burly men swung his whip down, cracking the thongs of leather against Yeshua's back. As he pulled the whip away, his companion aimed lower and lashed savagely from the other side. Shards of pottery raked Yeshua and curled around the inside of His thighs.

Incredibly, Yeshua did not cry out.

His silence spurred both men into an enthusiastic attack of alternating whips that caused instant rivers of blood to blossom across His shoulders, ribs, and legs.

Pilate kept waiting for the man to cry out. Instead, Pilate broke first. "Enough!" he barked.

Pilate turned his back as the soldiers swarmed in with the robe and the crown of thorns. Yet his ears could not block out the jeers of their taunts. Nor the thuds of their blows against the beaten man's face.

CHAPTER FIFTY-SEVEN

I discovered I could not do it. Standing at the edge of the cliff, I could not will myself to close my eyes and embrace death by diving forward. The spark of life burned too brightly.

I have searched myself many times since, wondering if fear or cowardice stopped me.

With all honesty, I believe it was neither.

As I closed my eyes to ready myself to jump, I could not hold the blue sky or red stone hills as my final image. Instead my daughter's face pushed its way into my mind. I saw it not defeated or in agony, but as it had been before the flames had melted the flesh of her legs: beautiful, innocent, and full of love for me. It reminded me of how much penalty I deserved because of my folly.

At that moment, I finally realized that death was too easy an escape. A more just punishment would be to live out my life with my daughter and her crippled, scarred legs as reminders of what I had done.

Pilate preceded Yeshua and His escort to the front of the crowd. The voices had become hoarse from shouting. Only a minority of

Jews wanted Yeshua dead, but their fanaticism made up for their lack of numbers.

At the sight of Pilate, the jostling and unruliness calmed.

"Look," Pilate said, "I am bringing Yeshua out to you. I want you to know that I find nothing against Him."

Pilate crossed his arms and stared at them. He did not want more of his own speech to diminish the pitiful horror of what he was about to do.

Moments later, the soldiers pushed Yeshua forward.

Pilate had guessed correctly. For a moment, no man in the crowd spoke as all strained to see the prophet from Galilee.

Yeshua was too exhausted to lift His head and face them squarely. He shivered from shock and pain. The purple robe was black with His blood. The crown of thorns had been jammed so securely on His head that more blood streamed down His cheeks and neck.

"Here is the man!" Pilate said.

Only a second passed before Caiaphas screamed, "Crucify Him! Crucify Him!"

It was enough to send the crowd into another frenzy. Not even Pilate's raised arms could stop it. He was forced to wait until the cries finally faded.

"You crucify Him," Pilate said, directing his words at Caiaphas. "I find Him not guilty."

Pilate spoke with a finality that was clear in the set of his square face. Enough had been done to the man. Pilate intended to provide an imperial escort to take Yeshua to Galilee.

Caiaphas saw that determination. Finally, forced to the wall, Caiaphas made known the true charge held against Yeshua. It explained, too, why Herod had sent the prophet back unjudged.

Caiaphas said, "By our laws, He ought to die because He called Himself the Son of God."

Pilate felt a lurch of sliding visceral fear. The Son of God.

Soldier or not, he was susceptible to superstition. The uncanny peace of his prisoner, the silence of the man against all accusations. What kind of spirit ruled this man, that He would make such a claim?

Then anger displaced the fear as Pilate realized the implications of Caiaphas's statement. Because, worse, the emperor was considered a god. If word were to reach Caesar that another had claimed divinity and had not received punishment . . .

"This is a new matter," Pilate snarled at Caiaphas. "I should throw the case out simply because you failed to cite this earlier. Instead, I will interview the prisoner again. In private."

* * *

"Where are You from?" Pilate asked Yeshua.

"But My kingdom is not of this world."

Yeshua gave Pilate no answer. Blood had crusted in His beard. He stood half crippled from torn flesh and muscles. But as always, He maintained the unearthly calm that so unnerved the Roman governor.

"You won't talk to me?" Pilate demanded, still angry that Caiaphas had manipulated him. "Don't You realize that I have the power to release You or crucify You?"

Yeshua answered, "You would have no power over Me at all unless it were given to you from above. So the one who brought Me to you has the greater sin."

"But My kingdom is not of this world."

* * *

"If you had not taken away our rights to capital punishment," Caiaphas told Pilate, "you would not be faced with this problem."

They stood at the edge of the restless crowd. Yeshua was still inside the palace.

"That is the past," Pilate answered. "The man will be set free. I have no grounds to order his death."

"There will be rioting."

"Over one man?"

"You Romans never understand the Jews," Caiaphas said. "This trial is not merely about a magician seducing the people with his heretical claims. Our freedom of religion is at stake. That is why the crowd is so determined to see Him crucified."

"You have a stench that offends me," Pilate said. "This is about you and a battle for power. You are jealous of what this man has because of all who follow Him. Don't try to dab perfume on a rotting carcass by claiming religious piety."

Caiaphas gave Pilate a silky smile of hatred. "As you well know," Caiaphas answered, "your own power is slipping. You have mishandled other affairs; Tiberius Caesar is tired of disturbances in Judea. He has charged you with upholding our religious customs."

"He has charged me with upholding the law."

Caiaphas shook his head, sensing victory. "If you release this man, you are not a friend of Caesar. Anyone who declares himself a king is a rebel against Caesar."

It was not a subtle threat.

On his index finger, Pilate wore the gold ring engraved "Caesar's friend," a symbol the emperor had bestowed on Pilate before his departure from Rome. Did he want to keep the ring?

Behind Caiaphas's accusation was obvious political blackmail. If Pilate did not do as requested, the Sanhedrin could send a delegation to Tiberius with two charges against him: direct disobedience to the emperor's wish that the Jews be allowed to handle their own religious affairs and neglect of duty for failing to punish a subversive attempting to set himself up as king.

Pilate had no place to go, unless he was willing to sacrifice his political career for a peasant.

He had Yeshua brought before the crowd.

"Here is your king!" Pilate said. These Jews had spent generations defying Rome, declaring allegiance only to their God. If Pilate was going to be defeated, at the very least he wanted to expose their hypocrisy.

"Away with Him," they yelled. "Away with Him—crucify Him!"

"What? Crucify your king?"

"We have no king but Caesar," Caiaphas and the other leaders shouted back.

Another time, Pilate might have enjoyed victory. Not only had he just heard Caiaphas pledge loyalty to Rome, but the chief religious leaders of the Jews had also just denied the lordship of their almighty God.

But this was not a moment to enjoy. The crowd had begun to shout again for crucifixion.

Pilate ordered a slave to fetch him a golden bowl with water. It was his last resort. Surely if he declared the execution of Yeshua a judicial murder, the crowd would respect this rarely used custom and let Yeshua go.

Pilate rose from the judgment seat to perform the symbolic act. He washed his hands in full view of the crowd.

"I am innocent of the blood of this man," he said. "The responsibility is yours!"

Caiaphas led the crowd by calling out the Old Testament formula reply for accountability. "We will take responsibility for His death—we and our children!" Caiaphas shouted.

The frenzied crowd picked up the chant. "We and our children will be responsible for His death!"

Pilate spoke with weariness to a nearby guard, pronouncing his final verdict in Latin for the records.

"Let Him be crucified."

CHAPTER FIFTY-EIGHT

I remained on the edge of the cliff, uncaring of the passage of time. I did not want to die; neither did I want to live.

What then, I asked myself again and again.

What then?

In a small courtyard surrounded by the soldiers' barracks, a centurion—his grizzled face reflecting his boredom with a duty he'd carried out dozens of times—organized the required soldiers and wood beams to execute the criminals sentenced earlier. A slave paced at the fringes of the group, carrying two bags—one with nails and a hammer, the other with the provisions to last the soldiers during their guard vigils beneath the crosses.

Outside the barracks, in the morning sunshine that already promised heat would later reflect from the city buildings, the narrow streets should have been quiet as the shops, bazaars, and markets had closed for a festival day. Yet a crowd of hundreds waited, lining both sides of the street into the quarter of Acra. Many in the crowd were the elders and Pharisees of the Sanhedrin, their gray beards bobbing as they discussed the events with great heat. Caiaphas and the chief priests had disappeared, choosing to present public disinterest once they had been assured of the death of the prophet. Many of the others, however, were friends of Yeshua and curious onlookers, astounded and helpless at hearing that the man from Galilee had been captured and sentenced privately and quickly.

The centurion was finally satisfied that everything was ready. He carried a substantial paunch, his knees were arthritic, and he did not look forward to walking the steep cobblestone streets and beyond to the place of execution. So, with a long sigh and a tired wave of his hand, he sent the procession ahead to the street and the waiting spectators.

Their expectations of drama were not disappointed.

They saw a man with a crown of thorns pressed into His head, a man haggard from the pain of betrayal, whose mental anguish had been great enough to draw blood from the pores of His skin. He had not had food or drink during a sleepless night of inquisition, and His welted and bruised skin had been flayed raw the length of His body. He bent nearly double as He dragged the heavy beam of lumber that rested on His shoulders.

The crowd's first view of the fallen Messiah drew a ripple of gasps of excited horror. Then the people closest to Yeshua read the inscription on the sign that dangled in Yeshua's face from the end of the beam, partially obscuring His vision. The gasps became exclamations of surprise, and the nearest elders quickly dispatched runners to Caiaphas.

Pilate had dispensed with the customary herald who carried a wooden board to proclaim the nature of the crime. Instead, he had ordered this sign, scrawled with a stick of gypsum, and written in Latin, Hebrew, and Greek so that no person would fail to understand the simple message:

"The King of the Jews!"

Women on both sides of the street wept openly. Even had they not known the man or the situation, the pitiful sight would have torn their hearts.

Yeshua fell repeatedly beneath the weight of the beam. Where His body was not too badly ripped from His earlier whipping, His taunt muscles lay flat against bone, showing a man accustomed to work and easily capable of such a load. But He had lost too much blood, suffered from physical shock, and reached the verge of unconsciousness from thirst. Because of the incline of the road and the uneven cobbles, He would have had difficulty simply walking without the burden of rough-hewn lumber scraping against His raw back.

When He fell, the grizzled centurion dispassionately beat Him with the side of his spear, as if Yeshua were a stubborn mule.

What tore most at the women's hearts was Yeshua's struggle to continue. He fell and bore the beatings silently, somehow getting to His feet one more time. Yet each time He stumbled it took Him longer to regain His feet, with effort so excruciatingly obvious that men in the crowd had to refrain from stepping forward to help Him.

Some who read of my small part in this from other sources might say I was a traveler, at that moment arriving in Jerusalem for the Passover. But what pilgrim would arrive after the Passover?

I had actually just slowly passed the villas and gardens of Bezetha on my way back into Jerusalem. As I had my own share of misery—though none to compare with His—and as I was full of my own sorrow and emptiness, I did not see the procession until I was almost upon it, just outside the Tower Gate.

When I did lift my eyes, I merely saw a bloody man on His knees with a beam of lumber lying across the backs of His calves. A centurion repeatedly struck His shoulders with the side of his spear. The bloody man tried to push Himself up, but simply collapsed again and again.

Behind Him were two other men, also carrying crossbeams. Each of the three was guarded by four soldiers.

Perhaps it was my sudden interest, or that the centurion faced my direction. Certainly it made a difference that I was a lone traveler heading into the city and easily noticed. Whatever the reason, the centurion's eyes met mine—and he beckoned me forward.

All eyes in the crowd turned on me.

"You," the centurion said to me, "come here."

CHAPTER FIFTY-NINE

One did not ignore the command of Roman soldiers, so I obeyed. But not with fear. For one thing, I didn't care enough about my own life. For another, I knew I had the protection of money. Unless the centurion struck me dead on the spot, if he accused me of some offense—though I couldn't imagine what—I could easily hire a defense. Romans are sticklers for the law, and I believed I would not be unfairly tried.

"Carry this cross," the centurion said, tapping me on the shoulder with his spear to conscript me into service. "We go as far as the Hill of the Skull."

Although I stood a head taller than the centurion, I obeyed without resistance. It would have been foolish to do otherwise.

Standing beside the man—who was still on His knees and gasping from exhaustion like a lathered, driven horse—I lifted the beam of wood and rested it on the meat of my right shoulder. He was so beaten, so bloody, that even then I paid no special attention to Him. And, knowing how it felt to be utterly drained, I shifted my position and offered my free hand to help Him up.

Not until He was on His feet, not until He lifted His face and shone those eternal eyes directly into my soul did I recognize Him.

Yeshua. The Messiah.

"Simon," He said, addressing me with the short form of my name. It came out as a mumbled whisper. His lips were swollen, and His tongue pushed against a snapped tooth. "Remember My instructions to you. And remember you are a child of God. Let Him provide the healing."

Simon. The man knew my name!

Later, I would contemplate the compassion of a man who, in the depths of this degradation, reached out to me. Later, I would come to realize that He knows each of us by name. But then, in that moment, I could only marvel that He knew me.

Simon.

Before I could speak, women broke into weeping wails. They had taken advantage of the procession's halt and had moved to surround us. They threw themselves on the road in front of us, begging the centurion to set Yeshua free.

On His entrance into Jerusalem on the Sunday before, Yeshua had wept over the women of Jerusalem. Now, they wept for Him.

Yeshua shook His head and spoke more clearly than I would have expected from a man so thoroughly beaten and exhausted. "Daughters of Jerusalem, don't weep for Me, but weep for yourselves and for your children. For the days are coming when they will say, 'Fortunate indeed are the women who are childless, the wombs that have not borne a child and the breasts that have never nursed.' People will beg the mountains to fall on them and the hills to bury them."

They stared at Him in amazement and bewildered disbelief. Infertility was a curse. She who did not bear her husband a child was looked down upon by all other women, in danger of being replaced by another wife. And, married or not, she faced poverty and lonely old age as a widow.

At that moment, with the weight of His cross firmly on my

back, I shared their shock at His response to their crying out on His behalf.

In my old age, of course, I would understand the literal prophecy of His words. When the Romans laid siege on Jerusalem, stories reached me in Cyrene of desperate, frenzied women roasting and eating their own children. And, with the scattering of the Jews, there was good reason to fear what awaited our people in the centuries ahead.

Yet since that moment of straining to rise with His cross, I have also come to believe that Yeshua was firmly rejecting their pity—and mine—because it was misplaced. When all we see is the man, the fallen prophet, we fail to see His kingdom beyond. We mourn His suffering when, instead, we should mourn the reason He suffered. Among the burdens He accepted by turning toward His place of execution were my own puny sins, my despair and hopelessness, and a selfishness that kept me apart from God.

I carried the cross for Him.

Too soon, the Hill of the Skull loomed above us.

CHAPTER SIXTY

The messengers dispatched by Caiaphas reached Pilate, who sat weary in his magistrate's chair.

By the way they were dressed, it was obvious who they were. And they could only be before him again for one reason. "Have I not finished your troublesome business?" Pilate asked.

"It is the sign on His cross," the first messenger said. "Change it from 'The King of the Jews' to 'He said, I am King of the Jews.'"

Pilate leaned forward and glared, then waved them away. "What I have written, I have written. It stays exactly as it is."

Golgotha, the Hill of the Skull, was just north of the city. It was not named, as many think, for the skulls of the dead abandoned around the execution sites; Jewish law forbids exposure of human bones. Instead, as anyone can see, the Hill of the Skull is just that: a high, rounded, rocky plateau like the dome of a man's head, worn by wind and rain to a dull gray. Two shallow caves, side by side, and a lower, larger cave centered below, form the eyes and gaping mouth. At certain times of day, when the sun's light casts black shadows across those depressions, it becomes such a vision of a gaunt face that any wind moaning across its barren stone seems to speak of the cries and groans and cursings of all those who have died tortured deaths on the hill.

As we arrived, I heard new voices join the crowd, voices that began to stridently jeer Yeshua. It wasn't until the centurion allowed me to set down the beam of wood that I saw who it was.

Caiaphas and the other priests had arrived, probably coming from temple services that allowed them, as always, to proclaim their holiness before God and man. They and other elders were circulating through the crowd, encouraging people to hurl insults at Yeshua as He stood bowed, waiting for the soldiers to begin the process of crucifixion.

Since Pilate had refused to alter the sign, it appeared that the distinguished members of the Sanhedrin were now forced to participate in the crucifixion, if only to incite derision, fearing that some in the crowd might take the sign to heart.

If any other man had been standing there—beaten, nearly naked, crusted with blood, hands bound, and about to be nailed to a cross—their fear of him would have been ridiculous. But Yeshua, swaying as He was from hunger and pain, still commanded respect. He was like a large rock jutting high above the ocean, impervious to the loud, vain splashing of the waves against its base.

Behind Him, into the ground the soldiers planted the beam I had carried to this place of execution.

◻ ◻ ◻ ◻ ◻ ◻ ◻ ◻ ◻

Crucifixion is a simple process.

After the upright beam is positioned on the ground, the crossbeam is set on it. The victim is forced onto his back and laid upon the upright beam with his arms extended on the crossbeam. A long sharp nail is driven into each hand. Sometimes, when executioners have little skill or time, they pound the nail halfway up the flesh of the forearm, confident that eventually the victim's weight will tear the arm's soft flesh until the bones of the wrist meet the nails and arrest the downward slide of the body. Once the victim has been secured to the crosspiece, soldiers use ropes to draw him upward, and bind the crosspiece to the upright with rope or nails.

At this point, however, the soldiers are far from finished. If the victim were left hanging in this manner, death would arrive too quickly from suffocation as the body's unsupported weight pulled against the lungs. So the soldiers turned the victim's lower body sideways and pushed the legs upward before driving spikes through the ankles.

Only then would the soldiers step aside.

The pain is so great that a man is sometimes unable to scream. His brain floods with agony from the different parts of his body. Flies arrive to settle on his blood and eyes and nose to torment him.

Yet the real pain has not yet begun. He will usually choose the lesser agony of shifting to hang from the nails in his hands, simply because it is unbearable to place any weight on the fragmented bones of his ankles.

But he will begin to suffocate. His lungs will strain for the sweetness of air until his throat rattles. A man's will to live is an unreasoning desperation, and it ignores his wish to die. So he fights for air by pushing up with cramping thigh muscles, supporting his weight on the iron spikes in his ankles.

When he can no longer endure this pain, he will sag again, until his lungs suck for air and he pushes his weight on his ankles again. He will alternate between these two agonies, knowing it may take hours and sometimes days before exhaustion and dehydration finally send him into black oblivion.

And the entire time it takes to die, his body will only be a scant foot or two off the ground.

This death is what awaited Yeshua.

□|□|□|□|□|□|□|□|□

There is a merciful Jewish tradition that allows women to offer the condemned a cup of strong wine mixed with a bitter gall, a brew that dulls pain. Yeshua tasted it when the soldiers passed it to Him, then refused it.

He said nothing as the soldiers drove Him to His knees. Nothing as they pushed Him onto His back. And nothing as the point of the first spike was pressed against His right palm.

As for me, I was a coward. I turned my head. The hammer came down with the peculiar clang and thud of iron hitting iron into wood. Against those two forces, iron's impact on the flesh is soundless, if not for the screams of the victim.

Yeshua, however, met the beginning of His death with full submission, as silent as a slaughtered Passover lamb before the altar.

When I found the courage to look again, blood streamed dark from His pierced palms and soaked into the hard, cold ground.

CYRENE

Upon my return home to Cyrene, I did not disembark from the two-masted sailing vessel that had carried me the final leg of my journey from Alexandria. Instead, I remained aboard the ship in the harbor.

I had traveled for six weeks after leaving Jerusalem. During that time, I had spent hours deciding what I must do. Even so, I had no certainty as to the right course of action.

I sent a messenger from the ship to Jaala, carrying the letters I had written during my Passover stay in Jerusalem. He also bore the scroll that would tell my wife the truth about the evening of the fire that had destroyed our family.

As had been my custom, I had worked late into the afternoon at my accounts in the small warehouse, long after most men had returned to their homes and families. And, as had also been my custom, I had eased my solitude with wine. I was close to drunk as I worked through some difficult transactions in the light of an oil lamp.

I had forgotten. Jaala had planned a celebration to mark Vashti's birth date. My daughter arrived to tell me herself, her dark hair combed and pinned back, her dark eyes flashing with importance. She carried a kitten in her arms, one of many strays that tried my patience.

I became surly at Vashti's insistence to return home. When she reminded me of the celebration, my irritation increased, more at myself for having forgotten than at her.

Vashti set the kitten down on my table. She clutched at my hem as she begged me to set aside my work. The kitten stepped onto my accounts, and I saw a place to vent my temper. I callously knocked the animal aside, and it tumbled into the oil lamp, beginning a horrible chain of events.

As the lamp fell, oil and fire spilled onto the fine wrap of silk around Vashti's legs. She shrieked in panic and pulled away from me before I could beat the flames into submission.

She ran.

A growing flame snaked around her tender legs.

I stumbled after her.

In her desperation, she fell against an unsteady table, which crashed to the floor, pinning her in a pile of dry rags beneath the table. The flames took hold of the rags instantly, and her legs became a torch.

I tried to pull her away. I felt useless because of my wine-addled brain. In her terror, Vashti clawed at my face and arms. When I finally disentangled her from the table and rags, the fire had begun to spread.

I had to save Vashti before I could turn my efforts to stopping the fire. I flailed ineffectually at the flames on her legs. I finally realized I could snuff the fire by rolling my child in a rug. But by this time, too many valuable seconds had passed.

The fire around me had flickered from piles of cloth to other piles of cloth. Stopping it was unlikely, obvious to me even in my impaired state. I picked Vashti up and, with her screams of agony in my ears, made an unsteady path of escape.

As smoke began to blind me, I fell twice. When I reached the air outside, I was grateful we were alive.

Vashti continued to scream. With a jolt, I became aware of a pattern in her screams and realized it was more than the crazed sounds of senseless desperation and pain. But I could not understand her hysterical words.

She tried to pull herself back into the warehouse and fought me as I restrained her.

By then, passersby had begun to run toward us, drawn by Vashti's shrieks. Others ran, shouting, to alert neighbors to the fire.

At some point in the confusion and screaming and roar of the growing fire, I became aware of Jaala shaking my shoulder.

She had come to the warehouse because she could not find Ithnan. She had hoped to find our firstborn son—only six years old—with his older sister, for he followed Vashti everywhere.

And in that moment of horror, I understood Vashti's hysteria. She'd brought her brother on her errand, knowing how he loved to explore the rolls of cloth and stacks of merchandise.

Ithnan was inside the burning warehouse.

I ran toward the great, roaring monster that held my firstborn son in its jaws. Just inside the door, swirling dense smoke drove me, choking, to my knees. I could see nothing.

I yelled in desperation, crawling and sweeping with my hands, hoping to clutch the tiny ankles of my son.

A narrow beam of burning wood fell, striking me on the left side of my face, searing through my beard and skin. I didn't even feel the pain.

My son was somewhere in the fire. A fire of my doing.

Another beam struck my head. In my last moments of consciousness, I hoped for my own death.

I had fallen so near the entrance that those who fought the fire doused me and the flames with their first buckets of water. I was pulled from the wreckage of my business, close to death, hours from reviving but alive.

Not so my firstborn son.

After the last of the fire had been tamed, someone discovered his body curled in a corner, spared from flame. But smoke had sucked the life from his lungs.

His body in death was as it had been in life. Perfect.

During the hours I had been unconscious, Vashti had shrieked over and over again that the fire had been her fault. In my first waking moments—unaware of Vashti's claim of responsibility and deeply ashamed—I had pretended confusion, determined to tell Jaala when the time was right.

Coward that I was, I delayed the truth again and again. The longer I let the lie continue and the more people heard it with grave sympathy, the more difficult it became to confess. Finally I could not turn back and take off the mantle of determined hero that had fallen upon me.

My torment had just begun.

My undivulged knowledge became a millstone of self-hatred, and as I closed myself off from Jaala, it destroyed what little love remained in our marriage.

Only a parent can truly comprehend the depths of my remorse, anguish, and self-loathing in the months that followed. Although I had not deliberately hurt my daughter, I was responsible. If, somehow, I could have blocked that responsibility from my mind and heart, her agony was there daily to remind me, not only in her cries of pain but also in the expression her eyes held and in how she recoiled from me when I tried to hug her.

I had burned her legs; I had seared her soul. I had once been her adored father, the man who could do anything and fix anything. Then in one horrible moment, I had betrayed her trust, destroyed her life, and killed my firstborn son.

Yet the world saw me as a valiant, heroic man for saving my daughter, for my struggle against the fire.

My remorse and anguish and self-loathing became the despair I had carried into Jerusalem.

CHAPTER SIXTY-TWO

As I waited on the ship during the first day in Cyrene, not ten minutes went by that I did not strain my eyes toward my villa on the nearby hillside.

My pleas to Jaala had been simple. If she could take me back after hearing my letters and confession, she should hang a dark blanket from a window, easily visible to my hoping eyes.

I had intended to be noble and romantic in my efforts to win back her heart, refusing to shame her with my unworthy presence.

The hours of bright sunshine and blue sky passed to mock my despair. Instead of nobility, I was a fool. I had to restrain myself from rushing up the streets to beg at the door for a glimpse of her face.

The entire day passed.

As I waited, I tried to imagine her reaction. I did not even know if she had decided to allow someone to read the letters to her. The messenger had been greeted at the door by a servant, who would only confirm that the mistress of the household would accept them.

I tried to remain in seclusion on the ship; if Jaala would not have me back, I did not want to shame myself further by making her rejection public knowledge. Because of the seclusion, however, I did not dare make inquiries of my household. I did not even know if my daughter still lived.

Night fell. I settled into the bowels of the ship, hoping that every creak and every sway would signal Jaala stepping on board to throw herself into my arms. I did not sleep.

Dawn arrived.

Jaala did not.

CHAPTER SIXTY-THREE

After another day, I could no longer fool myself. Enough time had passed. Jaala had made her decision. I could wait years and the blanket would not appear at a window of our villa.

Still, I did not order the boat to set sail.

This near, I could not leave. I imagined Jaala's every move in the villa. In my mind, I listened as she hummed, watched as she brushed her hair, stood beside her as she looked down on my ship in the harbor.

All the while, I knew a final good-bye was approaching. Once the ship left the harbor, I would not return. I planned to re-visit Jerusalem. I could manage my business affairs from there and see to it that Jaala lived a good life without me. It would not be a hopeless existence for me. Keen as I would miss her, despair no longer overwhelmed my soul. Pascal would welcome me in Je-rusalem, as would some of the followers of Yeshua, for I had turned to them in the days after the crucifixion, seeking answers about the man on the cross and the final events of that Friday.

I remained at the cross as the soldiers gambled for the rights to keep Yeshua's seamless clothing. I remained in the afternoon as a darkness covered the land—caused, perhaps, by a rare but not unheard of dust storm swirling above us or by an event astronomers could have predicted from the way stars moved in the sky. I remained until Yeshua cried out that it was finished, as the roar of an earthquake punctuated His last words, as the centurion was forced to exclaim that surely the man on the cross was the Son of God.

I watched the soldiers thrust a spear into Yeshua's motionless body to make sure He was dead. I saw watery blood spill from the hole in His side. I was there when the soldiers broke the legs of the two thieves to hasten their deaths before sundown, still there as the thieves rattled their last breaths, suffocating because their legs supported them no longer.

When Yeshua's body was taken from the cross, I finally returned to Pascal and Seraphine. Pascal had found my note to him along with the document and the sealed letters. He gave them all back to me without asking why I had intended to take my life and without asking why I had changed my mind. He was a good friend.

After, I searched out as many of Yeshua's followers as I could, asking questions about the man of miracles. My brief contact with Him as I carried the cross had further compelled me to learn about Him.

Judas, I discovered, had died hours before the man he had betrayed. After hearing the verdict against Yeshua, he had flung the silver back at the high priests, and remorse drove him to the act I could not do. He was discovered days later hanging from a branch by the same girdle he'd once used to store his thirty pieces of silver.

I am convinced, however, that Yeshua would have forgiven Judas. For I had watched as Yeshua died in agony on the cross, yet He was concerned not about Himself, but about others. To the thief beside Him, Yeshua had promised that heaven waited. Upon seeing His mother weeping, Yeshua had pledged her into a disciple's care. For the jeering crowd, He had prayed that God would forgive them.

Many times I have wondered about this request. What I have decided is this: Yeshua had a heart that saw much more than any other man. On the cross, looking down at the crowd, He felt and understood the pain and the burdens each person carried. A Pharisee, perhaps, had worries about a son who preferred wine and harlots to religious instruction. Maybe a woman was racked with the grief of losing a child. Or another man sleepless with the agony that accompanies doubts about his wife's faithfulness. Each of them—as with all of us—would have kept those fears private, unknown to the rest of the world. Each of them—as with all of us—had the heartaches, hurts, and sorrows that come with lives lived apart from God.

As Yeshua saw their pain, He saw, too, that most of the people in the crowd were so intent upon their own lives, so apart from God's presence that they failed even to look to God for help. He saw them as the poor, pitiable, weak creatures that they were.

Yet He knew what would heal them and give them peace: God's love, given freely. And so the plea from the man condemned to die because of His love for those in need: "Father, forgive these people, because they don't know what they are doing."

This is why I believe Yeshua would have embraced Judas, had Judas truly wished it.

All of this I believe to be true, even if Yeshua were only man.

But if He were only man, His forgiveness would not have erased my guilt as it did.

During my time in Jerusalem after His crucifixion, as I learned more about Yeshua and what He did and taught, I began to understand that He was the Passover lamb who had stood in my place. This Lamb, unlike any other lamb, had gone to His death willingly and aware. No other altar sacrifice was needed for me to be able to approach God, to have the mask of my selfishness removed so that I could see the warmth of the light that had always been there.

If Yeshua were only man, I would not have found the joy in the peace that had sent me home to Cyrene with hope.

When finally I gave reluctant orders for the ship to prepare to sail, I remained on deck, staring at the white of my villa so hard and long that my eyes ached from the brightness of the sun.

I still wanted to believe Jaala would take me back. Perhaps the activity on the ship—if she was watching—would show her I would act upon my word. Perhaps, with my departure looming, she would have a change of heart.

In those minutes before departure, I resigned myself to life without her. But I was not without a certain joy. In Jerusalem, I had found redemption. I knew I could begin to live life looking forward, not backward.

As two of the crew began to untie the heavy ropes that held the ship to the wharf, I heard a cry that was almost lost among the shrieking of the gulls overhead.

I saw a girl running toward the ship.

Vashti? Yes! Unless my eyes and my hope had deceived me.

I stopped the men and jumped from the ship.

The child continued to run toward me.

My daughter was running!

Her face was bright with joy as she jumped into my arms. Her body felt so tiny and vulnerable that it almost broke my heart to think I had to leave.

I set her down and squatted so I could look into her beautiful face.

"Mama wanted you to see that I can walk," she said proudly. "My legs are not pretty, but they don't hurt and I can walk and run."

I spoke slowly, afraid my voice would break and in so doing, alarm her. "I am so very glad," I said. For the healing. And that Jaala had sent her. As a gift, it would console me over the lonely years ahead. That the scars remained would always remind me of my own journey from desperation to healing.

I repeated myself. "I am so very glad to see you walking and running, my love."

"It was in a dream," she said. "An angel talked to me in a dream."

"Tell me about your dream," I said softly.

Her eyelids dropped.

"It's important to me," I said.

Vashti began shyly. "I felt silver light that was like a bright star alone in a dark sky. It turned brighter and warm until it filled the sky. An angel spoke to me from the light. He told me he wanted me to walk. When I woke up in the morning, I was happier and my legs started to get better."

"Was that yesterday?" I asked, teasing her with a smile. I was ready to believe her if she said yes.

"No, Papa. Since Passover."

Since Passover.

Miracle or coincidence?

Some, I am sure, will say that deep in her mind, my little girl needed to overcome her own guilt before allowing herself to heal, and that her mind brought forth the vision of an angel to do it. Some will say that the act of the Passover sacrifice sparked some form of self-forgiveness inside her. Some will say that she healed in the weeks since Passover as part of a natural process.

Yet her words echoed the description of what the once-blind beggar had told me in Jerusalem, the sensation of a silver light and the warmth. Passover was when I'd pleaded with Yeshua in Jerusalem to heal my daughter.

Others may scoff at miracles. I knew what I believed, however, and I closed my eyes in a prayer of gratitude.

When I opened my eyes, Vashti was looking at me gravely. With innocence. God must be thanked that our children love us without condition, that Vashti was too young to see me as the driven man who had disappointed her mother so badly. God must be thanked that the scars on her soul had begun to heal.

"Will you tell Mama that I love her very much?" I asked. "If she changes her mind, she can send word to Jerusalem. I will be there . . ." I lost my voice. It took several seconds to compose myself. "I will be there because of work."

An easy escape to give Vashti. She'd heard it often enough before.

"Don't you want to tell her yourself?" Vashti asked. She took my hand. "Mama sent me running down here to reach you before your ship left. She wants you to come home."

Away from the weeping chamber of my own tomb, I now sit in the shade of my villa. I occasionally stir, moving into the sun like a wrinkled lizard, warming the loose, leathered skin that wraps my old bones. Beyond my courtyard are the masts of ships in the harbor. The breathtaking blue expanse of the Mediterranean spreads beyond to meet a cloudless azure sky.

Forty years have passed since my firstborn son died. My thoughts return to the weeping chamber where I stood so recently to mourn him. I am saddened as much by my memories of him as by the knowledge that too soon I will return to the weeping chamber.

And forty years after the events of that Friday, I am able to see more clearly why an innocent man died.

The crowd before Pilate had no notion how prophetic their call for Yeshua's blood to be upon them and their children would be. Word has recently reached me that Jerusalem has fallen. After a six-month siege, the Romans—efficient, determined, ruthless—ended what was at the beginning plainly inevitable to all but the foolish rebel Jews who expected God to rescue them as He had patiently aided Moses, Joshua, David, and all the other heroes whom descending generations of Jews so proudly wear as cloaks of armor. Yet, despite the self-righteous, unceasing, directive prayers that surely rose from Jerusalem, no sea was parted, no pestilence destroyed the enemy, no trumpet calls brought them down, no angel of death visited the Roman army camps. Instead, the mighty city walls were finally broken, the Jewish rebels crucified, and, in the haze of the fire of destruction that drifted across the city, with the background yells of soldiers joyfully pursuing women in the rubble of torn streets, the temple stones were pushed off the plateau to tumble onto the tombs below.

Jerusalem—as Yeshua had predicted—is no more.

Some might say it is fanciful to assert that Jerusalem fell because a small minority of Jews slaughtered an innocent man, but I believe there is some truth in the statement.

Rome would have been content to coexist with Jerusalem for centuries—the mighty empire only fights back when prodded. Jerusalem fell because in the end Rome could no longer tolerate the unchanged blind selfishness, hypocrisy, and fanaticism that had killed Yeshua those four decades earlier.

Jerusalem is no more.

I am grateful that Pascal and Seraphine did not behold the siege. Pascal died gently in his sleep a dozen years ago, and the rich widow Seraphine married a silk trader in Alexandria.

Pilate is gone, recalled to Rome a few years after Yeshua's crucifixion for putting down a Samaritan riot with too much force. Some rumors have it that he killed himself as his career faded. Others say that his wife, Procula, became a follower and led Pilate to the same hope and belief in a man he had ordered crucified.

Peter is gone, too, martyred on a cross for refusing to deny Yeshua one more time. I have heard he declined the honor of dying the same way as his beloved master, however, and the executioners granted his request to be crucified upside down.

I do not know the fate of Caiaphas. Violent or peaceful, whatever end Caiaphas reached is one he deserved. Hatred is its own punishment. The riches his schemes continued to accumulate would not have been worth the last moments of consciousness and the sudden awareness of how utterly cold and lonely it will be for his soul's travel beyond.

My servant has appeared on the villa balcony to interrupt my thoughts. His hands are empty of the cooled juice I had expected. Instead, he has brought a message.

"She calls for you."

I don't ask why. The expression on my servant's face tells me enough.

Slowly, I push myself to my feet. I lean on his arm as he takes me inside. We enter a room in the upper corner; then the servant departs.

I smile at Vashti, who sits beside the bed where she has spent many hours away from her husband and family over the past weeks. Her face is barely composed. While I see in her grief the young girl who clung to me during the sorrows of her innocence, I also see strength and dark-haired beauty, much like Jaala's face in our early years together.

Vashti's younger brothers—our sons Alexander and Rufus, whom Jaala bore in the happier days that followed my return—

would be here, too, but they are helping to establish the Word in other parts of the empire. It is impossible for them to return in time.

Vashti rises and steps away from the bed, allowing me to move closer.

It is hot, but the woman I love shivers beneath her blankets.

Jaala. My wife. God's gift to me. Twice.

My chest is tight with grief. I go to her, blinking away tears.

Although, like me, she is old, and others might see wrinkles in her face, I see only the beauty that entranced me during the songs she softly sang throughout the years. Her body has become so tiny. Her once-dark hair is as white as mine. The delightful strong hands that stroked my face in our youth are now withered, knotted into fists as she fights occasional spasms of pain.

I sit beside her and take one of her hands. I brush her knuckles against my cheek. I do not trust my voice enough to speak first.

"I love you," she says when she finds the energy.

"As I do you."

A part of my mind notices that Vashti has left the room to give us privacy.

When, long ago in the temple, I begged Yeshua to heal Vashti, I had not understood His reply. I had yet to realize that forgiveness earned or bought is not forgiveness, but a transaction. Forgiveness must be given by the one who has been wronged, accepted as a gift by the one who has done wrong.

When a wrong cannot be righted, men have the power to punish.

But who has the power to forgive?

□□□□□□□□□

The sun is lower now, and shadows creep longer on the walls as I sit with Jaala, stroking her hair while she lays still with her eyes closed. I cannot imagine my life without her presence, yet the unimaginable is approaching as surely as the sun must disappear with the shadows that darken.

Jaala opens her eyes.

She sees that I am weeping.

Tears form in her eyes too.

With so many memories and so much I still want to say, I find I can only fall back on what means the most to me on earth.

"I love you," I say.

"And I you," she says. But her smile is small and her voice a whisper. We both know it will not be long.

Her eyes flutter and close.

As she fades from me, I can hardly bear my grief. To console myself, I remind myself I have something to grieve, when I once thought she was gone from me forever.

□□□□□□□□□

We are human, separated from God by our sins, our failings, our selfishness, a vileness abhorrent to God's pureness and righteousness. Much as He loves and wants to claim us, there must be atonement. With Yeshua's death as atonement to replace the sacrificial system that was later destroyed by the Romans, we can be cleansed of our sins.

If we believe in Yeshua and His message.

Indeed, I received forgiveness through Yeshua. It brought me home. But His forgiveness is worthless if He is only man, not Messiah. He cannot be accepted halfway. If the miracles did not truly happen as miracles, He died justly—insane, a fraud, a blasphemer.

How does one decide? Other men in the temple saw cripples walk at His touch, yet in their disbelief they looked for other explanations. Thus, it makes no difference whether a man witnesses miracles with his own eyes or hears of them later—even centuries later—from those who were there.

It is, of course, a matter of faith. But faith has two edges; some use determined disbelief to transform miracles into something natural, while others too eagerly transform natural wonders into miracles.

And so truth becomes lost in the confusion.

◻|◻|◻||◻|◻|◻||◻

Jaala wakes and squeezes my hand, this beautiful woman who pledged her life to me. There is sweat on her forehead. With a damp cloth, I soothe her heated skin.

Her eyes close again. I cannot help myself. I lean down and lightly touch my lips to hers, knowing all the tender kisses we shared will too soon be only memories.

Her eyes remain closed as she whispers her last request. "Sing to me, my love."

I am not sure I understand her words, such is her weakness.

"Sing to me, my love," she whispers again.

And so I sing to her. It is the first time. Always, in our many years together, she has sung to me.

◻|◻|◻||◻|◻|◻||◻

We each have a soul that continues beyond the body. This I know. As I also know ultimately, those who follow God will receive their own glorified physical resurrection. During our lives on earth, we hide ourselves from the One who created our souls—our self-absorption and our vain pursuits of the flesh become a chasm that prevents us from full awareness of Him. None of us can cross that chasm without acknowledging He is there and waiting, without asking for a bridge to reach Him.

That bridge is Yeshua—but only if we believe He is who He claimed to be.

And the ultimate question is this. Did He rise from the dead?

I have had all these years to decide for myself, armed with what witnesses have told me about the events. I now realize His resurrection appearances validated His predictions, His claims, and His message.

Because of those appearances, His disciples were transformed in purpose. Before the crucifixion, Yeshua's teachings were simply radical and almost revolutionary. After the empty tomb, His teachings had eternal significance.

His disciples were transformed in character. Before the crucifixion, they had fled into the night at the first sign of danger. After the empty tomb, they were lions of courage, uncaring of threats or arrest or death. Their joy, and the hope they carried, took this gospel far beyond the borders of their tiny country. Without the astonishing appearance of Yeshua alive from the dead, it is difficult to explain the incredible transformation that pushed the disciples to endure whippings, beatings, jailings, and martyrdom on His behalf.

To suggest that Yeshua didn't die on the cross but went into a brief coma and revived in the coolness of the tomb is hardly plausible. Not after His side was pierced by a spear. And if it did happen, and He woke trapped inside, who rolled the massive stone away for Him?

Certainly not Yeshua. If He were simply a man, revived from

a coma, where would He get the strength after the floggings, the hours of torture, the loss of so much blood? And would a man like this—in that pitiful state—convince anyone He had conquered death?

Certainly not the Roman soldiers, who faced possible execution for failing in their duty. Certainly not His enemies, who wanted the tomb guarded. If they stole the corpse to prevent the rise of a Yeshua cult, why would they not produce the body later when His resurrection was proclaimed?

And certainly not His disciples, so afraid of the Romans that they did not even take part in the burial of their master. If they had arrived to move away the stone, how? These were peasants, unskilled at fighting the soldiers who guarded it. Nor would they have been able to sneak in and move something that massive away—even sleeping soldiers would surely have been alerted by their efforts.

Was Yeshua's body somehow stolen by the disciples? That argument faces the same difficulties as finding an explanation for how the disciples fought the soldiers or moved the stone and took away the body unnoticed. And if somehow they had succeeded in this, why would they have done so? For it would ensure them the same fate as Yeshua—trouble with the Jewish and Roman authorities, with little gained except their deaths.

Some will rationally deny the resurrection of Yeshua because it seems impossible; yet with God, all things are possible. It is neither irrational nor foolish to believe on the basis of the evidence.

With belief, come hope and purpose. And peace.

<hr />

I am still quietly singing when life leaves Jaala. I only know she is gone because her hand relaxes in mine.

I continue to sing because I am determined not to let myself know she has died. As long as I sing, I tell myself, she is still listening to me.

But I am old. My voice begins to fail me.

When I can sing no longer, I place my head on her chest and let my tears soak into the blanket that covers her.

I was not there after the crucifixion when Joseph of Arimathea went to Pilate for permission to bury Yeshua in a private tomb. Nor when the Pharisees requested and received from Pilate continuous armed guards at the entrance of the tomb, worrying that Yeshua's followers might steal the body—who had been proven dead with the spear thrust in His side—and proclaim that the Messiah rose from the dead as He had promised. Nor was I there when another earthquake struck Jerusalem early on Sunday morning, scattering the guards and opening the sealed tomb.

I was, however, in the tomb later that Sunday, to look myself after the reports reached me that Yeshua was alive.

I had to stoop to enter the tomb. When I straightened, I stood in the weeping chamber, the very place where tears had anointed His still, pierced body as faithful followers had wrapped Him in linens and spices three days earlier.

I looked at His burial place and saw all that remained were the empty burial linens. A smile crossed my face as I noticed the wrap that had been used to cover Yeshua's face. The cloth had been folded in half, then folded in half again and left neatly on the stone floor beside the burial linens.

Standing in that weeping chamber, years after Yeshua had set aside His carpenter tools, I understood. And I began to feel an unfamiliar emotion. Joy.

The folded cloth was a simple method of communication, traditional among carpenters, for most could not write. At the completion of a project, a carpenter took water from a bowl to wash the sawdust off his arms and face, dried himself, and folded the towel in the same way, leaving it behind so anyone arriving later would understand the same message Yeshua had left for us in the empty tomb on that Sunday:

It is finished.

No one disturbs my grief.

My wife's hand is now cold. Since the fall of night, I have not moved from her bedside, nor have I let go of her hand.

Dawn has begun the new day. A day without Jaala.

But I am not without hope.

I will see her again.

I know this.

Because I believe.

Mark. But what the hell—he'd told Mark not to go out after returning from school. He'd be okay.

"*. . . Castro Valley. The doctor and his family . . .*"

Artie had a sudden premonition and turned up the volume.

"*. . . apparently were murdered before the house was set on fire. The suspect is in custody at the scene. The Paschelke family was well respected in the community . . .*"

Connie's breaker, had to be. It was the middle of the day and traffic was light; he could be there in maybe half an hour. Artie fumbled his cellular phone out of the glove compartment. He'd call the station and then phone Mitch, have him meet him there as soon as possible. Find out what had happened. This time they had the maniac who'd done it, though he definitely wouldn't be your ordinary murderer.

The drizzle had stopped, leaving little droplets of water glistening on the needles of the pine trees. It was chilly but the sun was out, and Artie guessed it would be warm by midafternoon. The town itself was idyllic, the kind you found on picture-postcard racks in drugstores. Not the proper setting for a brutal murder.

He could smell wet ashes two blocks away, then spotted the reeking heap of blackened timbers just beyond the line of trees that bordered the street. The ambulances had left but the fire trucks were still there, and several police cars. Mitch was watching Connie interview a fire captain.

"You're fast," Artie said. "I just called—"

"I had the radio on between patients and heard the first news flash an hour ago. Thought you might show up."

Artie showed his press pass to a curious cop, and he and Mitch walked over to the ruins. The cameraman was taping Connie's interview, the charred remains of the house in the background.

The house had been set back into a hill, so the rec room had actually been on the first floor. Artie could make out the few sofa spring-coils that marked where the couch had been and the half-melted bulk of the small refrigerator. A singed page from one of Paschelke's medical journals fluttered past and Artie grabbed it. Atenolol for arryhmias, "King of the Beta-Blockers."

He inspected the ruins a moment longer, then drifted over with Mitch to hear Connie's interview.

". . . the intruder apparently broke a window at the back—"

The fire captain was a big man with a mustache flecked with gray and rivulets of dirty sweat that had dried on his cheeks and neck. He was soot-smudged and tired, barely managing to tolerate Connie.

"We found Mrs. Paschelke in the bedroom. Dr. Paschelke and his two daughters were sitting on the couch in the rec room. Apparently they had fallen asleep watching TV."

"They had been"—Connie paused, professionally aware of the audience that would be watching the six-o'clock news—"murdered before the fire started?"

The fire captain nodded, knowing what she wanted. "Their throats were cut. Apparently the killer caught Mrs. Paschelke first, then the doctor and the little girls. All of them were probably asleep when he entered—no signs of any struggle."

"Robbery the motive?"

"Hard to tell. I don't think the police found anything on the guy they picked up. A neighbor phoned in the fire at the first sight of the flames." He sounded puzzled. "I don't know why the suspect hung around; he should have been long gone."

"Dumb," Mitch murmured to Artie. "Too dumb."

Artie spotted a figure huddled in the backseat of one of the police cars. "Let's ask him."

They walked over and peered in the closed windows, then a policeman came over to shoo them away. Artie flashed his press card again, but the cop ignored it. "Sorry, fellas, we've got to book him first. He'll be arraigned this afternoon or tomorrow morning. We'll have a statement then."

Artie had gotten a good look. A bewildered, skinny little man bundled up in dirty pants and a scarf and a worn overcoat two sizes too large. Salvation Army issue—the uniform you wore when you slept in hallways and pushed around a grocery cart with everything you owned in it.

"Some poor homeless bastard who hung around the town," the cop offered. "A few of the neighbors recognized him—he usually got to the recycle boxes an hour before the scavenger guys showed up, grabbed all the bundled newspapers and the bottles worth a refund. Probably how he lived."

"How'd he start the fire?"

"Would you believe it? Booze. The firemen said they could smell it, even over the stink of the ashes. Christ knows *he* smelled of it when we picked him up."

Artie glanced over again at the figure in the backseat of the patrol car. The man was pounding on the closed windows and shouting at them, a frantic look in his eyes. Artie couldn't make out the words.

Mitch said, "He's saying that he knew the two little girls, that he wouldn't have hurt them."

"You read lips?"

Mitch nodded and Artie walked away, embarrassed by the little man's pleading. At his car, Mitch asked, "Did he look like he was drunk to you?"

"Not really—but he's had time to sober up. Think he did it?"

"Do you?"

"Of course not—the devil made him do it." Artie caught Mitch's frown as he slipped into the driver's seat.

"I'm not being funny, Mitch. I'm serious."

CHAPTER 8

Connie would get back to the office before he did, but she'd be tied up most of the afternoon editing the story. Artie figured he had plenty of time to do what Hall had suggested: if seeing was believing, then he ought to see just what William Talbot had looked like. He was no expert but he might be able to glean something.

East Bay Medical Center was only a mile or so from Dr. Paschelke's home and, like the doctor's house, was nestled in among the redwoods. The nurses at the front desk were friendly; the doctor he was eventually referred to was less so.

An elderly Dr. Frank Lassiter, thin and dignified and smelling very faintly of aftershave and strong disinfectant, obviously resented anybody from the media. Artie guessed that sometime in the past he'd paid a heavy price for being misquoted.

Lassiter thumbed Artie's press pass, studied it, then dropped it on his desk and leaned back in his chair, his hands behind his head. "So how can I help you, Mr. Banks?"

"The front desk said you were a colleague of Dr. Paschelke's."

"I'm a senior partner in his medical group." Only the tiniest flicker told Artie that Lassiter had suddenly become more guarded than before. "The police have already been here. I couldn't tell them much of anything except how sorry I was. Apparently the world's going to hell in a

98

Safeway grocery cart." He was cool, distant, and Artie couldn't tell whether he was genuinely sorry or not. He was the opposite of Paschelke; there wasn't much chance the two had gotten along. Paschelke had been a beer and barbecue man: Lassiter would prefer poached salmon and a German white.

"You worked with Dr. Paschelke in the ER?"

Lassiter nodded. "I've worked in the ER from time to time." Then, abruptly, he added, "Why the hell are you here, Banks? My time is valuable; I imagine yours is as well."

"I was a friend of Larry Shea's; he used to work with Dr. Paschelke too."

Lassiter relented. "Affable man. Two of a kind, I'd say."

Which meant that Lassiter had nothing bad to say about them but nothing good, either.

"They worked together on an accident victim," Artie said slowly, watching for any sudden change of expression. "The victim was a man in his sixties named Talbot."

Lassiter studied his fingernails.

"I remember the man. Drs. Shea and Paschelke performed an autopsy on him. I didn't approve." He looked up. "I thought it was unnecessary. They should have waited a few more days, see if any relatives showed up. There was the danger of litigation if they had disapproved. In short, I thought they were a little too eager."

"Did you inspect the body yourself?"

Lassiter shrugged. "Shea wanted to point some things out to me one day. I was busy; I had other matters to attend to. I wasn't particularly interested." He made a show of glancing at his watch.

"What sort of things?" Artie asked.

Lassiter was running out of patience.

"I'm a doctor. I deal with the living, not the dead. I'm experienced in autopsies and postmortems, but I'll be the first to admit there are others more knowledgeable in the field than I. And more interested."

"But you did take a look," Artie persisted.

For the second time there was a small flash of expression.

"I thought they were wasting their time on an unethical procedure. They really should have talked to an anthropologist, not a fellow doctor. I told them that."

It was going to be a contest between him and Lassiter over how little the doctor would tell him.

"Why an anthropologist, Doctor? What was it you saw that made you recommend one?"

"I thought they were letting their fantasies run away with them. A good anthropologist would have brought them down to earth." Lassiter stood up. "Look, Mr. Banks, this conversation could go on forever and I'm a busy man—"

"I'd like to see the body."

Lassiter looked startled. "You're not a relative—it's against regulations. Even if it weren't, it's not possible."

Artie misread him. "Perhaps another doctor who has more time?"

"The family claimed the body this morning," Lassiter said, now bored with the whole conversation. "And that *is* all I know. I never saw them, I never signed the release papers. The nursing supervisor took care of all of that."

Artie stared at him. What family? Aside from the name, there had been no ID for Talbot, no family to notify.

The supervisor wasn't very helpful at all.

"We got a call that the mortuary had come to pick up the body. I countersigned the receipt and filed it and arranged for the showing of the body to the family. A younger brother and a woman, maybe a little older. A cousin, I believe she said. From Mr. Talbot's hometown in Illinois." The nurse smiled slightly. "A suburb of Chicago, Evanston. I had an old boyfriend who came from there."

"You didn't check them out?" Artie asked.

Like Lassiter, she was suddenly less friendly.

"They arrived right behind the mortuary van and had already made arrangements with an airline for shipping the body out. I didn't see any reason to hold them up." She read Artie's dissatisfaction in his face. "I'm not a policeman, Mr. Banks," she said stiffly. "They had ID; everything seemed to be in order."

And the medical center didn't have to foot the bill of a cheap cremation. Artie flipped open his wallet to his press card. "Do you have a phone or an address for them?"

She pursed her mouth, hesitated, then opened a file on her desk and scribbled some information on a piece of paper and slid it across the counter.

"That's their address. We definitely don't give out phone numbers and I probably shouldn't give you that."

Artie stopped at a public phone in the lobby and got the number from Information, then dropped in enough change to connect him to Evanston. The voice at the other end of the line was suspicious and curt and, surprisingly, without an Illinois twang. There was little that the voice would say about the late William Talbot except that they planned to cremate him tomorrow and scatter his ashes over Lake Michigan.

When he hung up, Artie's hand was shaking. Case closed, he thought.

Larry was dead and Talbot's body would be returned to the Mother of Waters.

The only people left who were suspicious of anything at all were he and Mitch.

It was the middle of the afternoon by the time Artie got back to the city. There was no sense in going to the office; Connie would be in the editing room getting the Castro Valley tape ready for the six-o'clock news. If he needed to grab a few hours for Christmas shopping, now was the time. He wanted to be home when Mark got there.

It was chilly for a San Francisco afternoon, cloudy and overcast, the temperature probably in the high thirties—damned cold for the Bay Area. The TV weathermen would call it unseasonal and blame it on the jet stream dropping down from Alaska. At least it wasn't the pineapple express, which picked up moisture in the mid-Pacific and dropped it by the bucketful along the coast and on the Sierras.

Macy's was jammed with shoppers, but he managed to get a ski sweater for Mark and a silver serving tray for Susan. Expensive, but a nice piece of work. He spent ten minutes admiring the displays in store windows, then walked back to Union Square and the underground garage. There was an ice-skating rink at one end of the square and Artie pushed through the crowd of spectators to catch a glimpse of the skaters.

"They've only had this for a couple of years—a few more and it'll be tradition."

The husky, pleasant voice belonged to a man about his own size and age, though Artie wasn't sure, what with his collar turned up and a woolen navy watch cap pulled down over his ears.

"Just like Rockefeller Center in New York," Artie said. "We've got a Christmas tree, too, maybe even bigger." San Francisco, the only city in the world with Christmas tree envy.

He concentrated on the skaters in the center of the rink. There were little kids pushing tentatively along on their blades and taking an occasional pratfall, and a covey of teenagers flashing around the edges of the enclosure showing off for the crowd and each other, trying figure eights and an occasional leap, usually badly. A solitary old man glided sedately through the swirl of other skaters around him.

Not a bad time of year, Artie thought. Skaters, fresh air, the municipal Christmas tree—if he didn't watch out, the spirit of the season would get to him yet. All he really needed was for Susan to be home. And for Larry to be at the other end of the phone line.

"The afternoons are sponsored," Watch Cap said. "This time, it's the AIDS Foundation. Poor bastards, something like seventeen thousand dead in the city and thousands more to go."

Artie knew the stats by heart; he'd lost enough friends to the disease. But right then he didn't want to think about it and spoil a pleasant afternoon.

Watch Cap wasn't about to take silence for an answer. "Not like Ebola, though. Now there's a disease for you—no cure and it's wiping out half of Africa. Or take Rift Valley TB—"

"I've lost friends," Artie interrupted. "I don't want to talk about diseases with strangers."

"Pardon me for living, fella." There was no anger in the voice, just a mild amusement, which annoyed Artie even more. His black mood returned in a flash and he swore quietly to himself. He started to edge away, trying to protect his packages from the crowd around him. He didn't have to fucking listen to this.

Watch Cap suddenly grabbed his arm.

"Catch the old man—can you believe that?"

Artie automatically turned back to the ice. It took a few seconds to spot the figure in the middle of the rink. He was doing jumps and turns with a grace Artie hadn't seen outside of competition or TV specials. Some visiting professional, probably. Then the skater flashed by fairly close to him.

He was better than good, Artie thought, astonished. At seventy, the old man was miraculous. Artie watched him intently, the crowd laughing and applauding every time he leaped into the air. A triple axel, and then another . . . the applause and the laughter died and the crowd was suddenly silent. What the old man was doing was impossible.

Not more than a dozen feet away, the skater folded his arms close to his chest and spun on his skates. He slowed, threw out his arms, and stopped, staring straight at Artie. The expression on his face was one of confusion and terror. A moment later, he slumped to the ice.

Heart attack, Artie thought. Had to be. No man his age could have done what he'd done without his muscles and joints freezing up, without his heart giving out.

Artie felt the cold sweats start then. It couldn't have been a senior citizen's idea to try to imitate Brian Boitano or Scott Hamilton. And it probably hadn't been a homeless man's idea to slit the throats of the Paschelke family and then burn down their house. And he doubted that it was the original intent of a roving pack of runaway dogs in the Tenderloin to tear the throat out of Larry Shea.

Nor had it been his idea the night before to play at being a seagull and soar over the city from the railing of a porch three stories above Noe Street.

He shivered. Last night *something* had put him on as easily as putting on its socks. He had thought what it had wanted him to think, had done what it had wanted him to do. So had the terror-stricken old man on the ice, so had the homeless arsonist, so had the dogs in the Tenderloin.

Larry Shea had been killed by a pack of dogs, Paschelke and his family had been murdered by a homeless drunk, the old man out for a lark on the skating rink had probably died of a heart attack, and if Mark hadn't stopped me, Artie thought, I would have been a suicide.

All of them had been murder by proxy.

Or would have been if he'd launched himself off the back porch. And the only connection was Larry Shea's research. Except that the old man didn't fit.

But, of course, he did. The murderer had been showing off. For his benefit.

Artie suddenly turned around. Watch Cap, the man whose face he'd never really seen, whose voice he hadn't recognized at the time but that now seemed oddly familiar, a voice he'd heard someplace before—

was gone.

I t   w a s   s i x   o ' c l o c k when Artie got home, and Mark wasn't back from school yet. He started to fix supper, then gave up and called up the House of Chen for takeout. Chinese from the House of Chen was second only to a Haystack pizza on Mark's scorecard of Good Things to Eat.

Artie made himself a cup of coffee and tried to remember Shea's notes—he'd have the Grub make another copy for him in the morning. But he knew Larry had been convinced he had autopsied a descendant of a . . . caveman. Artie half smiled. He preferred Hall's term. One of the Old People. It sounded a little more mysterious but also more acceptable. And Hall hadn't believed it in any event.

But *he* did, Artie thought. Talbot had been a member of another species that shared the planet with them. And that species would do anything to remain hidden. Murder? Sure. What would happen if people knew about them? *Something* had shown him just what had happened thirty-five thousand years ago. For an hour he had been a member of the Tribe; he had been one of the Old People. But the Tribe had been ambushed, slaughtered to the last man, woman, and child, and then butchered. Could it happen again? On a bigger scale?

Why not?

Homo sapiens wasn't about to share its world.

Artie got out a scratch pad and started listing points he wanted to remember, wishing to God he'd taken a course in anthro in college. Comparisons of William Talbot to . . . what? Shea would have drawn his control group from his own patients. But Larry's graphs and charts had been Greek to Artie. All he knew was what he remembered from what Paschelke had told him and what he had gathered from his interview with Hall. Talbot had shown great strength in extremis. So might anybody. Heavy bones, thick pads of cartilage for a man his age . . .

If Hall was right and Larry had been full of shit, maybe it was because Talbot had been a health nut, watching his diet and working out regularly.

The other things that Hall had said—the Old People in many ways could have been just as advanced as the New People. If anything, they could have been more "human" in some respects. And what if they'd had bigger brains? What would they have used them for? And finally, they might not have been as good hunters as the New People.

But certainly good enough.

Artie thought of the last scene with the Tribe, of the butchering. Could you call it cannibalism if it was another species? He vaguely remembered a photograph he'd seen in *National Geographic* of an African native roasting a too-human-looking monkey. The resemblance hadn't bothered the native—after all, the monkey had been another species.

Hall had been right on one score. The Old People would probably go to any length to remain hidden. Even to committing murder. It would never be traced back to them because the police would be fed the suspect who'd actually held the knife or fired the shot, or it would be a suicide, or "death from natural causes," or simply an accident.

And they were after *him,* Artie thought. He knew more than anybody else about Shea's research. Larry was dead and so was Paschelke, and he wouldn't bet a dime on Hall's life, even if the man hadn't believed the research he'd read. When it came to himself, they'd missed once—Mark had saved him then—but they'd try again. And sooner or later, they'd succeed.

Unless he got to them first.

The doorbell rang and Artie answered. He gave the delivery boy a two-dollar tip, walked back to the kitchen, and cleared the notes off the table. He got out several plates and the silver, then glanced at his watch.

Seven-thirty. Mark still wasn't home.

Goddammit, Mark knew they had an answering machine. If he wasn't coming straight home, he should have phoned and left a message. He always had before.

Artie called one of Mark's friends, a neighborhood kid who went to the same school and caught the same van. No, a friend had driven Mark right home—he hadn't stayed behind at school. When? About four-thirty, right after phys ed and a dozen laps in the pool.

Artie sat there, staring at the wall, the containers of chicken lo mein and moo shu pork untouched, his mind a blank. Then he spotted it out of the corner of his eye, the closet door off the kitchen—ajar. He got up very quietly and walked over to it, yanked it open, and stood there while a chill started in his chest and settled in the pit of his stomach.

Mark's wheelchair, neatly folded up and pushed against the back of the closet. He couldn't possibly have gone anyplace without it.

Artie searched the house then, even doing frantic, stupid things like looking under beds, sick to death that he would find a body someplace.

Nothing.

At nine o'clock, he called up Susan.

"I'm sorry, that number is out of service. . . ."

Twenty-four hours, Artie thought. It would be twenty-four hours before he could report either one as missing. The police would ask if he'd called all of Mark's friends, if he'd checked with the school, if he'd talked with the van driver. Sure, they could understand his worries about Mark, but he wouldn't be the first parent who'd sweated it out all for nothing. As for Susan, there were winter storms in northern California, nothing unusual about it. During the winter the phones went out all the time.

But Artie knew beyond a shadow of a doubt that Mark, at least, wasn't coming back.

CHAPTER 9

By three in the morning Artie had called every friend of Mark's for whom he had a phone number, checked in with the police—who sounded sympathetic but not very helpful, and questioned the neighbors on both sides of Noe and Twentieth Streets who might have seen or heard something.

He finally crashed on the living room couch, the windows and doors locked and a brown-painted, seventy-pound plaster elephant placed by the front door where anybody trying to enter would knock it over. The automatic was on the floor beside the couch, fully loaded. He slept only fitfully and when he woke at six, he called Mitch. A helluva time to be calling and Mitch had been sound asleep, but when Artie told him about Mark, he was instantly alert. He would be over as soon he could get there. Give him, say, half an hour.

Mitch lived across town—he rented a small house on Telegraph Hill—but there wouldn't be much traffic this early. And Christ, Artie thought, he desperately needed somebody he could talk to.

He went into the kitchen and made coffee, then called Susan again and got the same message he had the night before. He took in the morning paper and skimmed it, skipping the political and foreign news to read the small stories at the bottom of the inside pages of the second section where the paper chronicled the deaths of the petty criminals and the poor who lived in the rabbit warrens of the city, people whose names you forgot the moment you read them and people with no names at all.

Nobody fitting Mark's description was among them.

Mitch showed up ten minutes after Artie had finished the paper and was staring through the kitchen window at a city half hidden in morning mist, his mind fogged with a sense of helplessness. Mitch hadn't shaved and his coat still smelled faintly of wet wood ashes. He poured himself a cup of coffee and sat in silence at the table, waiting for Artie to begin.

Artie told him about Mark's failure to return home and his own failure when he tried to contact Susan.

When he'd finished, Mitch said quietly, "Mark's seventeen, almost a legal adult."

Artie shook his head in frustration. "How the hell can he go any-place without his chair?"

"Maybe he didn't need it. You said Susan wanted him up in Willow. If one of his instructors at school found that out, he probably told Mark to get his ass up there and make up the school time after the holidays. So a friend took him to the airport, helped him board, and Mark gave him the keys to drop the chair back here. Susan would've had one waiting at the other end."

Artie sipped at his coffee, not meeting Mitch's eyes. "Try and be helpful, for Christ's sake."

Mitch shrugged. "Okay, we'll check again with the cops this after-noon and remind them that Mark's missing. They'll contact the hospitals, his description will go out to all the beat cops to watch for him. They'll log him in as a runaway and wait for something to turn up. He's too old for them to put his picture on a milk carton or for your neighbors to hang yellow ribbons on their fences."

"Violence—" Artie started.

"I doubt it," Mitch interrupted. "He wouldn't have gone with any-body but a friend."

But somebody could have taken him away by force, Artie thought. He tried to block thinking about that possibility and concentrated on his coffee.

Mitch said gently, "Any friction, Artie? Any arguments with him? Anything that would make him run away? Any girlfriend who would shove him into her van and light out for a week of romance in Palm Springs?"

"There was no friction," Artie said finally. "If anything, I wanted to be more of a father. And I wanted him to be more of a son."

Mitch looked uncomfortable. "Chances are Mark will call within the next day or so; runaways usually do. A better guess is that he's with Susan up north and she doesn't know you're stewing down here. She'll contact you when the phones come back on line—probably complaining because you didn't insist he pack an extra pair of underwear."

"What's he going to do for money?"

"You ever give him a credit card?"

He'd forgotten. "Yeah, for his last birthday."

"Then we can trace him through the card."

Artie started to make another pot of coffee while Mitch watched him, an almost clinical look on his face. "You said you talked with some anthropologist at the museum?"

Mitch was trying to get Artie's mind off Mark. It took an effort.

"A Richard Hall. The Grub printed out the floppy and I took Hall the printout. Paschelke was right—Larry didn't think Talbot was human and he had a lot of measurements to prove it."

Mitch looked away, staring through the glass doors of the porch at the streets below. "Jesus Christ, our caveman again."

"The Old People, Hall called them," Artie said dryly. "He didn't believe it either. Said seeing might be believing so I went to the med center to see the body for myself. The relatives had already claimed it—I told you. Larry and Paschelke tried to convince one of Paschelke's colleagues and he didn't buy it any more than Hall did."

Mitch studied him for a moment.

"But you did." Artie nodded. "Why?"

How could he tell Mitch about his dream? About the Tribe? No more than he could have told him about Watch Cap or his almost suicide off the back porch. He remembered the look on Mark's face when he'd told him about Larry and what had happened on the porch, how he'd felt. Mark had been frightened; he hadn't understood. Would Mark have left because of that? He didn't know; he hoped not. But he couldn't think of any other reason. Except, of course, the obvious one. That somebody had Mark and might be willing to trade him for Shea's disk-ette and printout.

"No particular reason."

Mitch sighed. "Jesus, Artie, I'm your best friend and you're not willing to level with me." He opened the door of the refrigerator and started rummaging around. "What do we have for breakfast? Chinese . . . Chinese is good. No cold pizza, but you can't have everything. Leftover potato salad—not the season for it but that's good, too. . . ."

He found a plate and started serving himself. Artie stared at the mounds of food, wondering what the hell seemed strange. He knocked Mitch's arm away when he started to spoon out the potato salad.

"What's wrong?"

"Susan didn't make that. I never saw it before."

"Didn't make what? The potato salad?"

"She doesn't care for it. Neither does Mark."

Mitch stuck his finger in the salad to taste it. Artie grabbed his hand. "Don't do it."

Mitch frowned. "Come on, Artie, maybe a neighbor brought it over. Maybe it was on sale—why the hell else would it be in the fridge?"

Artie shook his head. "She wouldn't have bought it; no neighbor would have brought it over."

Mitch shrugged, wiped his hand on a paper towel, and pushed the plate away. "You're being paranoid but—Got a plastic sandwich bag?" Artie found him one and Mitch spooned some of the salad into it, then sealed it. "A friend of mine's a chemist—he can test it. If it turns out like you obviously think it will, then you're in deep shit, buddy. Somebody wants you dead."

"You're the one who was going to eat it," Artie said.

"Right. But it was meant for you. . . . Exactly what was it that Hall said about the Old People?"

"That they didn't exist—and if they did, they died out thirty-five thousand years ago. If any modern versions are around today, Hall thought they'd go to any lengths to keep us from knowing about them. Larry knew about them and Paschelke knew everything that Larry did. And now so do I." He hesitated. "And so do you."

"Larry was killed by a pack of feral dogs," Mitch said slowly, "and some homeless nut did in the Paschelke family."

"Yeah, sure."

Mitch shrugged. "Okay, I see the connection you're trying to make. I sure as hell don't know how they'd work it, but maybe the important thing at the moment is how you feel about it."

Artie was puzzled. "I don't follow you."

Levin slipped into his professional role. "Remember when you returned from 'Nam? Besides having served in my unit, you were one of the first patients I worked with—though not for long; you really didn't need that much help."

"Post-traumatic stress syndrome," Artie said carefully. "One of the souvenirs I brought back with me." The war was a long time ago; he hadn't thought about it for years.

"You said you hated the war, Artie. Your problem was that you really didn't, and you were deeply ashamed because you didn't. You didn't like killing people, you didn't like the idea of death, but just the same . . . it was the ultimate test of whatever it was that was *you,* and you finally admitted you had never felt more alive. You said you felt like a hunter in the middle of the hunting season."

"I wasn't proud of it," Artie said stiffly. "What's your point?"

"Just a thought, Artie. Something has scared you shitless, but if I were that something, I think I'd be afraid of you."

By the time Artie got to work, Connie had already loaded the desk with a dozen books and what looked like a hundred pages of computer printout. She held up a finger when he came in, finished the page she was reading, then looked up.

"Top of the morning, Artie—" Then: "What the hell happened? You look like shit."

Artie leaned his umbrella against the wall and struggled out of his coat. "Mark took off last night. I've no idea where to."

"So call the police."

"I already did. They said they'd check with the hospitals and have the beat cops watch for him. They think he might just have split—it's a little difficult to call a seventeen-year-old a runaway."

"He's still a minor and he's handicapped, for God's sake!"

"I can't prove he didn't leave willingly."

"A kid in a wheelchair shouldn't be that hard to find."

"He didn't take it with him," Artie said dryly. "Which means he's sitting in a car someplace or in somebody's house."

She struggled with it a moment, then gave up. "I don't know what to say, Artie. You want to take the day off, I'll cover for you with Hirschfield."

Artie didn't want to talk about it; it hurt too much.

"I've done everything I can, Connie." He pointed at the books. "What's up?"

"Research for the series." She looked relieved at the change in subject. "I've been doing my homework."

Artie looked at some of the titles, then thumbed the stack of computer printouts. Greenpeace apparently had a Web site.

"Anything interesting?"

"All of it—but depressing as hell. You read all the time about the ozone layer and then it becomes old news and you lose interest. But this winter it's thinned by half over Greenland, Scandinavia, and western Siberia. That's the worst it's been. Serious stuff."

"Wrong season for a suntan," Artie joked, then waited for Connie to come back with a snapper for his first and probably only yuck of the day.

She stared at him, sober-faced. "Not funny, Artie. The ultraviolet stands a good chance of frying the plankton in the Arctic ocean. That's the bottom of the food chain. No plankton, no krill, and pretty soon no fish, no seals, no sea lions, no whales."

Artie pulled out his yellow pad. "The world's going to hell," he muttered.

Connie slid one of the printouts across the table. "That's only the beginning of the bad news. Most of the forests will be gone within fifty years, ditto the animals that depend on them."

Artie read a few paragraphs.

"We're not going to do a once-over-lightly, are we?"

She looked offended. "Hell, no. Not when we've got a chance to make a difference."

The last time Artie had heard the phrase was fifteen years before, when he had dropped four hundred on an est seminar—the seminar assistants had chirped it like a mantra. Connie still wasn't Connie, he thought clinically, but it was more subtle this time, less confrontational.

Artie waved at the books. "That's a lot to absorb for the series."

Connie had gone back to reading. "Meaning am I going to be the one who's stuck with the research? Probably—but I don't mind. Really."

"Believe me, Connie, I didn't plan—"

"Hey, it's not my kid who's gone AWOL."

Artie's phone suddenly started ringing and he picked up. A confused Richard Hall asked why he'd changed his mind and taken the printout with him. Artie denied it and Hall was silent for a moment, then said he'd talked to the secretary for the department, who claimed that Artie had returned and told her he'd left the manuscript behind in Hall's locked office and that he needed it. She'd checked his ID, then sent a guard back with him.

"It wasn't me," Artie said slowly.

Hall now sounded angry. Both the secretary and the guard had given a detailed description, down to the clothes Artie had been wearing. It didn't matter a rat's ass to him if Artie wanted to keep the printout, he just didn't want to be jerked around.

"I'll be right over," Artie said and hung up. Connie was staring at him, puzzled, and Artie shook his head, annoyed. He had no idea what was going on, but somebody had passed himself off as him and apparently they had been damned convincing. He'd have the Grub print out two more copies, one for him and another one for Hall.

Jerry glanced up when he entered the computer cubbyhole, his expression sour. "Last time I do you any favors, Banks. You and your fucking mystery diskette . . ."

Artie felt the first chill of premonition. "What's wrong?"

"Virus, fella. I loaded it into the computer and opened the file to start cleaning it up and everything blew up in my face. It wiped my hard drive plus the main memory and then erased itself. Suicide virus. Nobody was ever supposed to look at it—your friend probably thought anybody wanting to snoop would not only check it on-screen, they would also print it out directly. What you got yesterday is all you're gonna get." He took a diskette off the worktable and flipped it at Artie. "Here you go, a Frisbee for midgets." He took a breath. "You have any idea what management's going to do to me? Only it's not going to be my ass, Banks—it's going to be yours."

. . .

H a l l   w a s n ' t   v e r y   f r i e n d l y . As soon as Artie showed up, he rang for the guard. "Fred, you know Mr. Banks, right? He was the one you let into my office yesterday."

The pudgy guard glanced at Artie, started to answer, then leaned closer. "I . . . don't think I know this gentleman, Dr. Hall. But I checked the man's ID yesterday—"

"Thanks, Fred."

Hall steered Artie back to his office.

"My apologies—to be honest, I don't know what the hell is going on." He wasn't the type actually to wring his hands, Artie thought, but he was doing a good job of it verbally. Hall managed a weak smile and tried to make a joke of it. "Maybe it was somebody from the *Journal of Forensic Pathology*—they would have had a field day with Dr. Shea's notes."

He closed his office door, settled himself in his chair, and motioned Artie to the other one.

"I'm sorry, I really am." Then, tentatively, "You understand that the Academy of Sciences can't be held responsible—"

Artie waved it aside. "Not your fault."

"You still have the original computer diskette, right?"

"Not anymore. A technician at work tried to print out two more copies and a virus on the diskette erased everything in the computer, including itself. He called it a suicide virus."

"There are no other copies?"

"I don't know of any."

Hall looked worried. "That doesn't make any sense—why would anybody want to erase the diskette? Or steal the printout?"

It made perfect sense to Artie. "Because of the information. Either they wanted it or they didn't want other people to have it."

Hall shook his head. "You steal facts; you don't steal speculation. Speculation is cheap."

"Maybe they thought they *were* stealing facts," Artie suggested.

The anthropologist studied him for a long moment. "You believe Dr. Shea, don't you? You think descendants of his Old People exist— right now, today."

"That's right."

Artie was mildly surprised at his own answer. Hall had put into words what he had been mulling over in the back of his mind ever since his first meeting with Paschelke. Since then, he had come very close to suicide and—probably—almost been poisoned. If a modern version of the Old People existed, then they were doing exactly what Hall had predicted: their very best to keep any knowledge of their existence secret. Any skepticism *he* had had about their existence had vanished after his hour with the Tribe.

Except you'd think they'd be trying to make him more skeptical, not less. The only explanation that made any sense was that the right hand didn't know what the left was doing.

Hall looked disappointed. "Then you're withholding information. You've made your decision based on something other than Dr. Shea's notes."

"You must have an opinion," Artie said stiffly.

"There's absolutely no proof that Dr. Shea's Old People ever existed, Mr. Banks. I told you that yesterday. Anything other than that is fantasy."

"If their descendants *did* exist," Artie persisted, "how would they differ from us today?"

Hall obviously didn't know whether to humor him or throw him out, then decided he owed Artie something for the loss of the printout.

"I couldn't tell you. All I can do is speculate about a species that never existed." He looked sour. "Since *we* exist, I suppose it's fair to speculate on any differences that there might have been."

"Yesterday you told me they might have been better than *Homo sapiens* in some respects," Artie said.

"Different, not better. 'Better' implies judgment, and we don't know enough to make one. They might have been humane, they might have taken care of their injured and their sick. They might have had ritual burials—or, as you suggested, cremations—indicating some sort of religion. They might have been good toolmakers, though toward the end they probably copied the tools and weapons that *sapiens* had. Again, a lot of might-have-beens."

"But they couldn't talk, right?"

Hall frowned. "How the hell would we know that? Admitted that most of my colleagues think it was language that enabled *sapiens* to make their big leap forward, culturally speaking. Your Old People might have had language too, but if they did, I doubt they could use it nearly as well."

"Then they probably couldn't sing," Artie mused, surprised at how wistful he sounded. "They had no music."

Hall looked intrigued in spite of himself. "Modern man is the only one of the hominids that makes music. I don't know of any chimps or gorillas that even come close. My guess is that if your Old People had music at all, it was a simple, percussive variety."

"Language would have been the key difference, then?"

"It would have been back then." Hall leaned toward him across the desk. "What we're doing right now—talking to each other—is an amazingly complex process. Language is much more than just naming things or passing along information. With it we can deal in concepts, things that have happened in the past, things that might happen in the future. We can talk about things that we can't see, that we can't touch. Consider the complexities of modern physics and then consider that we deal with all of them through language, either spoken or written. And all of it comes down to our ability to say *ay, eee, eye, oh*, and *you*. Pretty remarkable when you think about it. Then listen to opera sometime— say some tenor with the range of a Tagliavini—and think of all those sounds coming from that tube of flesh called a larynx, a simple voice box."

"Then language is one way the Old People could have been different from *sapiens,*" Artie said slowly. "There might have been others."

Hall smiled; he was on a roll.

"Let me count the ways. . . . The most obvious one is art. We can trace cave art back more than twenty thousand years. Fantastic images of animals drawn in charcoal, yellow ocher, and red hematite on cave walls in France. Many of the drawings would do credit to any modern artist. My guess is your Old People wouldn't have had art, Mr. Banks. Maybe they had body ornamentation, but there's no way of knowing. I don't think they would have been able to draw pictures, or decorate their tools or weapons. Maybe they strung beads or made necklaces, though it's more likely they would have traded for them. We know for sure that Cro-Magnons—archaic *Homo sapiens*—made necklaces."

Art and language, Artie thought. They were probably joined at the hip, anthropologically speaking, though he wasn't sure how. And there was always the possibility that the Old People didn't have language and art because they had something else as good . . . or better.

"And then something happened thirty-five thousand years ago."

"That's right. A tremendous explosion of creativity by *Homo sapiens*. For a hundred thousand years or more, nothing. Then, all of a sudden, language, art, and prodigious advances in tool and weapon making, everything from needles to spears. They made outdoor habitations of hide and wood, even huts of mammoth tusks and bones—they probably hunted the mammoth to extinction to get them."

Artie could believe that. "No wars, no conflict between *Homo sapiens* and any other group?"

Hall shrugged. "There's no indication of that; there aren't enough bones showing battle wounds or anything like it. Sure, there might have been some skirmishes. *Sapiens* probably penetrated into northern Europe from the Levant, following the migratory paths of the reindeer. Undoubtedly any other group would have hunted them as well. There could have been some localized conflicts, but nothing approaching war or genocide. That's tabloid thinking."

"The Old People disappeared, just like that?" Artie said.

Hall looked exasperated. "Mr. Banks, I'm debating with you as if the species existed. It didn't. But if it did, 'just like that' might have been over a period of at least several thousand years. *Homo sapiens* would have been more successful as a hunter, more innovative in making tools and weapons. If they hunted the same prey, *sapiens* would have won out. Your Old People would have been forced to shift their hunting grounds into areas that were relatively barren."

"Where they probably starved to death."

"Whatever."

"Lions and hyenas hunt the same prey," Artie said thoughtfully. "Neither one has disappeared."

"Apples and oranges." Hall's smile was the one Artie guessed he reserved for amateurs. "But we haven't considered breeding itself. If your Old People lived in a cold, inhospitable climate, then their gestation period might have been closer to twelve months than nine to give the baby a better chance of survival. With his shorter gestation period, *sapiens* could have simply outbred them."

"By producing babies not as well equipped to survive?" Artie shook his head in disbelief. "You're implying that if *sapiens* produced more children, then the Old People necessarily had to produce fewer, that the countryside could only support so many. But that would have depended on population, and I don't think anybody knows what population pressures were back then."

Hall suddenly smiled.

"You're picking on me, Banks. I'm only telling you what the theories are. Ask me again five years from now and I'll probably have a whole different set of them. But one thing for sure: When *Homo sapiens* invented agriculture ten thousand years ago, that was the name of the game. They settled down into villages, farmed for their food, domesticated cattle and pigs, organized trade routes, the whole bit. Once they could raise all the food they needed on the back forty instead of having to forage for nuts and berries, then there really was a population explosion."

Artie glanced at his watch. "Look, I've taken up enough of your time. I appreciate it."

"It's been fun. Buy you lunch—?" Hall looked at him questioningly.

Artie grinned. "Just 'Artie.' My car or yours?"

Hall shook his head. "Let's try the de Young Café, the other side of the music concourse—it's one of the best-kept secrets in town. Strictly high-class—cream of carrot soup and chocolate mousse if you want it, real San Francisco."

Artie promptly forgot his nostalgia for the hot dogs and hamburgers downstairs. He hadn't known the art museum had an upscale cafeteria.

They were almost to the front doors when a guard tapped Artie on the arm. "You Arthur Banks?" Artie nodded and he said, "Phone call for you at the Information Desk."

"Ask a docent for directions to the café," Hall called over his shoulder. He disappeared into the drizzle outside. Artie went back to the Information Desk and picked up the phone. "Hello, this is Banks." There was a click and then a dial tone.

He was still holding the phone, puzzled, when he heard a *pop-pop-pop* out front. A moment later, a woman started to scream. Artie stood frozen for a moment, then dashed for the doors.

Hall lay facedown on the concrete, his blood running slowly down the steps. The back of his head was a matted mixture of black, gray, and red. Artie felt numb with shock. 'Nam suddenly seemed very close—he remembered all too clearly friends who had been shot in the face, shattering their features and turning the back of their head into a muddy no-man's-land of blood and brains and hair.

He wished he'd gotten to know Hall better. He seemed a nice enough guy.

And that made it like 'Nam in still another way. People you'd grown close to over the months and then suddenly they were gone. They became just names on a casualty list or, worse, you stumbled across their mangled bodies half buried in the mud. After a while you grew numb; you couldn't cry anymore, you couldn't even grieve. You just walled off your memories of them in your mind. Larry Shea had been one of his best friends, Paschelke a friendly family doctor, the old man at the skating rink for whom he'd felt a brief burst of pity a stranger. Now Hall, and the only obit he could think of was: Nice Enough Guy.

The six-o'clock news would call it a drive-by shooting, a drug deal gone sour. Hall had been the right color to hang that one on him. And when the cops searched Hall's house they'd probably find a bag of crack someplace where his wife might have dusted two days before but not the night before, when something watching had seen them go out for dinner or to a movie and then slipped into their house.

Hall's sudden offer of lunch—what had suggested it to him? And if it hadn't been for the phone call, whoever had shot Hall would have gotten two for the price of one: the sophisticated crack dealer using his job at the museum as a cover, and the courageous KXAM reporter investigating a tip about him.

That somebody was trying to kill him wasn't exactly news, Artie thought.

That somebody was trying to save his ass was.

CHAPTER 10

Artie watched while the police cordoned off the steps of the museum and pushed back the sight-seers, pleased that they had been this close to tragedy but that it hadn't involved them. Two of the women were weeping, and Artie guessed they had been co-workers of Hall's.

There was nothing more to see—but that wasn't quite true. Artie inspected the faces in the crowd again. There was whoever had shot Hall and had come back to see how good a job they had done. Say somebody like Watch Cap who, for all Artie knew, was searching the crowd looking for him.

He started back to his car. The crime scene investigators and police photographers would show up any minute, and Schuler would wonder what the hell he was doing there. He glanced at the body once more. A spot on the six-o'clock news, a tragedy for Hall's family, and momentary curiosity on the part of the kids who came to the anthropology wing and wondered what had happened to the nice Mr. Hall who had always been so patient with answers to their questions.

Artie sat in his car for a long moment, then drove out of the park to Lincoln Way. Mitch had been wrong, he thought. He didn't like war, never had. He certainly didn't like this one. Larry, Paschelke, Hall, the old man in the park—all innocent bystanders in a conflict he didn't quite understand, whose participants he'd never met. Or at least didn't think he had, with the possible exception of Watch Cap.

Then there was Mark. He couldn't believe that Mark had just decided to leave, without any warning whatsoever. Had Mark gone up to see Susan? Maybe. He'd told Mark his mother wanted him up there. Mark knew his grandfather was doing badly—his going would have made sense.

Except he didn't believe it. Mark sometimes seemed remote; probably all teenagers did to their parents. But he would have left a note, would have called, would never have thought, Fuck you, hurray for me, and split. He knew Mark better than that.

Or thought he did.

Mitch didn't think there had been violence, but he wasn't sure of that, either. If *something* had slipped into Mark's head, he could have ended up doing anything it wanted or going anyplace it wanted him to. There were different levels of violence.

But what would have been the point? To hold Mark hostage for the return of Larry's research diskette? He had never gotten a call, there had been no note slipped under the door. Mark had vanished into thin air, with no indication of violence, no indication of abduction. And someone, *something,* had taken the diskette anyway.

He still hadn't been able to get hold of Susan, even though the operator assured him the lines were open—and always had been. She should have called him in any event, would certainly have phoned if Mark had shown up at the Eureka airport and called her in Willow to say he was there.

His world was slowly going to hell. His family had disappeared and something or somebody wanted him dead, as Mitch had put it. And he had no face to put to the somebody or something except the photographs that Larry had taken of a sixty-year-old man who seemed younger than he should have been and who had died after an automobile accident on 580 late on a Saturday night. Artie had looked at the photos in Larry's research a dozen times and could remember nothing about the man except that he'd seemed so ordinary—nobody you would have looked at twice.

The sun had come out and the drizzle had stopped, but Artie didn't notice either one. He had braked for a ten-year-old battered Mustang that cut in front of him, and his sudden surge of anger had blanked out the slight feeling of fingers plucking at his mind more subtly than they had done several nights before. For Artie the sky still seemed just as gray, the mist still condensing and running down his windshield in rivulets.

The car that had cut in front of him had swerved back into the outer lane and was now crowding him over toward the curb. Artie leaned on his horn and glanced over to look at the driver. Long brown hair, street kid, early twenties at best. The type Artie had come to hate for what they were doing to the city he loved. The kid turned toward him at the same time and flipped him off. Artie couldn't read lips but he knew what he was saying: "Get off the street, old man!"

They were on Kezar Drive now, then hit the light and turned onto Oak Street, paralleling the Panhandle. Artie twisted the wheel a little to the right and for a moment sparks flew from their fenders. He could feel his lips curl away from his teeth. Just like in the movies. Then his car jumped the curb and he hit the brakes to avoid a tree. The kid cut in front and stopped, jerked open the door of his car, and bolted out holding a tire iron.

Artie yanked open his own door, his hand on the automatic in his pocket. He had no clear idea of where he was or exactly what he was going to do, but he was mad enough to kill, his rage as thick as cotton in his head.

The kid came at him swinging the tire iron and screaming, "What the hell, you old bastard, you don't own the road!"

Suddenly a car directly behind Artie's turned out and raced on past. In his head Artie sensed bemused frustration, and then something cold as ice water slid into his mind and his anger faded. He glanced around, noticing with surprise the cloudless sky and the brilliant green of the Panhandle on his left, drops of water glistening jewel-like on the grass.

He turned to the kid and gaped. A student type with glasses, an inoffensive skinny nineteen, his face pale with fright. He stood there looking at the tire iron in his hand, shaking and trying frantically to piece together what had just happened.

"I don't know what the hell got into me, man—honest to Christ, I don't know! You all right, man? I didn't mean to cut in like that!"

A few minutes more and the fight would have escalated, Artie thought. He could have killed the kid, *would* have killed him. And if he'd tried to drive away, there were plenty of people around who would have gotten his license number. When the cops caught up with him it was more than an even-money bet that one of them would have shot him for resisting arrest.

Artie sat down on the curb, holding his head in his hands. "It's all right—anybody can lose control of a car. It happens." Especially if they had help.

The kid looked embarrassed. "Shit, my insurance has lapsed."

His own car was almost as old as the kid's, Artie thought. Why get the cops and the insurance companies into it?

"Forget it."

The incident was a reminder, Artie thought, as if he needed one.

Four times now, he'd been lucky.

He couldn't count on being lucky the fifth time.

What the hell was going on? Something had it in for him, and sooner or later they'd kill him and it would look like an accident or like it was all his own fault.

Artie pulled into a gas station and had the attendant fill his tank while he called Mitch on his cell phone. He got the answering machine, nobody at home. Office hours, noon to five— he could never keep it straight. He called the office and got a worried secretary. Mitch hadn't shown or called in, and she'd already had to cancel one appointment. No, she had no idea where he might be.

Artie held the phone for a minute after the line went dead. Mitch never failed to show for work, or if he couldn't make it, he never failed to cancel well in advance. An accident or . . .

Artie gunned the car and took off. He wasn't the only one who knew too much. Mitch knew almost as much as he did.

There wasn't much parking at the top of Telegraph Hill, and he left his car in a neighbor's driveway with the motor running. The door to Mitch's small cottage was locked, and Artie fumbled out his key ring and searched frantically for Mitch's key, a leftover from when Mitch had gone on vacation and asked him to look in on his cat and feed her.

The inside of the small cottage was quiet. A living room, bedroom, bath, and kitchen, all decorated like a Cape Cod cottage. The small office in one corner of the living room, pale blue chintz curtains by windows overlooking the bay, driftwood furniture and maple antiques, braided-wool space rugs over polished wood-plank floors. The hill itself could have been transposed from New England, with wooden walks leading off to the various cottages. It was a perfect bachelor's hideaway.

Mitch was stretched out on the kitchen floor, bleeding from a scalp wound where he'd hit his head on the table when he fell.

"Mitch!"

Levin was out cold, a half-empty bottle of scotch on the tiled sink ledge. Artie knelt down to feel his pulse. It was then he noticed the glass that had rolled beneath a chair and a small bottle of prescription pills. Valium—half the small yellow tablets were spilled on the linoleum. Bad combination if Mitch had taken them with the scotch, and he apparently had.

Artie lunged for the phone. The ambulance was there sooner than he thought possible, and he rode in the back while the attendant fixed an oxygen mask to Mitch's face and monitored his slow and laborious breathing.

At the hospital they pumped his stomach, but it was a good two hours in the emergency room before they let Artie in to see a pale Mitch, sitting on the side of his bed.

"You okay?"

"Yeah, I am now. It wasn't much of a lunch, but they took all of it. It'll be a week before I'm hungry again."

"What the hell happened?"

Mitch stared out the hospital window at the gray winter sky. There was a slight sheen of sweat on his forehead but his voice was steady enough. Only his eyes gave away how jumpy he really was.

"After I left you this morning, I went home. Looked over some patient folders and poured myself a drink before going to work. Two fingers of scotch, a few cubes, and half a bottle of five-milligram Valiums."

Mitch said it casually and Artie wasn't sure he'd heard right. "I don't get it."

Mitch sounded as if he couldn't quite bring himself to believe it either.

"A neighbor came over to bitch about my cat digging in her flower bed and when she left, I decided to make myself a quick drink before going to work. I knew what I was doing, Artie. I just didn't believe there was anything strange or dangerous about it."

Mitch struggled to keep his voice calm.

"I started to come out of it when I felt myself falling. Something just drained out of my head, like you'd pulled a plug. Something had been inside my mind and I didn't even know it. . . ."

After a long moment of silence, Artie said, "It's a strange feeling. You suddenly realize somebody's been pushing your buttons but you have no idea what it was. Or who."

Mitch looked at him in surprise.

"When? For you?"

"When I came home from seeing Paschelke that first time. I went out on my back porch and climbed up on the railing. I wanted to fly. I thought it was perfectly normal, too. Three stories down to solid concrete, Mitch." He didn't mention Mark; he didn't want to start talking about him again.

"You should have told me."

"Would you have believed me?"

"Not then. I sure would now."

A nurse looked in, disapproving, then pulled the curtains and left.

"Do you know how they do it?" Artie asked.

Mitch seemed more himself now, his voice calmer, his eyes less jumpy. He was still pasty-faced but that would clear up with a decent meal—whenever he felt like eating, which probably wouldn't be for a while.

"I've got my ideas. They're probably no better than yours."

"I don't have any at all." Artie hesitated. "I don't understand how anybody can manipulate my mind, Mitch. I just don't."

He sounded like a small boy asking his father for reassurance and felt like two-thirds of an idiot. It was Mitch who had almost died, not him.

Mitch glanced at the white curtains drawn around the bed and lowered his voice.

"Forget about free will, Artie—you don't have any. Physically speaking, you're an electrochemical machine. Especially your brain. The neurons fire, an electrical impulse travels along a nerve, and you think a thought or move your arm. If you were small enough to crawl inside somebody's head, you'd probably see little sparkles of light when their neurons fired. And like most electrical devices, your brain generates waves. You broadcast them and you receive them, too."

He leaned back against the pillows. For a moment, Artie thought Mitch was going to be sick, then he realized Mitch was probably so empty he couldn't even vomit green bile.

"We talk about it all the time, Artie. We feel the 'electricity' in the crowd when we're at a football game. You can feel the 'electricity' of a mob if you get caught up in one. And your mind can be taken over by that mob, Artie. You can end up going along with whatever the mob wants you to do, even if you don't really want to. The mob is doing your thinking for you."

"One on one," Artie objected, keeping his voice down. "We can't do it one on one."

Mitch managed a weak smile. "I read about it in the psychology newsletters all the time—talk to any biofeedback expert about your brain's alpha, beta, and theta waves. A few years back, the air force gave Stanford a grant to link computers with brain waves—they wanted to teach pilots how to fly planes with them. And I've seen demonstrations where the participants played Pong on a computer by controlling the ball with their minds. It's the next frontier, Artie."

"There's got to be an electrical connection," Artie said, unbelieving. "There's got to be a wire, some mechanical link."

Mitch shook his head.

"I told you, Artie, we broadcast. And we receive. How many times have you picked up the phone to call somebody and there they are, on the other end of the line? Or when somebody knows exactly what you're going to say a split second before you say it?"

Artie's memories of balancing on the porch railing, arms outstretched, the wind tugging at his hair, were suddenly very vivid.

"I'm sorry, Mitch—maybe I just don't want to think that somebody can make me do something by thinking at me."

Mitch looked away. "I can't blame you. I don't like to think that I did what I did this morning. We like to think the mind is truly private, that it's even more personal than our bodies. It's *us,* it's peculiarly our own, we operate it. But think of the last time you were 'drunk out of your mind,' or you were high on pot or had swallowed a tab of acid. Sure, it's ancient history. But we did it. We own our own minds, Artie, but we abdicate that ownership often enough. And all of us are susceptible to suggestion. With us, it's verbal. With something else, it's what we might consider a stray thought. It's a wild talent—one that we don't have. But something sure as hell does. Was it your idea to climb up on the porch railing?"

The nurse was back, pulling aside the curtains and looking at both of them suspiciously. Mitch peeled off the hospital gown and started to slip into his street clothes, ignoring the nurse's objections. "Let's get the hell out of here."

"Will they let you go?"

"They won't like it, but I'll sign myself out."

When Mitch had finished dressing, Artie said, "Where to?"

"You pick it."

It was one of Charlie Allen's days off, Artie thought. They could talk in his living room while Charlie puttered around with his computers and took on all comers in his Librarians Anonymous chat room.

They'd be in a friend's house.

And they'd be safe.

Charlie Allen was glad to see them, greeting them at the door dressed in a ratty bathrobe. "Come on in, guys— Franny's downtown, she'll be out most of the afternoon. And it's the last day of school for the kids; they won't be home until three so we got the house to ourselves. Want some lunch?" He didn't wait for an answer but swept into the kitchen and started pulling bread and luncheon meat out of the refrigerator. "There's some ice cream in the freezer, help yourselves—and I don't mind if I do."

He loaded up a cereal bowl with several scoops of strawberry and squirted chocolate sauce over the top. "What's up? You sounded pretty vague over the phone."

Artie wasn't very hungry. He dropped some deli ham on a single slice of unbuttered rye and folded it over. "We wanted to borrow your library for maybe an hour—talk over some business. We needed a place where it would be quiet and we wouldn't be disturbed." He took a breath. "So we thought of you."

Allen looked puzzled, turning from one to the other.

"What's wrong with your places? Not that I mind—it's great to see you."

"You were midway between," Mitch said, as if the answer made a lot of sense.

Artie watched Charlie turn it over in his mind and thought to himself, Jesus, what a lame idea. Charlie must think they were a little nuts.

"Okay, my casa is your casa—feel free." Allen led the way to the living room that doubled as a library, separated from the rest of the house by glass French doors. "Make yourselves at home."

"Thanks," Artie mumbled, "appreciate it." He passed a bookcase on his right when he entered, then suddenly paused. He'd been to Charlie's home dozens of times. He'd also walked past the same bookcase filled with its rows of little black notebooks at least twenty times and never really noticed them before. This time he did. Each notebook carried a neat red plastic label on the spine: SUICIDE CLUB. There was a book for every year since they'd started the Club when they were kids, sometimes two or three books to the year.

He waved at the shelves. "What gives, Charlie?"

Allen shrugged. "You guys elected me secretary way back when and I guess I never stopped." He looked embarrassed. "Call it a hobby. I probably know things about you guys that you forgot years ago."

Hero worship, Artie thought. Charlie had had a bad case of it back then and had never gotten over it. He was suddenly as embarrassed as Charlie was. "Have to look at them sometime—bring back memories."

"For you, any time." Allen waddled back toward his office, closing the French doors behind him.

"Strange guy," Artie muttered after he'd left.

Mitch shrugged. "Don't knock him, Artie. He's a generous, friendly slob, and we're charismatic. Neither of us can help it—and please don't take me seriously." He leaned back on the couch. Behind his steel-framed lenses his eyes were a bright ice-blue and he seemed a little remote, a little cold—the way Artie remembered him from the times they'd served together in 'Nam. "We haven't been using our heads. Who knew Larry was coming over to the city?"

Artie thought for a moment. "The people he worked with at Kaiser. The people at the restaurant—they took the reservations, they knew all of us would be there or were planning on being there."

"Who else?"

"All of us, of course—all the members of the Club."

"You're leaving somebody out."

"Anybody they might have talked to," Artie said slowly. "And maybe some of the kids."

"Who knew what he was going to talk about?"

"Probably only Cathy. Larry was writing an article, he wanted to go public with his findings. Maybe Cathy was apprehensive, maybe like Hall she figured that if there were one there had to be others and considering Talbot's lack of ID, they probably didn't want anybody to find them."

"You're giving her a lot of credit."

"She's nobody's dummy, Mitch. And she would have worried about the family. When the cops called with news of Larry's murder, it confirmed her fears and she grabbed the kids and ran."

"Who else?"

"I don't know." Artie frowned. "Paschelke didn't know about the meeting, though he must have known Larry was writing an article."

"You're not thinking, Artie. Would Cathy have kept Larry's research to herself or would she have confided in a close friend?"

Artie shrugged. "I suppose it would have been natural if she'd confided in a friend. Especially if she were scared. But Susan never mentioned it—she would have if Cathy had talked to her."

"I wasn't thinking of Susan. If Cathy had talked to her, Susan probably would have talked to you. Which leaves the other members. One of them didn't want the rest of the Club members knowing about Larry's research and definitely didn't want *Science* printing it. Which means the prime suspect is whoever Cathy made the mistake of confiding in. The danger for her is that she might not realize it."

"That's just a theory," Artie objected.

"You got a better one?"

Artie felt like a slow study. "Find Cathy, then, and maybe we've found our man. Or woman."

Mitch shook his head. "You're never going to find her, Artie. Or the kids. My guess is they've been dead for days." He was silent for a moment, thinking. "What did Talbot look like? You saw Larry's photos of the body."

"Ordinary. Nobody you'd look at twice."

"So what we've got is a group of people living among us who really aren't 'us,' who will kill to keep their existence a secret. All we know is that they can fuck with our minds and you'd never notice them in a crowd. Short of an autopsy, like Larry did on Talbot, there's no way of knowing who they are."

Artie thought about it. "You're driving at something."

"The obvious, Artie. The largest group of suspects are the members of the Club, or those related to the members. That means one of us, perhaps more than one, may not be who we've always thought he was. That for all the length of time that we've known him—or her—for them it's been a game of Let's Pretend. Worst of all, they're not human. Not human the way we're human. If Larry Shea was right, they're a different species."

Artie felt the small hairs stir on the back of his neck.

"So how does it affect us—you and me? Give me an example."

Mitch smiled. "I told you a cock-and-bull story at the hospital and you believed every word of it. You didn't doubt me for a moment."

Artie had the automatic out without even thinking. Jesus Christ, he'd walked right into it.

"You're my best friend, Mitch," he said slowly, "but if I were you, I wouldn't move." The gun was rock steady in his hand.

Mitch didn't even look surprised. "What I told you in the ER was true," he said dryly, "but you asked for an example and I gave you one. This is exactly how it affects us. And I could turn it around. How do I know that you're really you—somebody I've known for half my life? Because you're my friend? The ones who really screw you are your friends, not your enemies. You can watch out for your enemies." He smiled bleakly. "You could have lied about the porch railing bit. How do I know it's true? I wasn't there. You could have spent the last few days trying to sound me out for what I believe—or don't believe."

Artie sat there in silence, staring at him, the automatic never wavering. "Then that's a problem, isn't it?"

Mitch looked disgusted. "For Christ's sake, Artie, put it away. It goes off, you lose a friend and gain a murder rap."

There was a knock on the French doors and Allen opened them. Artie made the gun disappear before Allen had a chance to see it.

"If you guys are still hungry, there's some leftover potato salad—it's Franny's specialty." He caught the sudden shock on their faces and looked offended. "Hey, if you don't like it, that's fine—don't blame me for trying to be a good host."

Artie and Mitch listened to him shuffle back to the kitchen before speaking. Artie was sweating. He had to go to the bathroom, bad. Innocent, innocuous Charlie Allen. Why not?

Mitch shook his head.

"Relax, Artie—he's okay."

"Based on what?" Artie jerked a thumb at the notebooks in the bookcase. "He said he probably knows more about us than we do about ourselves. And he certainly knows more about Larry Shea than we ever did. He was close to Larry; if Cathy was going to confide in anybody about what Larry was working on, it could easily have been Charlie."

Mitch stood up and reached for his coat. "And there's always the chance that we're paranoid."

Outside, Artie shivered—it had turned chilly and gray again. Charlie had been miffed when they'd left so suddenly, but he'd get over it. All they had wanted was to get out of the house as quickly as possible.

Mitch stopped at his car and turned to Artie. "You're a good friend, Artie—one of my best."

"Yeah," Artie said, trying hard to sound convincing, "same here."

They looked at each other, each a little awkward, and then Mitch said, "Don't forget, Artie—you're the only one who saw Larry's research and is still alive." Artie nodded. "And I'm the only one you talked to about it, right? And I'm still alive. We've both had plenty of opportunity and we're still around. We both know the other is safe."

"Right," Artie said, still dubious.

Mitch blinked nervously behind his granny glasses.

"We're going to have to trust each other, Artie. We're the only ones we know for sure who know too much."

Artie nodded in agreement and got in his car.

Mitch was right: They were going to have to trust each other. But Jesus, right then he wasn't willing to trust anybody.

And he was sure Mitch wasn't willing either.

He got home and called the station, then went through a ritual of locking all the doors and windows and pulling down the shades and turning the lights low, keeping to the center of the rooms so his shadow wouldn't show on the window blinds. It was only after he finished his TV dinner of macaroni and cheese that he noticed the blinking red light on the answering machine.

"Artie? Susan. It's noon, Wednesday. Please call me at the following number—haven't heard from you."

That wasn't right. He had tried to get her two days running. He hastily dialed the number.

"Where have you been, Susan? I've been calling—"

"I'm at the hospital." A slight pause. "Dad's dying. . . ."

He had expected it but it was still a shock. "I'm sorry, Susan."

Her voice became sharper. "Where's Mark? I thought I asked you to send him up here—please try to get him on the next plane."

His throat suddenly felt very dry. He told her that Mark had disappeared, that he'd filed a missing persons report with the police but with no luck so far, that he'd tried to phone her—

Her voice turned frantic. "You've got to find him, Artie!"

"Can you come back?"

"I can't—I told you, Dad's dying. Find him, Artie! Please, you've got to find him!"

"Sure, Susan," he mumbled. "Sure, I'll do my best."

And then she had to go and he sat there holding the phone and all he could think of for a moment was that she had wanted Mark up there—she'd never mentioned him. Her father was dying and she'd lost her son, and he hated himself because what he'd thought of first was that she hadn't pleaded for him to come up.

Which made sense, because if he went up there, who would be left behind to look for Mark? And he sure as hell couldn't help her father.

He wore his heart on his sleeve, he thought. He had for fifteen years.

CHAPTER 11

Bayview Academy was located just off of Skyline Drive in Oakland, a pleasant ten acres that seemed a jumble of eucalyptus trees at first until Artie got a few hundred feet off the drive and saw the main building and the athletic grounds behind it. Beyond the track-and-field area the ground sloped sharply down to the bay and a view of San Francisco on the other side, partially hidden by tendrils of fog.

He had seen the school five years before, when he and Susan had first enrolled Mark there, but the ivy had grown since then. Now the redbrick buildings of Bayview Academy would look right at home in upstate New York or in some small town in Vermont.

Scott Fleming, the headmaster, was cordial enough, affable but careful to maintain a certain reserve as a protective barrier between himself and the parents of his students. He had been about to take his afternoon stroll around the grounds and invited Artie along. He looked in his early sixties, a small and somewhat placid man, thin and wiry. His hair was gray, and with his woolen jacket and thick scarf trailing behind him in the breeze, all Artie could think of was Mr. Chips. He even had a faintly English accent to go with his appearance.

Artie remembered when he'd first met Fleming and the headmaster had filled him in on the history of the academy.

"We were founded in the middle forties, just after the Second World War. Mr. Elias Putnam had his only boy come back badly wounded—he had lost a leg and the use of his right hand—and Putnam became interested in the plight of the crippled while overseeing the rehabilitation of his son."

" 'Crippled,' " Artie had repeated. He hadn't been sure he liked the sound of it. He had always considered Mark handicapped, not crippled.

"The students here are crippled, Mr. Banks," Fleming had said quietly. "We could use the phrase 'physically disadvantaged' but I'm afraid that being politically correct wouldn't help our students at all. They're crippled. We deliberately use the word and with usage, the word itself is defused. It's not the word, it's the baggage that goes along with it. The students are certainly going to hear the word on the outside; better they get used to hearing it at Bayview."

They were at the back of the building now, looking out over the track and the small baseball field. It was late in the afternoon and turning colder; Artie envied Fleming his thick woolen sweater. He waved at the diamond and the cinder track.

"I can't imagine those would get much use."

Fleming raised an eyebrow. "Physical activity is more difficult than it would be with ordinary boys and girls of the same age, but then they're not competing with ordinary boys and girls—they're competing with each other." He wrapped his arms around his chest for warmth. "There's not much to see beyond this, might as well start back. We can have some coffee in my office if you'd like."

They detoured through the gymnasium and Artie watched a wheel-chair basketball game in progress, then found himself distracted by a muscular sixteen-year-old climbing a rope to the ceiling, using only his arms.

"He can't walk," Fleming offered. "Nerve degeneration in his legs. But he's an ace gymnast and the star of our wheelchair basketball games—I've seen him sink one from the middle of the floor."

They had started for the exit when Fleming called to a student, his right arm hanging limply at his side, who was picking up towels from the benches. "Collins, I'll be in my office with Mr. Banks. When you finish, I'd appreciate two containers of coffee from the cafeteria. Tell Mrs. Deveny it's for me."

He glanced at Artie. "I've cream and sugar in the office, if you use it."

"Black," Artie said offhand. Collins had caught his eye and they stared at each other for a second. Sturdy kid, reddish hair, probably looked young for his age—more pretty than handsome, in a homely sort of way. The type of face where all the flaws made for an agreeable whole; the tough Irish kid who looked angelic as an altar boy.

In the office, Fleming relaxed in the black leather chair behind his desk and stared thoughtfully at Artie.

"Over the phone, you said Mark had disappeared. We thought he was sick and you had just forgotten to notify us."

Artie shook his head. "He vanished two days ago—he never came home from school. I called some of his friends; they said he'd done a few laps in the pool and then a friend had given him a lift home. Apparently he left again shortly afterward. No way he could have left by himself; his chair was still there."

Fleming nodded. "After you called, I did some checking here. Collins was the student who drove him home; you can talk to him later."

Artie wasn't sure how to approach what was on his mind. "I was wondering . . ." His voice trailed off.

Fleming didn't help. "Yes, Mr. Banks?" His face was impassive.

"I was wondering if . . . if Mark has any girlfriends. That sounds funny—I'm his father, I should know. I'm sure he would have brought any home but he never has and I was curious—"

"He's popular," Fleming interrupted shortly. "I would say he has his share of female friends. He's a very outgoing young man."

There was a knock on the door and Collins came in clutching a tray in his left hand with two sealed containers of coffee.

"Thank you, Collins. Stand by outside for a bit; I think Mr. Banks would like to talk to you."

Again, the brief spark of something in Collins' eyes, and then he was gone.

"You were saying, Mr. Banks?"

"How deep do the relationships go, Mr. Fleming? There's probably no way I would know—but you might."

Fleming looked puzzled.

"I'm not sure I follow you."

He was beating around the bush, Artie thought. But he didn't have all day and neither did Fleming.

"Sexually," he said bluntly. "I keep wondering if some girl . . . woman . . . might have gotten Mark to run off with her, say, for a week in Palm Springs or maybe Las Vegas."

Fleming looked amused. "I rather think it would have been a mutual decision, not the young lady's alone. But frankly, sexual activity isn't something we monitor, Mr. Banks. On campus, certainly. Off campus, it's none of our business." He paused. "You've never worked with crippled children, have you? As a counselor or anything like that?"

Artie shook his head.

"Being crippled creates a rapport among the students, Mr. Banks. It's a very strong one; they feel very close. You don't have the usual dating rituals you find in most high schools. Friends aren't chosen on the basis of beauty or physical prowess. They're very open with each other, they're very honest. To be truthful about it, I suspect our students are more sexually active than most. For one thing, to have sex at all usually requires close cooperation between them. The feelings of closeness and cooperation are already there, and I know they have great compassion for each other. I imagine that sexual activity is not far behind."

"And what do you do when students get pregnant?"

"They usually inform their parents—we don't have to. Pregnancy is uncommon, but when it happens it may interest you to know they invariably choose to keep the child."

"Mark—"

Fleming held up his hand.

"That's about all I can tell you. Mark is a very popular boy, it's my observation that he's much in demand. I'm somewhat surprised you aren't aware of that. I suppose his mother probably is; a lot of fathers seem to be remote from their sons. Too bad, but then I don't know the circumstances of your family life."

Artie felt his face color. "I don't see where—"

"Collins is waiting for you, Mr. Banks. It's the last day of school and I think he would like to go home."

It was a dismissal, but that wasn't what hurt. He'd been accused of being remote when it came to his son, and Fleming was probably right. Only he had blamed it on Mark when he should have been blaming it on himself.

C o l l i n s   w a s   w a i t i n g   f o r him just outside the door. He sized up Artie quickly, then said, "If you want more coffee, the cafeteria's still open." Artie followed him down the hallway, then caught himself watching Collins closely. Stocky build and athletic, his right arm useless but not withered. Physical therapy had to be a good part of their phys ed routine. But the kid walked with the same sort of confidence that Artie had noticed in Mark the last few years. Not cock-of-the-walk, but very confident in who he was.

They took a table in a corner of the almost deserted cafeteria and Artie sipped at his coffee and studied Collins over the edge of his cup.

"You gave Mark a lift home Tuesday night?"

Collins nodded, a faint curiosity in his deep-set eyes as he watched Artie in turn. "We left here at three-thirty and got to your house about ten after four. Traffic on the bridge was pretty light. I helped Mark get in his chair and he rolled up the walk and that was it."

"Any reason why Mark might have left the house again later? Anybody coming to pick him up?"

Collins shrugged. "He didn't mention any."

How the hell did you discuss sex with a seventeen-year-old? Artie wondered.

"Any girlfriends who might have showed up after you left?"

"Was he fucking anybody?" Collins asked coldly. "Is that what you want to know?" There was more than just belligerence in his voice; there was something else as well.

"He's been missing for two days," Artie said coldly. "He's handicapped"—he couldn't bring himself to use the word *crippled*—"and I don't think he could go anyplace by himself. Somebody had to help him."

Collins took pity on him. "He has a lot of girlfriends," he said, but once again something was hidden. "If he didn't . . . sleep with them, I'd figure he was a fool. And he's no fool. He might have had a date for later that evening; he acted like it but I didn't ask. There's a senior woman who likes him a lot. They're close."

"He gets around," Artie said bitterly, more because he hadn't really known about it than because of any bias against teenage promiscuity.

"More than I do," Collins said coolly.

"His mother's desperate," Artie said, pleading. "And so am I. Who is she? We'd like to find out if she and Mark went . . . somewhere."

Collins stood up; he wasn't about to be a snitch. "I'm sorry. I've told you everything I can. Mark can take care of himself. I wouldn't worry about him."

He was halfway across the cafeteria when he suddenly stopped and came back. He reached in his left pocket, took out Mark's earring, and put it on the table.

"We were wrestling in the gym earlier that day and this fell off. I found it on the mat the next morning. If Mark doesn't come back, then I guess you should have it."

Artie took the small piece of stone and what looked like worked silver, wrapped it carefully in a napkin, and dropped it in his shirt pocket. He glanced up at Collins to thank him for it, then realized with sudden shock that it wasn't a bad case of hero worship Collins had for Mark; it was something else.

"Mark didn't drop this—he gave it to you, didn't he?"

For a moment Collins looked like he was going to deny it, then shrugged, his face suddenly drawn. Whatever memory he had obviously hurt. "It was a consolation prize," he said quietly. "He said we would always be friends."

Collins got a few feet away, then turned back once again.

"Mark is still my best friend, Mr. Banks. He was generous with me—I've no complaint."

Artie stared after him, not quite sure what he should think. He didn't know what, if anything, had happened between Mark and Collins, but Collins had called Mark generous and the earring had been an heirloom. Mark hadn't given it away lightly. Artie felt like he had when he'd walked in on Mark that one morning.

Mark was way past puberty and besides, it wasn't any of his business.

. . .

It was eight in the evening. Artie sat alone in his car, the lights and radio off, the engine silent. He had put on two sweaters and the heaviest jacket he had and he was still cold. The Avenues in San Francisco were on rolling dunes west of the hills and nearest the ocean so they caught the brunt of the fog and the winds off the Pacific. When it was sunny in the Mission and the Castro, you could usually count on the Avenues being fogged in and chilly.

Tonight the fog had rolled in late in the afternoon and now blanketed the entire city. But he would bet the Avenues were still colder and clammier than the rest of the town. He shivered and hunkered down lower in his seat, watching the pink stuccoed house a few doors up at the corner of Ulloa and Thirtieth. It was a two-story affair with a huge garage beneath and surrounded by stubby little palm trees and rows of potted cactus plants on the front steps. Big house: Lyle Pace couldn't be doing too badly.

All Artie knew about stakeouts was what he'd seen in the movies, but they never let you know how the characters kept from feeling foolish—or guilty. He was going to spy on one of his friends and, once again, he wasn't even sure what he was looking for. Something out of the ordinary, something that didn't jibe with their character as he knew it. That was vague as hell, but presumably he would know what he was looking for when he saw it.

Or would he? His black mood was back in force and he reached for the key to start the engine. Enough of this bullshit.

But Larry Shea lying gray and torn in the morgue hadn't been bullshit, and neither had Hall, crumpled on the steps of the museum, his heart pumping his life's blood over the concrete. And it hadn't been bullshit when he'd stood on the railing of his porch about to plunge to the sidewalk three stories below.

He folded his arms and settled back in his seat, once more concentrating on the house on the corner. He'd been there half an hour now but nobody had come or gone and there were no lights on. Lyle obviously wasn't home, though Artie doubted he was out of town. He was manager of the Market Street Copeland's, and sporting goods were a popular item for Christmas. Maybe he had taken Anya, his live-in girlfriend, out to the movies or a holiday dinner.

Lyle Pace, one of the last members to join the Club. Artie had never gotten to know him well—a few months after Lyle had drifted into the coffee shop, Artie had enlisted. Lyle had followed a little later, but their paths had never crossed in 'Nam. After Lyle was discharged he'd enrolled in State and picked up a degree in psychology. Jenny Morrison, who'd dated him briefly back then, said he had never been more than a C student.

Lyle had been planning to work for the City but it hadn't panned out—like most things in his life. At State he'd been on the wrestling team and at one time had hopes of going to the Olympics, but he never even made the qualifying rounds. He'd had a three-year failed marriage, and then he'd drifted away from everybody. He'd surfaced again two years ago and showed up at a meeting—who'd brought him? Jenny?—and everybody had been glad to see him, but they knew they were dealing with damaged goods and had kept their distance. Artie had felt guilty about that. He should have extended himself more.

Lyle wasn't the star athlete he had once been. Now he was thicker in the middle, with a faint sag to the shoulders. Not especially handsome as a kid, a lot less so now. Broken nose, bushy black eyebrows, eyes that were too small and too bright, a face badly used by time. On the other hand, he had a way with women. Anya was exotic, a statuesque brunette ten years Lyle's junior with an executive position at Bank of America. What the hell had Lyle used for bait?

He'd picked Lyle for his first stakeout not because he knew so much about him but because he knew so little. He'd gotten over his paranoia about Charlie and Mitch—almost—and that hadn't left a whole lot of possibilities. Lyle had been first on the list of those who remained.

Artie scrunched around in his seat, trying to find a more comfortable position, then froze at a sudden tapping on the passenger-side window. He glanced over, thought *Shit!*, and rolled down the glass.

"Recognized your car from down the street," Lyle said cheerfully. "What the hell you sitting out here for?"

Artie fought his sense of shock, suddenly feeling like he was back in 'Nam and had stumbled into an ambush. Then once again the sense of unreality hit him and he felt faintly ashamed. He had never really tried to be Lyle's friend and now here he was compounding his guilt by spying on him.

"Waiting for you, Lyle. I just got here, you weren't home, and I thought I'd give you a few minutes to show up—glad I did."

"I was taking Fritzi for a walk." The rottweiler had put her paws on the edge of the window and was giving him a wait-and-see look, probably hoping he would be good for a biscuit or two. "Come on in. Anya's visiting relatives in San Jose so we've got the house to ourselves."

Artie climbed out and locked the car.

Everything was perfectly normal.

Why had he thought it would be otherwise?

The kitchen was clean and open, the dinnerware in the glass-front cupboards a pleasant delft blue pattern, no dishes in the sink, the linoleum floor freshly waxed, floral curtains over the windows. A woman's touch, Artie thought; a little too frilly for Lyle.

Lyle filled the dog's water bowl, then put on a pot of coffee. "You want to see the house?"

Lyle might not be the huge success in life he had wanted to be, but he was obviously far from down and out. If he wanted to show off or brag a little, he had the right.

"Sure, Lyle—sorry I haven't dropped in before."

"Really, Artie?"

The tour was cursory—nobody ever showed you their bedroom or the john. You usually saw only the rooms that were deliberately on display: the office, the library, the living room, the rec room if they had one. Lyle's office didn't amount to much, but the den in the basement was impressive. A bookcase full of CDs, a component music system that must have cost a fortune, a big-screen TV. Managing Copeland's obviously paid well, though Anya's salary undoubtedly helped.

Artie ran his hand over one of the shelves of CDs. "You must have spent a mint on these."

Lyle shrugged. "We all spend more than we should on our hobbies, right? And if you think that's something, you should see Mary's—she could set up her own store. Big on books, too, mostly poetry—didn't expect that, either."

Artie was surprised.

"You must be the first one in the Club that Mary ever invited over."

"Who said anything about being invited? I went over to see Jenny when Mary wasn't home."

Artie floundered for a moment. "You and Jenny—"

"—were a number before Mary cut in, remember? When I came back to town, I thought I'd look her up and try and fan the embers when the wicked witch was away. I never believed that lesbian shit. I thought she might at least be a switch hitter. When Jenny opened the door, I just walked in. Jenny wouldn't have any of it—she and Mary were for real—but I got a good look at the house. Nice decor if you care for turn-of-the-century."

He turned and switched on the light in a workout room just off the den. The room was small but laid out for efficiency. A NordicTrack machine and then several free-weight setups. A workout bench with two metal uprights holding a bar that was loaded with at least two and a quarter for bench presses. Lyle might have seemed like he was out of shape, but if he actually lifted those weights it was obvious he wasn't.

They returned to the kitchen and Lyle poured out two cups of coffee, then teetered back in a kitchen chair, looking at Artie with an expression that was vaguely unfriendly.

"Why did you come to see me, Artie? I mean, all of a sudden like? I've been going to meetings almost a year this time around and you're the first member who's dropped over. I thought for sure Larry or Charlie might, but they never did. You guys are friendly enough at meetings, but otherwise it's like I don't exist. You've got me pegged as a loser, right? And you decided to keep your distance because you were afraid it might be catching."

He'd never liked Lyle, Artie remembered, and now he knew why.

"You disappeared for eight years, Lyle. I don't remember you saying good-bye to anybody."

Lyle shrugged. "Okay, you've got a point. I should have."

It was difficult to keep it casual, not to take offense.

"It's kind of hard to pick up where you left off."

"Mea culpa, Artie." Lyle got up to fill his cup and gestured with the pot. "You want some more? Drink enough, you'll have to sleep in the bathtub tonight."

Artie shook his head. "One will do me."

"So why *did* you come over, Artie? And don't tell me it was because you were in the neighborhood."

If Lyle was Lyle, then he had a right to be pissed. If he was . . .

something else, then they were fencing. In either case, he was going to have to fake it. He wanted out of there, badly, but there was no way he could up and leave. Not right then.

There was a box of dog biscuits on the table and he shook one out for Fritzi to cover his nervousness. She was very dainty in taking it from his hand, her hindquarters wriggling as she tried to wag her docked tail, and Artie remembered the three dogs in Schuler's office and how friendly they'd been. It took an effort not to shiver.

"When you first joined the Club, I wasn't around long enough to really get to know you. When you came back, it was difficult to start all over again. Most of us are married and have families, and it's natural to stick with old friends. It's not so easy to make new ones when you get older, Lyle. So none of us volunteered. I felt bad about that, and since this is the Christmas season, I thought I'd drop by. Once here, I came down with cold feet and sat out in the car. I was afraid if you were home and I rang the bell, you'd tell me to get lost. You would have had every right to."

He meant it all. Every word of it. And he hoped, desperately, that Lyle believed him.

Lyle softened slightly. "Apology accepted, Artie. But to be honest, I don't know what the hell we've got in common to talk about."

"Larry . . ." Artie let his voice trail off, but there was no reaction on Lyle's part. He changed the subject. "It was something of a shock meeting Schuler again. He dredged up old times, at least for me. I imagine he did the same for you."

Lyle relaxed even more. "A real prick. He told me about the time he busted you guys. He busted me once and kept me in a jail for a week, said he didn't like my attitude."

And that was it for a good forty-five minutes, until Artie yawned and said if he were going to sleep in the bathtub, he'd better get started. It had been all old times, nothing about Larry's murder or Mark's disappearance. And toward the end, the nostalgic mood had worn rather thin.

Once outside in his car, Artie realized his shirt was sticking to him—he had sweated up a storm. Fritzi had even refused to come over when he offered her a third biscuit, probably because he smelled bad. But one minor mystery had been solved. Nobody had written Lyle off because he had failed at some time in the past. The reason was simpler than that: They didn't like him because he wasn't very likable.

Artie chose an indirect route on the way home, one nobody could have expected him to take to get from the Avenues to Noe and Twentieth. He was paranoid, he realized, but Jesus, who could blame him? The only time Lyle had struck him as real was when he'd let his hurt feelings surface at the very beginning.

And there had been all the other things that hadn't rung true, the little things. Lyle's workout room. What was Lyle now? Middle to late forties, like the rest of them? He looked like a schlump, but he was bench-pressing two and a quarter and the schedule pasted on the wall wasn't for casual workouts. He was stronger than he looked. But why the hell did he keep it hidden? At his age and in that shape, you'd think he'd be wearing tailored shirts and Italian suits to show it off.

Jesus, Mitch was right. The only thing he had to fear was paranoia itself. Anything he'd wanted to know about Lyle, he could probably have asked and Lyle would have told him. So Lyle was vain about his build and doing his damnedest to recapture the days when he'd yearned for the Olympics. What else was new?

But something had stuck in his mind.

Something about Mary Robards.

Mary was reclusive; nobody had ever been invited to her house. Ever. But Lyle had stormed his way in. He'd seen the inside of the house and commented on her extensive collection of CDs, enough to stock a store. Lyle had been right when he'd mentioned that everybody spent too much on their hobbies. They seldom kept quiet about them, though; hobbies were what you talked about when the conversation was on life support.

Mary had never mentioned her passion for music, and he never would have guessed her interest in poetry. But it was hardly strange for a lawyer to love the language.

Things started to swim into focus then and Artie felt like he'd just fallen into a pond of ice water. They couldn't sing, he'd told Hall when they had been discussing the Old People. *They had no music. . . .* And Hall had said they had little in the way of language.

There was an element of pathos about it, Artie thought. The descendants of the Old People probably loved the symphony; they probably went to the opera as often as they could, as well as to plays and poetry readings and probably art shows.

And if they collected anything at all, it was probably CDs and paintings.

And maybe chapbooks of poetry.

CHAPTER 12

Once home, Artie checked in with the police. There was nothing new on Mark—no runaways or young victims of violence who fit his description. Connie Lee was working late at KXAM and sounded a little plaintive when she asked Artie if he'd be in for work the following day. Artie assured her that he would; the rest of the conversation was devoted to Connie's growing belief that the world was going to hell.

Mitch's answering machine was on; he apparently wasn't home. For a few minutes Artie's mind was filled with possible scenarios of what might have happened to Mitch, then he forced himself to stop thinking about them. Things were scary enough without his imagination adding fuel to the flames.

He called Susan but there was no answer. She was at the hospital, he thought, and debated calling her there, then decided against it. He had nothing more he could tell her about Mark.

He slept fitfully and awoke the next morning with a splitting headache. He sat on the edge of his bed for a good five minutes, massaging his temples and trying not to think about what he was going to do that morning. He'd have to call Connie's voice mail and tell her he was going to be in late; there was no helping it.

He read the paper starting with the comics and ending with the front page, then dialed Mary Robards after nine. She was usually at her law office early—if she answered at home, he'd simply hang up.

Again, an answering machine.

He ate a quick breakfast of orange juice and oatmeal, then pocketed the automatic and drove over to the Potrero Hill section of town. Mary lived on Connecticut Street in a white clapboard house that seemed small from the front but extended back almost the full length of the lot. It was a large enough house for her and Jenny to have separate offices—neither one of them would feel cramped. The only drawback was that there was no garage tucked underneath. The house itself was on a hill that sloped away toward the back and Artie guessed that the first floor was set back into the hill. The floor that fronted on the street was actually the top floor.

Artie parked and watched for a few minutes. There was no movement behind the curtains and there were no cars parked on the street that he recognized as belonging to either Mary or Jenny. He glanced at his watch, then quietly got out of the car. Mary had cats, that much he knew, but she didn't care for dogs—"Dirty animals, always humping your leg and fouling the sidewalks." Mary had said the house had been painted that fall and it looked it. Certainly pretty enough from the front, the landscaping carefully groomed. That was Mary's one hobby that he knew of: gardening.

Artie spent a moment rehearsing a story to tell Mary in case he had miscalculated and she was home, then rang the bell. A minute of panic before he relaxed. Nobody had answered the door. He tried the knob—locked—and guessed there was a dead bolt on the inside. He stood there a moment, shivering in the cold, thinking about Mary. Serious, almost grim—and forgetful. She wouldn't rely on her memory when it came to taking along her keys when she left the house. She'd even joked about the time she'd locked herself out.

Artie lifted the mat—nothing—and glanced around the small front porch. The usual leaves that had blown into the corners, plus a half-empty bag of potting soil almost hidden in the shadows. He felt underneath it, found the key, and a moment later was inside the house. Heavy curtains and drapes kept out most of the sun and Artie stood for a moment in the gloom, listening. Nothing.

He took a breath and started exploring. The street floor was laid out like a railroad flat, with all the rooms opening off a long hallway that ran along one side of the house. A large living room in front with windows looking out on the street, then a dining room, and finally the bedroom with a kitchen opposite and a sunporch in back. The bathroom was across from the dining room just after a few steps that led down to a landing. Then more steps from the landing to . . . what? Probably offices and a family room downstairs, cut into the slope of the hill.

It was a turn-of-the-century atmosphere inside the house. Mary and Jenny had restored the interior, letting the outside of the house blend with the others on the block. Thick, heavy drapes and lacework curtains, dark oak furniture—probably all antiques. Area rugs carpeted the light oak flooring. The walls of the living room were covered with prints of famous paintings, all of them realistic, almost illustrative. Winslow Homer, Sargent, Gainsborough, Wyeth, Alma-Tadema, Eakins, Pyle, and a St. John of a cave girl being threatened by a saber-toothed cat. A lot of it kitsch, all of it romantic realism.

In the dining room, the table had a linen cloth spread over it and was set for two with antique dinnerware, obviously for show. The dining table and the setting went with the framed 1906 copy of the *Oakland Tribune,* the headlines about the San Francisco earthquake, that hung among the print gallery on one of the dining room walls. It was a room reserved for small dinner parties, Artie decided—Mary and Jenny probably ate most of their meals in the kitchen.

There was only one bedroom. Against the far wall was a king-sized four-poster with goose down pillows and a comforter that had probably won a prize in a county fair a century before. Large closets and two oak chests of drawers, one for each of them. Artie opened the bathroom door, then quickly closed it. The cat box by the toilet was overdue for changing.

He almost expected to find a woodstove in the kitchen, but when it came to cooking, Mary had the same taste for the modern as Cathy Shea, salted with a few antiques. Heavy cast-iron frying pans hung from wall hooks and an ancient butcher block squatted next to the sink. The surface was concave from usage but Artie guessed that Mary kept it mostly—again—for show.

Show for whom? He didn't know anybody in the Club who had

ever been there with the exception of Lyle, and he had hardly been a guest.

Artie walked quietly to the head of the stairs. There were no windows downstairs and the stairwell was pitch black. He couldn't find the light switch and fished around in his pocket for his cigarette lighter and flicked it on. He felt his way down the stairs, catching glimpses of more paintings in the faint glow from the lighter. Opening off the stairwell at the bottom were two offices—one somewhat spartan with a large poster of San Francisco on the wall, a plain, uncluttered desk, a single filing cabinet, and a computer table. Jenny's.

The other office was larger, with a bank of four filing cabinets and several large bookcases filled with law books. Mary's hideaway from her office downtown. A more ornate desk with two telephones on it, a fax machine, and another computer workstation. And on one corner of the desk, a large color photograph of Jenny, which must have been taken when they had first met. She wasn't a bad-looking woman now; she had been drop-dead gorgeous back then.

The room that lay beyond was the one Artie was most interested in. It was a huge recreation room with a conversation pit lined with black leather pillows around the rim. One wall was covered with more paintings, most of them prints of the Impressionists. The only exceptions were some Maxfield Parrish prints in thin black frames—covers from some old magazines. The far end of the room was taken up with an elaborate surround sound system.

The left wall held Mary's CD collection, one that made Lyle's seem tiny. Thousands of jewel boxes lined shelves that ran from the floor to the ceiling and extended from one end of the room to the other. Artie walked over and waved his lighter along the shelving. There were no instrumentals—all the CDs were voice. Popular, classical, operatic, jazz . . .

The opposite wall was taken up with bookcases, and Artie guessed they were filled with first editions. Mary probably hadn't been selective; he suspected she had everybody from Hemingway to Eliot to Ginsberg.

Such little things as art and music and poetry to give her away.

Artie never heard the creaking of the stairs, never heard anybody walking down them. The first he knew he was no longer alone was when the overhead track lights flashed on, blinding him. He dropped the lighter and the gun was in his hand without his even thinking. Then he had sense enough to freeze.

"You're a clever species," a voice behind him said. "Too clever by half."

A r t i e   s t o o d   s t i l l   a n o t h e r few seconds, then said, "I'd like to turn around."

"Please do," Mary Robards said. "I don't want to talk to your back all day." Her voice was heavy, gravelly. She was dressed in black with a looping strand of pearls. Your stereotypical old-fashioned matron, the perfect image of the motherly lawyer for the defense. To complete the picture she was holding a huge black cat with a splash of stiff white fur around its muzzle. A tom that Mary must have had for years.

"Congratulations, Artie—you've discovered the real me." She nodded toward the conversation pit. "We'll be more comfortable over there if you want to talk, and I assume you do." She turned her back on him and walked over to the pit. "And put away the cannon; you're the only one who's armed."

Artie sat gingerly on one of the leather cushions, hunching forward with his elbows on his knees. He was face-to-face with the enemy—and the enemy turned out to be a plump, middle-aged woman whom he considered his friend and whom he had once slept with when they both were younger. An enemy who wore reading glasses and held a basketful of knitting in her lap, her cat curled up next to her.

"You were waiting for me?"

"You paid a visit to Lyle last night; I guessed I would be next on your list."

Artie felt the first prickle of sweat.

"You're good—I never knew I was being followed."

She shook her head and pulled out a row of stitches, frowning. "Nothing so time-consuming. Lyle called Jenny after you left; they're still friends, he's closer to her than other members of the Club. I'll give him one thing—he's a game loser once he knows he's really lost."

To Artie, it sounded like a confirmation of what he'd suspected.

"Lyle's one of you?"

"Perhaps. But that's for you to find out, Artie. For your own protection, I'd certainly try to find out soon if I were you."

Artie could guess but asked anyway. "Why so important?"

She took a sip from a water glass on the coffee table in front of her. Vodka, Artie thought, or more likely gin. She'd been a drinker all her life but he'd never suspected she hit the bottle that early in the day; she was probably smart enough to limit herself to a glass in the morning and a martini in the evening. Who was it who said that as you grew older you didn't give up your vices, they gave you up?

"He could be a Hound, you know."

"Hound?" Artie felt lost.

"One of our soldiers, if you like. Or think of the children's game, Hare-and-Hounds, with the hounds out to catch the hare. Or the hound in *The Hound of the Baskervilles*. Better yet, the poem by Thompson. 'I fled Him, down the nights and down the days; I fled Him, down the arches of the years. . . .' It's one of my favorites— 'The Hound of Heaven'—but I think 'Hound from Hell' is more appropriate in this case." She smiled slightly. "I never knew, Artie—Do you like poetry? Your species has a way with words, I'll grant that." And then, deadly serious: "You're the hare, Artie. I think you've already met the Hound."

It was hard for Artie to think of her as one of the Old People. His mind kept slipping back to when he'd first met her. She'd had a peasant's stocky body and there had been occasions when he'd delighted in it. But there had also been a remoteness about her that he never understood until she and Jenny became a couple. He hadn't accepted that until much later.

"You're toying with me, aren't you, Mary?"

"Of course. I'm hardly going to point the finger at anybody; you wouldn't respect me if I did." Her voice was sarcastic.

"Did Lyle murder Larry Shea?"

She shrugged. Artie had always thought Mary and Larry Shea had been close friends. It didn't seem to matter to her now and it was obvious it never had.

"I don't know who our Hounds are, Artie. What we don't know, we can't tell. If I suspected, I would never ask and they would never say. Some Hound, maybe Lyle—if he is one. For all I know, he's *Homo sap,* just like you."

She chucked her cat under the chin one more time, then set it on the floor. It ran for the shadows in a far corner of the room and disappeared.

The house was made for entertaining, but nobody Artie knew had ever been there—or had admitted to it. She obviously had a different circle of friends from those in the Club, friends with whom she could let her hair down, friends with whom she could dispense with the act. Friends just like her.

"Who are you people, Mary?"

She didn't look at him but concentrated on her knitting, holding up a length of scarf that seemed a bizarre collection of colors—she had no sense of the artistic at all, Artie thought. But she wasn't fat, she didn't have a dowager's hump, and when she held up the scarf the flesh didn't hang in loose folds from her upper arms. Like Lyle, she was probably in damned good shape but kept it hidden under flowing dresses.

"Come on, Artie, you already know—we're the meek who were supposed to inherit the earth. Until your species came along. And that's not quite accurate, either. Did you know we managed to coexist for thousands of years?" She grimaced. "Then thirty-five thousand years ago nature gave you too many talents all at once. It was like giving an ape an arsenal of assault rifles and teaching him how to use them. Maybe it was a mutation, maybe it was a gene for violence—that's something your scientists ought to look into. But the problem isn't who *we* are, the problem is who *you* are." She shook her head in mock dismay. "You always want to know how other species differ from you, not how you might differ from them, unless all the differences are on the plus side."

"One of you killed Dr. Hall," Artie accused.

She took another sip from the glass and studied him, her eyes a crystalline blue in a remarkably unlined face.

"All I know about it is what I read in the papers, Artie. You apparently went to Hall and showed him Shea's research. Not very kind of you in the long run. You're as responsible for what happened to him as the Hound, whoever he is."

"And Paschelke?"

"Same thing."

She seemed friendly enough on the surface, but beneath it Mary struck him as being as alien as somebody from another planet. Artie kept trying to think of common ground, of points of rapport. She was willing to talk but he didn't know where to start asking questions. In 'Nam he'd sat in on interrogations with Mitch where the languages differed, but here it was the mind-set itself—and something more. Different species, he thought uneasily. How the hell *would* they talk to each other?

"You said that we're different from you."

She looked disapproving.

"Oh, you're different all right, in a way you don't suspect. Most of your anthropologists know it but they'll never tell you. You're a fluke of nature, a flawed species, Artie. Only a part of you is rational. The other part is mad as a hatter—as a species, you're committable."

Artie felt uncomfortable.

"That's a pretty harsh judgment."

"Is it? For starters, you breed uncontrollably, you war constantly, and you've made the world into a pigpen. Worst of all, you take no responsibility—you excuse yourselves by saying that somehow it's all part of God's grand design. I've got news for you, Artie. God sometimes makes mistakes, and you're one of them."

Artie remembered balancing on the railing of his balcony and the subtle urgings that had bubbled up in his head. He hadn't known what to call it then; he didn't now.

"You can read minds?"

She cocked her head, frowning.

"Don't be silly—nobody can read minds. We can't press a button on your mental computer and watch the words scroll up on a screen. We can see images in each other's minds and we can project them if you're receptive, that's all. It's like the Rhine experiments: The subjects weren't asked to identify words, they were asked to identify images. Many of your own children can do it when they're two years old. They mostly lose the ability as they grow older." She pointed to her glass. "You want something to drink?"

He might think about getting roaring drunk later on. But if Mitch was right, he knew he could never afford to lose control of his mind again.

"I'm fine. I didn't know that about kids."

"You should. When you're growing up, what's the one ability you always wished you had? To know what somebody else is thinking, right? When you're a teenager, it's 'will she or won't she' and how much you'd give if only you knew. To be able to glimpse an image of you and her together, to know that that's what she's thinking about. Wouldn't you have liked to be able to do that, Artie? You lose that ability early, but you never get over wishing you had it back."

"That must have given you a big advantage over your enemies."

For a fleeting moment she looked sad. "We could see pictures in other people's minds. It was useful on the hunt. And racial memories were our history books. A simple talent, but you more than made up for your lack of it."

Artie couldn't understand why she was telling him as much as she was. She had to be doing it for a reason, but he didn't have a clue what it might be.

"How?"

She put down the knitting and took another sip from her glass.

"Didn't your professor Hall explain the possibilities? Your species could make a far wider variety of sounds than we could, and eventually it led to language. We didn't need to describe what we saw in words. For much the same reason, we didn't need art. You needed both and you ran with them. And then you were clever enough to substitute paintings for mental images, the one talent we had that you envied."

She twisted her head to glance at the wall of CDs and books behind her.

"Nature not only made you handsome, it gave you language and music and art and you did wonders with all of them. From a personal viewpoint, I'm very glad that you did. I can't carry a tune—few of us can—and I couldn't draw a recognizable stick figure if you paid me. But it was a Faustian bargain, Banks. Nature also made you the most homicidal species the planet has ever seen."

She suddenly turned accusing.

"Your species learned to lie with language, Artie. Lying was a concept that was foreign to us; you can't lie very well with images. We believed you during truces, in battles, in negotiations—and by the time we understood you were lying, we were almost gone."

Artie tried in vain to see in her face the Mary Robards he'd once known, but that Mary had vanished for good. They had been lovers briefly and then friends for how long? Twenty years? Now she'd taken off the mask she had worn for so long and beneath it was the face of a stranger. It was like a death in the family.

"Language—that was your key to winning the world, Artie. Then you trumped it and organized the sounds you made into words you could carve in stone or print on paper. Remarkable! You could do with print the same things you could do with your voice. You didn't need racial memories; you could leave printed books behind. And you could lie with them just as easily as you could with the spoken word."

"You're afraid of us," Artie accused.

She looked surprised. "If you were us, wouldn't you be? What do you think would happen if everybody knew about us? How soon would it take your governments to launch the greatest pogrom the world has ever seen?"

He already knew the answer to that one; once again the memory of the Tribe was fresh in his mind.

"You're experts at genocide," she continued, her voice now heavy with anger. "It's in your blood. The genocides of the Second World War—"

"Committed by the Nazis—"

"Oh? And since then it's been the Hutus trying to exterminate the Tutsis, all those loser tribes in the Sudan killing each other off, the Serbs slaughtering the Muslims—That was another genocide where the murderers did their jobs with enthusiasm, an evening's entertainment! And remember 'Nam, remember My Lai?"

"Thousands died on both sides," Artie said angrily.

Mary's smile was sardonic.

"So what's your point, Artie? You want to go back to Tasmania a hundred and fifty years ago when the early settlers shot the natives for sport and exterminated an entire race?"

She resumed knitting, the needles flashing savagely.

"Or try your eden of Tahiti where warring tribes nailed children to their captive mothers with spears and drilled holes in the heads of other prisoners so they could be strung together like beads on a string. Consider the Turks and the Armenians or the Mayans, whose population dropped ninety-five percent in fifty years because of wars of extermination. Better yet, read your own Bible—"

"That's the dark side," Artie interrupted, desperate.

She sounded exasperated.

"My God, Artie, you think there's a bright side? Look at your history books. They're nothing but a recital of battles won and battles lost with the victors sitting atop a mound of skulls at the end! And the generals who engineered the slaughters become your heroes! What was it your General Grant said? That he could walk across the battlefield at Shiloh stepping on the bodies of the dead without his feet ever touching the ground?"

She drained what was left in her glass, hesitated, then refilled it from a bottle beneath the table.

"You should read your morning paper more often, Artie. Your species is monstrous when it comes to hypocrisy: you keep telling yourselves how much you prize human life when it's obvious there's nothing you value less. You love violence, you adore it. Three hundred years ago you even treated guns like works of art, decorating them with intricate carvings and inlaying them with mother-of-pearl. It's a wonder you're not doing the same thing with the stocks of AK-47s today. For all I know, maybe you are."

Mary turned colder now, her face masking her emotions. "History is a two-way street, Artie. You want to know what you were like in the distant past, look at what you are today. You're the same murderous species now that you were thirty-five thousand years ago. You exterminated the Neanderthals and then you went after us. You wanted our hunting grounds and our foraging areas, and the simplest way to get them was to kill us—men, women, children, babes in arms. And it was so easy! We looked different from you, so you could identify and kill us on sight. We were the 'other' and because we were, you didn't need an excuse."

Artie remembered the slaughter on the riverbank and turned away, sick. "You're still here, Mary," he said in a low voice.

"There were two groups of us. Those of us who lived in northern Europe were big nosed, heavy browed, stumpy people who had adapted to the cold. We were tribal, we tended to stay in the same areas, so we didn't get any images about what was happening until it was too late. We became the ogres of fairy tales, the hairy, ugly people who lived in the woods. It was open season on us and within a few thousand years we were gone."

Artie could see no trace of the primitive in her.

"You look no different from us."

Mary turned back to her knitting, her voice sad.

"I said there were two groups of us. The tribes who lived in southern Europe, around the Mediterranean, looked more like *Homo sapiens*. It was survival of the fittest, Artie, and the fittest were those of us who looked and spoke the most like you. Children who were throwbacks were killed by their parents for fear they would cast suspicion on their families. We were selected out by our environment and *you* were that environment, as selective as the glaciers or the veldt. We ended up breeding according to your specifications. We adapted to *you*; we had to."

"You interbred—"

"God, yes, we interbred, Artie—there was mating and there were offspring. But we were a different species, it was like donkeys mating with horses, where the offspring are mules, sterile. Since lives were short, there were few grandparents around to become suspicious. As a species, we survived through arranged marriages. It's an honorable practice; it just goes back much farther than you think."

Artie remembered the few times he had watched her in court. She was as passionate then as she was now. Except then it was a calculated passion and now it was spontaneous.

"Why are you telling me all this, Mary?"

This time her smile made his skin crawl.

"*We* were the species in a direct line of succession from ancient man. You came out of nowhere, a quantum leap in potential, and you looked like nothing that had gone before. You were flat-faced, relatively lightly built, comparatively hairless with well-shaped heads . . . an elegant species. And thirty-five thousand years ago you stole our world." She held the scarf up to check her stitches, the mismatched colors jittering in the light. "We want it back, Artie."

Once again, Artie wasn't sure what to say.

"What are you going to do?"

"That's the second question. The first is what are *you* going to do."

She wasn't making sense. "I don't understand."

Her voice was very calm, deliberate.

"You're going to exterminate yourselves, Artie. You don't stand a prayer of lasting another hundred years. For a while we thought all we had to do was wait."

Artie stood up. The feel of the small gun in his pocket was comforting.

"Larry and Dr. Paschelke and Richard Hall aren't examples of waiting."

Her expression was somber.

"Our original plan was simple: Stay hidden until all of you died in wars or starved to death in a habitat you had ruined beyond saving. Unfortunately, it's our habitat as well. In the meantime our chances of being discovered have grown immeasurably. Medicine has become more sophisticated, there are physicals for work and for the military—you're only a few years away from having DNA data included on everybody's birth certificate. You'd be shocked when you came to us. And we can't foresee accidents and autopsies like Talbot's. Shea was a curious doctor. There'll be others. We can't afford to wait any longer, Artie—we want you gone. Now."

"And you're going to use the Hounds as weapons."

She shrugged, as if somehow they didn't involve her. "They're a loose cannon, a wild card. I don't know what they plan or who they are, but even if I knew, I wouldn't try to stop them." She paused. "We breed them like you breed pit bulls. They're dangerous, Artie. But you know that."

He would give a lot for the old Mary, Artie thought. The former lover whom he could talk to about his problems at work, his problems with raising Mark. How did a Muslim and a Serb, who might have been lifelong friends, talk to each other now?

"Why did you join the Club, Mary?"

She took another small sip from her glass.

"You sweated testosterone, you and the others. And you were courageous, adventurous. More than any military academy, the Club was a natural breeding ground for your own Hounds. You proved it when all of you went to 'Nam and came back decorated. You were brave, you were resourceful—we knew you would be and we were curious about you, about what made you tick. So several of us joined to find out."

"I didn't enjoy 'Nam," Artie said somberly. "I didn't enjoy war."

She shook her head. "I don't say you enjoyed killing people.

But you enjoyed war, you enjoyed the hunt. You're ashamed of that now."

She sounded like Mitch, Artie thought with sudden anger. He knew what he was ashamed of and he knew what he was proud of.

"You could have talked me out of what I suspected when I came here, Mary. I thought it was going to be a wild goose chase."

She looked surprised.

"Does it really make any difference what I say? You have no proof of anything; all you have are fantasies. We claimed Talbot's body, your printout of Shea's diskette is gone, so is the diskette itself. And everybody who's read Shea's research is dead."

He remembered Shea and Paschelke and Hall, and for the first time he accepted Mary as a complete stranger—one who would probably consider it a victory when he was dead as well.

"Except me."

"Except you." She shook her head. "But nobody in authority is going to believe you. For everything that's happened, there's a reasonable answer."

"You've told me too much, Mary. You've played the traitor. Your own Hounds will be after you now."

She raised an eyebrow. "Traitor? Hardly. Call it a favor for a friend. Someday you might have to make a judgment based on what I've told you. And that's . . . important. But in any event, we don't kill each other like your species does. Incidentally, don't bother coming over here again. Jenny and I will be away on vacation."

Artie paused by the stairwell. It would probably be his last chance to ask a question that had bothered him for years. "Why you and Jenny, Mary?"

There was a flicker of tenderness on her face. "I mated outside of gender and outside of species, Artie. Jenny needed somebody to take care of her and I needed somebody to take care of. She was beautiful and I was lucky. It worked out."

Mark had been in the back of his mind ever since coming over. He had nothing to lose by asking about him now.

"Mark disappeared three days ago. You know he's handicapped, he has to use a wheelchair to get around. He couldn't have gone anyplace without help. I'm worried your people might have taken him."

He was pleading with her, gambling on any feelings that might still exist between them, and for a moment he thought she looked concerned.

"I'm sure none of us have him but I don't really know."

Artie heard a car drive up outside and started up the steps. It was time to leave; more than time.

Behind him, Mary said softly, "Artie?"

He turned.

"I'd like to help you but I can't." She hesitated. "I probably wouldn't, even if I could."

What surprised him was the sorrow in her voice when she said it.

CHAPTER 13

"**I thought I was** going to have to ask Accounting to mail you your check," Connie said. "Anything more on Mark?"

"I made a few phone calls trying to track down a possible girl-friend he might have left with. Either everybody's keeping silent out of loyalty or, more likely, nobody wants to get involved. He's underage and if she was over eighteen, then she probably broke the law and goddammit—"

Connie held up her hand. "Not being cruel, Artie, but the cops aren't going to get their water hot about a seventeen-year-old boy and a nineteen-year-old girl running off to Palm Springs or wherever for a little fun in the sun. If she were older, they might look into it, but only for a snicker or two."

Artie sagged into his chair and watched the bustle outside in the newsroom. "When do you stop being a parent, Connie? When do you decide to let them go out on their own?"

She looked sympathetic. "One, you never stop. And two, you don't do the deciding—they do. And please don't ask me how I handle Eliz-abeth and John. I don't. And it's not because they're adopted."

"I don't understand Mark," Artie said, his voice close to despair.

"You only think you don't. Wait a few years and when you talk to him, you'll be talking to a duplicate of yourself."

Artie glanced at the clock. Late afternoon. He'd spent more time at Mary's than he'd thought. She'd scared the crap out of him and he'd called Levin right after he had left. Mitch had been out of the office but he'd try him at home that night, tell him what Mary had said and scare the crap out of him, too.

The desk was still piled high with printouts and books and half a dozen tape cassettes. Artie thumbed through a stack: the Grub must be spending all his time searching the Internet and Nexis.

"You're going to have to bring me up to speed, Connie."

"Sure." She said it offhand and continued staring through the glass at the newsroom outside.

Artie watched for a second, worried, then figured Connie was herself, though it was the first time Artie had seen her in a blue funk.

"Earth to Connie Lee, Earth—"

"Sorry, Artie." She rubbed at her face and blinked open her eyes. "What'd you want to know?"

No jokes and funny stories today, Artie thought. "You're still you, right?"

She frowned. "Yeah," she said uncertainly, "we had an argument or something. I'd forgotten all about that."

Artie shrugged. "It doesn't matter." The Old People were keeping one step ahead of him.

Connie thumbed through a stack of reports. "To be honest, Artie, I'm sorry as shit I ever got involved in this. You read enough of these and after a while you begin to think you've got a ringside seat at the end of the world. It's all around us, nobody's doing anything about it, and you feel like you're barreling toward the edge of the cliff at full speed. Maybe we won't go over in my lifetime, but we sure as hell will in my kids'."

Artie was suddenly all attention. What was it Mary had said? They didn't stand a prayer of lasting another hundred years?

"What was such a downer?"

She waved a hand at the clutter on the desk. "For Christ's sake—everything! What do you want to start with? The shrinking penises of alligators in Florida? Declining sperm counts and growing sterility in human males? There's some argument about that, but in light of everything else, I wouldn't bet against it—the optimists are probably whistling in the dark. And on top of that, we can include the vanishing glaciers in Alaska and the Alps, the shrinking Arctic ice cap, the increasing failure of antibiotics, and the sudden increase in infectious diseases. . . . Or maybe just man's inhumanity to man, the social meltdown in Africa. . . ."

Connie was sounding like a *Homo sapiens* version of Mary Robards, but it was suddenly more involved than that. Who had thought up the series in the first place—and why? And why give him the assignment? It would have been a great research assignment for the Grub; Jerry knew all about the environment.

Artie stood up and covered the papers on the table with his arms. "We're just reporting it, Connie, and that's doing a lot. Go home and recycle, hope for the best, and live your life. So your kids are going to have big problems. So did you. So did your old man and his old man. Your great-granddaddy helped build the Southern Pacific and he was one of the lucky ones who lived through it. If you could ask him, he wouldn't think we have it so bad."

Connie sank back in her chair. "Okay, you win. But it's hard not to take it seriously."

"Didn't say you shouldn't—just keep it in perspective."

Sweetness and light and it was all lies, Artie thought. When it came to going over the cliff, if they didn't jump, they'd be pushed. But what the hell would an astronomer do if he spotted a comet heading right for the Earth and knew there was nothing that could be done? Put out a press release and have millions die in the resulting panic, or shut the hell up and let people enjoy whatever few months or weeks they had left?

Then there was a sudden stray thought that he knew wasn't his, a mere nibble at his consciousness.

no . . .

And a sense of deep disagreement.

A r t i e   t u r n e d   a w a y   f r o m the glass and started pawing through the printouts. Anything to look busy to anybody watching. And to hide his lips as he talked to Connie.

Somebody had just given themselves away.

"Connie, three days ago you talked to Security about possible visitors. Do you remember what they said?"

She looked at him blankly.

"Why the hell would I talk to Security? About what?"

"Forget it." Artie went back to fumbling with the papers on the desk, then after a few minutes picked up the phone and dialed the ad agency that did the station's self-promotion commercials. Connie was engrossed in one of the printouts; she wasn't listening.

The agency remembered Ms. Lee's call. No, they had no record of any of their messengers going over to the station. It had been a busy day. Right. All their messengers were out that day. Very busy. Did they ever use a professional messenger service when they were jammed? Yes, of course. Yes, she'd check which one.

The record was in another file. Deluxe Downtown Messengers. They had sent someone over. A quick delivery and pickup. A kid named Watson, James Watson. Artie called and got a complete description, and this time the guard remembered him. A skinny kid, black hair. He'd only been there a few minutes, a hasty in-and-out.

The messenger hadn't been there long enough, Artie thought slowly. It had to have been someone on the news floor who'd slipped into Connie's mind so easily. But if Mary was right, Connie had to have been receptive. And there was only one person she had noticed. Adrienne Jantzen, just as she was about to fuck up reading the 'Prompter.

Artie refrained from looking out on the floor. One quick glance and he knew he'd tip somebody off. But Jantzen had already given herself away. She'd looked toward their glassed-in cubicle several times. She was nervous. Was she a friend of Mary's? He'd seen her pick up the phone once and then look around the newsroom, her eyes lingering for just a second on the cubicle. She wasn't a Hound; they would never have made that mistake. But ten to one she'd been to a party at Mary's more than once.

"You haven't been keeping me up to date on Adrienne, Connie. How's she working out?"

Connie didn't look up. "Fine, I guess. She covered a five-alarmer in San Bruno around lunchtime, came back and wrote it up this afternoon for the six-o'clock. She's probably hanging around to watch it. Catch it yourself and make up your own mind."

"She dating anyone?"

"Got me—I hear she's a loner."

He'd bet on it. Artie glanced at his watch. About five-thirty; the station execs, the advertising and business staffs and the dayside reporters would be leaving soon. By six-fifteen or six-thirty the parking lot should be almost deserted.

He pushed away the papers, closed his briefcase, and yawned. "Time to hit it, Connie. See you tomorrow."

She looked at him over the top of her glasses, disapproving.

"How about making it a full day, Artie? I'm doing all the damned work here."

"You love it, Connie."

"Yeah, right. We're doing a series on the end of the world and it's a barrel of laughs. Make it in early tomorrow—we'll share a giggle or two."

Artie gave her a thumbs-up and headed out to the parking lot, behind the little outdoor plaza where the brown-baggers usually ate their lunch when the weather was decent. It was dark—the pole light had burned out the week before—and he felt his way across the flagstones past the little metal tables and the wire wicker chairs and the white plaster statue of Pan mottled with a year's worth of pigeon droppings. The parking lot was just beyond, only a few cars bellying up to the yellow line that separated the lot from the small luncheon plaza.

It wasn't hard to find Adrienne's car. In the darkness he could just make out the bumper sticker that said I LOVE SACRAMENTO with a big heart for "Love"—the standard imitation of the "I Love New York" poster. Artie checked his watch. Six o'clock on the button. The fire would be the top of the news, which meant that Jantzen should be coming out of the back door within ten minutes if she were going to leave right afterward.

He dropped his briefcase in his own car, then stood in the shadows one car away from Adrienne's Taurus. He concentrated on blending in with the dark, not thinking of anything at all. He had started to shiver in the chilly night air when she finally came out, pulling on her gloves as she walked. He'd always seen her sitting down; he hadn't been around enough this week to catch her at lunch or even walking around the news floor. She was there when he arrived and was still there when he left, always sitting at her desk, always working. He'd never even seen her go to the can. Which meant that every minute he was there, she was there. He'd been under constant surveillance and she had probably "seen" every word he spoke.

Her heels made little staccato clicking noises on the flagstones and Artie caught his breath, clutching the automatic in his pocket for reassurance. He watched as she stopped by her Taurus and fished around in her bag for the keys. Attractive woman. Not too tall, not what you would call willowy. Pretty but solid.

He stepped out from behind the nearby car. She heard the slight noise and looked up, her hand going to her throat. "You scared the life out of me!" And then immediate suspicion and anger: "Strange meeting you down here, Mr. Banks—hiding in the parking lot."

All the time her eyes were darting nervously around to see if he was alone. He couldn't quite believe the sudden fear, the apparent relief, and then the anger. It was all appropriate, but all it meant was that she was a good actress, that she knew why he was there.

"The lily pad was your idea, wasn't it?" he said, adding, "You're using Connie like a puppet, aren't you?"

She laughed.

"I haven't the slightest idea what you're talking about. I hardly know Miss Lee, but I have great respect for her."

She was still glancing nervously around the lot, which struck Artie as odd—she knew he was by himself.

She looked desperate. "I was trying to help—"

The expression on her face suddenly shifted to one of fear and then went slack. Artie guessed immediately what was wrong, but it was already too late to do anything about it. It was a setup and he'd walked right into it. They knew he'd follow her sooner or later, and tonight she had been delayed just long enough so the lot would be deserted.

She caught the look of awareness on his face and exploded. Her knee jutted through the folds of his coat and caught him in the groin and he doubled up at the same time she screamed.

He caught her foot and twisted, and she almost went down, then chopped at the back of his neck. She was strong, surprisingly so. Talbot had been strong too, according to Paschelke. Suddenly a different comparison occurred to him: the old man at the skating rink doing the impossible. But it hadn't been him. And it wasn't just her.

He'd gotten over his distaste for fighting women in 'Nam and now he backhanded her in the face. All he'd wanted was to ask questions, to try to start a dialogue. But Mary obviously had been the exception, not the rule. She *could* talk; Adrienne couldn't.

Her nails left his cheek bloody and then his heart started doing double time, thumping so wildly it felt like it was going to jump out of his chest.

try and scream, monkey. . . .

Something else was in the lot and Adrienne had become a mere extension of it, like a hand puppet. The same something that had stage-managed the whole affair. And now it was trying to get a grip on him. For a moment his heart felt like it was going to explode and he had to remind himself that the last time he'd had a physical, the doctor had made a point of telling him he never had to worry about a heart attack—

She suddenly caught him in the throat with the side of her hand. He couldn't scream now if he wanted to; he couldn't make a sound.

thought you would be better . . .

She threw him against the side of a car just as he was trying to fumble out the automatic. He realized with sudden shock that he had lost his peripheral vision, that his sight was dimming and within a second or two he'd be blind. He was fighting for his life and he was losing.

He was struggling in total blackness now, knowing where she was only by her scent and her breathing and the sudden puffs of warm air between them. It was like it had been in 'Nam when he'd been ambushed at night. He'd learned how to fight in the dark then and hadn't forgotten how. Then she had her fingers on his throat, her nails pressing into his windpipe, and he grasped his hands together and thrust them up to break her grip.

She whispered in his ear, "You're an asshole," but he wasn't sure it was really her. She drove her elbow into his ribs and he went down, the gun he'd never gotten to use flying from his coat pocket. He was helpless, crumpled against a car wheel, curled into a ball, his arms over his face to protect it from the stiletto heels of her shoes.

There was a pause and a sense of surprise in the air around him and the feeling that somebody else was in the parking lot. Artie was suddenly terrified more than he already was. He had stumbled into a whole group of them.

what . . .

He heard Adrienne get into her Taurus and gun the motor, then squeal toward the exit.

A snarl of rage in his mind.

next time, monkey . . .

His sight returned abruptly. He was sitting on the ground near the flagstone plaza, his back against a pickup, blood covering his face and the front of his coat. How the hell long had it been? And where the hell were *they*? There had been two of them, he was sure of that. He moved slightly, groaning with the effort, and glanced toward the rear door of the station. The clouds had parted just enough for the moon to peep through. Pan's face was staring down at him, its plaster lips curled in a smirk.

"Jesus Christ, Artie, what the hell happened to you?" Levin was leaning over him, reaching for his hand to help him up. "You look like you got hit by a truck."

He didn't want to admit whom he had lost to, but he knew he was going to have to tell Mitch everything. Most importantly what Mary had told him and why.

He went cold thinking how fortunate it was for Mitch to show up right then, for Mitch to save his life.

"I got your call when I checked in with the office," Mitch said, pulling him to his feet. "I came over as soon as I could break free."

And just in time, Artie thought. He must have seen something; he must have seen Adrienne and the other two.

"I guess I got here a minute too late," Mitch said.

And that was funny as hell because without even meaning to, Mitch was reading his mind.

T h e y   s a t   i n   A r t i e ' s car, the heater turned on, and Artie dabbed at the blood on his face with his handkerchief and filled Mitch in on everything Mary had told him. But the only enemy he had seen so far was a heavyset, matronly woman for whom he had once had a thing and a woman news reporter who had tried to kill him in the station parking lot. He told Mitch about the deadly game of Hare-and-Hounds with himself and Mitch and the others as hares and out there, somewhere, the unseen Hound.

After he had finished, Mitch fished out a cigarette and reached for the car lighter, then thought better of it.

"You don't believe me," Artie said.

"Two days ago I almost swallowed half a bottle of Valium and two fingers of lousy scotch. Why shouldn't I believe you?" Mitch glanced out the window at the parking lot, searching for figures in the shadows. "But there's no proof of anything. All you know is what Mary told you."

"You must have seen something when you drove in."

"I told you—I didn't see a damned thing. You were sitting on the ground looking like you wanted to puke your guts out and there was a lot of blood." He hesitated. "You sure you don't want to go to Emergency?"

"We'd probably never get there," Artie said bitterly. "And if we did, how could we be sure the doctor was who he claimed he was? Goddammit, there were two of them besides Adrienne, I could *feel* them!"

Mitch was silent for a moment. "I almost got hit by your lady friend's car barreling out of here and there you were. That's all I saw, Artie."

"We could go to the government," Artie said sullenly, and the moment he said it he regretted it. If Mary was right about who her people were, then she was also right about genocide. What would happen when you really couldn't tell friend from foe? It wouldn't be like the Serbs and the Muslims or the Tutsis and the Hutus, who'd known each other all their lives. In this case you didn't know who was who; your next-door neighbor could be the enemy, the guy who sat next to you at the office. It would start with suspicion and accusation and end up with . . . what? Burning people at the stake?

"We've got nothing to take to them, Artie. We don't have the diskette, we don't have the printout, all we have is Mary's crazy story. We believe it, but who the hell else would?"

Artie's ribs ached, but most of all he felt angry and embarrassed. He had been handled so easily. Not alone by Adrienne but by . . . somebody else. He could have been killed, probably would have been if Mitch hadn't showed up. And Adrienne would have said that she'd been at-tacked in the parking lot, that he'd come on to her the last day or so and she'd turned him down.

Behind his granny glasses, Mitch's eyes were bright and speculative.

"Who knows besides us, Artie?"

"Cathy Shea and whoever killed Larry—or had Larry killed. And Paschelke and Hall and they're dead as well."

"Somebody else believes, somebody else knows. And that some-body is somebody we know."

"Hardly anybody ever really keeps a secret," Artie said after a mo-ment. "Larry probably talked to Cathy. He might also have talked to ten or twenty other people that we never heard of. He couldn't have kept it to himself. Christ, people even talk in their sleep."

Mitch shook his head. "Sorry, Artie, I don't agree. He had too much riding on this one. Larry wouldn't have wanted to share it with anybody. It might have made his reputation." He looked at Artie, taking in his battered face again. "If you don't want to spend the night alone, you can bunk over at my place."

Artie had a sudden image of himself alone in the house without Susan working in the kitchen or Mark studying in his room, the music turned up loud. He'd be alone . . . and he'd be vulnerable. Somehow he'd forget and walk out on his balcony and the next morning they'd find him splattered on the sidewalk below.

But worst of all, he'd be alone.

"I'd be putting you out."

"Big deal."

It was quiet on Telegraph Hill, Mitch's small cot-tage peaceful. Mitch gave him sheets and blankets for the couch, plus a monogrammed towel and washrag. Artie stripped to his shorts and started placing the contents of his shirt pocket on the coffee table. Mark's earring was still wrapped in its napkin, and he unfolded it and held the ring in his hand for a moment.

Mitch noticed it and said, "Can I see that?"

Artie gave him the ring. "It belongs to Mark—gift from Susan. Family heirloom, I guess."

Mitch turned it over in the light.

"Looks Mayan. Let me borrow it for a day. I'd like a friend of mine to take a look at it."

"Go ahead. Just don't lose it. Mark would never forgive me." He reached for the phone on the table. "Mind if I make a call?"

There were no messages on his answering machine at home. Artie called the new number Susan had given him and a tape recorder repeated that the line had been disconnected. It didn't say when and there was no forwarding number. Artie dialed Information and asked for the number of the hospital in Willow and was startled when she said there was no hospital but she would connect him to the only medical clinic in town. Artie felt the sweat start when the puzzled voice at the other end of the line told him Susan's father wasn't there, that he never had been.

He was still sitting there holding the phone when Mitch walked through on his way to the kitchen.

"What's wrong?"

"Susan's gone."

"I thought you said she was in Willow, that her father was in the hospital there?"

"That's what she told me. He isn't, never was."

Mitch stared, not understanding.

"Susan's not in Willow." Artie was suddenly afraid his voice was going to break. "I don't think she ever went there."

CHAPTER 14

Artie lay on the couch staring out at the darkness through the front windows. It was a chill night with no overcast and the stars were bright, the moon a thin crescent above the streetlight at the top of the Filbert Street steps. By his watch it was almost two in the morning and he hadn't slept a wink; he was still sore and bruised from his fight with Adrienne. Mitch had knocked off about fifteen minutes after hitting the sack, he could tell by the snoring.

Not a worry in the world, Artie thought with envy. But then, in 'Nam Mitch had the reputation for being able to sleep through even the worst of the shelling.

Vietnam . . .

If he had to choose being here and being there, he wasn't sure which he would pick. You never knew who the enemy was over there: the little old lady hoeing her garden, the waiter at your table when you went to Saigon for R&R, the whore you slept with . . . You didn't know who the enemy might be here, either, but in both cases you knew what the enemy wanted. They wanted you out.

What the hell were the Old People planning? They were sure as hell plotting something. But he had only seen two of the enemy. There must be . . . what? Hundreds of them in the city? He probably ran into them every day and had no idea who they really were. They were in deep cover, had to be. It would cost them their lives and the lives of their families and friends if anybody found them out. It would probably cost the lives of their entire species except for a few who would end up in jails or zoos. And that was a lousy thing to think. My country, right or wrong. Who'd said that? Stephen Decatur? Patrick Henry?

He turned his pillow over and fluffed it for the twentieth time, then lay there trying to make up his mind whether to hit the john or get a drink of water. Telegraph Hill was quiet at night—at least during the middle of the week when the kids weren't cruising around Coit Tower—much more so than the Castro. When he and Susan had first moved to Noe Street, it was partying every night until two in the morning. It had slacked off some since, but hardly completely.

Susan . . .

He'd tried to wall her off in his mind; it hurt too much to think about her. She'd walked out on him, with Mark due to follow—except, for the moment, Mark apparently had other plans. He'd call the bank in the morning and see how much money Susan had taken with her. Walking out on him was the one thing he'd always dreaded, was always afraid that she might do. But he'd also thought she would discuss it in advance.

Try to forget it—for the moment. Too much of his world had collapsed all at once and there was little he could do about any of it.

Mitch . . .

Mitch had gotten to the station's outdoor parking lot just in time. Another few minutes and he would have been a dead man. It was hard to think it was coincidence but like Mitch said, you had to trust somebody. Everybody he met now would be suspect, from the postman to the taxi driver to the waitress at Welcome Home, where he sometimes ate breakfast.

Or would they congregate in the professions? Like they said most hairdressers and actors were supposed to be gay? Bullshit, but maybe most of the Old People were professors or accountants or . . . psychiatrists like Mitch or lawyers like Mary. All of them would be great ways of getting to know the enemy.

There was a rustle in the shrubbery outside and Artie suddenly tensed, waiting for the plucking at his mind, the little thoughts that weren't his, the suggestion to slash his wrists or swallow a can of Drano.

There was something out there, he knew it for sure, and then he slowly relaxed. Jesus, he was dreaming; he had finally slipped off. A lucid dream in which you know you're dreaming, like the first one he'd ever had about the Tribe when Susan was in bed with him. He turned and glanced around at the shadowy outlines of the furniture in the room. Everything seemed slightly fuzzy and out of focus, like you might expect in a dream. And he didn't feel a chill just beyond the margin of the blankets. If anything, it was almost a cocoonlike feeling of warmth and safety.

But why just lie there—why not walk around in it? He sat up and slowly started to put on his clothes, taking care not to make any noise. Which was silly—how could he wake up Mitch in a dream? He started to struggle into his shoes, then gave up and slipped his feet into the fancy leather slippers Mitch had lent him.

He let himself out, closing the door quietly behind him. He floated up the wooden steps to Montgomery, then left past the little corner grocery store and down the hill to Broadway. There weren't many people on the street and those few he passed were silent, huddled in their coats against the chill. The advantage of a dream, Artie thought: You didn't feel cold, you didn't feel heat. He'd put on his coat but hadn't buttoned it; he didn't feel the need to.

There was an all-night hamburger joint on Broadway and he stopped to stare through the windows. The night people were out in full force, the stools by the counter almost filled. Artie grinned to himself. Why not? When was the last time he'd had a burger and fries in a dream? He pushed in through the door and found himself a vacant stool.

An old man in dirty white pants and T-shirt with a stub of a pencil behind his ear moved down the counter taking orders. He stopped in front of Artie and mouthed something at him. Artie couldn't hear a word he was saying but made a guess and ordered a double cheeseburger with fries and a Coke.

A man sat down next to Artie and leaned over to pick up a menu. "What would you do with us, Banks?"

He was big, heavyset, but Artie couldn't quite make out his features. They were blurry, like almost everything else in his dream.

"You're the first person I can hear," Artie said, marveling.

The big man nodded.

"You can only hear the Old People. You've listened to *sapiens* long enough, it's time you listened to us. Like I said, what would you do with us?"

Artie stared at him blankly.

"What do you mean?"

The big man frowned.

"Put us in concentration camps? Feed us to the ovens?"

Artie suddenly wanted to wake up.

"We don't put people in concentration camps."

"Sure you do. You did once before."

It took Artie a moment to remember. He changed the subject. "What do you do? For a living."

"Construction. Dry wall, like the character used to do on *Roseanne*. How about yourself?"

"Newswriter for KXAM." Artie concentrated on his cheeseburger.

"You're ruining the world," the big man said, reaching for the napkin dispenser. "Did you know there's a sanitarium near Krakow, Poland, that has its patients sleep underground in salt mines because the air outside is so polluted?"

"You're an eco-nut," Artie said.

"Everybody talks about the weather and now you're doing something about it," the big man said. He stood up to go to the cash register. "It's your world. But it's ours, too."

The busboy came up to clear away the plates.

"The customer's always right," he said to Artie. "I mean the other one." He disappeared with his tray of dirty dishes into the kitchen.

Artie frowned and stared around the inside of the diner. Some faces he could make out, others were fuzzy and blurred. Deep cover, he thought. The Old People were all in deep cover. But Jesus, there were a lot of them. Maybe they all worked at night.

For a moment, outside the diner, he couldn't get his bearings. Which way back to Montgomery? There was a blurry-faced cop sitting in a patrol car on the corner and Artie drifted over to ask directions.

"They used helicopter gunships to kill the hippos in Mozambique," the cop said. "Carved the teeth and sold them for decorations in Asia."

Artie stared.

"Which way to Montgomery Street?" he asked.

"You can travel for miles in Mozambique today and not see anything larger than a bird." The cop jerked a thumb behind him. "Montgomery's that way."

Artie started back up the hill. There was a strip joint still open on the corner, the barker, a skinny, middle-aged man in a checkered sport coat, lounging out in front having a cigarette.

"Too bad about the frogs," he said.

Artie turned. "What?"

"The frogs," the barker repeated. "Billions of them. If the ultraviolet didn't get them the pollution probably did—they use their skin to exchange oxygen and carbon dioxide, you know. The air's going to kill you, too. Eventually." He took a final drag on his cigarette and ground the butt beneath his heel.

"Which way's Montgomery?" Artie asked.

"Bet you didn't know when fisheries net sharks with other fish they cut the fins off and dump the live sharks back in the ocean. The fins are worth ten bucks a pound for soup. Montgomery's next street up."

Artie tried to fix the barker's features in his mind and couldn't. His face was a blur, a hint of pocked cheeks, a suggestion of deep-set eyes and a nose that might have been broken, and that was it. Deep cover.

Artie turned toward Montgomery. At the corner, a cab slowed and the woman driver cranked down the window. "Need a lift, buddy?"

"I'm just going to the Filbert steps," Artie said, then hesitated. Another one; he could hear her but couldn't quite make out her face.

"I'll take you, on me. Hop in."

Artie climbed in and the cabbie drove up Montgomery in silence.

"You're too quiet," Artie said after a minute. "I thought you'd be an eco-fanatic, too."

"You're a self-endangered species," she said casually. "Why waste my breath?"

Artie let himself back into the house and closed the door quietly behind him. He took off his clothes and slipped between the blankets on the couch, surprised to realize that he was suddenly freezing cold and the blankets were a welcome patch of warmth. Something wasn't right, and then the thought drifted out of his mind and he could sense his breathing becoming deep and regular.

He wasn't aware at all of the first tendrils of smoke that drifted in from the back of the house.

I t   w a s   t h e   s o u n d of the fire engines that finally woke him. He coughed for a minute, then was suddenly wide awake. Somebody was hammering at the front door, shouting, and there were sounds of several men around in back. Mitch burst out of the bedroom, bleary-eyed, struggling into his bathrobe and fumbling with his glasses.

"What the hell's going on—Oh, Christ, fire!" He ran toward the rear of the cottage while Artie opened the front door. Several firemen crowded in lugging a hose, and one of them shouted, "Get your clothes and get out!" Artie could hear another engine drive up. Outside, he could see the lights turning on in the other cottages that lined the steps.

An hour later it was all over. Smoke damage and the wooden steps out back were the main casualties. One of Mitch's neighbors had seen the first flames and turned in the alarm. He thought he'd seen somebody at the back of the cottage but the fire chief had shrugged and said it was probably raccoons chewing on one of the hoses to the outdoor propane tank. Fast response time had saved the house. They probably had the fastest in the Bay Area, he said, otherwise the whole city would have burned down a dozen times. San Francisco had the highest percentage of wooden houses in the country this side of Baltimore.

After they'd left, Mitch made some coffee and he and Artie sat in the kitchen and stared at each other.

"I've never had raccoons before, Artie."

"It was two for the price of one, Mitch. Too good for them to pass up."

"What the hell do we do? Sleep in hotel lobbies?"

"Maybe." Artie got up to pour himself another cup.

"It's getting personal," Mitch said, thoughtful.

Artie raised an eyebrow. "The scotch and the Valium weren't personal enough? They want you dead too, you know."

Mitch looked frustrated. "The trouble is, neither one of us can prove a goddamned thing." He was quiet for a moment, the lines in his face gradually smoothing out. "It's a process of elimination, Artie. Mary and Jenny have left town, or so Mary said, right? Apparently she didn't want to be around for the kill. Charlie's not involved—at least we don't think he is."

"*You* don't think he is," Artie said. "I'm not so sure."

"Which leaves Lyle Pace—"

Artie shook his head. "Not Lyle. I saw him the other night; if he'd wanted to do me damage, he had plenty of opportunity."

Mitch didn't look convinced. "You were in the wrong place at the wrong time. What excuse could Pace offer if something happened to you in his own home? Even Schuler wouldn't believe him, no matter what the story."

"Dave Chandler," Artie said, turning the thought over in his head. Dave, the airhead of the Club. Nice guy, innocuous, deep cover at its very best. "Or maybe Cathy Shea. She's the one we know for sure who knew too much."

Mitch sipped at his coffee. "Not Cathy. She was home at the time Larry was killed. I'm not saying she couldn't be connected in some way, but she could hardly have killed Larry herself, even if she had wanted to. No time."

"Which leaves Chandler," Artie repeated.

"So what do we do? Both of us stop by to see him? He'd probably have difficulty handling two of us at the same time."

"Contact Schuler—"

Mitch looked disgusted. "And tell him what?" He tore open another pack of sweetener and dumped it in his coffee. "Is Chandler close to anybody?"

Artie thought for a moment. "Yes and no. He's close to everybody and close to nobody. Closer when we were younger and he was the class cutup and everybody's friend. The act got tired when we grew older. Dave never changed. But you know all that."

"So when do we pay him a visit?"

"Tomorrow? After work? I've got to check and see how much Susan left in the bank accounts. And put in a full day's work—Connie's beginning to bitch and I can't blame her."

Mitch yawned. "It's close to six—you want to hit the sack again? I could set the alarm for eight."

The thought was attractive but Artie was already wide awake.

"I'll just show up for work early. Surprise the hell out of Connie."

He finished dressing and folded up the couch and rearranged the pillows on top, piling the used sheets and pillowcase at the other end.

He was about to put the slippers on top, then held them for a moment in his hands, feeling slightly dizzy: the shiny patent-leather slippers that Mitch had lent him, probably a present from somebody. Nordstrom's finest pair, maybe a hundred dollars, two hundred a pop—

—were now water-stained and covered with mud.

He'd had growing suspicions that it hadn't been a dream at all, and now he knew for sure.

Somebody had just given him a guided tour behind enemy lines.

CHAPTER 15

The streets were quiet, the parking lot at KXAM almost empty. The attendant opened one eye when Artie drove up, then yawned and nodded off again. A moment later Artie was in his newsroom cubicle, staring dull-eyed at the plastic container of black coffee he'd bought on the trip in. Jesus, there were days God should have just deleted from the calendar, and this was one of them.

He dialed the Bank of America twenty-four-hour hot line and waited for voice mail to give him a number he could punch to ask for his balance.

Susan had taken exactly half of the almost five thousand in their savings account. She'd taken something like four hundred and fifty in cash from the checking. Again, exactly half.

She wasn't coming back. The next time he'd hear from her it would be through her lawyer.

She apparently hadn't used any of their credit cards, and Artie doubted that she would. She hadn't wanted him to find her, that was obvious. She wouldn't leave any tracks. Did she take any clothing? He'd check when he got home. She could have loaded up her car the day before, when he was at work. No way he would have thought of checking at the time.

Susan.

Aw, Christ . . .

It hit him then and for a moment he was afraid he was going to cry, something he hadn't done since he was fifteen and True Love had waltzed out of his life on the arm of the high school diving champ. His father had been sympathetic, his mother much less so.

"Women will break your heart all your life, Arthur. You're the thin-skinned type. Better get used to it now."

He never had gotten used to it and knew he never would, though he doubted there would be a successor to Susan.

Was Mark with her? Not right then, but had he known where she was going? Probably. He'd catch up with his mother later, after his own Christmas vacation.

What hurt Artie most was that he knew Mark as little as he knew Susan. Both of them apparently had been willing to stick it to him.

But he couldn't even be angry about it. Somehow it was his fault, though in what way he hadn't the foggiest idea. He'd been faithful; he hadn't cheated—had never even thought of it. He would have given his life for both of them, but that was an abstract that couldn't compare to a bigger house, a larger paycheck, a member of management—whatever the tangibles were by which success was measured these days.

He knew he was feeling sorry for himself and wallowed in it, only gradually acknowledging that something far more important was going on than his marriage coming apart at the seams. He was in the middle of an underground struggle that nobody knew about, and his very knowledge of it meant that sooner or later somebody was going to try to kill him again and probably succeed.

Susan and Mark hadn't left him at the worst of times; they had left him at the best of times. He should be damned glad that they had left when they did, that they were out of it and didn't run the risk of ending up like Paschelke's wife and kids.

"You're in early, Artie—first time I can remember you ever paying any attention to something I said." Connie hung her coat and umbrella on one of the back wall hooks, then glanced out at the newsroom. "I still think we ought to do our own morning show rather than pick up the feed from the network. We can do happy talk with the best of them—" She caught the haggard expression on his face. "Susan left you, didn't she?"

"How'd you know?"

"That expression on a married man's face goes with either death or separation. She walk out?"

Artie nodded. "She took half the money and split."

"Only half? Merry Christmas, Artie, you got off cheap." She suddenly looked apologetic. "Forgive the cynicism. I'm sorry, I really am. Anything I can do, just ask."

He shook his head. "I'll hear from her lawyer and we'll go from there. In the meantime, we've still got the series, right?"

"Right." Connie looked relieved. "I had the Grub pull some tape from the files and I wrote a preliminary script—give us an idea of where we're going with it. We might as well call in Jerry and go over it."

"Hirschfield's not bitching because I haven't been around?"

"I said you were out doing research."

"I owe you."

"Big-time, Banks."

When Jerry squeezed into the cubicle, Connie passed around copies of the script. Artie studied his. Connie, as he suspected she would, had done a better than excellent job. On the right of the page were Connie's narration and verbatims of the sound bites they would use; on the left were time codes and notes on the B-roll, the various pieces of field and file tape and stock footage they would use to "cover" the audio.

She had covered pretty much what he thought she would. Changing weather patterns, melting glaciers, rising sea levels . . . The Netherlands would catch it, so would Bangladesh and island nations like the Marshalls.

"You right about thirty thousand vanishing species, Connie?"

She nodded. "That's per *year,* Artie—and it's probably on the low side. Me, I'll miss the tigers."

After they had finished the script, Jerry shook his head. "Anybody who watches this is going to go out and slash their wrists. I don't think you guys know what you're doing."

Connie pointed at the door. "Scat, Jerry." After he had left, she said, "I figure we could interview some scientist on camera for an overview of what's happening. It would be a long interview, but we could cover some parts with video. Be a change from staring at me most of the time."

Adrienne had planted the seeds, and in Connie they were growing into a forest.

"You think Hirschfield is going to schedule that?"

"Why wouldn't he?"

"Because it's the world's worst downer, that's why. Five minutes into that and you'll be able to hear them changing channels all the way down to San Jose. We're not the *New York Times* of the air, Connie— leave that to PBS. We'll have to make it interesting and light with just enough real stuff to impress the FCC in case some citizens' group challenges our license. That's what the hell Hirschfield wants." He shrugged. "Feel free to disagree. If you're confident with it, show it to Hirschfield yourself."

"I thought you of all people would back me up."

"I will—after we lighten it up."

She leaned back in her chair.

"I wanted to do another segment, but I didn't think we could get away with it. Social meltdown, kids murdering kids. The kids over in England who stoned the four-year-old and placed the body on the railroad track and the six-year-old over here who almost beat a baby to death in his crib."

"That's not ecology."

"I'm not so sure. You seen the studies on rat behavior when they get overcrowded?" She rubbed her forehead. "You still got coffee in that cup?"

"It's probably cold."

"Doesn't matter—I can use the caffeine." He shoved over the container and she sipped at it, looking drained and listless. Adrienne had pushed Connie over the edge.

"How much time you been putting in on it?" He hesitated, apologetic. "I know I haven't been as much help as I should."

"It wouldn't have mattered. The last few days I've been going at it for twelve, fourteen hours a day. . . ." She waved a hand helplessly at the printouts and magazine articles and books that covered the desktop. "There's too much of it; there's no end to it."

"The trick in doing research is knowing when to stop," Artie said. "You taught me that when I came here."

Connie stood up and walked over to the window, glanced out at the newsroom, then turned around to lean against the glass. Artie felt embarrassed. He had never seen her look so vulnerable before.

"It's an end-of-the-world story, Artie. We make a few gains here and there, but then they're lost in the disasters."

He managed a smile. "Hey, c'mon, you're supposed to be the perky one."

"Yeah, right. Boy, was that a long time ago."

His phone rang and Artie picked up. At first he couldn't make out the voice, a slurred combination of lisp and grunt as if the caller had a serious speech impediment or a throat wound. "Say again?" This time he got it: a desperate Dave Chandler who needed to see somebody. He sounded in pain, and an alarmed Artie suggested an ambulance. Chandler said no, he'd just come from the hospital, he needed somebody to talk to.

Sure, Artie said slowly, he'd get there as soon as possible. Yeah, he knew he was a prince.

He hung up and dialed Mitch. No way was he going over alone—he needed backup. Mitch came on the line and they agreed to meet outside Chandler's apartment in the Marina. And yes, it might be smart to be armed.

Connie had been watching him and when he hung up said, "You're off again, right? Something about Mark?"

"Not this time. A friend—needs help apparently. Couldn't talk straight. I've no idea what's wrong. Sorry, Connie."

Artie was almost out the door when Connie suddenly said, "I've had this strange feeling lately, Artie. Like all of us are at the tail end of the third act and pretty soon the curtain's going to fall and the play will be over. And I've no idea at all what's going to happen to us next. I even read the cards about it."

"And?"

"All the cards were bad."

She was feeling the same way he'd felt for a month, Artie thought. But he didn't need anybody else's troubles to add to his own. Chandler was spinning a web and he was about to walk into it.

Or maybe, once again, he was just being paranoid.

.   .   .

I t   w a s   l a t e   i n   the afternoon and the sun was already
starting to dip behind the hills of the Presidio. It was hell finding a
parking place, and when he finally found one and got to the whitewashed
stucco building where Chandler lived, Mitch was waiting for him.

"I didn't buzz—thought I'd wait until you showed."

"Lousy parking."

Mitch pressed the buzzer, waited a minute, then pressed it again.
"Who is it?"

It was a strange voice, as if its owner had difficulty talking. It didn't
sound like Chandler at all. The few times Artie had been over, Dave
usually answered with some clever line from a play or a movie—"I'm
Dave Chandler and I coulda been a contendah! Who are you?"

Mitch leaned closer to the intercom.

"Artie and Mitch, Dave."

The buzzer sounded and they pushed the door open. It was dark
inside, no hall light. A voice at the top of the stairs mumbled, "Come
on up," in the same combination of lisp and grunt. Artie looked at Mitch
and muttered, "Think it's a setup?"

Mitch shrugged. "We'll never know down here."

Artie felt for the automatic nestled in his pocket and started up the
stairs. At the top, a voice said, "I'm in the office, in back." Mitch found
a wall switch and turned on the hall light and the voice became almost
hysterical. "Turn it down! It's on a dimmer."

The long hallway was lined with framed theater posters and the
occasional signed photograph: *To Dave, with love—Sharon* or *For Dave,
I'll never forget you—Brad*. At least Chandler was nondenominational,
Artie thought.

The office in back was large and equipped like a small theater with
a row of upholstered fold-up seats facing a fifty-inch rear-projection TV
flanked by large, floor-standing speakers. Chandler had had the room
soundproofed years ago so he could show films late at night without the
neighbors complaining. An old-time popcorn machine was in one corner, while in the other was a small desk and filing cabinet and an easy
chair with an ottoman. The windows had been covered with black
drapes, and the only light in the room came from a small red bulb above
the door.

Chandler's party room, not as cool as it must have been fifteen years ago. Artie wondered how many hours Chandler spent watching old movies in the dark.

The figure in the easy chair moved and mumbled, "Thanks for coming," and Artie almost yanked out his gun. It sounded like Chandler but it didn't sound like Chandler, and it didn't look much like him. Just a dark shape in the oversized chair.

There was the sound of a small tug on a pull chain and the floor lamp by Chandler's chair came on. Artie caught his breath. It was Chandler all right, but he recognized him more by his standard uniform of chinos, loafers, and light blue woolen sweater than by his face.

He couldn't make out Chandler's features at all; some kind of white ointment covered his face like a mask with small holes for his eyes.

Artie said, "What the hell happened, Dave?"

Chandler leaned forward in his chair, taking a moment to catch his breath. It obviously hurt to talk. "The other night at the theater—Theater DuPre—I was in the dressing room putting on a makeup base and five minutes after I got it on, it started to burn. I wiped it off and then I guess I went nuts. The cast called an ambulance"—he tried to grimace but it was clearly agony—"a little late."

Chandler took a towel from the desktop and wiped off the ointment from part of his face. Beneath it, the skin was pink and seamed with red furrows. Artie thought it looked like a lightly plowed field.

"The doctors said it could have killed me if it had been poisonous. They got me to the emergency room just in time; it might have burned right through the flesh. They told me there'll definitely be scarring." Chandler's voice was pushing hysteria. "Who the hell would do that? Put whatever they did in the base? They knew it was mine—they knew it was my personal kit!"

Nobody was going to envy him anymore for looking like the youngest member of the Club. And no way was anybody going to cast him in the occasional TV or movie role when they shot locally. Not unless they were doing a *Nightmare on Elm Street* segment.

"Who would do something like that?" Chandler asked again, his voice breaking. "Christ, I can't even cry, it's too painful. . . ."

Artie didn't know what to say. Mitch said, "I know some plastic surgeons, Dave—the best there are."

"My insurance," Chandler mumbled. "I don't know what it will cover. It wasn't an accident—somebody did it deliberately."

Next to castrating him, it was probably the worst thing anybody could have done to Chandler, Artie thought—to any actor, but especially to one whose face had been his fortune, if only a small one.

"I wouldn't worry about the cost," Mitch said, trying his best to be reassuring. "We'll figure out something. The surgeons work out of St. Mary's and there's probably some fund someplace that they can tap."

"Thanks," Chandler said. It took a moment for him to control his voice, and Artie could make out several tears trickling down through the ointment. It probably hurt Chandler like hell.

"Anything else we can do?" Artie offered tentatively. "We'll drop by as often as we can."

Chandler turned away and there was a long pause. It must be torture to want to rub your eyes and be unable to because you knew it would hurt so much. Artie touched him lightly on the shoulder.

"Appreciate it," Chandler said and reached up and squeezed his hand.

They stayed for a while and talked, mostly about Chandler's past "triumphs" in the theater, and then left when it became apparent that it hurt Chandler to talk much.

Outside in the chill night air, Mitch murmured, "And a Merry Christmas to you, too."

"Who would have done it?" Artie asked.

Mitch shrugged. "Who knows? There's nobody who doesn't have enemies. Maybe an ex-lover, maybe somebody who wanted a part and Dave wouldn't give it to him. Or her."

"You don't think it was connected with Larry?"

"I didn't say that. After we saw Schuler and met in that south-of-Market diner, Chandler said he'd had lunch with Larry, that Larry had told him he was working on an article for *Science*."

"He never said Larry told him what it was about."

"Maybe Larry did and it was over his head so he forgot about it."

"Dave seldom remembers anything that isn't about Dave."

"Not kind, Artie—and it looks like somebody at that table would have disagreed with you. Somebody evidently thought Larry had told Dave something. It's a wonder the poor bastard's still alive."

"Sorry about the comment," Artie muttered. "We've joked about Dave for so many years it's become habit." He started back to his car, then suddenly turned.

"Mitch? If we eliminate Dave, that means we've eliminated everybody."

"Yeah, I know. Which means we've eliminated nobody."

CHAPTER 16

The Marriott near the Moscone Center was big, expensive, and fireproof. Artie was convinced somebody would have to splash gasoline around their room to set it ablaze. Hotel security seemed to be good, though any Hound could get around it if he or she wanted. But at first glimpse it was safer than either his house or Mitch's Telegraph Hill cottage.

Mitch turned on the television set and they channel-surfed until the six-o'clock news. The usual depressing local coverage and a foreign affairs segment that wasn't much better. Another mini-uprising in what was left of Yugoslavia, a network story on the Russian mafia, and another on a standoff in the mid-Pacific between a Greenpeace boat and a Japanese whaling ship, plus there were eighty more dead in Africa from Rift Valley TB.

Locally, a suburban father had been shot by his son because he'd had a date and been refused the family car, and there was a fire in a Tenderloin hotel, one transient dead of smoke inhalation, fifty evacuated . . .

"The *National Enquirer* of the Air," Mitch muttered at the half-hour break. "No wonder I end up prescribing so much Prozac."

" 'If it bleeds, it leads,' " Artie quoted. " 'If it's fire, play it higher.'

But you missed the biggest story, and most of the rest of the hour will be devoted to it, with the sports wrap at the end."

"So what was the biggest story?"

"Barring wars and plane accidents, what it always is: the weather. You're so used to it being the mainstay of the nightly news, you don't even notice. The Tenderloin fire wasn't much more than a teaser and they didn't waste much airtime on the father-and-son bit before they switched to a live feed from a mountain road impassable because of snow. It never rains, Mitch, it pours; and if it snows, it's a blizzard. If it isn't, you better make it one or, trust me, your ratings go into the toilet."

"I'm glad it's your job and not mine," Mitch muttered. He picked up the phone and Artie looked at him, alarmed.

"What the hell are you doing?"

"Letting my answering service know where I am—sometimes I get late-night calls from patients."

Artie took the phone out of his hand and replaced it in its cradle. "*They* already know your phone number—it's probably been tapped for the last three days. You want to let them know where we are?"

"You're telling me they're all over out there?" Then he added soberly, "Of course they are."

"They're not just Mary and Adrienne and whoever killed Larry," Artie said. "They're not a group or a gang, they're a *species*. They're all around. And there's no way of telling who they are."

"You're paranoid," Mitch said.

"You better be paranoid too, Mitch. You'll live longer."

There was a knock on the door, and a voice outside said, "House-keeping."

Artie muttered, "You get it," and stood just out of sight in the bathroom, the automatic in his hand.

Mitch opened the door to the limit of the chain.

"Yes?"

A slightly muffled voice: "Housekeeping—I forget some towels when I clean room earlier."

Mitch stuck his hand through the opening. "I'll take them."

He closed the door and bolted it. "One maid, Hispanic. Late thir-ties. Probably an illegal."

Artie shrugged. "So?"

"Christ, Artie, just check the towels."

A moment later Artie called from the john, "We were shy a set of hand and bath towels."

"So I was right. No way she could have known we were going to check in. You're paranoid."

T h e y   h a d   b e e n   i n bed by eleven, but Artie was still wide awake. Mitch wasn't snoring, which meant he was wide awake as well.

"It's not a small conspiracy," Artie said into the dark. "First there was Larry Shea and the Hound, and then it became Larry and the Hound and Paschelke and Hall and you and me and probably Cathy. The circle keeps getting larger."

"You can deduct Larry and Hall and Paschelke," Mitch said.

"And add Mary and probably Jenny and maybe Lyle and just maybe Charlie Allen. And God knows who else."

"It's getting risky," Mitch said. "For *them*." After a moment: "You keep saying it's a conspiracy, that it involves a lot of people. But where's the organization? Who's running it? There's got to be some sort of organization."

Artie thought about it, feeling increasingly uncomfortable.

"Mary said that the Old People are tribal. Maybe there is no central organization. Maybe everybody more or less knows what to do without somebody telling them."

"Which is what?"

Artie gave a mental shrug. "Stay hidden. Stay undercover. Wait."

Mitch was starting to doze off.

"Strange sort of organization."

"It's like some ethnic groups, Mitch. There's usually little in the way of national organization but at the local level, depending on the city, it's something else."

Mitch sounded irritated at not being left alone to sleep.

"There's a difference. We don't know who the Old People are. And the potential for violence is there when you don't know who the enemy is. It would be a chance for terrorism on a gigantic scale. We live in a technological society: one person could throw a monkey wrench into it and bring it all down."

It wouldn't take a massive organization, Artie thought. Maybe it would be more like whatever organization the IRA had in Ireland.

"Cathy Shea," he said into the darkness. "What do you remember about Cathy, Mitch?"

Silence for a moment.

"Maiden name, Cathy Deutsch. I think she joined the Club about the same time I did. She dropped out when she got married and had kids. A looker, but then they all were back then."

"Everybody's handsome and everybody's pretty when you're in your early twenties," Artie said.

"Thanks for reminding me I'm getting older, Artie."

"Did you ever ball her?"

"Jesus Christ, you're talking about Larry's wife. She's an old married woman now. She's got two kids."

"I'm talking about twenty years ago. I'm not asking if you laid Larry's wife—I'm asking if you slept with Cathy Deutsch."

"I thought everybody made it with Cathy. . . . You want to know how she was, right?"

"Sure."

Mitch laughed quietly.

"We were all young and we were all horny; I doubt that any of us lasted longer than five minutes with her. I think we stripped down; I nuzzled her breasts a couple of times, she touched my prick once, and then it was all over and I told everybody how great she was afterward. By the looks I got from the other women, she said the same about me. I've been in her debt ever since."

Artie was starting to drift off again when he had another thought.

"Lyle and Jenny," he said aloud in the dark.

He sensed that Mitch was suddenly wide awake.

"Why do you ask?"

"Because it's still going on."

He could hear Mitch moving around in the other bed and suddenly the lamp on the bed table came on.

"You never told me that."

"I told you I'd seen Lyle the night before I went over to Mary's. He dropped in to hit on Jenny when Mary wasn't home. Nothing happened, they're still good friends, according to Mary."

"They were a number twenty years ago, you remember."

"He's got a new lady—Anya."

"I've met her." Mitch yawned and turned out the light. "Exotic."

"So why is Lyle still interested in Jenny? I mean—you know, after twenty years."

"Nobody forgets first love, Artie. Doesn't matter how old you get, given the chance you'll still try to breathe life into the embers if only to make sure they're out."

"Would Jenny have talked? She must know a lot."

Mitch was silent, thinking about it.

"I don't think she'd ever betray Mary intentionally. But she might drop a stitch here and there and, before you knew it, the whole scarf would be unraveled. She might have ended up saying more than she thought she did."

Artie tossed it around in his mind. If Lyle wasn't one of the Old People, then he could be in real danger. If he and Mitch had thought of the possibility, somebody else could have thought of it as well. Maybe Jenny was smart enough not to drop any stitches, but the possibility of it endangered Lyle as much as the reality.

And there was somebody else they hadn't considered.

"What about Charlie Allen and Franny?"

There was no answer. Artie listened for a moment, heard the faint sounds of snoring, and turned over on his side to go to sleep. There was no sense of anything or anybody outside the windows—there couldn't be, they were twenty stories up—and no sense of anybody standing outside their door.

How long had it been since he'd had a good night's sleep?

It was eight o'clock when Artie rolled out of bed. Mitch had already showered and shaved and was staring out the window, waiting for him. It had started to rain again, the drops pelting against the glass. It was going to be a damp and dismal Christmas, Artie thought. Both Susan and Mark gone . . . Bad timing. Like most of his life lately.

"Downstairs or room service?" Mitch asked when he had finished dressing.

"Downstairs—less chance of somebody messing with the food."

It was nine o'clock when they finished breakfast. Mitch gave his credit card to the waiter, then pushed slightly back in his chair and turned to Artie.

"So who's it going to be? Charlie Allen, to ask him what he remembers about Cathy and any bright ideas where she could be? Or Lyle, to ask him what Jenny might have said at one time or another."

"Lyle," Artie said at last. "I don't think anybody would be after Charlie; he wouldn't have any direct information. Lyle might."

"See him at work?"

Artie shook his head. "It's the Christmas season—he's probably working his tail off. Call him and try and see him tonight."

Mitch stood up. "Be right back."

Artie was halfway through his second cup of coffee when Mitch returned, looking concerned. "Called the store, they said he hadn't come in yet—that he was usually there at eight. They were apologetic—he's never late. So I called him at home. No Lyle."

"Try Anya?"

"You know what she does? I don't, I only met her once and I got the impression she didn't do much of anything."

"She works at BofA. Lyle said she was visiting relatives in San Jose but maybe she's back by now."

Mitch sipped his coffee in silence until the waiter brought back his credit card. He tucked it away in his wallet. "Let's go check out his house."

Ten o'clock on a windy, rainy day in San Francisco. The neighborhood around Thirtieth and Ulloa was deserted, the only person on the street a mailman working his way slowly up the block.

"You want to watch for a while?" Artie asked.

Mitch shook his head. "What for? There's not going to be anybody coming and going. And all we want to do is ask him a few questions."

"Without giving the game away," Artie said. "And we're depending on Lyle being . . . Lyle."

"Big gamble." Mitch got out of the car and Artie tagged along after him, standing at the bottom of the steps while he rang the doorbell. There was no answer. Mitch tried again, then out of impulse tried the door itself. It opened easily; it wasn't locked.

"Cute," Mitch said. "It's deliberate, Artie, a signature. If anybody was here, they've come and gone and we're supposed to know it."

He pulled on a pair of surgeon's gloves and Artie followed suit. It would make it difficult handling the automatic, but they wouldn't leave any prints if they touched something in the house. And he could pray he didn't have to use the gun.

The house was quiet, the kitchen area clean. Dishes had been washed from the previous night's supper and were in the drainer on the sink. Two plates, two cups, two sets of silverware—Anya had returned from San Jose, had probably cooked the meal.

But nothing had been set out for breakfast. There was no carton of milk slowly growing warm on the table, no butter slumping in its dish, no half-filled bowls of cereal or frying pan crusted with egg.

The bedroom was deserted. The bed hadn't been slept in, the towels in the bathroom were dry and neatly hung on their racks.

"That's a three- to four-hour window," Mitch said quietly. "After supper but before bedtime."

"Window for what?" Artie asked.

"We know they ate supper here. If they'd gone to a movie, they would have returned sometime before midnight or shortly afterward. Maybe they went out of town, but like you said, Lyle is manager at Copeland's and this is one of their busiest seasons; he wouldn't have left in the middle of it. My guess is they're still here." There was a ripple of excitement beneath the calm in his voice. "I think they're dead, Artie. The reason we had such a peaceful night last night is because they probably didn't."

They found Fritzi first, at the bottom of the stairs to the basement. The rottweiler was balled up in a corner, its eyes glazed. Both hind legs were broken, and it looked like its chest had been crushed.

Mitch knelt and ran his fingers lightly over the body. "Maybe muscle contractions could do this, but they'd have to be stronger than anything I know of."

Artie knew.

Lyle was in the exercise room, lying flat on his workout bench, the barbell with its load of two hundred and twenty-five pounds on his chest where it had fallen and crushed his rib cage. His workout shirt was soaked in blood, and it took a moment for Artie to spot the several holes in his chest. He stared in silence for a long moment, once again feeling a wave of guilt. It really hadn't been one for all and all for one—ever.

That had been a happy bit of hypocrisy on his part. Would he have liked Lyle any more if he had known him better? Probably not. He was a valued member of the Club when they were younger, but that was because he could score a lid whenever you wanted one. Nobody had really been close to him. He had been too aggressive, too brash, and while they all liked what the vintner sold, nobody had cared much for the vintner himself. None of them had been perceptive enough to realize that Lyle probably knew it and resented it and had used them as much as they had used him, though Jenny might have guessed.

"He was shot while he was working out," Mitch said. "When he would have been helpless."

"Any idea who shot him?"

"My guess is Anya. Ten to one her body's around here someplace."

They found her in Lyle's office, slumped in the big, black leather chair behind his desk. She had put a gun to her head and blown blood and brains all over the books in the bookcase behind her. Artie felt sick and had to force himself to be as clinical as Mitch. She was dressed in a black see-through nightgown that Artie had absolutely no desire to see through. Lyle had taken her to one club meeting and Artie remembered the faint surge of lust that all the men had felt, the momentary envy of Lyle. God, that was another thing to feel guilty about.

Artie glanced around the floor, frowning. "Where's the gun?"

"Not near her—at the instant of death she probably threw it across the room, again because of involuntary muscular contractions. Not the same as Fritzi's, though."

Artie found it near the door. Mitch picked it up with a pencil through the trigger guard and dropped it on the desk. There was a smear of red on the barrel and Artie bent down for a closer look, then jerked his head back. Lipstick.

Mitch studied the papers on the desk, then pushed one over to Artie with the eraser end of a pencil.

"She left a note."

Artie glanced over the first few lines, then read them more carefully. She had been faithful to him but she knew Lyle was cheating on her and that after everything he had promised her, he deserved to die. After she had shot him, she had realized she couldn't live without him, that life would be empty for her . . .

Soap-opera time.

"I didn't know her very well," Artie said when he had finished. "From the few times I met her, I got the impression that it was an open relationship—that she wasn't the jealous type."

Mitch looked dubious. "Maybe she wasn't, maybe she was. She probably got a phone call that set her off and a few minutes later I suspect somebody was around to help her build up a jealous head of steam. Cut and dried, Artie. The police will have the weapon, they'll have the motive, and there's nobody left alive to contradict her suicide note."

It had been the pattern all along, Artie thought. Plausible, open-and-shut, no loose ends. No real reason to investigate anything.

"Do you believe that letter, Mitch?"

"Of course not. But it doesn't matter. I don't think the police will look very far."

Artie let his breath out, realizing for the first time how long he had been holding it. "Should we call them?"

Mitch shook his head.

"Somebody from Copeland's will show up looking for Lyle. We'll leave the door unlocked, just like we found it. If we call in the police, Schuler will be all over us. What do you want to tell him?"

"Nothing," Artie said.

"Neither do I."

Mitch hooked the gun with the pencil again and placed it back on the floor in the same position where it had fallen. They made sure nobody was around, then left the house. Once in his car, Mitch picked up the cellular phone and started dialing.

Artie looked at him, surprised. "Change your mind?"

"Calling the office. Getting my messages. Life goes on, Artie." He listened for a few minutes, then snapped it off and turned to Artie, a bemused look on his face. "Got the report back from the chemist on the potato salad."

Artie had almost forgotten about it.

"What did he find?"

"Red herring, Artie—better check with your neighbors as to who went out of their way to do Susan a favor. The only thing wrong with it was too much Miracle Whip."

CHAPTER 17

Artie sat at his desk going over Connie's script and jotting down notes. It was an uneasy balance between documentary and propaganda, and Connie had fallen off the high wire. It was a matter of emphasis more than anything else. The world was as dark as you cared to paint it, and Connie had deliberately chosen a black palette. And yet . . .

He scribbled another note, then tore the pages from his notepad, crumpled them up, and tossed them in the wastebasket. The problem was not that she was right or wrong—he knew she was right—but how the hell did you sell it? People would watch the bad news only if you told them somebody was doing something about it, that there was progress, that the water was safer to drink, the air safer to breathe, and a number 50 sunblock would take care of the hole in the ozone layer.

"Did you hear anything from Mark?" Connie had come up behind him and was looking over his shoulder at the script.

It took an effort to keep from jumping.

"Don't do that, Connie—I'm not in the best of moods. And no, I haven't heard anything from Mark." He wished to hell she hadn't asked. He had tried to wall it off in his mind and had almost succeeded. "I called the cops this morning—they don't know anything. They're not too excited about it."

"Susan?"

"Called our lawyer. He hasn't heard from her. She'll undoubtedly want her own lawyer anyway." He waved at the pages of the script spread out on the desk. "I was wrong: It needs work but it's honest and it's something people need to know. Trying to market it will be something else. Our ratings will suck—we'll only hold the PBS crowd—but what the hell, we'll have done our bit. As you put it, maybe we'll make a difference, and God forgive me the cliché."

Mary would be proud of him, wherever she was. Then he wondered if she would even see it.

For one of the few times he could remember, Connie leaned back in her chair and lit a cigarette. "I'm afraid we've got a problem."

Artie couldn't possibly think of any problem more serious than those he already had.

"Like what? We can always cut it if we have to, juggle sequences to make it more linear. . . ."

"I'm talking about Adrienne—who turns out to have been a prize bitch."

He looked at her, suddenly wary. "What about her?"

"You may have noticed she wasn't here yesterday. She didn't come in today. We called, nobody home. I sent Jerry over to check her apartment, expecting God knows what. The apartment was clean. She wasn't there and neither was anything else. No furniture, no dishes, no rugs, no books, no nothing. Jerry talked to the landlord and it seems she moved in with a futon and a hot plate and a telephone and that was it. That woman really traveled light."

"Surprise," Artie muttered. Which was no surprise at all. After the fight in the parking lot, nobody was ever going to see Adrienne again. "Anything else?"

"Oh, yes. I went over her résumé. She claimed she'd gotten her bachelor's in communications at McMurphy University in some little town in Nebraska. It doesn't exist. I called previous stations where she said she'd worked. Half of those don't exist either, and the other half never heard of her."

"She *did* work in Sacramento, right?" Artie sensed where all of this was going and wasn't sure he wanted to hear it.

"Right. But the news director who hired her left three months ago and seems to have disappeared. He didn't leave a forwarding address."

Artie definitely didn't want to hear it. "So? What do we do now?"

"You haven't asked me what her last assignment was."

He already knew. "Let me guess."

"You've got it—she was working on a series about the environment. I asked if anybody had seen her tape and they had so I asked them to describe it."

"And ours is the same as hers."

"Down to the same exact examples. Cookie-cutter time." She shook her head. "How the hell is that possible?"

Artie knew how it was possible: Adrienne had orchestrated the series from the very beginning. And how many other Adriennes were scattered about the country, all of them pushing the same special?

He felt as if somebody had just opened up a window and a cold draft had blown in. There were the Hounds and the bystanders like Mary, and now a different branch of the Old People. One devoted to a last-ditch effort to convince *Homo sapiens* of the errors of its ways. In one sense, not dangerous. A lot of people would agree with them. But it was an indication that there *was* a conspiracy, and it might be more tightly organized than he'd thought.

"I don't know, Connie. I haven't the foggiest. Did you talk to Hirschfield about her?"

"He said he was shocked. I'm not so sure. I checked and it turns out he'd interviewed her for only about five minutes and decided the station couldn't get along without her. Maybe he banged her after all."

Artie waved at the pages on the desk.

"Did you show this to him?"

"This morning, before you came in."

"And?"

"He loved it. He thought it was great."

Artie suddenly realized he had to go to the bathroom, bad. Maybe not all the Old People were lawyers or Hounds or TV news reporters after all. Maybe some of them were news directors.

Connie shook her head in disbelief.

"What the hell's going on, Artie? There's no way in the world two different people could think this much alike. Adrienne and I never had a conversation all the time she was here; we barely nodded to each other when we passed in the hallway. I always considered her an ice queen."

"So let's change the script."

Connie snuffed out her cigarette. "You're right. She's good, we're better."

They worked on the script for the next few hours, rearranging segments and rewriting Connie's voice-over. Adrienne's Sacramento tape was being held for the same after-the-holidays doldrums. Theirs had to be different, which meant drastic shifting and cutting. It was two in the afternoon before Connie called a break.

"You want lunch, Artie? My treat."

He shook his head. "Go finish your Christmas shopping while you're at it. I'm going to grab a cameraman and go to the zoo."

"What for?"

"The zoo's part of a nationwide cooperative breeding program to preserve endangered species. Some species you can only find in zoos nowadays—they've disappeared completely from the wild. A lot of the specimens we've got—here, in the San Diego, the Brookfield and the Berlin Zoos, and a couple of dozen others around the world—are all there are; there ain't no more."

She looked surprised. "How come you know all this?"

"The Grub knows everything, Connie. I had him print me out a list of the different endangered species; it's as thick as a small phone directory."

He was slipping into his raincoat when Connie said, "Artie? I hear they've got a Siberian tiger out there—shoot some tape of it for me, will you? I'm kind of fond of tigers."

It was after three by the time they got to the zoo and the daylight was already fading. It was cloudy and misting by the ocean; they wouldn't be able to shoot outside for much more than an hour and Artie wasn't sure whatever they got would be usable; the zoo had insisted they not shine lights on the animals. But at least it would serve as a guide if they had to come back another day.

Almost all the big cats were inside, and Artie watched while the cameraman shot tape of them moving around inside the large cages, then angled for what might be used as a head shot. The King of Beasts, with the background out of focus behind him, looking majestic. It was humid and, as usual in the cat house, it stank. After ten minutes Artie was ready for fresh air, even if it was chilly.

The Siberian tiger was in a special outdoor display, a large moat and high iron fence separating it from the curious spectators. It would make for better tape if it were spring and there were dozens of people around staring and pointing. As it was, the only people there besides himself were a middle-aged woman in a heavy cloth coat with the collar up around her ears and a teenager with a colorful scarf half wrapped around his face, the ends trailing in the stiff breeze. They were a good ten feet apart, obviously not a family group; not much in the way of human interest when it came to an interview.

Artie watched the tiger for a few minutes, letting the cameraman shoot as much tape as he wanted. It was a gift from the Cincinnati Zoo, and Artie wondered what they'd gotten in return. A dozen buffalo? Maybe a couple of Kodiak bears—that might be more fitting for a zoo in the heartland. But if he were a zookeeper and had to choose between them, he'd pick the tiger, a good five hundred pounds with long, pale fur and sheer grace to its movements.

How many were left in the world now? he wondered. Less than five hundred, at best? Less than fifty? Connie would make a copy of the tape for her home library and her kids would show it to their kids and by that time wild Siberian tigers would be long gone, a fading memory along with their original habitat, probably destined to be a collection of resort towns, fancy hotels, and upscale restaurants in a distant, crowded future. The tigers would be nothing more than photographs in encyclopedias and "Mammals of the Twentieth Century," or creatures captured for a moment in time on scratchy videotape. With luck some natural history museums would have animatronic versions, and a few zoos would be desperately trying to breed them back.

Connie would have an odd sort of memento. Or maybe memorial, and that might be a line he should use.

Artie squinted at the sky. Not much more than half an hour of light left; they'd have to come back in the morning or preferably on a day when it was sunny.

He walked into the Primate Discovery Center, the new monkey house, stopping at a small cage complete with waterfall, rocks, and trees.

The plaque on the railing identified the monkeys as macaques, the most widely ranging primate genus outside of man. You could find them in almost every country in Africa and Asia, from Morocco to the Philippines.

There were three white-faced monkeys inside the enclosure, all lined up behind the glass, staring at him. Artie stared back, feeling vaguely uneasy. There was rope netting inside the cage on which they could swing and climb: why the hell weren't they? He moved on to another cage to stare at more monkeys staring back. He was the only visitor on a chill and windy day and apparently the prime attraction.

He shivered and went back outside, stopping at the small island of rocks surrounded by a deep moat that was home to the chimpanzees. How long ago was it that several of the chimps had escaped from the island and scared the hell out of a dozen housewives who reported prowlers in the backyard? Years now—it had been a different, low-tech zoo back then.

He leaned against the railing and watched the few chimps shivering on top of the pile of artificial rocks, searching for any scraps of food they might have missed earlier in the day. One patriarch with graying fur sat at the edge of the moat and glared back at him.

A moment in time, Artie thought. A moat, five million years, and less than two percent of encoded genes separated them. How surprised the chimp's ancestors must have been when they saw the first primitive hominids venture out of the forest, creatures not that much different from themselves but swaying awkwardly from side to side as they tried to walk upright on two legs. Larger heads, flatter faces, and less fur. Ugly creatures who didn't have sense enough to stay in the forest where they at least had a chance of escaping the big cats and the other predators.

And how shocked a similar patriarch and his fellow chimps must have been to see the hominids make fires outside their caves to keep them safe during the long night. Artie imagined the years rolling past and the upright creatures becoming taller and heavier, shedding more of their hair while their heads grew ever larger and their faces flatter and their noses more defined. About the same time something curious must have started to appear in their eyes, something that frightened that early patriarch when he first saw it. Something that made it difficult for him to look the new creatures in the eyes for any length of time before he had to drop his own.

That patriarch was undoubtedly familiar with tools; he probably used sticks that he thrust into termite mounds and pulled out with a dozen juicy termites sticking to it. And he probably knew how to use logs and rocks to crack nuts and how to drive away predators by throwing rocks at them from the safety of a tree limb. But the new creatures did something else with the stones: They struck them together and used the chips that cracked off to cut meat and clean bloody skins so they could wrap them around their waists to take the place of the hair they no longer had.

That ancient ape might even have tried to imitate them and struck two rocks together and watched the sparks fly, but that was all that happened. There was probably a dim thought in the back of his mind that perhaps the other creatures used different rocks, but it was a difficult thought to grab hold of and he probably couldn't tell the difference between the rocks anyway.

He must have been afraid of this strange animal and the curious things it did, more afraid than he was of the big cats or the protowolves that hunted in packs. The new creature was more dangerous than all of them.

Artie smiled at the old chimp staring back at him. He was probably very much like that patriarch of long ago. Now he was too old and too slow to fight for mates and most likely considered himself fortunate to be in a zoo where old age might be a problem but not survival itself, and where the zoo veterinarian gave him odd-tasting stuff to ward off the chills he occasionally felt and where the keepers might save a particularly juicy piece of meat for him that was easy to eat because he had long since lost most of his teeth.

he might trade it all for a real forest, monkey. . . .

Artie suddenly felt sweaty and frightened. He glanced quickly around. There was nobody there, at least nobody he could see. He was alone in the middle of an almost deserted zoo and suddenly imagined all the cage doors swinging open to leave the animals free to roam the walks and buildings. What better place to be hunted than in a zoo?

take another look. . . .

Artie turned back to the island and caught his breath. The old chimp had disappeared and in its place was a naked man sitting on his haunches at the moat's edge, his eyes dull and only casually curious. It took a moment before Artie realized he was looking at himself.

your future home, monkey . . .

Artie waited, but there was nothing more in his mind than the sound of raucous laughter. It faded and he was looking at the elderly chimp again, slowly scratching itself and turning away from the fence to amble back to the center of the island. The middle-aged woman—probably a schoolteacher—and the teenager were now at the far side of the enclosure, staring at the little group on the rocks.

It was almost dusk now and all he wanted was to get the hell out of there. He'd sent the cameraman over to the Primate Center to get some close-ups of some of the monkeys on Jerry's list of endangered species, but it was time to go; he didn't dare stay longer. Connie would want to know just what they had shot, but he'd draw up a list for her back at the office. At least she'd be pleased with the tiger.

Besides, he had more important things to think about than a television series. He'd try Susan's phone number once again, hoping against hope that the disconnect message had been a mistake. She might even have called him; she'd have to sooner or later. And maybe Mark had checked in.

Wishful thinking, but that was all that was left to him.

He was suffering from terminal frustration, Artie thought. He was in the middle of a conspiracy that nobody but him and Mitch even realized existed, and if he tried to tell somebody, they'd think he was nuts. He had to try to stay alive and find his family—and work on the series as if nothing was happening around him.

He glanced at his watch. He'd check again with the police, then he'd call Mitch and they'd pay Charlie Allen a visit. Charlie knew everything about everybody.

Maybe he even knew where Cathy Shea was hiding.

" A n y t h i n g I c a n g e t you guys? More coffee, soda, some cake? Franny made a chocolate one for the kids—it was Nathan's birthday today and chocolate's his favorite."

Artie settled back on the living room sofa and shot a glance at

Mitch in the big easy chair, concentrating on his coffee and trying to ignore Charlie Allen overdoing his role as host.

"We were thinking about Larry and Cathy," Artie said. "You were closer to Larry than we were. We wondered if there was anything you remembered about him that might be relevant."

Charlie looked confused. "Relevant to what? His murder? I told Schuler everything I knew. It wasn't much—no more than you guys know." He cut into his slice of cake. "Somebody cut him down in the city and I've no idea why. He was a sweetheart; he didn't have any enemies."

"What about Cathy?" Mitch asked.

"What about her?" Charlie washed down a bite of cake with a sip of coffee and leaned back in the chair by his desk, the inner man temporarily satisfied. "Cathy was a goddamned saint, if you ask me. Took care of Larry and the kids like nobody else, believe me."

Franny was almost a shadow in the room, filling their coffee cups and murmuring offers of more cake, then sitting on the edge of the chair by the doorway, ready to fly into the kitchen at the slightest indication of hunger or thirst.

"Cathy have relatives here in town? Anyplace where she might have gone with the kids?" Mitch was doing his best to cut to the chase.

Charlie shook his head. "Nobody in the Bay Area, not that I know of. A cousin in San Luis Obispo, another in Seattle. Think she was an only kid—both parents died in a car accident about ten years ago."

"Any close friends?" Mitch asked.

"Aside from everybody associated with the Club? Hell, I don't know. Probably the parents of some of her kids' school friends—I think she was active in the PTA."

"Any lovers?" Mitch asked it as if it were the most natural question in the world.

Charlie looked from one to the other, frowning. "Something going on that I don't know about? Why do you want to know stuff like that?"

He was irritated more by the idea that he might have been left out of the loop than by anything else. Mitch tried to soothe him.

"We're just trying to figure out where she might have gone. She's the only one who might have some information that could lead to Larry's killer."

Charlie concentrated on his cake. "That was one happy marriage, Mitch. She idolized Larry."

It was Artie who caught Franny's expression, the slightly sour look of disapproval that fled across her face to disappear into the rolls of happy fat that framed it.

"What do you think, Franny?"

She looked surprised and faintly annoyed at being caught out. "Oh, I agree with Charlie. Completely. She was very committed to her family. But . . ." She let it dangle out there, a worm on a conversational hook.

Mitch leaned forward in his chair, looking at her over the top of his glasses, clinically curious. "But what, Franny?"

A wave of the hand. "Nothing, really."

She wanted it teased out of her, Artie thought. She wanted to be encouraged to damn with faint praise and vomit twenty years of resentment all over the living room floor. Franny had been a member of the Club when it started, then had married Charlie early on and vanished into her family. She would still show up at occasional parties, though never at meetings. She hadn't cared for the other women in the Club and never bothered to hide her opinion that they were all a bunch of elitists.

Charlie stared at her in surprised silence and Mitch and Artie let the silence grow. Franny turned to her husband.

"Come on, Charlie. You remember how Cathy used to flirt with every man who came to our parties? She toned it down after she got married, but she still did it."

The jealousy flickered in her eyes like flames while she glanced from one to another searching for encouragement that wasn't there. She shrugged and began to backpedal. "It really wasn't anything serious. I suspect most of you weren't aware of it at all. But the other women were."

He *had* been aware of it, Artie thought, though he never would have called it flirting. Cathy was the type of woman whom men found easy to talk to, even to confide in. She didn't represent a threat to any happy marriage, but if you were in an unhappy one, you would have been drawn to her. Not that anything would have happened. Cathy drank too much at parties and she liked to kiss all the men good night and sometimes the kisses were really sloppy, depending on how much she'd had to drink. If you couldn't avoid it, you made a joke of it. Larry never noticed, or he'd spent so many years deliberately not noticing that he'd become genuinely oblivious to it.

The typical suburban housewife's night out: You knew instinctively when to avoid her at the door and nobody held it against her afterward. It rated the same as Charlie's occasional belch at the dinner table.

Franny was up and busy with the coffeepot to cover her own embarrassment. "I'm sure she never meant anything by it."

"No, I'm sure she didn't," Mitch murmured. Charlie looked slightly put out and Artie made a big thing about changing his mind over the cake. Give Franny a chance to excel at the things she was good at, rather than regretting that she hadn't been the belle of the ball like Cathy.

But still, there was something there.

When Franny had left the room on a mercy errand to get more cake, Artie said tactfully; "Anything you can remember about the early years with Cathy . . ." If there was anything to be found, it would be early on. There wouldn't be many surprises in the later years.

Charlie waved at the shelf of notebooks about the Club. "Hell, it's all in there. You're free to look through them."

"I wouldn't know where to begin."

"I'll flip through the early ones and pick out those that include anything about her. I don't remember much, but there may be something. Tell you what—I'll put those copies aside and take them down to the library. You can pick them up there."

If Charlie pulled more than a dozen, it would take longer than one night to go through them, Artie thought. But any information on Cathy's background might be useful.

He forced himself to eat another slice of cake and sit through half an hour more of start-and-stop conversation with an unhappy Franny sitting silent and sullen in the corner. Then Mitch yawned and Artie muttered something about early-morning work on the series.

Outside, on the porch, Charlie closed the door firmly behind him, looked faintly uneasy, and coughed. Mitch tried to anticipate him.

"I don't blame Franny, I can see—"

Charlie said, "It's not about Franny. She's a little on the jealous side, always has been. I take it as a compliment. It's about Nathan."

Nathan was the eight-year-old boy, Artie remembered. Quiet kid, a little on the chubby side, like his father.

Mitch was all professional calm. "Something wrong, Charlie?"

Allen took a breath. "He's been playing with matches."

"Normal enough, nothing serious. Just talk to him—"

"I have. Three times now. We had to call the fire department the last time. He started a fire in the basement—two of them, actually: a pile of rags soaked in kerosene beneath the bottom of the stairs, another by the water heater and the gas line. The firemen said they were very . . . workmanlike."

"You sure it was Nathan?"

Charlie was looking progressively more unhappy. "We caught him a couple of times before, in the kitchen and in his own room. Little fires, easy to put out. But the firemen said we found these just in time."

Artie could feel the hair stir on the nape of his neck. Nathan hadn't thought of it all by himself. He'd had help. If the house had gone up and Charlie and the family with it, somehow Nathan would have survived and confessed and once again it would have been murder by proxy.

But why Charlie? He didn't know a damned thing.

Mitch clapped Charlie on the back and said briskly, "Call me at the office tomorrow—we'll make an appointment for the boy."

The consummate professional, Artie thought with a trace of irritation. Levin was friend and clinician, but seldom both at the same time.

CHAPTER 18

They spent that night at the Ritz-Carlton on Stockton and Artie dimly remembered taking an est seminar in the building. What had it looked like back then? He couldn't remember and there was little about the building now to remind him; the renovation had been very thorough.

"A little rich for my blood, Mitch."

Mitch loosened his tie and dropped his coat on a chair.

"I wouldn't worry about it. We're getting it for half—the manager's a former patient of mine."

Artie ran his fingers over the pillow; both beds had already been turned down.

"You're ethically challenged, Mitch, but I accept."

"I said 'former,' Artie. I try to discourage it, but sometimes you end up sounding like you're being unfriendly. If I were still counseling him, I would have rejected it automatically." He pulled the curtains; there wasn't much of a view: Chinatown and the towers of the business district. "If we're going to have to hide out, might as well do it in style. He recommended room service, by the way—offered to put it on his tab."

The alarm bells started ringing in Artie's head. "How well do you know him?"

"Well enough not to worry."

Would Mitch trust his friend with his life? Artie wondered. But that was a little like asking how far he and Connie would trust Hirschfield. The station manager seemed reliable, but that's where the crunch came. You really couldn't be sure of anybody. Mitch ought to know that. It wasn't a case of better-the-people-you-knew-than-the-people-you-didn't-know. It didn't matter if you knew them or not; the only thing safe to assume was that you didn't know them. Not really.

"What did you think of Franny?"

Mitch was leafing through the room-service menu and didn't bother looking up.

"Aside from the fact that she's a bitch? I felt sorry for her—she's been holding it in all these years and tonight was the first chance she had to vent. She's not going to be a happy woman to live with for the next few days. Charlie didn't give her any support at all."

"Maybe he made it with Cathy Deutsch, too." It was still hard for him to connect the sexy Cathy Deutsch of his youth with suburban housewife Cathy Shea, Larry's widow and mother of two young boys. Artie yawned and stretched out on his bed, flicking on the TV with the remote but keeping the sound low. "What about Nathan?"

"He was set up. I'll get the kid alone and ask him why he did it and I'll be lucky if he even knows what I'm talking about."

"And the two times before last?"

"Normal playing around. Ordinarily he'd forget all about it. Our Hound picked it up from the kid's mind and saw a way he could use it."

Artie was halfway through a baked potato with the works and a small filet when he remembered the question that had worried him at Charlie Allen's house.

"Why would Charlie be in danger? He never saw Larry's research."

Mitch wiped his mouth and took a sip of chardonnay. "Think, Artie: Why did we go to see Charlie in the first place?"

Levin was playing the role of intelligence officer talking down to a subordinate, and Artie resented it. Mitch had been a top interrogator in 'Nam, and on more than one occasion Artie had looked on with a mix of admiration and horror as Mitch worked on a prisoner. At such times he'd had to struggle to remain friends with Mitch, to remind himself that it was war and a lot of lives depended on Mitch's skill.

"Come on, Mitch—to find out about Cathy Shea."

"Because we think she knows something that would shed some light on Larry's murder, right? Because she probably knew what Larry was working on, knew that he intended to publish it. Because she was the last one we personally know who saw Larry alive. She may know who our Hound is, Artie, might even have been friends with him—or her—at one time without realizing it. And Charlie Allen knows more about all of us than we do about ourselves—I'm willing to take his word on that. Poor Charlie has his memories and his diaries and could very well know too much—or know where to look for it. He probably doesn't give a damn, but that's beside the point."

He couldn't deny that Levin had a good sense of summary, Artie thought, but he resented having to play Dr. Watson to Mitch's Holmes. He set the trays and dirty dishes out in the hallway, then double-locked the door and stripped to his shorts for bed. He channel-surfed for a few minutes, then tossed the remote over to Mitch. He started to doze, the aftermath of a good meal, and made a mental note to tell Mitch to thank his friend.

Mitch finally flicked off the tube and Artie was alone in the darkness, thinking of Mark and Susan and what they might be doing now. He was sitting on his ass waiting for Susan to call him, and that was a mistake. He should try to find out where she had gone, talk it out in person . . .

There was no noise at all in the room except for the murmur of the ventilation system and the muffled sounds of the city outside. With the drapes drawn, it was pitch black and Artie let his mind drift, then turned over and tugged on the blanket to cover his ear. The one mystery story that had left an indelible impression on him when he was a kid was one where the murderer killed his victims by pouring hot lead into their ears while they slept.

He'd never forgotten it.

T h e   c o l d   w a s   n u m b i n g just beyond the mouth of the cave and the small night fire that Deep Wood was tending. The spirits of the dead were twinkling in the evening sky, and as Artie watched, he saw one of them flash across the blackness and disappear just over the trees that lined the other side of the river. One of the spirits returning to the earth to be reborn as who knew what? One of the giant bears that lived deep in the forest, maybe a beaver, maybe even a wolf.

He remembered the wolves that came around and watched him from just outside the ring of firelight, their eyes gleaming in the dark. He imagined that the spirits of the dead were looking at him through the eyes of the wolves, and when he told White Beard what he thought, the chief had nodded wisely and said, of course that was so.

There was one particular wolf who came quite often to sit just beyond the firelight, a huge male with a dirty white coat and black splotches on its muzzle. It stared at him with intelligent eyes, and lately Artie had taken to throwing it small pieces of meat, which it would grab out of midair. Artie wondered how close he could get to it without it biting him. There was a dim picture in the back of his head of the wolf standing where he was in the mouth of the cave, howling whenever danger approached and being rewarded with more chunks of meat.

But that was a foolish thought. Why would any animal from the forest want to protect them? It could get all the meat it wanted on its own.

The wind had picked up strength now and was howling through the branches of the trees and making the fire spirits dance as they ate the twigs and leaves Deep Wood fed them. Deep Wood was afraid of the dark, and Artie caught images in his mind of monsters hiding in the gloom, ready to pounce on him. They were marvelously inventive monsters and Artie felt an occasional flicker of fear himself, then shrugged it off.

White Beard had said the reindeer would be passing through in two more risings of the sun and they had already picked out where they would drive them, a small cliff with a thirty-foot drop, but not so steep that members of the Tribe couldn't scramble down the face and butcher their dead or crippled prey. There would be no problem in preserving the meat. They'd stack it outside the cave, away from the fire, and it would keep frozen until the sun lingered longer in the sky and the blue and yellow flowers dotted the valleys again. They would, of course, have to mount guard to keep away the wolves and the big cats.

White Beard had warned that the Flat Faces might follow the reindeer and if they did, then the hunt would be very dangerous. There were enough reindeer to feed many tribes but the Flat Faces acted as if the reindeer belonged to them, though Artie couldn't imagine the Flat Faces eating them all.

He shivered and wrapped his furs tighter around his chest, letting the fire keep his backside warm. The furs reminded him of what Clear Stream had gotten from one of the Flat Faces she met fishing in a small river nearby.

The Flat Face had shown some interest in a cutter she had and traded her several very thin strips of hide and a slender length of bone with a point at one end and a hole at the other. You forced the point through two furs, then pushed one of the thin strips through the hole. When you pulled on the bone the thin strip slid through both furs and you could tie them together. Clear Stream had demonstrated on the skins that Artie wore, tying together several pieces so they wouldn't fall off his shoulders. The Flat Faces had been good for something after all.

He shifted around so he was standing in front of the fire and could feel the warmth on his face and hands. It was a cloudless night, the sun's pale companion just a hand's-width above the top of the trees. It was almost time to wake Tall Tree to take over guarding the cave mouth and keep Deep Wood from falling asleep despite his fearsome monsters.

But first he wanted to spend a little more time staring up into the night sky and wondering how the spirits traveled to the inky blackness overhead after their ashes had been returned to the Mother of Waters. But it must be easy for them; there were so many up there.

He yawned and moved closer to the fire, shivering. The wind had shifted once again, blowing off the huge river of ice that crept through the mountains two marches away. He was puzzled why White Beard insisted the Tribe live here, when they had all heard of pleasant meadows where the sun traveled higher in the sky and stayed there longer.

It was more marches away than they could count, White Beard had said. And none of the other Tribe members seemed anxious to leave, to make a journey to places they had never seen but had only heard about and that might hold unimaginable dangers.

There was a sudden hooting in the forest across the river and Artie tensed. White Beard had warned that the Flat Faces constantly watched them, that sometimes when it was dark and they heard hooting it was actually the Flat Faces talking to one another.

But there was no more noise, only the crackling of the fire and the usual sounds of the forest. Artie turned and walked to the corner of the cave where Tall Tree was sleeping and kicked him in the rump. It took two more kicks before he was awake and stumbling toward the cave entrance.

Artie watched for a moment to make sure he didn't go back to his furs, then crept to his side of the cave, his mind alive with the dream images from those around him. Some were fighting off bears and wolves as they slept; others, especially those of the boys, were exciting in a different way. He crawled under his own sleeping furs, stiffening for a moment when he felt somebody else there. He recognized Soft Skin by her smell and pulled her closer to him, cursing the thin strips of hide that knotted the skins around his chest and waist. But it took only seconds to slip out of them and a moment later he felt her breath upon his face. He sighed with pleasure and let his hands dance over her breasts and slide down her stomach and between her legs.

It was very good to be alive, he thought. The spirits were watching overhead, the fire was blazing at the mouth of the cave, he had a full belly, and the hunt would begin as soon as the sun awoke. Soft Skin was moving steadily beneath him now and he could feel his own excitement build.

Somewhere in the cave a baby cried and Artie could hear the shushing sound of its mother. He could feel the rough surface of the cave floor beneath the furs and smell the air thick with the odors of a hundred meals and the assorted stinks of the other members of the Tribe. Just beyond the cavern's mouth he knew there were creatures who could tear him in two or delight in eating him while he was still alive.

But if he lived twice as many winters as White Beard had, he knew life would never be much better than it was right then.

"Let's go, Artie." Somebody was shaking him by the shoulder, and it took a moment for Artie to wake up. Another visit with the Tribe, but this time no killing, no slaughter by the river's edge. It had been much more like the dreams he used to have with Susan beside him in bed, then he realized that Soft Skin had been far too real and his shorts were sticking to him. Jesus, that hadn't happened to him since he'd been a kid.

Susan had been gone for . . . how long now?

Mitch was already dressed and pacing nervously by the window.

"What's up?"

"We're going to have to get out of here. Right now, no time for breakfast."

Artie sat on the edge of the bed, blinking the sleep out of his eyes and feeling sudden alarm growing inside.

"Why the hurry?"

"I checked my calls—Schuler phoned in at seven-thirty. He wants to see both of us as soon as possible."

"They found Pace and Anya?"

Mitch shook his head. "Don't think so. Said he'd meet us at an address in the Upper Haight."

"You ask him what about?"

"He wouldn't say. Said he'd call Charlie Allen and Chandler later."

Schuler had to know that he'd been present when Professor Hall had been shot, but since he'd mentioned contacting Allen and Chandler, this couldn't be about that.

"No Mary and Jenny?"

"I thought you'd told me they were leaving town? Schuler didn't mention either one, and I assumed he'd already tried to call them."

Artie vaguely missed the warmth and energy of Soft Skin; it was hard to adjust to the real world.

"You sure it was Schuler?"

Mitch searched the bureau drawer for the phone book and leafed through it. He grabbed the phone and dialed, asked for Schuler and got confirmation.

"Sorry, Artie, I should've checked. Let's go—we'll take my car."

Schuler was waiting for them outside a combination redbrick and stucco three-story on Woodland. The house was already cordoned off with yellow police tapes. Schuler was leaning against a police car holding a plastic container of coffee in his hands.

"Sorry to get you two up so early. Allen and Chandler both said they'd be down a little later, though Chandler didn't sound very happy about it."

Artie could understand why. Chandler had looked like hell in his dimly lit office; he'd look frightening in daylight.

Mitch said, "What happened?"

Schuler nodded at the house. "Homicide. Neighbors saw a light go on in the upper bedroom about two in the morning—then screaming half an hour later that abruptly cut off. Apparently two kids started in then, but they were choked off within seconds. Literally, as it turned out. The uniforms got here too late to do anybody any good."

Artie couldn't think of anybody he knew who lived in the Upper Haight, not since his hippie days. But Schuler must have had a good reason to call them down to identify the bodies.

Mitch asked the obvious. "Anybody we know?"

Schuler hesitated. "I know what her ID says. You'll have to tell me if it matches. One woman, two kids. Apparently she was house-sitting for the owners. They're up in Tahoe for the holidays; got hold of them half an hour ago but they can't make it back until this afternoon."

Artie glanced at Mitch, who nodded slightly. They both knew who it was without asking.

Cathy Shea was in the bedroom, naked on the bed, a torn pillowcase knotted around her throat. Her face was purple with blood; there was no expression in her bulging eyes. She was a larger woman than Artie remembered, then he realized that personality can add to or diminish the size of a person. Cathy had never struck him as very big in life. Quiet, basically insecure, sexy when she was drunk, though it always struck him as more of a parody than a reality. All he could think of was that he would have to tell Susan and when he did, she'd come apart. For himself, he was numb. Maybe tomorrow he would feel something. Right then, he felt cold, professional. She had kept the house neat as a pin, had loved her kids, had dutifully supported her husband, had been a good friend to her friends . . .

It was a crappy epitaph.

She had struggled, and her hands were bloody where her nails had scraped flesh. The coroner's assistants were still taking photographs and measurements. Schuler watched the expression on Artie's face, then asked, "Mrs. Shea, right?"

Artie nodded.

"We found an ID in the purse in the john. Didn't guarantee it was her, but ninety-nine percent sure. Time of death—maybe two in the morning. What you see is what you get; she was strangled."

"Raped?" Mitch asked.

Schuler didn't answer but started downstairs. "The two boys were in the living room; they were camping out on a futon. Must have been fun for a while."

It was harder for Artie to look at them than it had been Cathy. Both were sprawled on the futon, presumably in the same position they were in when they had died. Both wore shorts, now soiled and smelling. The aftermath of death. Andy's face was contorted and Artie guessed he had fought. His head had been bashed in by a table lamp, which was now lying nearby, its base covered with blood and pale blond hair. James, the youngest and thinnest, looked almost peaceful. He had probably been suffocated by the pillow next to him, his skinny arms spread out like the arms of a crucifix.

They'd been spoiled rotten. They'd also been full of life and mischief. For the first time Artie thought he was going to break down.

"Why?"

"They probably saw whoever it was. It's even possible it was somebody they knew."

"Breaking and entering?"

Again, Schuler didn't answer.

"We've got prints—a lot of them. One of the neighbors saw somebody leave the house and run down the street toward Golden Gate Park. We're rousting all the homeless encampments, checking IDs and possessions, that sort of thing. They might have lifted something on the way out, something that won't go with their usual collections of tin cans and bottles."

The cops would find something, Artie thought. He'd make book on it. Once again, murder by proxy.

In the kitchen a tired Schuler sprawled in one of the chairs by a large distressed-oak table, and motioned them to take two of the others. "You guys want some coffee? I can send one of the uniforms down to McDonald's. I could use some more—I've been up a long time."

Artie nodded and Mitch said "Thanks." They sat around the table in silence while Schuler jotted notations in a small notebook.

"Curious, isn't it? A few days ago the doctor was killed, his wife disappears, and here we are again wondering who the hell did it. And—tell me if I'm wrong—both you guys have a pretty good idea who. Right?"

Artie shifted uneasily in his chair.

"We can prove where we were—"

Schuler looked disgusted. "Nobody said you were suspects. I'm just saying you know something I don't and I wish to hell you'd tell me."

"Was she raped?" Mitch asked again.

Schuler considered it. "That's a hard question to answer. Did she have sex before she was strangled? The pathologist says so. Was it consensual? Probably. Neighbors saw lights go on in the upper bedroom maybe twenty, thirty minutes before they heard any screaming. There were no signs of breaking and entering. Whoever it was, she let them in."

"A friend," Mitch said.

"You don't let strangers in at two in the morning. A personal friend, maybe a friend of the family."

"Not a friend of Larry's, that's for sure," Artie murmured.

Mitch looked thoughtful. "Maybe more than one."

"Oh?" Schuler sounded sarcastic. "Tell me why."

"The kids. She was killed first so they must have been awake—they heard her screaming. They could have run or cried for help themselves, unless somebody was holding them."

"Or her screams could have woken them up, they ran up the stairs to help her, and met the murderer on the way down. He could have grabbed them both and thrown them back on the futon. They started screaming right after she stopped. Probably died seconds later."

"How many were seen running to the park?"

"Only one, but the witness could have been wrong." A policeman walked in with a sack of muffins and half a dozen coffees along with tiny plastic creamers and little packets of sugar. Schuler shoved several containers of coffee toward Mitch and Artie.

"How well did the two of you know Mrs. Shea?"

Artie was deliberately vague. "Well enough—she was a member of the Club, that's where she met Larry. We've known her for more than twenty years. My wife, Susan, and Cathy were good friends."

"I understand your wife and son have disappeared too, Banks."

Artie flushed. "It's divorce time, Lieutenant. I imagine I'll hear from her lawyer before I hear from her."

"My sympathies," Schuler said dryly. Then: "I gather neither of you two found anything of importance in the Shea home."

Artie looked surprised; Mitch kept his face blank.

"The neighbors." Schuler sighed. "The eyes and ears of the world. The Oakland police called us. A woman one house over got your license number but nothing was missing, so I didn't figure there was any hurry questioning you about it. Happens all the time. Friends of the deceased, angry about the murder, decide to do some investigating of their own. Granted that the two of you were better equipped to do that than most."

There was silence, then Mitch said, "I don't think there's much we can tell you, Lieutenant."

Schuler nodded and took a sip of coffee, jotted something more in his notebook, and shoved it back in his pocket.

"I might have done the same if I were you. But you were operating under a handicap. One, you were friends of Dr. Shea's, which means you probably weren't objective to begin with. Two, you didn't have the authority so you couldn't approach those who might have been in a position to tell you something: the people who lived next door and across the street."

"I assume the Oakland police questioned them," Mitch said. His voice was curt, and Artie guessed he resented Schuler for implying incompetence on his part. As a military investigator, Mitch had been top flight and proud of it.

"That's right, Doctor. I asked for copies of their records and they were kind enough to turn them over to me."

"And?"

Schuler shrugged.

"Apparently Mrs. Shea was one hot lady. Dr. Shea was buried in his work; he was blind to it. My guess is that the rest of you knew it but who the hell wants to tell the husband, who isn't going to believe it in any event but will hate whoever tells him? She had visitors when the kids were at school. There aren't many pool boys in Oakland, but there are enough delivery men familiar with the lonely-housewife syndrome. Probably a fringe benefit of working the Oakland hills."

"Some of us knew it," Mitch said. "There wasn't much to be gained by blowing the whistle."

"You might be right, Doctor. And then again, you might not. We've got one dead lady and two dead kids. Maybe blowing the whistle would have been the kindest thing in the long run."

Schuler looked from one to the other.

"I'm willing to listen to any ideas either one of you might have."

Artie didn't say anything. Mitch said, "You must have some of your own, Lieutenant."

Schuler looked disappointed. "I was hoping this would be a conversation, not a monologue. My take is Mrs. Shea hears about her husband's murder and she figures she's in danger too, so she runs, so frightened she doesn't pack anything at all. She doesn't tell a soul where she's hiding. Barring any evidence to the contrary, I think somebody tracked her down, somebody she was glad to see, because she let him in the house of her own free will. Maybe she got tired of being alone after a few days and called him. If I had to go further, I'd guess the lady was in love but hadn't been about to leave her husband and fight for the kids. Men have mistresses on the side. She had a boyfriend stashed away. But sometime in that half hour she figured out that he wasn't just a terrific bed partner after all, that he'd had something to do with her husband's murder. Maybe she confronted him with it, more likely it was a slip of the tongue, or maybe he just suspected she knew. But that was all it took."

Schuler helped himself to a muffin and took another sip of coffee. "What bothers me is that I think I'm right—and I'm not right. That there's a lot more to it than that but I haven't the slightest clue as to what. I still don't know what she was running from, what frightened her so badly. You two care to help me out?"

They were silent for a moment, then Artie said, "Did you check out the dogs that killed Larry?"

"Two of them were strays, the third—the one with the tags—had been reported missing two days before. Owner was some old guy about to retire from the Health Department. Claimed Fido wouldn't hurt a flea."

Schuler stood up, capping his container of coffee to take with him.

"Tomorrow I think I would like to talk to both of you some more about the Suicide Club. Dangerous club to belong to—the members keep dying like flies. Maybe you can tell me something about Lyle Pace and Anya Robbins. A friend of his at Copeland's stopped by Lyle's home last night to see if he was okay; he hadn't showed for work, didn't answer his phone."

He stared at them for a long moment. "I would like to think I surprised you, but somehow I'm not sure I have. And maybe you can fill me in on Professor Hall, Banks. Ten o'clock sound all right by you?" He didn't wait for an answer. "Fine. See you then."

On the sidewalk outside, a few neighbors had started to gather, whispering among themselves and watching the coroner's men wheel out the bodies.

Schuler opened the door to his car, then paused to glance back at Artie and Mitch. Schuler's face looked drawn and tired, and it occurred to Artie that Schuler was thinning down, becoming frail, that he must be close to retirement.

"I'm getting too old for this. The wife and I have a vacation cottage up in Victoria and I think it's time we put our feet to the fire and let the world take care of itself." He looked depressed. "You probably write obits for your station, Banks. How long do you give the world? Fifty years? Twenty?"

Just before the car pulled away from the curb, he cranked down the window to say, "If I were you guys, I'd watch my back." A thoughtful look, then, "Take care of yourselves."

The scary part, Artie thought, was that he wasn't just being polite.

CHAPTER 19

They had breakfast at a small restaurant on Haight Street, sitting in the back, half hidden by a magazine and paperback-book rack. The fried eggs were passable, the bacon cold and greasy, the orange juice fresh frozen.

But Artie could have been eating hay and he wouldn't have complained. "Schuler's no dummy," he said at last.

Mitch dug into a jar of grape jam to spread on his toast, then gave up and shoved his plate away. "Never said he was. He was just in a better position to know some things about Cathy Shea than we were. He was right—we were too close to Larry and we didn't have the authority to interview the neighborhood. But we still know a lot more than he does."

"I wish to hell I didn't," Artie muttered.

"Probably wouldn't make much difference. We knew Larry—that's the major sin. Our homicidal Hound would have assumed Larry told us everything in any event and things would have happened just as they did."

"Professor Hall might still be alive."

"Paschelke would still have been killed—and so would Lyle."

The coffee was enough to gag on, but Artie drained half his cup.

"So what's next on the agenda? Cathy's a closed book—there's nothing she can tell us."

Mitch pulled several bills from his wallet and dropped them on the table. "Right in one sense, wrong in another. She was good friends with whoever killed her and there's a good chance he's mentioned in Charlie's diaries."

Artie dug in his pocket for some coins as a tip. "The only thing that's wrong with that is apparently she was good friends with almost everybody."

Mitch's smile was bleak. "Except you."

"Except me," Artie agreed.

"When you get around to the diaries all you have to do is pick out the right boyfriend, Artie." Out on the street, Mitch asked, "When are you going to get them from Charlie?"

"He said he'd call me at work so I could drop over to the library after hours."

Mitch leaned against a newspaper box and flipped open his cellular phone. "I'll help you run through them when I get back to the hotel." He looked apologetic. "I've got to check my messages and tell Linda I'll be in today—I've postponed too many sessions already."

He concentrated on his phone, punching in his code for message retrieval. A few nods—Artie assumed that patients had called in to make appointments or cancel them. Then Mitch's face suddenly became starched and flat of emotion. He glanced at Artie, then turned away. He punched in another number, looked again at Artie to see if he was listening, then held the phone so it was partly muffled by his coat. Artie could hear what he was saying but not the other half of the conversation. The only thing that gave Mitch away was his eyes, blinking furiously behind his granny glasses as they always did when he was excited.

Artie was insulted at first, then curious. What the hell? Mitch listened intently to the voice message he was getting, glanced again at Artie after the voice stopped, then punched in still another number.

Artie kept his own face blank and looked away, making a show of giving him some privacy. What was going on? Mitch had obviously received his messages, then punched in for a repeat of one of them, and now presumably was calling the caller back.

Mitch made his connection, then said in a soft voice, "Stu? Levin.

Don't want to talk about it now, just repeat the date." A moment of tense silence. Then: "Got it. Yeah, unbelievable."

He clicked off and slipped the phone back in his pocket.

Artie looked at him, ready to be sympathetic.

"Bad news?"

"You could say that." Then a failed attempt at a smile. "Just business."

It was business that had something to do with him, Artie thought. He'd stake his life on it. Mitch suddenly seemed remote, a hundred miles away.

"I've got to meet somebody, Artie—you can get back to the hotel okay?"

"I'll grab a cab, go right to work. You sure you're all right?"

"I'm fine." But when Mitch looked at him, it was with the eyes of a stranger sizing up somebody he had met for the first time.

"See you at the hotel tonight?" Artie asked, suddenly tentative.

For a moment Mitch seemed surprised, then nodded. "Yeah, sure." He started up the street to his car. He didn't look back.

Artie stared after him. He had known Mitch Levin almost all his life, but inside of a few minutes it suddenly seemed like he didn't know him at all.

"I've changed it a lot," Connie said nervously. "Jim and I had to go ahead without you—sorry about that, Artie, but Hirschfield wants it sooner rather than later."

"Have I made Hirschfield's shit list yet?"

She shook her head. "Not yet—but close."

She looked worn out, Artie thought—she must have shed five pounds in the last few days.

"You stayed here and worked on it all night?" He felt a brief twinge of guilt, then realized there was no way he could have helped her any more than he had.

"Not quite—we were here until three in an editing booth. Most of the audio track and sound bites are laid down and Jim started covering it with B-roll."

Jim Austin was their star editor, and he and Connie had been friends from the day she'd started working at KXAM.

"What's the standard, Connie? A bottle of Chivas?"

She gave him a long look. "Beam—and make it half a case. We took him away from his family at Christmastime."

He pulled a stool over in front of the monitor, sitting close to Connie, who had balanced her yellow notepad on her knees. Jerry asked, "Ready?" and, when she nodded, started the tape rolling.

It was more of a PBS opener than Artie had figured Connie would use. Stock tape of lush forests of oak and pine with eagles flashing through blue skies, tumbling rivers with salmon leaping over rocks, grasslands spreading as far as the eye could see with a herd of buffalo on the distant horizon. Eden, Artie thought. Then the camera dipped for a view of an Asian forest and a tiger padded into the frame, high-lighted for a moment against a patch of waving grass. It looked over-whelmingly majestic. Then a dissolve into the field tape they had shot of the Siberian tiger the day before, pacing back and forth in its tiny enclosure of weeds and artificial rocks.

And finally a shop in some unknown Chinatown with a shelf of mounted tiger's paws, tins of something unknown but with the logo of a tiger on it—dried gall bladder? Powdered tiger's blood? Aph-rodisiacs of some sort? And in the back of the shop, draped over a small mound of boxes, a tiger's skin, its teeth bared in a taxidermist's idea of a snarl, muted by the poorly painted plastic buttons that served as eyes.

The skin could have come from the same tiger they had seen a few seconds earlier.

"I'm not sure about this title setup," Connie murmured in his ear.

On the monitor was an animated version of an artist's palette with splotches of brilliant paints: greens and blues and reds and yellows and purples and pinks. Then an animated brush started mixing the colors, slowly at first, then speeding up into a flurry of motion. The different splashes of pigment were swirled into various tints and shades, which gradually lost any sense of purity and merged into a brown that covered the palette and then the entire screen. The title "World Without End?" was reversed out on the muddy background.

All the brilliant colors at the start had been reduced to a shit brown, Artie thought. The analogy was obvious: a pristine world that had been reduced to ... what?

"We took it from the opening of a Disney cartoon," Connie said in a low whisper. "We can do a variation if we can't get permission."

Artie was fascinated by the images on the tube. She had taken the assignment and run with it; he'd been egotistical to think she had needed his help at all.

Now the screen was filled with portraits of various animals while Connie narrated the names of the endangered species: the Siberian tiger—fewer than five hundred remaining in the wild; the Florida panther—thirty to fifty; the black-footed ferret—less than five hundred; the red wolf—fewer than three hundred; the ocelot—a hundred. . . .

Her voice faded into a chroma-key shot with Connie standing in front of what would have been the weather map, only with the zoo footage rolling behind her while she explained the "sixth extinction": the thirty thousand officially threatened species, including more than five hundred mammals, almost a thousand each of birds and fishes, more than twenty-five thousand plants.

Species went extinct all the time due to natural causes, she continued. But this time the culprit wasn't nature; it was man. Take Mozambique, where a dozen different armies had used everything from assault rifles to helicopters to slaughter the animals. The white rhinoceros was now extinct, only a few black rhinos were left, the elephant population had fallen by ninety percent.

The image behind her now changed to a large commercial fishing boat, pulling in nets and dumping the day's catch on the deck. The situation was no better in the oceans, where overfishing was gradually emptying the waters. Bluefin tuna in the Western Atlantic was down by ninety percent and due to drop farther—it was selling for three hundred and fifty dollars a pound in popular sashimi restaurants in Tokyo.

Overfishing had gotten so bad that Canada had shut down its fishery in the Grand Banks of Newfoundland, throwing forty thousand people out of work. Poaching inside its two-hundred-mile coastal limits had already led to shooting with Canada firing on and boarding a Spanish fishing trawler; Icelandic fishing ships and Norwegian patrol boats had exchanged gunfire. Were these the first shots in the coming wars over the spoils of the sea? And inland, streams where fish had once been so plentiful early explorers claimed you could cross the water by walking on their backs were now so polluted they ran brown and empty.

Few fish caught within coastal waters were suitable for eating, the on-screen Connie said in the wrap-up.

Jerry stopped the tape after the end of the segment.

"How long did it run, Jerry?"

"Under five minutes—four forty-two. It's still a little over."

Connie frowned. "We'll have to take the time out of the final segment." She looked at Artie. "So? What do you think?"

Artie was impressed. "You did a great job—so did Jim."

"It gets better. Okay, Jerry."

The second segment was titled "Garbage World" and opened with squirrels gathering acorns at the bottom of an ancient oak, then panned to a stream a hundred feet away where the banks were spattered with rusting cans and empty bottles while the water was iridescent with oil and toxics spewing from a waste pipe jutting out from one of the sandy banks. Finally, shots of women washing clothing in the Ganges, a river that had "died of detergent."

A stand-up with Connie talking about a consumer society while she wandered through the aisles of a Costco packed to the ceiling with electronics and household furnishings, racks of clothing, pallets of detergent and twelve-packs of soda and beer, refrigerator cases filled with TV dinners and frozen chicken parts, and a meat department with ground beef in five-pound packages and steaks a dozen to the plastic tray. "And it all comes packaged," Connie said.

Jerry stopped the tape again. Connie turned to Artie and asked, "You want to take a break?"

Artie's coffee was cold but he didn't care.

"Let's go through the whole thing—after that I'll go home and kill myself."

Half an hour later the tape finished and Gottlieb ejected the cassette.

"Thanks a heap, Jerry." Connie left for their glassed-in cubicle overlooking the newsroom, Artie trailing after her in silence. They sat and watched the activity outside for a minute or two, then Connie said, "Okay, tell me what's wrong with it. I already know it can be polished."

"I think it's a great piece of work," Artie said. "Also, depressing as shit."

Connie nodded. "You read an article here and an article there, the newspapers run stories, once in a while you see a review of a book about it or watch a PBS special. But you don't read or see them all at the same time—you don't add them up. It's easier to worry about your next raise, your heartburn, what the kids are doing to each other after dark and what about a curfew. You feel you can do something about those. This kind of stuff just makes you feel . . . helpless. What the hell, you don't fish, you don't farm, you recycle and hope the problems will go away."

"Hirschfield seen the tape?"

She dumped some sugar in her cold coffee and stirred it with the cap of her pen.

"You hit the one bright spot. He loved the script, he loves this more—thinks he can get the network to carry it in six weeks or so, after the February sweeps. Hell, they've got nothing else important scheduled then."

Maybe it was their one last chance to change things before the Hounds of Hell came up with something really final, Artie thought.

Connie was studying him. "You don't think it's my cup of tea, do you?"

Artie looked at her in surprise. "The series? I can't think of anybody who could have done it better."

"You really mean it?"

"If I didn't think so, I wouldn't say so."

She looked away. "Thanks, Artie. A lot." Then: "I'm thinking of doing one on Russia."

"Why Russia?"

Jerry knocked on the door and came in with a cardboard tray and two containers of hot coffee.

Connie took one, glanced at it, and said "No cream?" in mock dismay. Jerry muttered "Jesus" and left, Connie's "Thanks" floating after him. She took a gulp. "The Russians are like the deer on Angel Island: they're crashing. But almost all we ever hear about are the politics and the crime. They destroyed themselves twenty years ago and they've been walking around ever since not knowing they're dead."

Artie felt uneasy. "I don't follow you."

"Terminal poisoning of their own environment. Almost all of the major rivers are polluted, and they've dammed the ones that fed the Aral

Sea so they could use the water for irrigation; now the Aral is maybe half its former size and dying. They even have salt storms that blow off the crusted shores. It was fish versus cotton, and the planners in Moscow chose cotton because it paid better. They've dumped nuclear wastes into rivers and the sea, there's pollution from leaking pipes in the older oil fields, heavy metals have contaminated the countryside around smelters. . . . It's hurting, badly. The average life span of Russian men has dropped from sixty-five to fifty-eight. . . ."

Artie didn't want to hear any more.

"Connie, get the hell out of here."

She grimaced. "I'll be okay. But the next time I do a special, maybe it should be one on soccer moms. What I'm going to do right now is go home, curl up on the couch with half a gallon of eggnog, and get smashed. Let Kris take care of me for a change. She'll bitch but she'll love the novelty."

Artie turned to leave and behind him Connie said, "You got a call earlier. A Charlie Allen at the library. Said he had some books for you."

"Thanks—I'll pick them up." He slipped out of the door, leaving Connie to her demons.

CHAPTER 20

It was dark when Artie left the station, the air cold and misting. Lately when he'd been getting up in the morning, he could see frost on the railings of his back porch. How cold was it now, high thirties? Maybe tonight it would even snow; there had been a dusting of it on Mount Tam a few mornings ago. He'd called for a cab before leaving the office and waited ten minutes behind the bulletproof glass of the front lobby until it showed up.

"We'll be closing in fifteen minutes," the library guard warned. People were already streaming out the doors, on their way to the Muni or BART.

Artie showed his press card. "Charles Allen?"

The guard consulted a printed listing on his desk. "Main Library Administration—that's on five. Elevators are across the rotunda on the Fulton Street side."

Artie started across the granite floor, stopping for a moment in the middle to glance up at the skylight six floors overhead with the staircases circling beneath it. The rotunda and its skylight were the architectural center of the building; the different reading rooms and cultural centers led off the staircases on each floor. A teenager a dozen feet away, his back to him, was also staring up at the skylight; he'd probably just signed off the Internet and was getting ready to go home and had stopped to look up at what he'd heard so much about. There wasn't much to see now—too dark—but during the day the sunshine streaming through the massive skylight illuminated the whole interior of the building.

Supposedly it was the first step to the electronic library, though Artie would have been happier with fewer computers and more books. There was something about the feel of paper and cloth that a computer screen could never replace.

"Hi, Artie. Come on in and close the door."

Charlie's office was hidden behind the stacks across from the rotunda. It was just big enough for a desk, a spare chair, a coat rack, a bookcase, and the ubiquitous computer. Charlie finished what he was working on and powered down.

Artie asked the obvious: "Working late?"

"Not this time of year—most everybody's doing their last-minute shopping. We get some young kids in the audio/visual center and some of the winos for the warmth, but that's about it." Allen locked his fingers behind his head and leaned back in his chair, yawned, then opened his eyes wide and stared at him. The stare of a too-curious man, Artie thought, with misgiving.

"Artie, what's going on?" Allen sounded plaintive and a little angry.

Artie tried to look surprised. "You tell me."

Charlie shoved the afternoon paper across the desk. Artie picked it up, afraid for a moment that Cathy had made the headlines.

"First Larry, then Lyle and his lady. Lyle wasn't the most likable guy on the face of the earth, but I keep getting this feeling that somebody out there is gunning for us."

Artie read the story carefully, taking his time though he already knew the details. Charlie didn't know about Cathy or Chandler yet and when he found out, the shit would really hit the fan.

"I got a right to know," Charlie said quietly. "You better believe Nathan already has Franny and me pretty upset. The kid could have killed us all. I feel like we're characters in *Ten Little Indians,* where one by one the suspects are knocked off." He pointed at the paper. "Did you know anything about this? And if you did, why the hell didn't you tell me? I'm not exactly an innocent bystander, Artie, not after the other night."

He was referring to Nathan again, Artie thought. He shook his head. "That's the first I've read about it, Charlie. Scout's honor."

Charlie studied him, trying to decipher the expression on his face. "You're lying like a rug, Artie. How long have you and I and Mitch been friends? More than twenty years now? You and he know something, and you're not letting me in on it. We all have our secrets, but this time it looks like my family's concerned. Not good."

He stared at Artie a moment longer, then motioned toward the bookcase. "The diaries are in the shopping bag there—I flipped through them and pulled the ones where I saw a mention of Cathy. I didn't read them closely. Why spoil the memories, right? Though right now they seem to be rotting pretty badly."

"Sorry you feel that way," Artie said quietly. "All Mitch and I are doing is trying to find out who killed Larry. I don't know about Lyle and Anya, though it looks like a lovers' quarrel."

"Coincidence stretched to the breaking point," Charlie snorted.

Something on his desk caught Artie's eye and he changed the subject. A box with a Walkman and a set of headphones draped over the sides. He pointed at it. "They won't let you have a radio in here?"

"Just trying it out—Christmas present for Nathan. This and a dozen tapes of his favorite bands. He loves 'em, I hate 'em, but this way he's the only one who's going to hear them."

Artie suddenly stiffened. When he got off the elevator, he hadn't seen anybody on the floor. It had been silent, the study rooms had been empty, and the Magazines and Newspapers Center was deserted. Now he sensed there was somebody outside the door. Probably the guard making his rounds, he thought frantically, and knew immediately he was wrong.

He smiled crookedly at Charlie, hoping it really was the guard and waiting for a knock on the door. A minute of staring at a puzzled Charlie. There was no rap on the door, no further sound of somebody walking in the corridor outside.

But somebody was sure as hell out there; he could *feel* him.

"You know," Charlie said in a suddenly smug voice, "Mitch wasn't the only one who banged Cathy Deutsch. I had a piece of her too."

Artie suddenly felt panicked. He had left the automatic back in the hotel room, hidden under the dirty clothes he'd stuffed in a drawer. Jesus, he should have known better.

Charlie had asked him to drop in at the library after hours, when he knew it would be deserted, and he had cheerfully obliged.

you're a fool, monkey. . . .

F o r   a   m o m e n t   l i f e was a series of freeze-frames. Charlie Allen, looking both smug and surprised at what he'd just said. The box with the Walkman and the tapes open on the desk, a long pair of newspaper shears at the top of the desk pad. The look on Charlie's face slowly shifting from one of surprise to one of watchful hostility. Then the little things: the telephone out of its cradle, the small green light signifying "On" for the phone recording system.

Setup, Artie thought chaotically. Whatever happened in that office would be recorded for Schuler to find later.

"You never struck me as a cocksman, Charlie," Artie said in a thin voice.

Charlie was a pudgy man but now there was a subtle change. He suddenly didn't strike Artie as weak or slow on his feet. Charlie was like a glove that something had put on and was now flexing its fingers.

"Those who do don't talk about it, Banks. I don't think Mitch ever got as far as he said he did."

"But *you* did?"

Charlie smirked.

"Why not, she was easy. So were Jenny and Mary." There was something behind his eyes that Artie couldn't read. "So was Susan."

Artie almost leaped over the desk at Allen, then realized that it wasn't Charlie speaking to him at all.

the voice on tape is all that counts, monkey. . . .

"You're a liar," Artie croaked.

Charlie shook his head in mock anger.

"It's okay for you and Mitch to talk about Cathy, right? But you ought to take a good look at Susan. She had a two-year-old kid, the boy needed a father, you were the closest thing to a virgin in the Club, and you even had something of a future. You were shy, she was physical, and a taste of flesh went a long way with you, didn't it? She's probably been a good wife and loyal, so you've had no complaints." He looked at Artie quizzically. "Or has she been? Loyal, I mean. She never struck me as very demonstrative, not the kind to run her fingernails down your back and spend half an hour telling you how great you were and how much she loves you. She ever done that, Artie?" He paused for a fraction of a second. "You don't have to answer—I never thought so anyway."

Artie felt himself go white.

"Has Franny ever done that for you, Allen? She bowed out of the competition early, probably realized she was a loser all around."

He was almost shocked when he saw Charlie's fingers curl around the handle of the shears. Newspaper shears were long and pointed, and the grip would be great for either an underhand or an overhand thrust.

"Stop it, Charlie—he's trying to get to both of us!" For a moment the real Charlie flickered in Allen's eyes, frightened and confused. Then Artie found himself saying, "Cathy Deutsch wasn't the only punchboard. You sure Nathan's all yours, Charlie?"

First one, then the other. They were being played against each other. The argument was childish, but it wouldn't sound like that on the tape when Schuler discovered blood all over the desk and the walls, and a body on the floor, maybe two.

Raucous laughter inside his head . . .

too late, monkey . . .

He thought for a moment of going after Charlie, but Charlie beat him to it. He gripped the shears in his right hand and launched himself over the desk, rolling to his feet on the other side. Charlie shouldn't be able to do that, not even on a good day, and then Artie remembered the old man skating in Union Square.

The shears slashed through his coat and Artie felt a stinging sensation in his shoulder. A scratch, but probably a bloody one. He rolled backward in his chair and twisted so he was sitting on the floor, then caught Charlie in the stomach with a foot and the pudgy man went down. Artie rolled away and was on his feet, yanking at the doorknob.

He got as far as the corridor outside when Charlie was clawing at his back, and he went down again. Repeated jabs with the shears, catching mostly overcoat. Artie caught his wrist and tried to bend it back. Charlie was too pudgy, too out of shape—it should have been easy to take the shears away. It wasn't.

Charlie's other fist came up and caught him in the throat. Artie rolled backward into an aisle in the stacks, shelves of books looming up on both sides. Charlie came after him, his face red with anger, using the shears like a broadsword to carve the space in front of him.

Artie reached out and swept books off the shelves onto the floor. Charlie danced out of the way, then slipped on one that had fallen open and went down in a flurry of torn paper. Artie turned and ran for the rotunda stairs.

He had started down when once again he was hit from behind, then was being forced over the railing. He grabbed the steel-pipe railing with both hands, caught a glimpse of the floor five stories below, then started to hoist himself back onto the stairs. When he looked up he was staring full into the face of Charlie Allen.

A very normal Charlie Allen who looked terrified and bewildered. He threw away the bloody shears and helped Artie over the railing.

"Christ, Artie, what's happening! What the hell are we doing?"

"Killing each other," Artie mumbled. His ribs ached and his shoulder felt sticky and wet. He sat on the steps, sagging back against the railing.

Charlie's face suddenly went blank and Artie tensed. "Wait!" Charlie turned and ran off.

If he had the brains God gave a goose, Artie thought, he'd get the hell out of there. Now.

Something was fingering the back of his mind again and the shelves of books just beyond seemed to ripple like the reflection of trees in a windswept pond. How easy it would be to hide in the stacks and catch Charlie when he returned. It would be Charlie Allen they'd find splattered over the floor below.

Suddenly he sensed confusion and anger, and his mind was free. He heard steps and turned to see Charlie running toward him, clutching the bag of diaries, the Walkman headphones covering his ears. He looked scared to death.

"What the hell's going on, Artie? It was me and it wasn't me. . . ."

Artie pointed at the headset.

"Why the phones?"

"So I can't hear myself think—and nothing else can, either. Metallica, Nathan's favorite. I can't stand them." He pushed the bag into

Artie's hands. "Get the hell out of here. I got hold of the guard and he'll call the cops. I'll tell them some story about an intruder."

Artie grabbed him by the arm. "Let's both get out of here."

Charlie shook his head. "It can't follow both of us if we separate. My guess is it'll follow you—sorry, Artie, it's probably after the diaries. I'll be okay, just get out of here."

Artie clutched the bag and ran down the steps. Just before he reached the doors he staggered and almost fell, his mind caught for the moment like a baseball in a glove.

you'll come to me, monkey. . . .

There was nobody back at the hotel and Artie waited half an hour, patching up his shoulder with supplies he'd bought from a nearby drugstore. The shears hadn't gone very deep but the cut was bloody and hurt like hell. He cleaned it with alcohol and put heavy gauze and tape over it, then rinsed his bloody shirt in cold water and hung it over a towel rack in the john, turning on the ceiling heat lamp to help dry it. He watched the news on TV for a while, got bored, and ordered a ham sandwich and a chef's salad from room service—Mitch could order something for himself later.

He didn't want to start plowing through Charlie's diaries until Mitch showed. Best thing to do would be to skim one and turn it over to Mitch when he finished. Maybe Levin would catch something he hadn't.

By eight o'clock, Mitch still hadn't showed up. Artie called Mitch's office, but there was only a recorded message telling the caller to leave his or her name and number and Dr. Mitchell Levin would get back to them. It was the same at home. No Mitch. He called his own house; no messages on his answering machine. And no messages from Levin at KXAM.

Mitch should at least have called him if something had come up, Artie thought, and that was funny because he'd blamed Mark for not doing it either. But something could have happened to him; Mitch was as much a target as he was.

Or was he?

He trusted Mitch because . . . he trusted Mitch. They were good friends who went back forever, but then so had he and Mary. So had he and everybody else in the Club.

He finished half the salad but had no appetite for the sandwich. Eight-thirty—where the hell was Mitch?

It gradually occurred to him that Mitch wasn't coming back and he remembered the phone call that morning. He'd had no idea what it was about except that it had concerned him.

And Levin had hardly been friendly afterward: "See you at the hotel tonight?" "Yeah, sure." But Mitch had said it offhand; he hadn't meant it.

By nine o'clock Artie had made up his mind, wondering if he wasn't already too late. Only one person knew where he was, but that might be one person too many. He put on his still-damp shirt and managed to slip into his coat, his shoulder protesting vigorously. He pocketed the automatic, picked up the bag of diaries, and took the elevator down to the lobby. He nodded at the desk clerk but didn't bother checking out. As far as anybody was concerned, that was where he was going to spend the night.

It was misting again but it was late enough so there was no difficulty getting a cab. In case the doorman might overhear, he told the driver to take him to the Washington Square Bar and Grill. Once there, he got out, waited until the cab had disappeared from view, then caught another to Lombard Street.

There were dozens of cheap motels lining Lombard and he picked one at random. Checking in sans luggage was no problem; as long as your credit card cleared, you were golden.

The room was serviceable, the bed sheets on the gray side but clean, the towels worn but ditto. He took off his coat, set the gun on the other pillow, and lay down to watch the top of the late news. There was no story about the fight in the library, which was interesting. If somewhere Mitch were watching, he'd have no reason to believe that for ten minutes he and Charlie Allen had been intent on killing each other.

Unless, of course, Levin had been the prime mover all along, the Hound who had murdered Larry Shea a week ago and apparently had declared war against almost everybody in the Club.

Except . . .

He really didn't believe that. Nor did he believe the Hound had finally caught up with Mitch. No, Mitch had abandoned him and the only reason Artie could think of was that it had something to do with him.

For a moment he felt like he was back in the library, dangling from a railing in the rotunda, five stories above the floor. The only one he was sure of now was Charlie Allen. He'd *seen* what had happened to Charlie, just like he'd seen what had happened to the old man ice-skating in the square. Both had been subject to . . . control.

He wondered if Charlie had managed to get away, then guessed that he had. There was no way that the guard and a platoon of cops could have been manipulated all at the same time.

Artie closed his eyes and tried to will himself back to the cave beside a meandering stream so many thousands of years ago, and when that failed tried to visualize himself at the breakfast table with Susan and Mark, wishing Susan well on her visit to her folks and bitching about almost everything Mark did that he thought was strange or uncalled for.

It had been so easy to forget that he was a teenager once. If he ever got the chance . . .

But he wouldn't.

Susan was gone, and so was Mark.

He opened his eyes and stared at the ceiling for a long moment, blanking his mind of everything, then spread the diaries out on the bed table and switched on the light.

He had a lot of reading to do.

CHAPTER 21

Reading about yourself twenty years before was bittersweet, Artie thought. Charlie had been something of a naive writer at the start, but he hadn't missed much. He'd had a flair for characterization and description, even if his vocabulary had been that of a teenager, and he had been a meticulous chronicler of times and places. The later diaries were undoubtedly more sophisticated, but Artie couldn't believe they'd be as interesting to read.

You forgot so much: the characters drifting in and out of the coffee shop, a lot of students and a thick scattering of hippies. The early members of the Club would sit around a little table in back, sipping coffee and picking out which of the younger patrons might be interested in joining and those whom they wanted to ask. Arch—was anybody still named Archibald?—had been a jock from State and laughed a lot when they asked him to join, thinking they were putting him on. When he was convinced they were serious, he said he thought it would be a hoot. He had been the first to reach the top of the north tower of the bridge.

Arch. Gone now, a boobytrap in 'Nam. Screamed his lungs out until they got him to an evac unit and then he slipped away from an overdose of morphine. What the hell, it was front-line medical and everybody was so scared they were pissing in their pants; you couldn't blame them for occasional mistakes. Arch probably wouldn't have made it anyway.

A friend of Arch's had enlisted with him, and after being mustered out dropped in at the coffee shop to tell somebody, anybody, what had happened. How long had it been since he'd thought of Arch now? Ten years? Fifteen? If he ever wanted to feel guilty about something, he could always pick on that.

And the other members as they had drifted in. Mitchell Levin, toothy and nerdy and wearing John Lennon glasses even back then. Smart, the kind who bragged about it. His family had lived in the St. Francis Wood district and he'd gone to a private high school and bragged about that, too. But what you saw wasn't what you got. He'd had a wicked sense of humor, had taken martial arts classes along with Shakespeare and the History of the Renaissance, was fond of camping trips, and even had a small gun collection back then, carefully hidden from his father, who was one of the city's leading cardiologists.

Artie smiled to himself. Maybe it was because Mitch had been a fan of the Three Stooges that they'd gotten along so well. It had been strictly serendipity when they'd met up in 'Nam and he'd asked to be transferred to Mitch's unit. Intelligence was better than front-line duty, but then, to Artie's regret, the friendship had turned formal. It had been "Sergeant, I'd like you to do this" and "Yes, sir" unless things were really hairy and there was no time for bullshit. He'd been damned glad once the war was over and the friendship got back to normal. Or had it?

Larry Shea had been your typical average guy, so average they'd debated whether to ask him to join. He'd wanted to be a doctor even back then and had found a pigeon in Golden Gate Park with a busted wing, set it, and nursed the bird back to health. There was no debate after that; everybody wanted him in, even Mitch. Charlie Allen had been Larry's buddy and Larry had campaigned hard for him. For his part, Charlie had a flair for making himself useful. And he bugged them, showing up on escapades whether he was asked or not, dogging their footsteps no matter where they went. Finally it had been easier to ask him in than to try to keep him out.

Lyle had won the women's vote. He was somewhat surly, somewhat mysterious, and overwhelmingly sexy. A star of State's wrestling team, a below-average student, probably because he was a pothead but nobody had really objected to that—if you wanted a lid, Lyle could always turn you on to one.

The women had been something else. Mary had a stocky build and was somewhat self-conscious about it. She had been a music buff even back then, though she had no favorite among the rock groups—she liked them all. Her idea of a good time was to hang out at a rock concert, any rock concert. Somebody had reported seeing her going to the opera one night, but the idea was so outrageous that nobody had believed it.

She also loved art, and that was when Artie had become interested. She not only liked it, she studied it, and when he went to the museum with her it was like having his own private docent to explain the artists and their paintings. Mary had been his opposite, Artie thought. She had been energetic and extroverted. He had been fairly quiet, a bookworm with the saving grace of cycling and playing handball so he wasn't stoop-shouldered by age twenty.

It was Mary who had introduced him to sex, though he realized later that she had taken pity on him. He had tormented himself about masturbation; he hadn't been willing to admit that he was hormonally driven and had instead blamed it on his lack of enough courage to approach a girl. Mary had figured out the cause behind his occasional moody silences and invited him over for dinner when her roommates were away for the weekend, suggesting they play cards afterwards.

It had been a strange way to spend the evening, but he'd shrugged and thought, Why not? Mary had teased him into strip poker—later insisting it was his idea, which was all part of her therapy—and when he was naked and could no longer hide his feelings, Mary had sex with him. His first impression was that she had more teeth than the shark in *Jaws*. It was more comfortable face-to-face, but it was all over impossibly soon. Mary went out of her way to compliment him and help build up his ego. For all of a day or two afterward he'd lorded it over the girls in the Club because he had a prick and they didn't. Mary and he had slept together several more times after that until he figured out that for Mary it was more of a mercy fuck, and for himself it was because of loneliness. But they had been good friends ever since.

Until now.

After he had come back from 'Nam, it was Mary who had introduced him to Susan Albright, a widow with a two-year-old son. It had been love if not at first sight, then certainly by third. Ordinarily a little reserved and more thoughtful than adventurous, Susan was anything but that in bed. Mary had showed him how, but it was Susan who taught him to let go and enjoy the intricacies of lovemaking. One time when he'd held back—because, as Susan had told him afterward, of outdated "moral" reasons—she'd defiantly said, "It's my body and I'll do what I want with it," then smiled and added boldly, "and so should you."

But she soon became a lot more than a bed partner. When he walked into a room and she was there, he knew his eyes lit up and so did hers. He *liked* her, he finally decided. He liked the way she moved, her sense of self, how she thought and, of course, the fact that she liked him, that she seemed to like everything about him. When he realized she had become his best friend, he asked her to marry him. She had known he would all along; the only thing she had wondered about was when.

In his own mind—though not in Charlie's diaries—the other women seemed to play a minor role. Jenny had been the quiet goddess, the good scout who went everyplace you did and did everything you did and somehow never got her hair out of place. He couldn't remember her using much makeup but she was still a knockout. Quiet, too quiet, and she eventually gravitated to the company of Mary, who was brash and outspoken enough for both of them.

Franny had been the plump girl, too much aware that she was overweight, too anxious to please, too eager to do whatever the group wanted to do. She could be depended upon to show up with sandwiches and cookies for whatever trip they went on, sort of a self-nominated commissary. Charlie had caught her one day in a corner of the coffee shop crying to herself about her awkwardness when it came to the men in the Club. He had felt sorry for her, and they were a couple ever after. No regrets, Charlie had written enthusiastically. He'd found a diamond in the rough that all the others had overlooked. What he didn't admit in the diary was that Franny had figured out the road to his heart was through his stomach and, in his case, it had been a freeway.

Cathy had been the strangest one of the group. A beautiful girl who worried about her figure, worried about her complexion, worried that even in ordinary conversations she might say the wrong thing. She was driven by her insecurities and finally found a way to triumph over them, if only for a short time. She liked sex—a lot—and she was very good at it. It was in bed that she felt the most secure. It was the one place where she didn't have to worry about doing the wrong thing, because the "wrong" thing was usually the most exciting. And in bed, she had power over the boys.

According to Charlie's diaries, she spent a lot of time there.

But Charlie had been curious and didn't stop at merely reporting it. He had wanted to know why. As a fat little kid he had known what insecurity was all about—he'd had bouts of it himself—and wondered why a beautiful girl like Cathy should be insecure about anything. Her family was well off, the boys fell all over her, and she was certainly no dummy.

So, according to his diary, Charlie got himself invited over to the house for dinner and met the family. Her father had been a vice-president of Wells Fargo, her mother a socialite who went to every opera and play opening in town. She was very proud that she could call most of the singers and actors and actresses by their first names. There had been several members of the touring cast of *Jesus Christ, Superstar* at the house for dinner the night Charlie was there, and he had been properly impressed.

It was in Charlie's third diary that Artie found what he was look-ing for.

Cathy's great ambition in the world had been to be an actress.

But according to Charlie—Artie had no idea how he'd found out—her mother had discouraged her. Not that she disapproved of the pro-fession, but compared to the professionals she'd met, her daughter had no talent and the mother didn't want her disgracing the family.

The lack of approval had bled into all phases of Cathy's life: she was no good at that, she was no good at anything.

But her mother's disapproval hadn't dampened her ambitions. She'd decided she needed a guru when it came to acting and she'd found one in the Club, one who'd played bit parts when touring companies filled out their casts with locals. One who had already made inroads in the suburban theater scene playing juveniles.

The laugh-a-minute cutup, everybody's friend, one who knew by heart every play on Broadway since the Depression and could regale you for hours on end with anecdotes that he'd plucked out of actors' biographies and tell-all books about Broadway and Hollywood.

One who even then was talking about starting his own theater company.

Dave Chandler.

But hardly anybody had known about Cathy's secret desire. She had kept her ambitions under wraps until she was "ready," and in Charlie's estimation—he'd caught her in a minor role in a play Chandler had directed for summer stock—she was never going to be ready. A year later she finally bit the bullet, acknowledged her lack of talent, and married Larry Shea, the runner-up for her affections. Whatever else he was, Chandler wasn't the marrying sort.

Had she ever gotten over Chandler, to whom she had undoubtedly given heart, body, and soul? Charlie Allen's precise handwriting indicated that he didn't think so and expressed sympathy for Larry.

Artie put the diary aside and walked over to the window, watching the first signs of sleet whirl around a street lamp outside. There wasn't any doubt that Chandler had been Cathy's first true love. And when she'd fled her home in the Oakland hills last week and wound up housesitting for friends in the city, Chandler had to have been the one she'd called when the loneliness had gotten to be too much for her. She hadn't been afraid of him; she had trusted him implicitly.

It never occurred to her that the man with whom she had carried on a love affair for years, and in whom she'd probably confided everything about her life—and Larry's as well, including his latest project—was a Hound from Hell for another species. Somebody who regarded her with all the affection that a spectator regards a chimpanzee in the zoo.

Jesus.

It had been Dave all along, the one Artie would have voted least likely. Except that somebody had tried to dissolve Chandler's face with acid. It didn't make sense, but there was only one way to find out.

It was chilly in the room but he could feel the flop sweat start then. He and Mitch had been trying for days to find out who the Hound might be. Now he knew and he was the only one left who could go after it. Mitch had deserted him, and Charlie didn't even know what was going on.

He took a deep breath, held it for a moment, then let it out slowly and pushed everything else out of his mind. It was like going on night patrol in 'Nam, and God knew he had gone on enough of those. You never knew what was out there, who was waiting, but he had always managed to make it back. Mitch had once said that maybe whoever was the Hound should be afraid of him.

Maybe he was overmatched. But, with a little luck, maybe he wasn't.

And who was he kidding?

It was three in the morning, the witching hour for the city. The theaters had let out hours before, the bars had long closed, the Marina was deserted except for the occasional 7-Eleven. Artie had the cab circle the block twice to check who was on the street, then got out around the corner. There was a small side entrance leading to a walkway between Chandler's building and the one next door. It wasn't difficult to break the small lock and walk to the back. No dogs, no alarms.

Chandler's studio was three flights up.

Artie took his time climbing the stairs, slowly putting his weight on each tread so the squeak of wood wouldn't give away his presence. There were two apartments opening off the back porch, and he hesitated for a long moment, trying to decide which one was Dave's. There was a litter box outside of one door, waiting to be emptied in the morning. Did Dave keep cats? He couldn't remember any, then found a wooden slat on the porch and carefully dug into the box. It definitely hadn't been for a kitten, so the chances it was for a pet Chandler had recently acquired dropped considerably.

He worked with the lock of the other door for a minute, a simple eyebolt-and-latch affair, and managed to lift the latch with the thin blade of his pocketknife. The Manhattan mania for half a dozen dead bolts and chain locks hadn't hit this part of the Marina yet. There had been a time when almost nobody in San Francisco locked their doors and hardly anybody was ripped off, a far more innocent era that was now one with the ages.

He opened the door and slipped through, closing it noiselessly behind him. With good luck he'd find Chandler asleep; with bad luck he was probably in his theater/office watching an old movie.

He started down the long hallway that led to the front of the apartment. The office and home theater were about in the middle. It was gloomy but not completely dark; the door to the office/theater was open and the glow from the television screen suffused into the corridor enough so Artie could just make out the framed photographs and posters on the wall. Dave had been acting all of his life and was mediocre in most roles but superb in the most important one he had ever played: that of the *Homo sapiens* "Dave Chandler."

If Chandler were really the Hound.

Artie caught himself wishing desperately for Mitch Levin. With Mitch along, he'd have a decent chance. Without Mitch, he didn't stand much of one at all unless he caught Chandler by surprise and didn't make the fatal mistake of waiting. But what was he going to do, walk in and shoot Chandler where he sat? So far it was all surmise. If he were wrong, he'd spend the rest of his life regretting it. If he were right, then it was either him or Chandler—and he would have to be damned fast.

The Hound had come very close in the library. The next time, it wouldn't miss. He, Mitch, and Charlie Allen, all friends of Larry Shea's, were the only three left. And maybe Chandler, if he were wrong.

But he knew instinctively he wasn't.

A movement to his left caught his eye and he whirled. There was nothing there but one of the posters, the one of the beach scene in *From Here to Eternity*. But Burt Lancaster and Deborah Kerr were naked—and moving.

Artie swore quietly to himself. His hand holding the automatic was suddenly slick with sweat.

"It'd be easier if you turned on the lights, Artie. The switch is on the wall, a foot ahead to your right."

Artie froze, then reached out and flipped it on. The lights weren't blinding, as they had been in Mary's house. They were just about as bright as they would be in a theater auditorium before the feature started.

"Come on in, Artie—have a seat. Popcorn?" Chandler turned off the DVD player and the television screen flashed blue, then turned black.

I said you'd come to me, monkey. . . .

It was only a wisp of a thought, just enough to convince Artie he'd made no mistake. He should have shot Chandler when he came in the door but he'd hesitated a fraction of a second too long. Now he couldn't move a muscle.

Chandler was sitting behind his desk like he had been two days before. Artie stared. His voice was normal but his face was still covered with white ointment, though it obviously didn't hurt so much now because Chandler was smiling at him. Artie caught his breath. Chandler had disguised his voice the last time he and Levin had seen him. Now it was the familiar voice and a face he couldn't quite see.

Like Watch Cap at the skating rink.

"No sense in keeping this shit on any longer, though some of the neighbors might think I've made a miraculous recovery. But it wasn't for them, it was for you and Mitch." Chandler wiped at the ointment with a makeup towel. The red-furrowed, pink mask was peeping out at Artie now, and Chandler started peeling it off in strips. He had never gone to the emergency room, Artie thought. If he had, it would have been reported and Schuler would have been all over them the next day.

Then Artie stiffened. Under the makeup were raw, red scratches. The signs of Cathy's fight for life.

"I thought for sure I wouldn't fool you guys—you knew I was an actor, you knew I'd lived with makeup all my life. If you were watching a movie with special effects or a blue screen, you'd know it immediately. I guess this was just too simple." He looked at Artie in mock amazement. "And I was sure I'd blown it in the restaurant when I said I'd had lunch with Larry and he told me about his article for *Science*. Hell, you guys knew I wasn't that tight with Larry. Cathy told me about the article, what was in it." He shook his head. "A real no-no."

"What are you going to do?" Artie tried to keep the question casual but didn't succeed.

"What am I going to do? With you?" Chandler made a temple of his fingers and leaned back in his chair, his fingers directly beneath his chin. "How's your health, Artie?"

Artie could feel the sweat pop in his armpits and on his forehead.

"Fine. Why?"

Chandler shrugged. "Perfectly healthy people with normal check-ups have heart attacks all the time. They're unpredictable. Little flaws in the pump or the circulatory system that doctors never catch before-hand. Fairly decent way to go, all things considered."

"And my body?" Artie asked.

Chandler glanced at his watch. "They're hardly going to find it here. I think the appropriate place for you to die would be home in bed, all tucked in and peaceful. A quick, painless exit from this world and the only people you'll be able to tell about me and mine will be those in the next."

"Mitch—"

"Levin? I'll catch up with him. I'm surprised you trusted him so much, Artie. You had almost as much to fear from him as you did from me. In one sense, even more."

He'd known it all along, Artie thought, he just hadn't wanted to admit it.

"He's one of you, one of the Hounds."

Chandler looked surprised. "Not one of ours, Artie. One of yours. You mean to tell me you never knew? And I thought he was one of your best friends." He studied Artie a moment. "You're something of a Hound yourself"—he shrugged, contemptuous—"but not a very good one. More of a hare."

Artie decided to try to bluff it out.

"You can't just give me a heart attack at will. . . ."

Chandler leaned across the desk and stared at him, his blue eyes hypnotic.

"Try and lift your right arm, Artie—the one holding your auto-matic."

Artie tried again. His right arm was as limp as spaghetti—he couldn't budge it.

"How do you do that?" He was more curious than frightened now.

"I can't tell you how, Artie. The best I can do is give you an ex-ample. Your species does it all the time, but mostly when you're kids. You're in a crowd at a theater or a store and just for fun you concentrate on the back of somebody's head and eventually they turn around in annoyance, wondering who in hell has been staring at them. A rather simplistic example of controlling somebody else with your mind. Give yourself thirty-five thousand years and you might become quite good at it. Even to the point of controlling somebody's autonomic nervous system."

"That's impossible," Artie said.

"Is it? A species can change a lot in thirty-five thousand years. You can learn to do a bunch of impossible things in that amount of time."

"And you pass it on, I suppose."

Chandler half smiled. "You have books, we have racial memory. They each have their advantages."

"Too bad you don't have a conscience," Artie said.

"Hey, good B-movie line, Artie. I'm impressed." Then, indignantly: "And you do? Jesus Christ, you were in 'Nam. Bad things happen in wars; that's the nature of them. You gave out medals for a lot worse than anything I've done. And whether you care to admit it or not, we're in a war. You and yours against me and mine. Like the IRA and the Brits, Hamas and the Israelis. You want a declaration of war? Hell, nobody declares them anymore."

"War," Artie said, feeling stupid.

Chandler looked surprised.

"War, Artie. The one that started thirty-five thousand years ago. You won all the battles back then but now it's our turn."

What did you do when the enemy looked like you, sounded like you, and wasn't wearing a uniform? It would be worse than the Civil War, much worse. You'd never know where the front lines were until it was too late.

"Cathy and the kids," Artie said slowly.

Chandler's handsome face was shadowed.

"Cathy knew more than the rest of you, and she knew it first. Whatever I did, no matter how much I stopped the leaks—Paschelke, Hall, Lyle—she was the important one who'd gotten away. I never would have found her if she'd stayed hidden. But then she called and asked me to come over." He shook his head. "I couldn't believe my luck."

"First you laid her, then you killed her," Artie said in disgust.

"I slept with the enemy and you think that was a bad thing." Chandler looked amused. "Everything's fair in love and war, Artie—it was love for her and war for me. I'm probably species amoral but then, we're not all alike any more than you're all alike. But I didn't rape her—she asked. I think she lived half her life in bed. They may be different species, but donkeys don't refuse to screw mares. And I'm sure they both enjoy it."

"And the boys?"

"They knew me, they saw me come down the stairs, and I had no idea how much they might have heard about Larry's project around the house. The stakes were too high; I couldn't take the chance. I did what was necessary."

He studied Artie's expression. "Okay, I see I'm still a monster. And you an ex-military man! Didn't the army ever give you a course in ethics? Or maybe it's morals, I'm always confusing the two—or maybe I've got the wrong word entirely. Say your platoon is lying in ambush along a roadside, waiting for the enemy. A young boy who doesn't know you're there starts across the road and doesn't see the first enemy tank coming—don't ask me why he doesn't hear it. Do you jump up and save the kid, thus giving away your position and endangering all your men, or do you let the tank run the poor kid down? Maybe it's a bad analogy, but you see what I mean."

Artie sat there, silent. Chandler suddenly hit the top of the desk with the flat of his hand, his face grim.

"Don't talk to me about innocent bystanders, Banks! Nobody gives a shit about innocent bystanders in a war! How many women and children died in Dresden and Hiroshima and London? Tell me whether it makes a difference if you kill them face-to-face or from ten thousand feet up! I'd like to think that matters to your species, that you couldn't kill if it had to be done face-to-face. If it did, you would have had far fewer wars, wouldn't you? But then there were the ovens, and face-to-face it turned out nobody was exempt. Or go back to Agincourt, when Henry the Fifth had his soldiers slaughter the helpless French prisoners. Did you applaud in the movie when the English won? But that's right— they didn't show the slaughter of the prisoners, did they? Maybe if they had, the applause wouldn't have been quite so loud."

"That was war—"

"And what the hell do you call *this*?"

For a brief moment, Artie was back on the path by the river's edge, a member of the Tribe watching a Flat Face hold a young boy over the river and cut his throat.

"One of our racial memories," Chandler said. "Some things we wish we could forget but can't."

"That was thousands of years ago—"

"Not to us. If you're cursed with racial memories, it might as well have been yesterday, Banks."

"You have plans—" Artie started, desperate to stall.

"In the short run? To see that you have a heart attack—back home, safely in bed. It could be a lot worse. Artie. In the long run?" Chandler thought for a moment. "I'm not sure—not my department. But it's time for your species to go; nature made a mistake and it's time to rectify it. Frankly, I don't think it will be that hard. Your society is so interconnected that, technologically speaking, one man could bring it all down. But in what part of the machinery should he throw his wrench? It'll probably be something along biological lines—you're more vulnerable than you might think."

Artie didn't say anything and Chandler looked amused.

"Do you honestly believe your world can totter on for another thousand years? You know it can't, no way. Another hundred? Would you bet on it? A few years ago your Pat Robertson gave it all of five— five years to the end of your world! He's probably more correct than he thinks."

Chandler had become preoccupied with his arguments and Artie could feel a little strength flow back into his arm. He was careful not to move a muscle.

"We've been in tight spots before—"

"Meaning *Homo sapiens*? Come *on,* Banks, be real. The Black Plague nearly did you in, and that was only a few hundred years ago. You've survived this long only because you've been separated by oceans and your technology was primitive. You've tried to substitute political systems for wars and what's been the result? There hasn't been a year since World War Two without one. And each political system is convinced it's the best and anxious to convert the political heathen—by force, if necessary. Wasn't it Churchill who said that as a system democracy was crap, it was just better than any of the others?"

Artie could feel the butt of the gun in his hand and casually rested his finger on the trigger.

"What was it like, pretending to be human?"

"You mean pretending to be one of you?" Chandler leaned back in his chair, the light from the lamp illuminating the shadows of his face and reflecting off his vividly blue eyes. Artie was startled. He had never really looked at Chandler before, probably because nobody ever takes a clown seriously. Except for his slightly buck teeth, Chandler was one of the handsomest men he had ever seen. Cathy must have been obsessed with him.

"Fun, in a way. You learn what buttons to push and you can have almost anything you want from anybody if your stomach is strong enough. You saw the photographs in the hallway? They're special, Artie—I slept with all of them. They're handsome or pretty, all of them famous, and most of you have wet dreams about them. But to be honest, few of them are any good in bed—or at much of anything else. I remember going to a party at a film convention in Vegas and by two in the morning everybody was either dead drunk or balling their brains out in the various bedrooms. I wandered into one looking for a place to crash and here was one of the biggest movie stars in the country screwing some hooker from the Strip. A big education for me, Artie. Take away the soft lights and the music and the romantic camera angles and what you've got left are smells and sweat and grunting. No whispered endearments, no tender moments. Just two animals rolling around on satin sheets rather than in the dirt." He laughed. "I know what you're going to say—'Hey, they're only human!' I couldn't agree more."

"Not as romantic as you and Cathy?" Artie said sarcastically. His finger was on the trigger and he had angled the barrel up just enough so he could catch Chandler in the groin.

Chandler shrugged.

"I suppose I meant something to her, but I never encouraged her. She fed her own fantasies. But she was a danger to us, Banks. She could have been responsible for the deaths of thousands—"

Artie tried to pull the trigger and his hand jumped slightly in the attempt. His fingers suddenly froze.

Chandler's face changed then. No longer smiling, no longer casually amused or arrogant. It was hard, furious, all angles and hollows, the lips thin bands against his large white teeth, which showed in a snarl. It was like somebody had morphed Chandler's face and White Beard's when the old chief had been angry and his heavy brows had become like stone, his eyes slitted and rimmed with red.

you shouldn't have tried that. . . .

Artie felt like somebody had jumped on his chest, knocking the wind out of him. He couldn't breathe and he started to struggle in his chair, then felt his sphincter give way and realized he had shit in his pants. His heart was going crazy and he could feel it tumble into a fast, erratic beating.

your species or mine, monkey—you think I ever had a choice?

Artie forced the chair sidewise and managed to fall to the floor and for just a moment felt the pressure on his heart lessen and his hand loosen up. He managed to get off one shot and heard it shatter the front of the television set. But nobody would hear it outside the soundproofed room. The pressure abruptly returned and his vision started to fade, the room turning black. He was going to die right then and there. It was more than his heart now; it felt like something was tearing up his insides. His stomach was spasming with cramps and somebody's hands were squeezing the rest of his guts. In the distance he heard screaming and realized with mild surprise that it was himself.

He managed to roll behind a couch and for a second was free. He could feel a sly probing in the air around him and tried to crawl for the doorway. Then Chandler caught him again and Artie felt himself being squeezed like somebody might squeeze a balloon. It felt like his head was blowing up to a monstrous size and he could look down on the room and see himself lying on the floor and Chandler sitting calmly behind his desk, staring at him. He had no sensation of a body at all.

This was it.

Then there was the faint sound of another shot and he was back on the floor, acutely aware of his own stink. There was no pressure on his chest or guts, but he ached as if he'd run a marathon. On top of everything else, he was going to be sick from sheer exhaustion. It took a moment for him to realize he hadn't managed to get off a second shot after all. Somebody else—

"Artie!"

He was being helped off the floor and onto a chair. It took a moment for his eyes to focus.

"Charlie," he mumbled. "What the hell . . ."

He looked over at Chandler, who was slumped back in his chair, his eyes a dull watery blue with no life in them at all. Artie watched the blood pump from Chandler's chest onto his desk and then simply flow over his shirt and down to the floor.

Artie desperately wanted to get out of his clothes; he needed to shower badly. He looked up at Charlie Allen, staring in sick fascination at Chandler slumped in his chair.

"What the hell was he, Artie?"

"A hero to his own kind," Artie muttered. "To us, a homicidal maniac. Maybe we all are, depending on which side we're on."

Allen didn't know what he was talking about. "I listened to him for a couple of minutes. He never saw me—he was concentrating on you."

Artie took a breath. His heart had slowed, but it didn't seem by much.

"How did you know I was here? You must have reread your diaries after all—you must have figured it out."

Allen shook his head. "I never had time to go through them. But when I got home Franny and I started talking and she told me all about Cathy and Chandler. She was pretty hurt back then, pretty envious. She remembered everything. She insisted Cathy was still tight with Chandler. After you read the diaries, I figured you'd come right over here. Dave was a night person; he'd still be up."

Artie held his head; he had the start of a whopper of a headache. He couldn't think straight. Not everything Charlie was saying made sense but he couldn't argue with his timing.

Charlie was looking at him with an almost belligerent expression on his face. "I'm not going to be left out this time, Artie. Larry and Cathy were friends of mine."

"He killed Cathy and the boys."

Charlie nodded sadly. "I heard him."

"Your gun," Artie said. Charlie was still holding it. "I didn't know you owned one."

Charlie looked down, surprised. His hand immediately started to tremble and he put the gun on the desk. "It isn't mine. I found it in the library months ago. Somebody had left it there, believe it or not. So I stuck it in my desk—too late to turn it in, the guard had gone home—and forgot about it. Until tonight."

He stepped closer to Chandler to look at him, and Artie was afraid Charlie was going to be sick.

"You didn't do a bad thing, Charlie, you—"

"Don't worry about me. Larry Shea was one of my best friends. So was Cathy. She played around but she was still a good person." He reached out to touch Chandler, his hand jerking back when he made contact. "I don't know how he did . . . what he did, I didn't understand a lot of what he was talking about." He glanced back at Artie, his face grim. "You're going to have to tell me, Artie. I'm serious—you owe me."

"Someday," Artie said. Then: "Take me home, Charlie. I need to shower down. I stink."

Charlie glanced around the room, frowning. Something had just occurred to him.

"Where's Mitch? I thought he'd be here with you."

CHAPTER 22

Mitch's house on Telegraph Hill was eerily quiet. It was midmorning and everybody on the Hill had left for work and their maids hadn't yet arrived to clean up the mess from the night before. The BMW wasn't parked on the street above, and Artie sat in his car for twenty minutes, just watching. There had been a black-and-white at the corner and Artie guessed that Schuler was finally going to bring him and Mitch in, that too many members of the Club had died for Schuler not to think they were involved in some way. Especially with Chandler's death.

The police had left their squad car five minutes ago and sauntered down the hill to a coffee shop. They wouldn't return for a good half hour. Artie still had the keys Mitch had lent him some time back, and he let himself in the back door, hesitating a long moment for any sound of Mitch in the bathroom or his office. Nothing. Nobody. As far as Artie could tell, the house was pretty much as he had left it three mornings before. The sink had a coffee cup in it, and a rinsed-out cereal bowl sat in the drainer. Artie opened the cupboard out of curiosity. One box of bran flakes. The life story of the American male: you started with Cocoa Puffs and ended with All-Bran.

He glanced around the kitchen again and noticed the Mr. Coffee still plugged in, the little On light glowing orange. The glass carafe was half full and Artie rummaged around in the cupboard for another cup, poured some of the coffee in it, and tasted it. It was still light colored and not bitter; the unit hadn't been left on overnight. His guess was that Mitch had left the house probably not more than an hour before.

The good news was that Mitch was still alive. The bad news was that he had no idea where Mitch had gone.

Or why.

Artie wandered into the bedroom, feeling more like a spy than ever. Jesus, what was he doing here? For twenty years, Mitch Levin had been his best friend, ever since they had both collapsed in laughter watching old tapes of the Three Stooges in a crash pad just off Haight Street. For twenty years, they had been as close as brothers. He and Susan and Mitch had gone on vacations together, he had confided in Mitch about almost everything he had ever done or ever thought of doing, he had even asked Mitch to be a latter-day godfather to Mark.

He started for the door to leave, then shrugged. It was Mitch who'd failed to show up the other night, who had left him to face the Hound by himself. He didn't owe Mitch any apologies.

He glanced around the bedroom again. What the hell did he hope to find?

He hadn't been to Mitch's house all that often—when Mitch had offered to let him spend the night, he'd been surprised and touched. He couldn't remember Mitch ever throwing any parties there. But that made a sort of sense: it was easier for a bachelor to visit his married friends than the other way around. If you invited people over it meant you had to do the dishes and pick up your dirty underwear from where you'd dropped it on the floor.

He pulled open the drawers of the bureau and did a quick and careful search. Fancy-label boxers and T-shirts, a stack of carefully folded linen handkerchiefs. Along with his suits, Mitch's shirts were hung in the closet on hangers; they didn't come neatly folded with a thin paper band around them. Expensive designer shirts, Italian suits—nothing really ostentatious but enough good taste to choke on.

There were no surprises in the john. Two electric razors, one a barber's special for trimming sideburns, an electric toothbrush, a stand-up canister of Mentadent, mint-flavored Listerine, dental floss, a row of nonprescription cure-alls for headaches, constipation, and diarrhea. A small prescription container of Valium, another of Percodan. Apparently psychiatry had its occupational hazards.

One thing was missing, which left Artie puzzled. There had been no condoms in the drawer of the bedside table and there were none in the medicine chest, which surprised him. Mitch wouldn't have led a risky life in that respect. Which meant Mitch was something of an ascetic, reputation aside. Maybe it was a reputation he'd deliberately fostered, man-about-town, so none of the wives would keep asking why he didn't settle down and they knew a woman he would love to meet. Or maybe after listening to hundreds of patients over the years, he'd just turned off to sex.

Or maybe his personal life was more professional than that. Casual encounters deliberately kept casual, maybe play for pay, though in that case you'd think his medicine chest would be loaded with condoms and ditto the bed table.

But there was nothing very exotic about the average man's sexual life. It was when you looked at the emotional one that you found the variations, the odd and the unusual and the pathetic.

The largest room in the house was in the back, with a huge picture window overlooking the bay. Every home had one room for show, the one that usually sold the house to prospective buyers. Mitch had taken it and turned it into a combination office and den. The desk was separate from the computer area and clean of papers. A small table radio, a combination phone and answering machine, a notepad, desk calendar . . .

And two photographs, one a candid shot in a small, black frame and the other a studio portrait sandwiched between two sheets of clear plastic and standing upright in a black plastic base.

Artie picked up the smaller one first. The photograph was faded but he could make out a very young Captain Levin standing on the top of a small Japanese-style bridge in a city park, his arm around a young Oriental girl of perhaps sixteen or seventeen. They were both smiling for the camera. There was an inscription in the lower right corner that he could barely make out.

Love you alway, your honeybunch Cleo . . . Saigon, 1975.

An unlikely partner for Mitchell Levin, but there it was. A wartime romance in which Madame Butterfly had disappeared completely when the city had fallen. No way for Mitch to trace her even if he had wanted to. If he did now and succeeded he'd probably discover she was forty and graying, had a husband and three kids but no memory of Mitch from among the hundreds of GIs she'd serviced when she was a working girl so many years before.

The studio portrait was signed simply *For Mitch, all my love—Pat.* No indication who she was or what part she had played in Mitch's life, though it was obvious she must have had an important role. Artie started to replace it on the desk, then noticed a newspaper clipping taped to the back of the frame. It was dated September of 1981. A tabloid tragedy—Patricia Bailey had apparently dumped a boyfriend, who then showed up at her small carriage-house apartment late at night, dragged her into the courtyard, shot her, and then shot himself. The boyfriend had been a law student at a local university and had a history of mental instability.

Artie knew who she had dumped him for. Mitch would have had his first courses in psychiatry by then. Maybe he'd taken it upon himself to suggest she drop the old boyfriend, about whom she must have already had her doubts, and take up with good old stable, lovable Mitch. Perhaps she already had, and the old b.f. had shown up one evening after weeks of brooding about it.

Mitch had never told anybody. But it was obvious that he'd never really been a man-about-town—that had been a role he'd played, helped along by Cathy Shea's friendly praise when they were younger. In reality, he had been disappointed in love twice, and the last time must have been traumatic. After that he had become a man for whom life was all work and definitely little play. He was a top psychiatrist, but Artie now wondered whom he went to himself. It was like the quatrain from *The Rubaiyat*: "I often wonder what the Vintners buy one half so precious as the Goods they sell."

But what about the stories Mitch had told him and the others about his affairs? Not that many, not that gamey, but enough so nobody would wonder about his personal life. Or lack of it.

Artie glanced around the room, frowning. He'd overlooked something. He went back to the bedroom and opened the doors of the chiffonier. Behind them was Mitch's gun collection. Most of the guns dated from 'Nam, but the Uzi looked new and so did several of the others. All of them were polished and oiled and appeared ready for action. Disturbingly, there were four empty spaces, vague shadows on the wood indicating where the guns had been.

Artie hurried back to the closet and brushed aside the suits and shirts hanging in a neat row. At the back were a Samsonite two-suiter and several briefcases. Mitch should have had an overnight bag or two to go along with them, but there weren't any.

Among the lineup of suits and coats were several empty hangers, and Artie wondered what had been on them. One overcoat, that was for sure. Trousers, probably a jacket, and maybe a couple of sweaters.

When Mitch had left him in the Haight, he'd returned home and spent the rest of the day catching up on work and rescheduling appointments. This morning he had packed and left. For where? He'd taken an overnight bag and his car; he hadn't packed for an extended trip nor had he chosen to fly. Wherever he had gone, it was relatively close by. Not more than a day's driving, if that.

Artie wandered back to the office-den. Through the picture window he could see clouds rolling in from the ocean. The mist was turning into a light rain and he thanked God he'd stopped by the hotel to pick up his car. It would be hell trying to get a cab up there once the rain hit in earnest.

He looked around, then settled into the chair in the office area of the room. Unlike the desk, the computer table was cluttered with notebooks and a pile of opened letters. Mitch probably didn't use his computer much except for typing and maybe billing—though Artie was sure Linda did that—and E-mail. There was a small stack of it that Mitch had printed out.

Artie hesitated, then picked up the stack. If you were going to be a snoop, you might as well be thorough. He'd already checked out Mitch's sex life, or lack of one. This couldn't be any more embarrassing.

He riffled through the stack, then stopped abruptly at one message. DOD, Department of Defense. From a colonel in Intelligence, somebody Mitch had apparently kept in touch with from his 'Nam days.

No, the colonel had written, they had no information on other species, aliens, or flying saucers. But if Mitch had proof . . . The humor was heavy-handed but friendly. Artie checked the date. A little more than a week ago. It had been sent the day after they had first talked to

Paschelke. Mitch had been a true believer after all. When he'd gotten home that night, it was too late to phone so he had told his old colonel all about it via E-mail.

Artie hastily leafed through the rest of the correspondence. The ones from Washington got increasingly serious, the bantering tone dropping away. Mitch had kept them fully apprised. Paschelke's death, Hall's murder, Lyle's, Cathy's, the near suicide with the bottle of Valium and the scotch.

Artie felt his face gradually go white. There were mentions of himself, references to the various incidents he had told Mitch about. Not all the mentions were flattering, and he felt his face flush. The last E-mail said simply that the information Mitch had fed them was being bucked upstairs, but that they needed proof for the situation to be taken seriously. If Levin could offer something really solid, they would move on it immediately.

They hadn't trusted phones; they could be tapped. The E-mail had undoubtedly been encoded, and Mitch had a program for decoding when he printed it out.

Artie pulled open one of the drawers in the filing cabinet next to the table and started checking the correspondence at random. Mitch had never stopped playing the intelligence officer. He had kept a line open to Washington even after he had been mustered out, a part-time agent for the Bay Area. Attend the protest meetings for this and that— the Bay Area was full of them—and report back. He'd been something of an agent provocateur on at least one occasion. There had probably been others, but Artie didn't bother checking the rest of the files.

Even after his two true romances had fallen apart, Mitch still had a life. A lousy one.

What was it Chandler had said? That he thought Artie had as much to fear from Mitch as he did from Chandler? That he was surprised Artie had trusted Mitch? Levin, he had said, was a Hound.

For the other side.

It didn't make sense, Artie thought. He'd suggested to Mitch that they call in the feds and Mitch had advised against it. Why? Because they hadn't known enough about what was going on? So Mitch could hog all the glory? So he could still play the game of intelligence officer?

The answer was probably simpler than that. A good Hound wouldn't trust anybody, and Mitch had never really trusted him. Mitch had wanted to watch him a little longer, see what he did, where he went, what happened to him. After Larry and Cathy, he had been the major player, and Mitch had treated him as bait.

Now Mitch had packed and split, and there was no indication of where he had gone. But after that morning, Artie knew it had to have something to do with him.

He leaned back in the chair and let the small stack of mail slip to the floor.

Twenty years of friendship had just turned to ashes. Twenty years of looking forward to nights of racquetball, to Sunday picnics, to drinking beer in one of the local bars and shooting the shit about the Good Old Days, which had never been all that good but you wanted to think they were. Susan had liked Mitch, had always looked forward to having him over for dinner. And when Mark had been younger, he'd doted on Mitch, who had played the role of uncle to perfection.

But the truth was that he'd been far more of a friend to Mitch than Mitch had ever been to him. He and Susan and Mark had been merely grist for Mitch's psychological mill, a family that provided occasional companionship and amusement but was more important as a family to be watched and studied.

For twenty years Mitch had pretended to be his best friend.

And for twenty years Mitch had lied to him.

The campus of Bayview Academy was deserted; apparently everybody had left for the holidays. The day had turned sunny and there were few clouds; the view of San Francisco across the bay was dazzling. With a little imagination you could almost believe the claim that when some visitors first saw the city, it struck them as something out of *The Arabian Nights*.

Artie felt tired but, for the first time in more than a week, relaxed. Schuler was probably out there looking for him but at least the Hound was dead. And then he suddenly wondered about Schuler. Had Chandler reported to anybody higher up? He must have. And who better than Schuler, who knew everything that happened in the city, who knew where the bodies were buried—literally, where people might hide, the places where people might run to. Lyle had never trusted Schuler and Artie would be a fool if he did.

Schuler was probably as good an actor as Chandler, maybe better. Probably all the Old People were. Acting, the ability to convince the observer that you were somebody else, would have become second nature. Kids were natural actors, but most of them lost the ability as they grew up. The Old People hadn't. For them the ability to masquerade as somebody else probably meant the difference between life and death. Schuler—

Paranoia. He would never be without it.

But at least he now had time to look up Susan and talk about any possible divorce. What had she chosen for grounds? The situation didn't make any sense but she wouldn't be at a loss for answers; he knew that. The immediate thing was to try to find Mark, put some pressure on Headmaster Fleming to tell him more than he had. He was Mark's father—he had a right to know everything that Fleming knew. Somebody at the school must know where Mark had gone.

Artie called out "Anybody home?" a couple of times, then circled the administration building looking for the caretaker. Nobody. At the rear, the door to the gym hung open, creaking back and forth slightly in the wind. Artie walked in.

The gym was empty. Even if nobody was there, he still had expected to see the equipment, the climbing ropes, the benches, the tumbling apparatus and trampoline, the barbells and exercise machines in the corner, the punching bag, the canvas-covered mats on the floor.

It had been cleaned out. There was nothing but the walls and the bare basketball floor.

The kitchen was as empty as the gymnasium. No pots, no pans, no knife racks, empty china cupboards. Artie opened several of the industrial-sized refrigerators that remained. Some shreds of lettuce in one of the bottom bins, a lone, half-filled plastic jug of spoiled milk, half a stick of butter.

Empty, all of it gone. No silverware, no boxes of cereal, no toasters, no waffle irons, no stainless-steel trays for the steam table.

He wandered into the big dining room. It was cleaned out to the walls. No tables, no chairs, no steam table, no setup for a cafeteria serving line. If he hadn't had coffee there once, he wouldn't know the room had ever been used as a dining hall.

The classrooms were just as barren, though the blackboards still remained. On one of them, somebody had chalked *Have a Merry Christmas!* and in another room a small plastic Santa Claus dangled from a window shade. But the teachers' desks and the one-arm student chairs were gone.

Artie hurried down to the one room he had wanted to visit, the headmaster's office. The neatly lettered inscription on the door reading HEADMASTER: SCOTT V. FLEMING was all that remained. The inside of the office was vacant. No desk, no lamp, no chairs, no filing cabinets.

Schools closed for the holidays but there were usually caretakers, janitors, somebody around. And the equipment was usually still in place, the tables and chairs still there, the library still had books, the gym still had its equipment, the dining hall its steam table and the kitchen its pots and pans and knives.

Bayview Academy hadn't closed for the holidays.

It had closed, period.

He walked outside to go back to his car when behind him, a familiar voice said, "What are you doing here?"

Artie turned. Collins.

"I could ask the same of you, Collins."

The boy studied him, wary.

"You didn't get the notice?"

"What notice?"

"The school's closed for good. The notices were sent out a week ago."

If Susan had gotten one, she would have told him. Christmas deliveries, the mails were slow.

"I haven't been home the last few days." But if the school had been due to close, it would have been discussed with the parents months ago to give them time to make other arrangements. He knew from experience there weren't that many schools for handicapped kids. "Kind of sudden, wasn't it?"

Collins shrugged, "I thought everybody knew."

Everybody but himself, Artie thought.

"They cleaned it out in a hurry, didn't they?"

Another shrug and Collins looked vague. He was an expert at looking vague.

"After the buildings and grounds were sold, I guess they sold the
furnishings and equipment."

They'd had a week to do it, Artie thought. Everything was probably
on consignment with an auction warehouse, and in another week or two
there would be an ad in some newspaper. Or maybe a trade magazine
that covered institutions; they would be the logical buyers.

"Somebody liked the view," Collins added. "I think they're going
to turn the campus into a resort complex like the Claremont."

The breeze had started to pick up and Artie buttoned his coat.
Collins was wearing a wool sweater and the sudden chill to the air didn't
seem to bother him.

"You haven't told me what you're doing here, Collins. School's
out—in more ways than one. Why hang around?"

Collins was staring out at the bay. He didn't look at Artie and Artie
guessed that he didn't like being asked questions. When he was seventeen he hadn't liked talking to strangers either.

"Mr. Fleming asked me to drop around every few days, check for
vandalism."

Artie didn't believe him. Collins was there because *he* was there.

"What does he care? It's been sold."

Another faint shrug. "I dunno, maybe the final papers haven't been
signed yet."

When he'd seen the gymnasium door standing open, Artie had
guessed that the school had closed for the holidays but had hoped that
Fleming would still be there. When he hadn't seen anybody around,
he'd thought of breaking into Fleming's office and going through the
filing cabinets to see what records they kept on Mark. Maybe something
in them would have given him a clue.

Now there was nothing at all. Except Collins, who had been something more than just a friend to Mark. Had Mark confided in Collins?
And if so, what had he told him? Had he talked to Collins about running
away, about the girl he was presumably running away with?

Hell, he must have. Kids didn't talk to their parents, they talked
to each other, and a lot of what they thought they knew about the world
they got from other kids as ignorant as themselves. He had, and so had

everybody else he'd ever known. It took a lifetime to figure things out as they really were.

He'd expected Collins to turn and walk away but the boy had jammed his left fist in the pocket of his sweater and was staring out at San Francisco across the bay. He was, Artie suddenly realized, waiting.

"What's your father do, Collins?"

"Nothing fancy, Mr. Banks." Collins started to walk back to the gymnasium. Artie didn't move. If Collins was really cutting him off, he'd chase after the little bastard and find out what he knew about Mark if he had to beat him bloody.

A dozen steps away, Collins stopped and waited for him to catch up.

They walked into the gymnasium together. Collins pulled the door closed after him. It was still cold—there was no heat in the empty building—but at least they were out of the wind.

Collins sat on the floor with his back to the wall. He pulled his legs up, gripped his right hand with his left, and wrapped his arms around his knees. Artie sat a few feet away.

"Your father, Collins."

"I told you, nothing fancy—we're not rich. He's in construction." He hesitated, as if he were trying to remember. "Dry wall, I think."

Artie stared at him.

"Like the character in *Roseanne*."

"The old TV show? I never watched it."

"You're putting me on, right, Collins?" He didn't try to keep the menace out of his voice.

Collins managed to look both surprised and hurt. "I told you it was nothing fancy, that we weren't rich."

Artie turned away. "Right. Sorry, Collins."

It was time for Collins to get up and split, saying he had to be back home. Collins didn't move.

"Where is he, Collins?"

Collins picked at his shoelaces.

"Where's who?"

"Mark."

Collins shrugged. "I wouldn't tell you if I knew. I wouldn't rat on Mark."

Collins knew all right. He was lying. Artie pulled the automatic out of his pocket and placed it on the floor in front of him, out of Collins' reach or where his feet might kick it away.

"Mark is my son," Artie said quietly. "I will do absolutely anything to find out where he is. Do you understand, Collins? We're all alone; nobody saw me drive up. I don't think anybody will see me drive away."

Collins didn't look impressed.

"Then I couldn't tell you anything, could I?"

Artie kicked the gun across the floor and held his head in his hands.

"Okay, Collins, beat it."

Collins didn't move.

Collins was a lock and there had to be a key, Artie thought. Did he know where Mark had gone? Yes. Was Collins going to tell him? No. Why? Because Mark had told him not to tell anybody. But there was a key and Collins was waiting for him to use it.

Then he had the answer. All Collins really needed was an excuse.

"You love Mark, don't you, Collins?"

Collins nodded, mute.

"I don't care what happened," Artie said.

"I told you. Not much." Collins looked like he wanted to cry.

"Collins." Artie hesitated. "I can't tell you everything that's been going on but I can tell you one thing. I don't give a damn if Mark has chased off for a week's fling. More power to him—I had my own when I was his age."

He thought momentarily about Mary and wondered if his brief affair constituted a fling and if it had been anything like that for Mark. He doubted it; Mark seemed much more pragmatic about sex than he had ever been.

"I want to find Mark," Artie continued, "because his life's in danger."

Collins looked worried. "Medication?"

Artie shook his head. "No."

Collins said quietly, "Look me in the eyes and tell me his life's in danger."

Kid stuff, Artie thought with surprise; Collins was older than that. Then he looked into Collins' eyes and changed his mind. The boy's eyes were a steady gray, his face expressionless, and Artie had the uncomfortable feeling that Collins could tell a lie from the truth at a glance. For a moment all Artie could think about was Cathy and James and Andy and Chandler's face just before Charlie Allen had shot him. There was a chance, maybe only a small chance, that another Hound for the Old People would come after him and by extension Susan and Mark. He wasn't out of it; he'd probably never be out of it. But he desperately wanted them out of it. At the very least he owed it to them to tell them what they faced. There were no innocent bystanders, Chandler had made that pretty clear.

Artie said, "His life's in danger, Collins."

Collins stared at him a moment longer, then glanced away.

"Mark went up to Willow. To meet his mother."

"When?"

"This morning. A friend drove him up."

Nobody had answered when he'd called; communications had broken down somewhere up there. Mark's weeklong fling was over, but Artie had the oppressive feeling that Mark was driving into danger and Susan was probably up to her neck in it.

He stood up.

"Thanks, Collins."

What he had told Collins was the truth and it had been the key that had released Collins from whatever promise he'd given Mark. The thing that bothered Artie was the small expression of satisfaction on Collins' face just before the boy had turned away.

CHAPTER 23

It was a long day's trip to Willow and it was getting dark by the time Artie drove into town. He hadn't bothered to pack anything—just stopped at an ATM to pick up several hundred dollars, then hit the road. He could buy a toothbrush when he got there and rinse his shorts out in the sink at some motel.

He'd never been close to Susan's parents, Harold and Sharon Albright. They'd been at the wedding, but they'd been openly hostile to him and he'd never visited them. For whatever reason, they hadn't approved of the marriage and made it plain they didn't care to see much of him. He'd obliged them, and Susan had taken care of the parental obligations, remembering them at Christmas and sending out birthday cards, calling occasionally, though Artie couldn't remember any time when *they* had called until the week or so ago when Susan's mother had phoned to say her father wasn't doing well. They had never sent cards or presents, not even at Christmas, not even to Mark.

Chalk one up for Mark: he'd never complained about them. Occasionally when Susan had visited them she had taken Mark along, but Mark never had much to say about them afterward. Probably out of deference to him.

Willow was a little town of a thousand at the foot of the Cascades. A Motel 6 on the outskirts, then a three-block-long Main Street with a clothing store and two small restaurants, a combination gift shop and bookstore, a small grocery plus some shops catering to occasional tourists.

Artie glanced at his watch—almost dinnertime. But if he showed up at the Albrights in time to eat, he knew damned well Susan's mother would be annoyed.

He parked in front of a little restaurant that had red-checked curtains in the window. The cold evening air cut through his thin jacket and half a foot of snow crunched under his shoes when he got out of the car. He should have taken the time at least to grab a sweater before leaving.

Inside, the restaurant was small but spotless, with half a dozen tables and a counter with eight stools. Only one of them was occupied— an old man reading a copy of what looked like the county weekly. Two teenagers were in back playing a pinball machine, and a middle-aged couple with two kids sat at a table along the side.

It looked very comfortable, very cozy.

Artie picked a table close to the front door. They probably didn't have much business this time of year, so there wouldn't be a draft with people running in and out. The table was covered with oilcloth that matched the curtains, the menu neatly typed and inserted in a little clip holder that also held an ad for Budweiser.

It was the little things that counted, Artie thought. The ketchup and mustard bottles were full, the tops carefully wiped off. And there were no signs of the previous diner on the oilcloth. It was a high-class establishment for a small town.

"Hi, stranger. What can I get you?"

She was chubby and smiling, midthirties, hair done up in a loose bun, wearing a spotless white apron and holding a little notepad, ready for his order.

Artie looked at the menu without really seeing it. "Any recommendations?"

"Everything's good." She pointed to one of the items. "I had the ham and sweets earlier this evening. The green beans are frozen but the biscuits and gravy were made tonight." Another smile. "Try the apple pie for dessert—my mother bakes it special."

"You own the place?"

"Me and Terry—he works the kitchen, I wait the tables. Good division of labor."

Artie had glimpsed a thickset man in a white apron in the kitchen just off the dining area. He'd caught Artie's eye when he came in, flashed a smile, then went back to his stove.

Friendly town, even the dogs were friendly. A shaggy collie lying on the floor at the far end of the counter had eyed him when he first came in, then went back to dozing.

The waitress left a copy of the paper for him to read while he waited, and Artie leafed through it. The usual small-town board meetings, apparently centering around getting prepared for a sudden influx of visitors. It didn't say why or when, but then small towns probably spent most of the winter getting ready for the rest of the year unless they were ski resorts.

The ham and sweet potatoes were the best Artie ever had—the hogs were raised on a farm just down the pike, the waitress said, and the farmer did his own slaughtering. The biscuits and gravy melted in his mouth, and the cook had even done something special to the beans. The apple pie was superb, and Artie ordered another slice, which he couldn't quite finish.

When he had finished the meal, he felt stuffed. There was nothing he wanted more than to go back to the motel and collapse on the bed—except one thing: to see Susan and Mark.

He dawdled over his coffee and stared around the restaurant again. The kids in back were still going at it, the old man at the counter had been replaced by two giggling girls of high school age, and the middle-aged couple and their two kids had been exchanged for a younger family with a baby in a high chair.

Middle America, Artie thought.

Norman Rockwell country.

He paid his check, then just before leaving turned to the waitress and asked, "Do you have a hospital in town?"

She looked alarmed. "You sick?"

"Just wanting to check on a friend."

"We're kind of small for a hospital. Doc Ryan has something of a clinic—two or three beds—his wife helps out as his nurse. But that's the closest we come. Anything really serious, LifeFlight flies them to

Redding or Eureka or some bigger town, depending on what's wrong."
She looked dubious. "I didn't know Doc had an overnighter but you
can never tell, I guess."

He hadn't really expected there would be a hospital in Willow.
When he'd called they had told him there was only a clinic and old man
Albright wasn't there. He'd hoped there had been a mistake and now it
looked like there wasn't. Maybe Willow was a dry hole after all.

"We had one last year—young tourist girl was lost in the brush. It
was three days before they found her and she was suffering from exposure pretty bad. I think they flew her to Redding for treatment."

Artie got the doctor's address, then went outside and stood on the
sidewalk for a moment, filling his lungs with the chill night air.

Beautiful little town. He should have found an excuse to come up
with Susan more often; the hell with her parents.

He started for his car, then glanced back at the restaurant. Not a
gourmet's paradise, but some of the best food he'd had in years. He
could see through the windows that the boys in back were still playing
pinball, the young couple were spoon-feeding the baby, and the girls at
the counter had their heads together in animated conversation.

Norman Rockwell country all right.

Kids in the city playing pinball wouldn't be nearly that quiet and
well behaved.

The Albright home was a small, white clap-
board house with a neatly tended lawn in front, familiar from the photographs Susan had shown him. Even in the dusk Artie could see it was
well kept up. An old black Chevy in the driveway, a swing on the front
porch, doghouse to the side.

The porch light was on and so were lights in the living room. Artie
took a deep breath, got out of the car, and crunched through the snow
to the door. It opened on the second ring.

"Yes?"

The man who answered certainly wasn't Harold Albright. He was
twenty years too young and twenty pounds too thin. And friendly. He
was still holding the paper he'd been reading and looked at Artie ex-
pectantly.

"I was looking for the Albrights," Artie said, expecting to be told that the whole family was up in Eureka or Redding because of the old man's illness and friends were house-sitting for him.

The man in the doorway looked apologetic.

"Sorry, but nobody by that name lives here, Mister."

Artie stared at him, not sure what to say.

"They . . . used to some years back." He hesitated, uncertain. "You have any idea where they might have gone?"

Somewhere in the house behind him a woman's voice said reprovingly, "Ask him in, Tom. It's cold out there—he'll catch his death."

The man opened the door wider.

"Come on in. No sense letting all the heat out."

Artie carefully wiped his shoes on the doormat. On the inside, the house had all the warm, rustic appeal of a country bed-and-breakfast. A slender woman in her forties was sitting on the couch knitting. She looked up at him over the tops of her glasses, then stood up, waiting to be introduced.

"My wife, Maude." Her husband turned his head slightly. "Maudie, our friend here is looking for the Albrights. You ever heard of them? Apparently they used to live in this house."

She shook her head, frowning and trying to look helpful at the same time. "Name doesn't ring a bell."

The man turned back to Artie and shrugged. "We bought the place seven years ago from the MacDougalls. Got no idea who owned it before them." Still friendly but curious, "Why you looking for the Albrights?"

"I'm married to one of them—their daughter. She came up to visit them and I said I'd follow on the weekend." Artie started to back away toward the door. "Must have got the address wrong."

"Sorry, Mister." He looked genuinely regretful when he said it. "Ask at the gas station just out of town—they usually know where everybody lives."

He should have asked the waitress, Artie thought. She would've known. But then he had an even better source of information: the doctor.

In the door, Artie paused and said, "Thanks—thanks a lot." He turned and trudged back to his car. Friendly couple, but for a small town you would have expected them to have asked more questions, or else to have been curt and slammed the door in his face.

. . .

The doctor looked like he might have stepped out of an old Marcus Welby television show, white-haired, late sixties, ruddy-cheeked. And, like everybody else Artie had met, he went out of his way to be friendly and helpful.

"Hal Albright in the hospital?" He looked mystified. "I didn't even know the old coot was sick. Who told you that?"

He invited Artie into the living room, one with lace curtains and old, dark oak furniture whose legs had been carved or decorated. A lamp with a beaded fringe stood guard over the ancient rolltop desk and there were lace doilies on the arms of the big easy chair the doctor sat in and on those of the couch.

"My wife—I'm married to their daughter. Her mother called up and said that Hal was in a bad way, that he was in the hospital."

The doctor squinted at him, suddenly making the connection. "You're the fella who called, aren't cha?" Artie nodded. "Well, if Hal was in a bad way, he sure wasn't here then. Most serious thing I've handled aside from births and emergencies was an appendectomy with Liz handling the anesthesia." He turned and hollered to his wife in the kitchen. "Lizzie, that coffee ready yet?" Then back to Artie. "Your wife say what was wrong with him?"

Artie shook his head. "It was a short conversation. She sounded under a lot of stress. Maybe it was something the doctors hadn't diagnosed yet."

The doctor motioned him to a chair. "How's Susan? I haven't seen her in a coon's age. I remember when she was a little girl, all pigtails and energy."

Artie stared at him. Susan had gone up there, but the doctor, who should know everything in town, hadn't seen her or even heard she was around. Something was falling apart, Artie thought. If her father was as sick as Susan had implied, they would have airlifted him out to a hospital in a bigger town. Maybe Susan had called from a nearby city—one with a hospital—and just forgotten to tell him. But Mark would certainly have checked with her, would have known where she was. He wouldn't have driven all the way to Willow for nothing.

"I haven't seen her father in years," Artie said slowly. "We never got along very well; I never came with her when she visited him. I went to the address I had and they're not there. The couple in the house had never heard of them."

The doctor frowned.

"Your wife never told you her folks had moved or where to?"

Liz bustled in from the kitchen with coffee and a small plate with slices of coffee cake on it. "Thanks, Lizzie." They sipped their coffee in silence until she retreated to the kitchen.

"Sounds like you and your wife are having a bit of trouble." Ryan shook his head. "Not my business, of course."

"We're thinking of divorce," Artie said, surprised how painful it sounded when he mentioned it aloud. "That's what I drove up to see her about."

"Divorce." The doctor concentrated on his coffee cake. "Bad business, divorce."

"You know where they moved to?" Artie asked.

The doctor looked at him shrewdly.

"I'm taking a lot on faith, young man. How do I know you're who you say you are?"

"If you know their phone number, you could call them," Artie suggested. "Talk to Susan."

"I suppose I could do that." Ryan put down his coffee cake and walked to the phone on the desk and dialed. He waited for a long minute, then finally hung up. "Out of luck, young fella, just the damned machine. Nobody's home, or else they're not answering, which would be unusual for these parts."

"I need to see her," Artie said desperately.

The doctor hesitated, then said, "Let me see your driver's license."

Artie pulled it out and the doctor checked it over, squinting at Artie to see if he matched the photograph. He wrote some information on a piece of paper.

"Just in case anything happens, the state police will know who to look for. Sorry if all this seems unfriendly, but all I've got is your word and I don't know you from Adam." He scribbled something on another piece of paper and gave it to Artie.

"The Albrights moved out of town, oh, I'd say ten years or more ago. Didn't ask why, they never told me—but Hal just never got along with people. Their place is back in the woods a ways, five miles out on

Route 89. A little county road connects just about there. There's a white mailbox at the front of the driveway, can't miss it. They're about a hundred feet in, sort of a fancy log-cabin affair."

Artie stood up, tucking the piece of paper in his pocket.

"Thanks a lot, Doctor."

Ryan clapped him on the shoulder.

"Glad to help, son—sorry if I came across as too suspicious. Try and talk your wife out of that divorce—only people who benefit are the lawyers."

Artie left and drove slowly through the few blocks of the business district. A sweet shoppe—they even spelled it with two "p"s—with three or four cars out front, the type his father used to call jalopies. Young kids huddled in the booths, and Artie could hear music blaring from the jukebox but no rock, no rap. The residential part of town was a few blocks of old wooden houses with porches and dormers and big lawns, now covered with snow. There was a small brick schoolhouse, and right before the town ended and the woods began, a classic white painted church with a tall steeple and a cross silhouetted against the starlit sky.

Artie was on a slight rise and pulled over to the side of the road, stopping to look back. The perfect dinner in the perfect small-town restaurant with perfect small-town customers. The motherly waitress, the friendly cook, the well-behaved kids playing the pinball machine, the friendly couple who didn't know where the Albrights had gone and were genuinely sorry they didn't know, the country doctor right out of central casting.

A small village on a starry night, the snow softly falling, holiday lights twinkling in the windows below. It could have been the model for a Hallmark Christmas card.

A village right out of the nostalgic past with people to match, everybody in costume and playing their parts, like the characters at Disneyland.

If you were driving up Highway One along the coast, Willow might not have looked out of place next to Carmel or Mendocino, pretty little towns overrun with cars and noisy kids and chockablock with tourist traps. But inland, you got a different type of small town. Old working towns with an ancient grain elevator or lumbermill and the occasional dilapidated tractor sitting in a farmer's front yard, roadhouses with a dozen pickups and beat-up cars parked out front with large furry dice or small plastic skeletons jiggling in the rear window.

In the back of Artie's head a flag went up.

Willow was too good to be true. It was in the wrong place to be what it seemed to be—a picture-perfect tourist town—when there was no lake or mountain or seashore nearby to draw the tourists.

What was the old expression? A Potemkin village: one of the fake villages that Catherine the Great's lover built along the roads she traveled so she would never see the poverty of the peasants.

Willow was a Potemkin village.

A few days ago somebody had given him a guided tour of the Old People in the city. But they were in the country, too.

In one sense, Willow wasn't a village at all.

It was a nest.

A nest of the Old People.

And then he took one last look and changed his mind. It was probably an experimental village by, of, and for the Old People. An example of what the whole world could have been like if *Homo sapiens* hadn't fucked it up.

CHAPTER 24

The white mailbox was just where the doctor had said it would be, a few yards beyond the intersection of Route 89 with the county blacktop. Artie could see the driveway and the shadowy form of the house, the lights on in the living room downstairs. Nobody had answered the phone but somebody was home, or maybe they'd just left the lights on to make people think they were, a standard ploy in the city.

He cut the engine a hundred yards away and watched for a few minutes, then got silently out of his car and started up the road. There was a car in the driveway and he knew by the blocky outline that it was Susan's old Volvo. Hers was the only car there, which meant Susan was home unless she'd gone out with her mother and father for the evening. A few steps farther and he walked across the intersection with the county road. He automatically glanced down it, then abruptly stopped. There was another car on the road, he could tell by its silhouette against the starry sky. It had been parked about as far away from the Albright house as his, and for the same reason. The driver had probably killed his engine at the top of a small hill and coasted down the slight incline to a stop, trying to keep his approach as silent as possible.

Artie hesitated, felt for the reassuring bulge of the automatic in his pocket, and walked up the road to the car.

Mitch's BMW. He had driven around the town on the back roads because he didn't want to be seen. A BMW in a small country town would be a little hard to forget.

Artie felt like somebody had slugged him in the stomach. He'd probably been as blind as Larry. It had been a nice, little, incestuous club—everybody had been balling everybody else. Susan and Mitch had probably been a number back then. And they probably still were. Nobody would have told him, any more than they would have told Larry about Cathy.

And now Mitch had done what he hadn't been able to do. He'd found Susan and immediately gone up to see her.

Artie felt sweaty and sick. Why hadn't Mitch told him he was driving up? Because Mitch hadn't wanted him to know. After the phone call he'd made the previous morning, Mitch hadn't told him anything. Maybe Susan had left a message on his machine telling Mitch where she was staying.

Artie turned to the house and walked quietly across the lawn, keeping out of a direct line of sight with the front windows. With good luck, it would turn out that Susan's father was too mean to keep a dog. At least he prayed he didn't.

He sidled up to the edge of one of the living room windows and looked in. He felt the sweat start all over then. Mitch was seated with his back to the front door, Susan and Mark were sitting together on the couch, Mark with his arm around his mother. Mitch was talking but Artie couldn't make out what he was saying.

What the hell should he do? Artie wondered. Go around to the rear of the house and hope the back door was open? Crash through the window? Break down the front door?

He walked to the front door and rang the bell.

There was a pause, and then Mitch said in a loud voice, "Come on in, Banks—door's open."

Mitch was using his Captain Levin voice and Artie felt a momentary flash of relief. He wasn't interrupting lovers. This was about . . . something else. He tried the knob and walked in. Mitch was seated in a big easy chair, his legs crossed, relaxed and in charge. Susan and Mark sat on the floral-printed couch, both of them looking pale and frightened.

It was the same scene that Artie had glimpsed from the window except now he could see that Mitch was wearing his camouflage fatigues and had a gun in his hand. Strangely enough, over by the couch where Susan and Mark sat, no crutches or wheelchairs were in sight.

It was a different scene from the one he'd expected. One that didn't make much sense.

Cautiously Artie asked, "How did you know it was me, Mitch?"

"Just a guess—the old folks had left for the evening and I couldn't think of anybody else it might be. I don't think people drop in at this time of night without calling first." He looked curious. "That was you a few minutes ago, wasn't it?"

Mitch must have watched the house until Susan's parents had left and he knew Susan and Mark were alone.

"That's right." Artie glanced from Mitch to Mark and Susan and then back again. This time he took a closer look and felt the blood drain from his face. There were bruises and an open cut on Mark's cheek. Mitch had pistol-whipped him, one of the first steps in breaking down a prisoner.

"What the hell's going on?"

Mitch cracked a thin smile.

"Good question, Banks, one I came up here to find the answer to. And I think I have." He waved the gun at Mark. "Stand up, son. Take a few steps forward."

Mark looked shame-faced at Artie, then stood up, took a few steps, and sat back down.

"That should give you a clue, Banks."

Mark was taller than Artie had thought. How many years had it been since he'd seen Mark stand up straight, without leaning on crutches? Since he was twelve? For five years it had all been pretense, an act. Mark could probably walk and run with the best of them.

Artie's first reaction was to try to hold back tears, grateful that Mark wasn't crippled after all. But why?

"Things weren't quite how they appeared, Banks. Apparently, they never have been."

Artie looked at Susan, at the agony and fear on her face, then over at Mark, who was trying to keep a poker face but was plainly scared to death.

"What's going on?" Artie repeated. His voice was empty of emotion.

Levin dug in his pocket with his free hand and pulled something out. He held it up to the light so Artie could see it. Mark's earring, the one that Collins had given him a few days ago and that Mitch had borrowed to show a friend.

Artie glanced at it.

"Was it really Mayan?"

"A little older than that, Banks. My friend had it dated—it goes back something like thirty-five thousand years. You said it was a family heirloom, right?"

Artie could feel the hair stand up on the back of his neck. That had been the call Levin got on Haight Street. His friend had left a message about the date and Levin had called back to confirm it.

"That's what I was told."

Levin's expression was sardonic. "Apparently the family tree goes back a ways. But the boy's not yours, so it looks like you're strictly a recent graft. Did you and she"—he waved his pistol at Susan—"ever try to have children?"

"Susan said she couldn't."

"Oh, I think she probably could. The children would have been sterile, of course."

Artie took a breath.

"What are you trying to say?"

Levin stared at him in mock surprise.

"Christ, Banks. All the time you're looking for the Old People and they're right under your nose—you married one of them. Sort of like Jenny and Mary, though I suspect Jenny knew what she was getting into and you didn't. Right?"

Artie looked over at Susan and didn't know what he felt—relief at finally finding her, anger at the deception. She'd never told him she loved him because she never had. She wouldn't have been able to, even if she had wanted. And he was sure she'd never wanted.

"That right, Susan?"

Her face was expressionless, her eyes bleak. He had seen the expression once before, on the faces of the members of the Tribe when they were being massacred on the riverbank. None of them had expected mercy.

It was Mark who said quietly, "That's right, Artie."

For fifteen years his life had been a sham. Susan had married him, but not for love, and he had no idea what other reasons she might have had. At the time she'd certainly had her choice of men. Why him?

"How'd you find them, Levin?"

"You said Susan had left for Willow. Then you said she hadn't. Logical thing to do was check out Willow anyway, find out where her parents lived and pay them a visit. We"—Artie knew he meant the DOD—"went through the records. She never used her regular credit cards after she left San Francisco, but she had a Shell card and used that—it wasn't a joint card, it was in her name only. She bought gas twice on the way up and after that it was simply connect the dots. The manager at the Shell station just outside town had an address for the old folks."

How easy, Artie thought. But then Levin had the resources of the federal government. Chandler had been right. Levin was a Hound. For the other side.

Levin glanced at Artie, curious. "You drive through town?"

Artie nodded.

"I guessed it would be full of them—Christ, they had to be some-place—so I circled and came in from the back. I was right, wasn't I? The town's a staging area."

"In a sense," Artie said bleakly.

He was staring at Susan and Mark and trying to figure out the emotions that kept welling up in him. His marriage had been a sham; they had deliberately used him. As a cover, as a convenience. But why had they picked on him?

What had Susan told him about Mark's biological father? Killed in an industrial accident of some sort? He had never pushed her for details; it had obviously been painful for her. Painful because Mark's father must have been the man she had really loved, had probably never gotten over.

Levin glanced at his watch. "I figure we've got an hour."

Artie suddenly felt apprehensive.

"An hour for what?"

"Backup, Banks. There should be at least two choppers on their way; I phoned in and left a message for my old colonel. We can sweat the people in town after we get the proof back to Washington."

"Proof," Artie repeated, feeling stupid.

Levin nodded at Susan and Mark.

"Them. Government doctors and psychiatrists will examine them. There won't be any secrets then." Levin leaned back in his chair, the hand holding his gun never wavering, and whistled. "For thirty-five thousand years they've lived among us, Banks. Think of that. And nobody knew, nobody suspected."

Mark shifted on the couch and Levin was suddenly on the edge of his chair. "Don't try anything, son. The doctors can do an autopsy when you're dead. They'll take you apart bone by bone, do X rays and CAT scans and blood tests and come up with just as much information as they could if you were alive."

"Be careful, Levin. He's my son," Artie said in a dead voice.

Imagine the genocide, Mary had said.

The expression on Levin's face was one of genuine pity.

"I feel for you, Banks, I really do. You lived with them for fifteen years and from everything you said it was a happy marriage. But they were using you, can't you see that? It was probably the same all over the country, infiltration. Married to you, why should anybody suspect them? But don't forget, Cathy Shea left town the night of Larry's murder, and your wife left for Willow the next morning. Ask yourself why. Because she knew what was coming down? You were almost killed too. Being married to you was protection for her—it wasn't protection for you. Think she shed any tears over the possibility? You knew too much, even though you didn't think you did. She could have asked you to go to Willow with her but she didn't. She told you her father was sick; you could have gotten time off from work."

He studied Artie, reading the expressions flitting across his face. It's what Levin had done in 'Nam, Artie thought. It's what he did for a living in the States. The ace psychiatrist who listened to his patients and watched the flood of emotions on their faces and read them like a book.

Artie tried his best to look blank-faced. He'd had his own experiences in 'Nam, too, including the three months in a Charlie prison camp until he'd managed to escape. He'd learned to hide his feelings then.

"She didn't want you along," Levin continued, "but she wanted the boy, didn't she?"

Levin was an expert at painting the picture of a wasted marriage, of betrayal, but of necessity it was a distorted portrait. He had been there; Levin hadn't.

"Banks." In the light from the lamp, Levin looked hostile. "She's a different *species*. She's as different from you as you are from an ape. It doesn't take a military genius to figure out we're in a war. What do you think they want? Easy answer: They want their world back. The losers always want to turn back the clock. How do you think they'll get it? How *can* they get it? By eliminating us. It's the only way." He turned cajoling. "We're in a war, Artie, and war is vicious and brutal—you know that. Think of Dr. Paschelke and Professor Hall, Lyle, poor Cathy and the kids. Tell me what compassion they were shown."

"It was the Hound—" Mark started feebly.

"Shut up, son. You talk when I tell you to."

Captain Levin, Artie thought again. Levin loved it. And then he had a flash of guilt. So had he when he was in 'Nam, but not in the same way. He had loved the danger, the hunt. Levin had loved the kill. After you got out, you pushed it out of your mind. Everybody had done things they weren't proud of. But he guessed Levin had never forgotten it and never worried about it. He'd slipped into the friendly, slightly sardonic role of psychiatrist with no trouble at all. And Artie had taken him at face value. The Captain Levin in 'Nam had gradually become a vague memory. Now here he was, come back to life, the 'Nam Levin whom Artie had never really liked. The captain who inspired both admiration and horror. The captain who loved his job too well.

Levin was still staring at Mark.

"There're no Germans here but us good Germans, that it?"

The river's edge, Artie thought. The young boy being held over the rushing waters while his throat was cut. For a brief time he had been a member of the Tribe, he had been one of *them,* and they had been . . . had been . . . What? Human. Very human. Even Professor Hall had suggested that.

"What are you going to do with them?"

"These two?"

"All of them."

Levin shrugged. "I imagine we'll develop DNA tests so we can identify them. I suppose they'll be camps for them, like there were for the Nisei during World War Two."

"Gas chambers, Levin? Down the road?"

"Christ, Banks, what the hell are you thinking of?"

He couldn't tell whether Levin was really shocked or not. Everybody had committed genocide at one time or another, Artie thought. Nobody had clean hands. And then he realized that after all of this was over, Levin would be a hero. And he thought of Mary again: *If you want to know what you were like in the past, look at what you are today.*

"Susan's my wife," Artie said slowly. "Mark's my son."

Levin's eyes narrowed.

"Do you remember what Cathy looked like?" he asked softly. "James and Andy? Their Hound did that, all by himself—no proxy murder that time. Remember Lyle? Nobody liked Lyle, but he didn't deserve what happened to him. And Paschelke and Hall, did they deserve it? And what about yourself? You almost did a swan dive off your rear balcony—three stories up onto concrete, Artie. Think you would have survived? They would have picked you up with a blotter." He waved his gun at Susan and Mark again. "Do you think they would have shed any tears?"

That was one of the few things he had never told Levin. That somebody had cried "Dad!" and the next thing he knew Mark had pulled him off the railing and was kneeling over him on the porch, the rain beating in his face, his wheelchair left behind in the doorway. Mark had dropped the pretense to save him; he had risked betraying his own species to do so.

"We can't give up the world, Banks—you know that. For events that only anthropologists care about, events that happened thirty-five thousand years ago? It's tragic but it's simple. It's us versus Professor Hall's Old People. Do you think they would let us live?"

No, Artie thought bleakly, no they wouldn't. They couldn't. But that didn't stop him from loving Susan and Mark. He'd always loved them more than they loved him, always would. That equation hadn't changed.

Or had it? In the back of his mind, a part of him was wavering. Levin shrugged again.

"It's war, Artie. When you look at the world twenty years from now, what do you want to see?"

Garbage world, Artie thought chaotically. Poisoned streams, empty oceans, thousands of species that had died and hundreds of others that existed only in the concrete and steel confines of a zoo.

Levin cocked his head, listening.

"The choppers are coming."

Artie thought he heard something in the distance but he wasn't sure Levin was right; he'd served in 'Nam too long to be mistaken. Enlisted men knew the sound of choppers better than officers, probably because they spent more time in the front lines.

Mark suddenly lunged off the couch in a desperate leap at Levin. Susan screamed. Levin fired once and Mark crumpled to the floor.

For a split second time was stationary, impressions and thoughts flashing through Artie's mind. Levin would take Susan and Mark back to Washington and he would be the interrogator, the one who always got the information he wanted but whose methods would make you sick. Levin would ask Susan and Mark to identify the Hounds. He would never believe them when they said they couldn't. Captain Levin was firmly convinced there was always an answer, that there *had* to be an answer.

Artie fired twice then, right through his jacket pocket. His first shot hit the bulb in the lamp and the room abruptly went dark. There were only the stars and a full moon lighting up the room now—just enough moonlight to glint off the frame of Mitch's granny glasses.

After all these days of doubt and indecision, Artie finally knew exactly who he was and where his loyalties lay. Above all else, he was a man whose whole life was his family. How in the world could Mitch have misjudged that?

His second shot shattered the left lens of Mitch's glasses.

CHAPTER 25

They got back to San Francisco on Christmas Eve, driving the whole way in silence. Dr. Ryan had patched up Mark's shoulder, urging Artie to get further treatment for him in the city. The muscles had been torn, nothing serious, but somebody should check him for possible infection once he got home.

Levin had been mistaken. They weren't choppers, though perhaps he had thought so because he'd been operating with a 'Nam mind-set plus a bad case of wishful thinking. It was his chance for an intelligence coup, to become a national hero. He must have called Washington, but the message had never been delivered. The Old People had Hounds in D.C. as well as San Francisco and besides, Levin's old friend was probably tucked away in a minor bureaucracy of the DOD. Without proof, who would pay attention to what a semiretired intelligence officer told them?

The "choppers" had actually been several cars from Willow, the passengers armed. They had been too late, and for that Artie had been grateful. Susan and Mark would never have survived any shootout; it had been bad enough as it was. Doc Ryan had been along and helped Mark, but there was nothing to be done for Levin. It had been a lucky shot, an instant kill.

Artie had left the house with his arm protectively around Mark's good shoulder. He'd glanced once at Levin lying on the floor and had felt everything from grief to pity to relief that he had been so lucky and Susan and Mark were still alive. Then he'd had a brief flashback to the days in the Haight when he had lived in a crashpad with half a dozen others, including Mitch, and spent more than one evening smoking joints and laughing uproariously at the Three Stooges on the tube.

But there was little connection between that Mitch and this.

The doctor and the others would take care of the body. Levin had left San Francisco in his BMW and disappeared. There would be an investigation, but nobody in Willow had seen either him or his car. The case would end up in an open file, be shuffled toward the back, and eventually forgotten.

Susan's parents had told her they would be back at midnight but Artie didn't want to stick around to meet them. Somebody else could fill them in. Susan had left them a note; she didn't want to stay either. He hadn't argued with her one way or the other; he couldn't care less.

Back at the house on Noe, he and Mark had taken a nap, then gone out shopping for a Christmas tree. Afterward he called Connie to wish her and the Grub a Merry Christmas and to report that his family was together again. He'd bitten his tongue when he said it, but was glad he'd told her. A little of the Christmas spirit had managed to infect Connie and the news had cheered her even more.

"Merry Christmas, Artie, and don't drink too much eggnog. Oh, yeah, Monday's a working day and you better be here, damn it—you've just run out of excuses."

They had spent late afternoon trimming the tree and Susan had eventually joined in. Mark was cheerful and talkative; Artie didn't have much to say. Susan said nothing at all.

They ordered out for pizza, waited an hour and a half for it to show up, and ate a cold mushroom-and-double-sausage in stony silence.

After he had finished one slice, Mark shoved his plate away, angry.

"You two got something to talk about but I don't think I want to hear it."

He stalked out to the porch and yanked the sliding glass doors shut behind him. Artie could see him leaning on the railing, looking out at the lights of the city twinkling in the gathering dusk. San Francisco at its prettiest. A fairly warm evening, the fog just beginning to roll in and a sea of colored lights below that seemed to go on forever.

Artie pushed his own plate aside and walked into the living room, Susan following. He sat on the edge of the couch, Susan on the edge of the big recliner, tense and uneasy. She still hadn't looked him in the eyes.

"Where do you want to start?" she finally asked.

"Why did you marry me?" He had wanted to be dispassionate and objective, but to himself he sounded despairing. *Women will break your heart all your life, Arthur.*

"Because I wanted a father for Mark. And for protection. I was afraid of what might be coming."

Like a few Jewish women did in Nazi Germany, Artie thought. Married to an Aryan, they had hoped for protection during the holocaust that had followed. If they married high enough up, it helped. But not always.

"Why me?" Artie repeated.

She looked at him then, a slight flush of anger on her cheeks.

"You want me to read off your virtues? You're brave, you're stable, and you're a family man. I realized that early on. You wanted a family badly and when you got one, I knew it would mean everything in life to you. Do you remember the conversations we had after we first met? You wanted me, but you really wanted a family more. I couldn't give you everything you wanted—I warned you about that—but I could give you enough, and with Mark I could give it to you all at once. As I remember, you said you liked that."

"Protection," Artie said, sullen.

"That's right, and for protection. For myself and Mark. Especially Mark."

"But not for love," Artie said. It hurt to say it.

She looked away.

"No, not for love."

He had asked for the truth and gotten it, and now he was sorry he had asked. But he couldn't blame her for that.

"Your first husband—you've never told me much about him."

"I'd known Michael in college. We graduated during a recession and he ended up in construction, as labor. He was on a work site one day and a wall collapsed on him. He died immediately."

Artie knew better but he had to ask it anyway.

"You loved him."

"No."

He looked surprised and she said, "He was a friend. I wanted children and if you're one of us that means an arranged marriage. You have to be matched—both of you have to be species typed. My family knew his, and both families approved. My father thought the world of him."

Which explained why her parents hated him, Artie thought. They would probably have hated anybody who followed Michael.

"I hoped to grow to love him." Her voice was dry, emotionless. "I think I might have."

"You told me you couldn't have any more children. The truth is you didn't want any more, right?"

"That's not true. But they would have been sterile and nothing on heaven or earth would have enabled them to have children in turn. How do you think they would have felt? How do you think I would have? I would have condemned them to a childless marriage. It wouldn't have been fair. Not to them. And not to you, either—you would have wanted grandchildren."

"They could have adopted," Artie said. "It wouldn't have mattered to me."

She stared at him, contemptuous.

"And you're so sure you can speak for them?"

H u b r i s ,   A r t i e   t h o u g h t . He was guilty of it, guilty as sin. But he couldn't help himself.

"Chandler was your Hound," he said. "Cathy was his lover and told him everything about Larry's research. She didn't know what he was." For just a moment he was back in Chandler's little theater, watching as Dave peeled off his makeup and became somebody Artie had never known, somebody who had almost squashed him like a bug. "Charlie Allen shot him."

"Chandler?" She looked surprised.

"You never knew?"

She shook her head.

"Of course not." Then: "You don't understand how . . . underground we've had to be. Nobody knows who the Hounds are. They're the only army we have, if you want to call it that. We couldn't tell you who they are even under torture because we don't know. We live in cells, little groups of us scattered around the country. There aren't many of us—there never were. A town like Willow, of almost a thousand, is unusual. I don't know of any others, though I'm sure there are some. A very few of us have contacts outside the group, like Dr. Ryan has contacts in Washington. But otherwise, we're in—"

"—deep cover," Artie finished.

"That's right. We have to be."

"Mark's school," he said. "It never was a school for the handicapped, was it?"

She looked tired.

"Schools, even private ones, have too many physical examinations, too much probing by doctors and nurses from the state. Maybe they never would have discovered anything unusual. Maybe they would have. We don't get sick very often—we're immune to most of your diseases. We couldn't take the chance that somewhere along the line somebody would get curious. Perfect attendance records, an *A* in health. Always. And stronger, much stronger, than average . . ."

"So you opened your own schools. Like Bayview."

"Mark and I have our own family doctor, too. You never knew."

"What happened with the academy? I met one of the students there; he said it had been sold."

She shrugged.

"It was time to fold it. State examiners were suspicious the last time they came around. They were due again right after the first of the year and we felt we couldn't risk it."

"Why not?"

She half smiled then.

"You saw Mark. None of the students were handicapped; it was a sham, a show for anybody who came around."

"Like me."

"Like you."

Collins had been very good. Artie would have sworn he had a withered right arm. And Mark had fooled him for five years. The car accident had been faked. Both he and Susan had gone out of their way to deceive him.

"You knew Larry was going to be killed."

She shook her head, denying it.

"I didn't know. Certainly not then. Cathy had told me what Larry was working on, swearing me to secrecy, and I knew it would be dangerous. I knew . . . eventually . . . a Hound would come after him. But aside from Mary and myself, I didn't even know there were any others of us in the Club. The police called Cathy shortly after Larry's death and she called me just before she left the house. She wouldn't say where she was going."

The timing would have been right, Artie thought. He wouldn't have known about the call; he'd been at Soriano's, waiting for Larry to show.

"So you called your folks and said you'd be coming up—maybe for an extended stay—and they were delighted. You decided to fake your father's illness."

"Something like that. Hal suggested it—I needed a last-minute reason for going. They didn't want you to come along, said you'd just bring danger up with you."

"You never left the house when you were in Willow, did you?"

"I didn't want anybody to know I had gone up there. After Larry was killed, I knew there would be an investigation, that sooner or later the police would want to talk to me. Perhaps to Mark. I didn't want to risk it."

Artie was suddenly angry again.

"You knew I was a good friend of Larry's, that I was one of those with his neck in a noose. You knew it all along, and you never warned me. That morning when you left, you asked me what Larry had to say at the meeting, and all the time you knew he was dead. You lied to me."

She sighed.

"Yes, Artie, I lied to you." Then it was her turn to be angry. "If I had warned you, I would have had to betray my own species and betray Mark. I couldn't do that. You should know about divided loyalties—they're not easy to handle, are they?"

He had a glimmering of the truth then, only a glimpse, and then it was gone.

"I would have sacrificed everything for you and Mark." He cursed the plaintive tone in his voice.

"That's why I married you. In turn, I would have sacrificed everything for Mark. I still would, I would offer up my own life for him as easily as I would offer up yours. I did my best to get him out of here. I ordered him to come up to Willow and he refused. We agreed on a day or two later, as soon as school was out. But school wasn't his reason for staying."

Artie couldn't hide his bitterness. "A week of romance. An early Christmas present to himself."

She looked at him, startled.

"You can't really believe that!"

Artie didn't answer her. He was lost in a flashback of the last dream he'd had, when he had stood watch in front of the cave, looking at the wolf just beyond the firelight and wondering if it could be trained to guard the cave in return for scraps of meat.

"You married me to be a watchdog," he said with sudden insight.

She had shifted slightly so her face was in shadow. "Not against any of our Hounds—against yours. And you were a very good watchdog. You more than lived up to expectations." There was a sudden tinge of pity in her voice. "I knew that somewhere along the line you would have to make a choice. I didn't think it would turn out to be the particular one you had to make."

Moe and Curly and Larry on the tube and a very young Mitch Levin sitting beside him on the dirty floor mattress, doubled up in laughter.

"You felt nothing for Shea?" he said at last. "For Lyle? For Cathy? I thought she was your closest friend."

She started to cry then, silently, the tears glistening in the glow from the lights on the Christmas tree.

"Yes. They were good friends, and I betrayed them by keeping quiet. It was just as difficult a choice to make as yours." She was suddenly furious, at him, at herself, at the choice she'd had to make. "And there was no way I would betray Mark!"

Artie sank back in his chair. Everything had gone to hell; everything bad that could happen to him had happened.

"Mitch was right," he said slowly, "and so was Chandler. It was war and it was either you or us. I was as familiar with that as Mitch was—we were both graduates of the same killing fields."

Pity flowed over her face like water.

"There isn't going to be any war, Artie. We've won and you've lost."

Artie frowned. "What the hell are you talking about?"

She looked away. "Go ask your son."

"He's not my son," he said angrily.

"He thinks he is. You raised him; he's got your values, your outlook. He might as well be your flesh and blood. He earned it. He saved your life. He stayed behind to take care of the beloved watchdog. I hadn't planned on that."

"I owe him," Artie said reluctantly, remembering the time on the porch.

She saw the image in his mind. "That wasn't the only time."

He held his head in his hands, trying to make sense of everything she was telling him. There were huge gaps, but he was too tired to ask her to fill them in now.

"There were other times?"

Her voice was curt. "How do you think you stayed alive? You should have died a dozen times over. Ask him."

"Maybe tomorrow."

"Tonight. You don't know him—you should at least make a start. He's not like you, but he's not like me either. I would like to think he has the best of me." She paused. "And the best of you. You should be proud of him. And you should be willing to show it."

"If he saved my life more than once," Artie said sarcastically, "then he must have known Chandler was the Hound. Why didn't he just kill the bastard? You people seem able to do anything else."

"He doesn't have the genes for it," she said, her voice ice. "He didn't kill him because he couldn't kill him."

Artie looked up, confused and angry once again.

"You're going to have to explain that one."

She shook her head.

"Not me—Mark. Go talk to your son, Arthur."

THE ENDING

It was darker now, and a wind had started to whip the trees along the side of the house. Artie had brought out a sweater for Mark and handed it to him, then leaned on the railing beside him and looked down the block at the decorations on the houses and the flickering Christmas lights in the windows. A few doors away a window sign was blinking MERRY CHRISTMAS, HAPPY YOU-ALL.

It wasn't like back East, where he'd grown up as a kid. In Chicago there would be a foot of snow on the ground and he'd be bundled up to his ears with a thick coat and gloves stiff from making snowballs, plus a woolen cap and earmuffs and heavy galoshes. He missed it, but if he ever moved back there, he knew the winters would kill him.

"I heard some of the argument," Mark said.

He had to talk to Mark about it sooner or later, Artie thought.

"Your mother and I—"

"Yeah, I know." Then, curious: "Are you and Mom still friends?"

Artie felt defeated. "I don't know, Mark. I just don't know. She doesn't—"

"Has she asked for a divorce?"

Artie suprised himself with the answer.

"No she hasn't."

"Maybe you asked the wrong questions," Mark said quietly.

He would have to think about that. Marriages among the Old People were usually arranged, they were seldom for love. Why should he and Susan have the same frame of reference? She had married him because she had wanted a father for Mark and protection for them both. He had married her because he had wanted a family. Both of them had gotten what they wanted.

"I don't know if I ever thanked you."

"For what?" Mark asked.

"Saving my life. Here on the porch."

Mark grunted.

"Susan told me there were other times," Artie said.

"Yeah." Mark laughed quietly at the memory. "You almost ran into me at the museum that first day. I thought for sure you'd seen me."

Artie remembered the hour spent with the Tribe in the Visions of the Past room and he was suddenly uneasy.

"Those were *your* memories, weren't they? Racial memories?"

Mark shrugged.

"You were there to find out about us, where we came from. I thought I ought to show you. It was pretty grim, but I thought you needed to know about us, what it had been like for us back then."

It had all been part of his education as a watchdog. You have to know who you're guarding—and against what. He was suddenly puzzled.

"I used to have dreams—"

Out of the corner of his eye he could see Mark smile.

"Those were supposed to be my wet dreams, not yours. I was broadcasting in my sleep and didn't realize it."

Artie laughed and then immediately sobered.

"You placed the phone call to me when I was about to leave the museum that day with Dr. Hall."

He could sense Mark nod in the dark.

"I followed you when you drove away. Chandler almost got you then—you would have killed the guy in the car."

"How did you stop him?"

"Set up an interference pattern. That was about the only thing I could ever do. . . . And I was at the zoo, admiring the Siberian tiger. I almost got to the station parking lot too late." He was silent, remembering. "It was the same thing at the library. And I had Charlie Allen chase after you early in the morning when you went to Chandler's apartment. His wife didn't want him to go." Another silence. "He could do what I couldn't."

"There's a lot that Charlie is going to insist on knowing."

"He won't remember," Mark said gently. "I'll see that he doesn't."

He had a lot to ask Mark, Artie thought, but he didn't know where to begin.

"I gave you the guided tour of the city when you were staying at Levin's house," Mark continued. "Maybe I should have stuck around longer, but I was pretty tired by then. I read about the fire later."

"I was worried about you," Artie said slowly. "You could have let me know you were still alive."

Mark laughed in the darkness. "I was too busy keeping you alive. And I had Collins tell you his father was in dry wall. I guess you didn't pick up on that one—I thought you were sharper than that."

"You arranged with Collins to tell me at the end, didn't you?"

"It was time you found us; it was time you came up to Willow. I knew Chandler was dead, that you were no longer in danger. And I knew your friend"—Mark paused, aware he had used the wrong word—"was looking for Mom and me. I knew he would come to Willow searching for us." He suddenly sounded distant, remote. "I had done my best to save you. It was time for you to save us. You just made it."

All his married life he had been their faithful Hound. And to save them he had killed his best friend. But that wasn't true. Mitch hadn't had any friends, only patients and old army buddies.

Cautiously: "Collins struck me as a decent kid."

"Collins likes me too well," Mark said easily.

"I guessed that."

"I think the world of Collins—I wouldn't have turned him down. But what he wanted meant so much to him and so little to me his pride would have been hurt. I could have lied to him but he would have known." Mark hesitated. "A friend of his loves him, but Collins doesn't realize it yet."

Artie didn't say anything. It wasn't any of his business—and then he realized that of course it was. If it mattered to Mark, it mattered to him. He stared into the gathering night and after a moment said, "Susan claims the war is over. That it was over before it really began. That we lost—that is, *Homo sapiens* lost."

It was Mark's turn to be quiet, and Artie had a sudden premonition about what he was going to say.

"Doc Ryan talked to me about it before we left Willow. He'd just gotten a message from a friend at the Centers for Disease Control."

Artie was silent, waiting.

"He said it was in the papers, though they didn't print everything. Maybe they couldn't. Rift Valley TB. That's where they found 'Lucy,' isn't it? One of the earliest fossils? In the Great Rift Valley?"

"I think so." It took a moment for Artie to recall where he'd heard of the disease, then he had it. A TV news show in the hotel room with Mitch. And Watch Cap—Chandler—had mentioned it.

He knew Mark was looking at him in the dark, uneasy.

"Where the Rift Valley cuts through Ethiopia . . . there were a lot of mercenaries involved in their latest civil war and they were the first to come down with it. You go fighting in old boneyards and I guess you run the risk of catching whatever killed the owners of those bones to begin with."

"What's it like?"

"Doc Ryan said it's something like TB—but a lot worse. He said it was multidrug resistant and ultraviolet radiation doesn't kill it. Incubation period of a month or so, then a week of vomiting blood and that's it."

"They'll find something for it."

Mark shook his head.

"Doc didn't think so. Said there's only one drug that's good for TB now and it doesn't touch this. It's incurable."

Artie felt the first touch of fear.

"Did he say anything else?"

Mark cleared his throat. He suddenly seemed reluctant to talk about it.

"That it's species specific. That we're immune."

But *Homo sapiens* wasn't. Mary had been right. They had done it to themselves. But if it wasn't this, it would have been something else. TB was airborne and by now it would have spread all over the world, mercenaries going home and passing through Heathrow—all of London would have been exposed. You couldn't quarantine a city, and it was too late now, anyway. After that, New York, Paris—wherever the flights went. There were no oceans to protect them, no mountain ranges that would seal it off.

"Doc said the Old People are withdrawing. Moving out of the cities into the country, into uninhabited areas. Collins knows of a little town in Alaska, about a hundred miles out of Anchorage. Kodiak Creek. It's one of ours." Mark looked over at Artie. "We could move there."

"Maybe," Artie said. He'd like it in Alaska, he thought. "And maybe we'll be lucky."

But he knew they wouldn't be.

Mark changed the subject.

"Did you love your grandfather?" he asked.

Artie turned, surprised, trying to read his face in the darkness.

"Yes, of course."

"And your father?"

Artie smiled. "Him, too."

"Neither one of them were like you, were they?"

"In some ways, of course they were. In a lot of other ways, I suppose not. But that didn't affect my loving them."

"I'm not like you," Mark said.

"I know that."

"I'm not like Mom, either."

Something was bothering Mark, and Artie remembered what Susan had said: "He doesn't have the genes for it. . . ."

"Susan told me that. I didn't understand her."

Mark walked over to the porch light and stood beneath it.

"Look me in the eyes," he said quietly.

Mark's eyes were just as gray as Collins', but there was a depth to them that Artie had never seen in anybody's eyes before. Mark was suddenly more naked than if he had stripped off all his clothes. The only thing Artie could compare it to was when he was on the line in 'Nam and friends who were scared shitless talked to each other about themselves and their lives with absolutely no pretense and no lies. How they felt, things they had done, what they thought. It was when they were in extremis that you finally saw the real person beneath all the bullshit and the real person was usually . . . beautiful.

He was seeing everything Mark was or ever would be. Mark could show his soul at will and it was overwhelming.

And there was something else.

Mark could also see him as he really was, without the mask that everybody wore almost all their lives.

Artie looked away.

He had been staring into the eyes of the Buddha.

How long had Susan known? he wondered. Probably shortly after Mark was born. She had kept his secret ever since. Mark was the person who meant the most to her, the one person she could never betray, the one person she would gladly die for. She had never lied to him about that.

Mark suddenly yawned.

"Would you have shot Collins?"

Artie shook his head. "I was trying to bluff him. That was silly, I know."

"Yeah. He thought so, too." Mark opened the sliding glass doors and stepped inside.

"Good night, Dad."

Ever since he was a kid, he had thought it would *be fun to play God. Most kids probably did.*

But he'd had his chance.

And it hadn't been fun at all.

Artie leaned against the railing and looked out at the city below, the lights winking in the darkness. The streets downtown would be jammed with last-minute shoppers, the restaurants crowded, the theaters filled. It was probably the same across the country, around the entire world. *Homo sapiens* going about its business of shopping, eating, making children, making war, making plans for a thousand tomorrows that would steadily diminish until finally there were no more.

A few might linger for a while in small patches here and there. The species was too genetically diverse to be wiped out by a single bug. There might be a few farmers, maybe even a tiny village. An insignificant self-endangered species dependent upon the kindness of the other species surrounding them. Chances were they would still be warring among themselves until Cain once again slew Abel and they vanished for good.

They were going to go away. All of them. How many years? He didn't know. But sooner rather than later.

Something would take their place. Something that had been in hiding for thousands of years. Mankind would dwindle, realizing what was happening but powerless to stop it. As powerless as the dinosaurs had been when the meteorite had plunged into the sea millions of years ago and they had gone away, leaving their world to the tiny mammals hiding under the leaves of the forest.

But of all the teeming billions, he was the one truly Damned because in whatever small way, he had been the Instrument. He'd had to make a choice: his best friend or his family, his species or theirs.

But even if he had chosen Mitch—and he knew he never could have—it wouldn't have made a bit of difference in the outcome, only in how bloody it might have been. The Old People would have been blamed for spreading Rift Valley TB, and the pogrom that followed would have been everything that Mary feared.

Perhaps the Old People deserved the earth. Perhaps they had been meant to own it after all, at least for a while. Evolution had stopped for *Homo sapiens*; there were no isolated pockets of them that could throw up a mutation and then breed true. The world of *Homo sapiens* was all one; the constant mixing would have diluted it all too soon. But it hadn't been like that for the Old People. They had lived in tiny patches scattered around the world, isolated socially if not geographically. Evolution might have hesitated for them, but it had never stopped. And they'd had thirty-five thousand years for a change to show up. Time enough plus the tides of chance.

Artie turned away from the railing. The world would continue. The genus would continue. Hominids would continue. But *Homo sapiens* would disappear and so, eventually, would the Old People. Mark's genes would dominate, and after so many millennia the Old People would be replaced themselves, like every species was slated to be.

With Mark, nature had thrown the dice once again, willing to try a new combination rather than giving up the game altogether.

Artie smiled to himself.

Mark would be a surprise to them, one the Old People hadn't

counted on. But at least they would let him live rather than burn him at the stake or dissect him in a laboratory or cage him in a zoo.

He wondered what their scientists would call Mark.

Homo what?